"Myriam J. A. Chancy is a masterful writer. *What Storm, What Thunder* is an ecstatic collage of grief in the aftermath of the Haitian earthquake of 2010. The book is devastating and tender, but it is not a spectacle of sadness—it is a show of humanity and care in the midst of great violence. Though there is much pain in the novel, Chancy reminds us through her careful narration that none of her characters ever went unloved."

—JOSÉ OLIVAREZ, author of *Citizen Illegal*

"*What Storm, What Thunder* refracts the tragic events of the 2010 Haitian earthquake through multiple perspectives and voices. The result is an affecting and immersive—an important—book."

—DAN VYLETA, author of *Soot*

WHAT STORM, WHAT THUNDER

WHAT STORM, WHAT THUNDER

MYRIAM J. A. CHANCY

 TIN HOUSE / Portland, Oregon

Published by Tin House, Portland, Oregon

Distributed by W. W. Norton and Company

Library of Congress Cataloging-in-Publication Data

Names: Chancy, Myriam J. A., 1970- author.
Title: What storm, what thunder / Myriam J.A. Chancy.
Description: Portland, Oregon : Tin House, [2021]
Identifiers: LCCN 2021019399 | ISBN 9781951142766 (hardcover) | ISBN 9781951142841 (ebook)
Classification: LCC PR9260.9.C43 W48 2021 | DDC 813/.6--dc23
LC record available at https://lccn.loc.gov/2021019399

First US Edition 2021
Printed in the USA
Interior design by Diane Chonette
www.tinhouse.com

This novel is dedicated to the 250,000 to 300,000 individuals estimated to have perished in the January 12, 2010, earthquake in Haiti.

It is also dedicated to my mother, (Marie-Carmel) Adeline Lamour Chancy (December 29, 1932–January 5, 2019), in honor of her courage and persistence.

Atibo Legba, ouvri pòt la pou mwen,
Papa Legba, ouvri pòt la pou mwen,
Ouvri pòt la pou mwen kab entre,
Pou mwen kab tounin.

[Atibo Legba, open the door for me,
Papa Legba, open the door for me,
Open the door so that I can enter,
So that I can return.]

—*Vodou invocation to Legba, opener of doors*

. . .

At a time like this, scorching irony, not convincing argument, is needed. O! had I the ability, and could reach the nation's ear, I would, today, pour out a fiery stream of biting ridicule, blasting reproach, withering sarcasm, and stern rebuke. For it is not light that is needed, but fire; it is not the gentle shower, but thunder. We need the storm, the whirlwind, and the earthquake.

—*Frederick Douglass* (1852)

. . .

If you don't speak for the dead, who will?

—*Concussion* (2015)

MA LOU

Ezili, o! M san zo, ey!

Ezili m san zo!

M san zo lan tout kòm!

Ezili, o! M san zo, ey!

M san zo lan tout kòm!

Ezili o! M san zo.

Oh Ezili! Hey, I have no bones!

Ezili I have no bones!

I have no bones in my entire body!

Oh Ezili! Hey, I have no bones!

I have no bones in my entire body!

Oh Ezili! I have no bones.

—Vodou traditional for Grann Ezili

Port-au-Prince, November 25, 2014

"*Oh. Oh ye, oh ye. Manman'mwen. Oh ye, oh ye, oye. M'pa gen zo ankò!*"
My old mama used to say these words when she grew too old to
draw water from her own well. I remember. When I made my way
back to see her in her last days—standing in the tap-tap truck for

long hours as we traveled the serpentine road leading out of the capital to the villages of the coast, all the way to Saint Marc, where I was born, and my mother was born, and her mother before her—I was troubled to see her diminished frame in her bed. I could see her bones through the frail, wrinkled skin that lay limply across them. I could see the bones, but still she moaned to the goddess plaintively: "I have no bones; I have no bones."

Now that I am old like her, I understand the moaning of her last hours. Yes, Mama, you had no bones, and I did not understand you. I did not understand. She complained of cold during the hot days and of heat in the coolness of night. I rubbed a cloth dipped in river water over her flaccid skin, slowly, slowly, in circular motions, to warm her, to cool her. She sighed as I did this, sighed for the temporary relief, without a sense of hope, as a soldier of war would after being shot, waiting in the trenches to be found by enemy or kin, hoping not to be found by an enemy. At night, I lay beside her and put my arms around her, two blankets covering us. She shivered in the night even when it was still hot. She died July 15, the day that the devotees climb the waterfalls in Saut d'Eau, seeking penance from Metrès Dlo, seeking healing and renewal. "No bones," she said, her eyes wide open, looking through me. "No bones."

But, in the end, all that remained was skin and bones. When she died, the wick of light in her eyes flickered, then disappeared, a lifetime of misery extinguished, very slowly. Just a heap of bones.

A month ago, the dictator's son died. I wonder who mourned his lifeless body. What the gods had to say. Whether his passing meant that we would be delivered of whatever curse his father, the god of death, had set upon us. Thinking about it, I realized that he was a man like other men. A heap of bones like my mother.

I thought about going to Saut d'Eau for a long time after Douz, to bury my mother's bones. I had never been but had always wanted to go. I thought about the stories that my husband, Lou, told me about the place. He went there just before we met, on the feast day in July. He asked the gods to bring him to someone like me. Not someone, he corrected himself, you. A soul mate. You, he said emphatically. Lou was a *vodouisant* all his days, made altars, offerings, participated in the feast days. I watched him without saying anything. I was a Catholic, and that was that. We never discussed our difference. Had he been here after what happened, happened, he would have danced with the mourners. I would have watched him. Lou's memories were my own. That's why it didn't bother me that once we were married, everyone took to calling me Ma Lou, echoing my constant references to him in my speech ("my Lou," "my Lou," I always said, as I still do, as if everything he told me were sacred and true; I wanted to believe that this was so). Everyone still calls me by his name, though Lou is long gone. After what happened, happened, it seemed to me then that it would be best to believe in gods that had not harmed me. Lou's gods. My mother's gods. Being sent to Catholic school early on severed me from them, even if I was only to become a market woman. At least I could read, count, and pray the catechism. I thought this made me lucky, but in other ways, it made me poor, like a pocket turned inside out, empty of coins.

My Lou had told me about the *mapou* cut down when the priest and a parish official stationed at Saut d'Eau were told that Ezili Wèdo, goddess of the waters, had made a shimmering apparition. Saut d'Eau was made up of two waterfalls and it was said that the second belonged to Damballah, the serpent god, giver of all life.

The priest had the tree cut down, but the gods remained. That priest later lost both his legs in a freak accident. The police captain who had overseen the cutting down of the tree temporarily lost his mind. His faculties returned when he went into the waterfalls and asked for forgiveness. Now, everyone goes to the falls. Even I went, some two years ago, when I could begin to stand on my own two legs, move forward again, to cleanse the bones.

Before going, I thought a long time about the priest who'd lost his legs. Thought about the boy in the camp whose leg they'd cut off, whose mother had lost her hold on reality. Were they being punished for something? For not believing? But I could not believe in gods that would punish the helpless. No. The earth had buckled and, in that movement, all that was not in its place fell upon the earth's children, upon the blameless as well as the guilty, without discrimination. It wasn't the boy who'd lost his leg, who was guilty, it was the rest of us who looked away from people like him, people who could have been us, lame, stumbling, afraid to go out of their houses in the light of day for fear of what could happen next. We'd lost our legs—sea legs, land legs, the ability to stand up for ourselves. I needed to cleanse the bones myself, to put all this behind me, return to the land, to my mother's land, remember everything, and forget the last two years of death begetting death. But, for some time, before going to the waterfalls, I did not know where to start. How to rise again and set out. I am just an old market woman. A relic.

Yes, yes, me, Ma Lou, I admit, finally, that these bones of mine are old, worn out, fragile like the eggs I take to market that everyone wants, even the Dominicans. I never thought I would see the day that Dominicans would want anything we produced for ourselves.

But all they *really* want is to sell us their good-for-nothing eggs produced in factories. My eggs are warm from being dropped from the hens' insides. That's how fresh they are. That fresh.

Fresh like Jonas, who used to count his steps all over the market. Counted how many of everything I had to sell, how much I made with every sale. Counted the eggs I had, to see how many his family might purchase. They were five all together. Not the poorest. Not the richest. Just counting their pennies like all of us, counting and putting them away when there weren't enough to buy what they wanted. "Don't worry," I told him, when he would come to me with his fingers filled with grimy folds of paper, our useless *gouds*. "Don't worry," I'd say. "You save, and one day you'll have enough to purchase the whole dozen! For you, and for your family, the whole carton just for you." He would smile when I said that, be less embarrassed if that day he had been sent to purchase two or three eggs, sometimes only one. He came, that day, to get one egg for his mother, but he never reached home.

He's gone, that boy, along with his sisters, wee things that came to the market only when the mother was there, trailing behind like ducklings, with the same odd waddle of a walk that only winged creatures have. Perhaps this is why they weren't for this earth for very long. The girls five and two, the boy all of eleven in that New Year. She sent the boy, alone sometimes, to run errands for the family, sometimes let me have him run errands so he could make a little of his own money on the side, a few *gouds* to call his own, to make him feel grown, or growing. I knew him well, as did my clients for whom I had him run errands, especially up at the hotel on the mountain, perched above the city. He was quick, quick, and mostly reliable. He reminded me of my own son, Richard, at that

age, except that I had a presentiment that unlike mine, he would
grow up to be a fine man. I had been wrong concerning them both.
My son grew to be a wealthy, respected man, though I no longer
knew him by then. Jonas would never become the man I could see
hovering already in the shadows of his eyes and vanishing smiles.

The girls were crushed beneath a house over there, not far from
the market. Playing in the streets. Darting in and out of the houses,
nothing unusual. I watched them do this daily from my seat low
to the ground. Watched the boy count his steps from his stoop to
the market, then to my stall, backward, forward, as if he could solve
a mystery with his calculations—so much like his father, the ac-
countant with hardly a cent to his name, but rich in other ways: his
family, for one. Anyone could see that he had married the love of
his life, ran to her like a man runs to water in a desert. No wonder
it would be fire we would have to save her from, in the end, months
after the disaster. The boy had left my stall with his one egg for his
mother in hand, then gone down the street and into a house with
a television on, turned out to face the street so that everyone could
gather inside and outside to watch the *futbòl* games or, that day,
a soap opera. The woman who owned the house was a childless
woman, a widow or a divorcée. She, too, would not survive.

When the earth moved, the houses fell to the ground within
seconds, jolted when the ground stopped swaying and crushed
everything that had remained. The girls were not the only ones
left crying below: the whole street swayed; the earth rippled like
a carpet heaving itself of crumbs and dirt that a distracted house-
keeper had forgotten to sweep away. I left my stand and all my
wares—the piles of mango, the eggs (they would fall, smash against
the ground), the packs of Chiclets, the ripe avocadoes—and made

my way toward the voices, not thinking of my own small house up and away in the hills. I was not worried for my own: Anne, my granddaughter, had left for her work, far away in another country, after her mother's funeral, and Richard, her father, my son, well, we had stopped worrying for him long ago, carrying with us solely the memory of him as the small child we had raised, before he left us, leaving behind, carelessly, a stray seed for us to water. We buried our grief in the process, watching Anne grow. Our son, the man, we did not know.

I watched. That's what old market women do: we watch. But this time, the lot of us market women sprang to action, even as our bones creaked for lack of cartilage and oil. Like the others on the street, we used anything in hand we could find. Useless things like spoons and forks, the metal ends of umbrellas, as if our puny things, our fingernails, could move all that. Only the lucky were saved. Being lucky meant simply that you were closer to the surface, or that fewer things blocked the way to being found. We heard people on their cell phones, all up and down the street, begging frantically for help, giving directions to where they thought they were beneath the rubble, within the rooms of their houses. Phones rang and we heard people answer them. Then—fewer and fewer voices. The tinny, persistent ringing of cell phone tones: different songs rising like wind from underground with no answer.

We heard our own voices, screaming at each other, asking for help, not knowing what to do. Faces covered with dust, and sweat, and other things later to be determined. What to do? There was nothing to do but to scream, try anything, flail our hands, scratch at the earth like my chickens when they get confused because their fresh-laid eggs disappear, one by one, and still they lay more. Try anything and still, it's too little. After the earth rose and split open, yes, I saw angels walking, but there had also been dust, white dust, everywhere, caking all objects and every moving thing. The dust came from the concrete crumbling to pieces as buildings flattened, but there were also other things mixed in, blood and bones. Had I mistaken the walking dead for angels, survivors stumbling through the debris with the same white flakes covering their bodies from head to toe that covered mine?

Eventually, we, the market women, remembered our oil lamps and lit them, one by one, those of us who could. Only part of the market had been crushed, the part against a wall. Still, it was impossible to tell what belonged to whom, and at that point, no one cared. We worked at freeing those we could, said prayers for the others, promising deliverance to those we could not get to, to give them some solace, some hope in their final moments, because salvation would soon be theirs. Then back down the street, darting back and forth. Using the goods from the market to feed those working at rescue. Doing what we could, as we always did, our large bodies moving through the rubble as if we were land whales, made for swimming through dust-laden air, made for parting human waves.

We treated everyone alike. They had become all the same, were always the same. Something we had always known from our low-to-the-ground perches, observing life like budgies, our heads wrapped in colorful scarfs to keep the heat of the sun from roasting our brains, sweat slipping down our necks, draping the half-moon of our chests exposed above the breasts. We fanned ourselves, but it didn't help. *Chalè!* Heat came with the territory. But not this. Not this. A different kind of heat. Sitting here under the hot sun all day, we ripen.

The saints, the crooks, the foreigners, the white saviors, the bleeding hearts, they all need sustenance, and we give it to them. Close my eyes. Look away. It's all the same. The need to shut everything down, slow my breathing, take in what's there to take in, let all the rest go. If only I could get rid of the images, of the smells still clogging my nostrils. *Ha!* You would think that after so many years working in the market, nothing would offend this nose. Look what surrounds us every day: the mounds of smoldering garbage, the spoiling fruits with skins speckled with loitering flies, the leavings of dogs, the runoff of dirty water weaving its way through the alleyways, that dense acrid stink of urine.

A marketplace is a world of colliding senses, not all of it pretty or fruitful, much of it decay, especially at the end of the day, when the best of what's available is gone and all that remain are castoffs, the leftovers. This is the part of the day when those of us who work the market blend into the dust and the loam, become one with the elements, the odors of sweat and dung, the sweet sap of fleshy fruits ground underfoot, the nothing that we are, the all. We sweep up what's left of the day, knowing that striving toward perfection is beyond our reach.

A little corner of peace. That's all we want. I found mine after the trip to the waterfalls, but it would take some time to get there. Peace is what others want from me, from us, the market women they imagine sit immobile, rooted to the earth but without extensions, no lives and families of our own, waiting patiently for them to come with their grimy dollars, their smiles full of need, to unload money and stories of desire, a desire to be free of worry, to be freed.

A little corner of peace is all they want.

And I give it to them.

Like a sponge, I absorb and grow fat and round. The weight of their words like leaves imprinted into my flesh, hanging heavy from my frail bones, rooting myself to the ground because it is the only thing that I can be sure of, then, now. Who's to say that the red of the earth of this island isn't drawn from the blood of women like me, sitting in the markets, pooling?

A little corner of peace is all that is wanted.

Now I know how to give it to them. I do so freely: I listen.

Little did I know that my work was only beginning.

SARA

Port-au-Prince, IDP Camp, July 2010

It started with a tug on her right elbow as she was sleeping, sometime earlier that spring, after the last of her loves had disappeared, two at once, then the other two, one after the next, over a matter of a few weeks, after she had come to the camp set up beneath the broken cathedral in the middle of the neighborhood. It didn't disturb her at first. She mistook the feeling for her own hand, holding herself close in slumber.

She liked to sleep on her side, with a distinct preference for lying on her left, because everything changed, in a way, once she came to share a marriage bed. It was something that took some time to get used to though she'd never had much room to herself: what she'd had before was a space the narrow width of a military cot, or so Olivier had said the first time he'd been inside the little cement block house she had been living in then, when they'd met, with her aunt, uncle, and five cousins. Being born in scarcity—in a shack by the ocean on a stretch of beach an hour out from the big city, a stretch that had since been privatized for the wealthy, and for the tourists who were given run of the place—had been preparation for a life of gratitude. A lack of personal space had never bothered her because the house had overflowed with laughter and touch, things she missed when she moved away from her grandmother to town, when her grandmother had found it too difficult to take care of her after each of her parents died, also one after the other, like flies, of some mysterious illness one couldn't get from drinking unclean water. Her memories of them wasted away until she couldn't remember them anymore and had to ask every day for some morsel of who they had been or to catch a glimpse of what they might have looked like, or what remnant of themselves they might have left upon her features. Her grandmother understood and pointed out things like the length of her narrow, thin fingers (like her mother's), or the way her cheekbones protruded into the shape of small apples from which hinged a square jaw (unfeminine, she thought, but like her father's face, and so she grew to be proud of it). Gradually, her grandmother started to speak of the things she'd inherited from her as well—the thickness of her long hair, the arch of her right brow, the way her top lip curled when she smiled—and she understood from these confidences that her grandmother didn't believe herself to be long for their world. So, when Sara was sent away to the city to live with her aunt and uncle, she didn't hold it against her grandmother, but she was deeply sad that she would not see her again, though each of them (grandmother, aunt, uncle, and the chirping cousins who were small, then) kept repeating over and over and over again about how she would come back on vacations to visit, how her grandmother would be fine, how it was all for her "betterment" and so that she could get a real education. She wanted to tell them that she didn't need to be "citified." She could live like her parents had, off the land, like her grandmother, until a ripe old age, and be perfectly happy. But she didn't say anything, because she recognized that the old life was over, that she would have to get used to seeing her grandmother, and parents, not in person but when she looked at herself in a mirror. This is what her parents' deaths had taught her: there was only one direction for evolution: a lateral movement sideways—like the movement of crabs upon the beach at sunset.

By the time she met Olivier, in an accounting course she had signed up for at a local technical college, after she realized that studying literature (as her aunt and uncle and cousins had all pointed out) would nourish dreams but never reality (she needed a job), she had learned to shift her priorities. Olivier liked expansive and expensive things. She began to acquire a taste for space. She began to expand.

After they married, their house was in a slightly better neighborhood than her aunt and uncle's. It had sidewalks and gutters, even if they overflowed whenever it rained and, sometimes, when there was no rain in sight. The house was no bigger than her aunt and uncle's, but it was only the two of them at first, and Olivier had outfitted the bedroom with a double bed like she had reported seeing in the children's rooms in homes where she had taken part-time work tutoring to make extra money to help pay for her school books and fees. The bed wasn't large, but the pleasure of feeling the warmth of Olivier's body next to hers was both a comfort and a blessing. How could she mind? He was everything she had (not) dreamed of and imagined, more of the world than she could conceive.

It all took some getting used to but she was glad for it even when she could no longer toss and turn at will, or turn on her stomach with arms spread out along her sides, tips of fingers dangling down to touch the coolness of the tiles below the bed on hot days when not a breeze moved, when a fan was futile (it only called attention to the oppressive heat as it stirred humid, hot air thick as porridge—*acassan*, like her grandmother used to make for her when Sara was still small and wobbly on her feet). Such heat made her think of loss and suffocation, watching her parents gasp for last breaths before they expired. It was a cloying heat, like tentacles reaching up from the depths, from another place. That's what the tug at her elbow reminded her of: warm, suffocating summer heat, not of this world.

When it was that hot, she would lie with her back to Olivier, facing out from the bed, the contrast with the heat emanating from his body giving her an illusion of coolness wafting between bed and tiles, in the open space between the furniture and themselves, the walls and ceilings. At times like these, in the heat, she wondered what such minute freedom might be like, if she could make herself small and disappear. Such thoughts were always brief and fleeting, less than a few seconds in length, because she was happy. Too happy, she thought now, when she allowed herself the luxury of deep thought. It was easier these days to bumble along, not think of anything too much, of what was going to happen in the next hour, and the one after that, and the one after that, until the day was done, and she could lie down and hope only for dreamlessness.

When the children came (three tadpoles, Olivier called them, because every time he asked how it felt to have them growing in her belly, all she could think of was fish, tiny little sardines, or frogs), one after the other as if they had been waiting an eternity for a way into the world, for Olivier and her to find each other, settle down, move into the little brick house with the green shutters and pink, chipped cement stoop. When they were big enough to get out of their cribs and patter through the house (their little footsteps made her think of rain), they would come into her and Olivier's room and tug at the sheets, then at whatever they could grasp, their parents' arms and legs protruding from the bed. This always caused much merriment that sometimes turned into pillow fights or tickling contests as they got older. Sometimes she and Olivier let the children win; sometimes they came up with excuses for why the children had to go back to their rooms and leave them alone, but that never lasted long: they missed the children's faces even when they had already seen them many times in the day. The longing for them became more intense, she found, when each child started pre-school, then elementary school, and had found new preoccupations. She missed the tugging at her after the last one was sent to school, though on weekends the three would remember the old rituals and return, pulling the sheets off her and Olivier, demanding breakfasts in bed (which were never delivered).

It was a happy, boisterous home, something she never dreamed for herself the day she left her grandmother, holding a bag made of rough green fabric tightly against her chest, containing all her worldly possessions: a pair of slacks for working in; two pairs of shoes (one for school, the other for work and leisure); a simple navy-blue dress for school days and a fancier one that her grandmother had a neighbor woman make for her to wear on Sundays and special occasions (of which there were few out in the country: they were pleased to greet the day, as her grandmother always was accustomed to say, and to wave the sun to sleep); two pairs of socks for when shoes were necessary; five pairs of ribbons for her hair; two T-shirts; three pieces of underwear; handmade thong sandals with red leather straps that had been her mother's; a small Bible made for children; and a silver cross on a silver chain she had received at First Communion.

The years with her aunt, uncle, and cousins were fine, but she was always aware of being a guest in the house, someone from the outside, even as they took care to include her in everything and take her everywhere the other children went: some things simply can't be manufactured. This house, with Olivier and the children, was hers.

They both found work as accountants and were happy. Life was simple but good, and Olivier continued to dream of the next steps they should take for a bigger house, a better car, better jobs, vacations abroad. She let him dream since she had all she wanted, for the most part, though, secretly, back then, what she would have liked was a bigger bed, what some people called a "family bed," where they could fit together like on Noah's ark, and she could have a square of space entirely her own and smile to herself because her mind would be empty of worry with all the beings she cared most for in the world (this included a raggedy family cat who liked to scratch at things) around her, suspended as if on a barge floating out to sea, contained, inseparable. She had an image in her mind of each of them sprawled in a different place on the mattress covered in white linens, and how she and Olivier would watch the tadpoles grow into their full size until every inch of the mattress surface was covered up. The image used to make her laugh. She could not imagine her babies with a mustache, or long hair, long-armed, heavy, thick-limbed. But she imagined them beautiful nonetheless, better reflections of both Olivier and herself, more supple, athletic, smarter, improved versions in every way.

When the tugging started on her right elbow, as she slept folded in on herself as she used to sleep, that image of all of them growing old together had begun to fade. She had begun to forget what each of them looked like. Not because Douz had happened so long ago (was it, now, only a few months ago, six months ago? It seemed so much longer), but because the shock of their sudden disappearance had broken something in her mind, the part that was able to take things in and let them go, that wanted for little more than she had. The violence of this loss was like nothing she had ever experienced before, not like her parents' departures or her grandmother waving goodbye to her as she climbed into the back of her aunt and uncle's four-wheel drive, where she sat between two of the cousins, their sweaty thighs touching stickily together in the heat, forming an unexpected bond in place of the tearing away from all that she had held dear and familiar.

The morning of the Event, she remembered, they were there, eating breakfast, fighting over something that would soon be forgotten; they went off to school, hair combed or plaited, looking smart in their school clothes. They came home from school, washed up, changed into play clothes, did their homework, then asked for permission to go play with their friends as they waited for Olivier to return home and sit down to dinner. She'd said yes, as she almost always did (why had she said yes, why hadn't she been stricter, as Olivier had started to insist that she be?). Out they went, little arms flailing in that smooth, devil-may-care way that only children have—miniature dancers with hidden internal choreographers named happiness and simplicity, love. That's what they were—love in movement, her love, Olivier's, all the world's love wrapped up in their little fists pumping through the air, feet following, drumming the earth for joy.

Jonas, their oldest, she'd sent to get an egg from Ma Lou, the old woman in the market who doted on her son as if he were her own, sent him to and from the market to run errands for other clients when she could spare him. He loved the attention, feeling grown. But the boy had turned eleven, though he had been a brooding ten going on eleven, a ruminator like his father. He was often distracted as he made his way to and from the market, counting his steps in every direction that he went. Televisions and radios caught his attention, other children from school, or the market women themselves, with their *teledyòl* and tall tales. He listened to it all and sometimes reported back. He loved to tell her about the soap opera named *Frijolito*, or little bean, which everyone liked to watch at a house down the road from them, the house of a woman whose name she didn't know but who had a sullen-looking nephew who had helped her to install a used television in her living room that she turned toward a window so that neighbors could watch, too. She didn't watch telenovelas, didn't have any use for them. And what did romance have to do with "little beans," anyway? That day, she'd told him to come right back with the egg. She needed it to strengthen a thin soup, was already imagining the filaments of egg, beaten and swirled into the broth, thickening it to a lustrous yellow. Why had he not done as she'd asked, that day, come right back with the egg? Why had he dallied and gone to take a peek at the soap opera with the neighborhood children? Why had he entered the house rather than stood outside, like the others (because he was too short, this she knew, so always minced his way through alcoves and doorjambs, but still she asked herself the questions, over and over again, as if the answers might come back differently, though they never did)? Why had he always, like her husband, his father, been so distracted by everything around him? Why couldn't he stay on a straight path? She thought this, now, lying on the cot, knowing that if Olivier, her husband, had stayed on a straight path, one that would have brought him greater wealth, maybe better class standing, they might have never met, never made the children, who, all, were gone. Maybe this was why she asked the question, Why? If they had never met—which would have been better?

The tug, insistent, in the middle of the night: she had turned to the darkness next to her, inches above the ground, and said to it: "Please, please leave." Then turned her head back against the thin mattress she had been given in the camp by some act of grace because she'd come there with nothing more than the stitch of clothes on her back, a headdress, some flat-heeled shoes, a ribbon from one of their daughters' heads (had she come alone?).

Her children came to define her. Not even Olivier had been able to mark her in that way. They taught her who she was and who she wanted to be. Something more than a mother, something of the divine, an intermediary between heaven and earth, the vessel that brought them from over there to here, who'd made flesh out of spirit. They made her believe in holy things, for a time, until they all disappeared, in a matter of seconds, and the miracles that they were became dust, leaving her above ground only to preach about their passage, a passage she no longer believed in, and for which she refused to testify.

She turned to the heavy presence settled next to the mattress, pawing at her, and said: "I can't see you. Would you please stop? Can't you see I'm tired? There's nothing left for you here. Go back where you came from." Then her face rough against the fabric of the mattress; Olivier gone as well. No warmth next to her. What had happened to Olivier? That, she didn't know. But the tadpoles, yes, if she allowed herself to think about it, she knew.

Two had been left beneath the neighbor's house. They had me-owed like kittens for her, for anyone, for hours, until they stopped making a sound, and when the men from the neighborhood at-tempting rescues with bare hands moved the broken slabs from above the space that housed them, she knew already that they were unlikely to be breathing, moving, dancing flowers on supple stems; she knew, so she turned away when they brought them out, one by one, those limp bodies not the ones she had birthed, one after the other. The third was still writhing with life, bloody like afterbirth, and men in masks spirited him away with Olivier at his side, Oliv-ier saying he would return (where had he gone?). Olivier, who had not been there when the first two were unearthed, but who had emerged, miraculously, to take the boy away.

No, she said, these bodies are not mine, and walked away from the bloodied and broken bones, the glassy, bulging eyes, the tears frozen to the skin by dust. She saw but pretended not to see and let them take the bodies of her two little girls away. They would never dance, or move, or grow long hair down their backs. They would never sway against a sea wave or a lover or the sheer bliss of their own bodies at rest. They would never know her again, or Olivier. Where was he? She turned away from the question in the same way that she had turned away from the children's bodies. The bod-ies that were no longer the children. Rather, she should say: those husks. "Leave me be," she said, at the source of the tugging.

Inside herself she was in a rage. How dare it pretend to be one of them, to tug at her like that, and torture her with a memory she strove to forget? Olivier had come back a few days after Douz with the third, Jonas, one of his legs cut off, bandaged, two vials of pills for the boy to take for several weeks, until the sutures healed, fell off (which they never would). Olivier would count the pills into her hand, one white, two pink, until she learned that it would be up to her to continue, after Olivier left, against her will. She didn't think the boy would ever heal; didn't want to look. Olivier took care of it at first, then, after two or three weeks, when faint lesions started to appear above the bandages, and the level of pills in the vials lowered, he'd left her with what was left of what had been their son. She dared not look at what remained. Every time she did, the dimming features of the small face made her heart ache, took the breath out of her. If she stopped breathing, she would no longer be able to take care of it. She might float away. So, instead, at first, she fretted about the tent, tried to keep things in order, used the water from the silver bowl that appeared at the mouth of the tent every day, set there by Loko's gnarled and rivered hand. Loko was old, kind. Said he had a daughter who looked like her. She didn't respond when he spoke to her (let him speak), took the water, bathed the thing on the mattress, changed the dressings and kept the gashed wound dry (tried not to look at it), asked Ma Lou how to treat the faint, reddish lesions staring at her angrily from what was left of her son's leg (Ma Lou promised to get more pills and a special ointment from the foreigners), wondered when all of this would stop. Where was Olivier? Everything made her angry, deep down, an anger she could not show.

Her rage manifested itself in a refusal to conform to camp life: the lining up for rice delivery (the rice was meted out by the plastic cupful from fat white burlap-like bags emblazoned with the red, white, and blue of the American flag; scrawny children who seemed to belong to no one moved through the sinew of legs with eyes trained to the ground, picking up fallen grains into the palms of their hands); the lining up for water when the big truck with the rounded back came trundling down the broken cement, spilling half its contents along the way and more when it stopped to open the faucets installed at the back before anyone was ready to fill their ramshackle containers, ranging from small, chipped china cups, to emptied coffee cans, to multicolored Tupperware, to, at the beginning, the large translucent containers designed for hauling water from distant wells that some had had the foresight of toting with them rather than attempting to save photographs and whatever trinkets they held dear that meant nothing at all to anyone else on earth; the lining up to take a piss in the trenches dug out along the extremities of the camp by men who spoke a language no one could understand, though some looked like them (dark of skin, and gaunt—as if they came from a place where food was also scarce). The lining up. The lining up. And now, the pawing at night. Why had the ground opened up and swallowed them whole only to leave her, alone, walking the broken roads?

She had crossed over. That was what it was. She had crossed into an in-between world in which the ghosts could see her, but she could not see or touch their shimmering contours. In the heat of late afternoon, when everything and everyone was burdened from accumulated weariness and humidity, she thought she could see their silvery shapes bump into the living, push their way through crowds, lingering over the dead as if recognizing themselves, only to continue on to some unknown destination where they seemed to melt away. Only these shapes—huge, tear-shaped globes—moved her temporarily out of her state of lethargy. Blind to the other camp dwellers all around her and deaf to their cries, she followed them. Some dwellers were fighting over the right to a piece of dirt where another had already pitched a tent; the *madansara* already devising ways to set up stalls to sell God knows what—what was there left to sell? Soon, they would be making food from the rations being handed out by NGOs (Not God's Own, she thought—who were they?); some less-fortunates would revert to making the mud cookies that outside fundraisers argued never existed so that their charges would seem less desolate; some yelled after her: "*Wou la-a, kote'ou prale?*" (you, you there, where are you going?); some shook their heads in recognition of madness when they saw it: "*Li te gayen twa pitit*" (three little ones she had). Sometimes the mention of the children made her lose concentration and she retreated back to her tent, a dirty gray tarp the color of hurricane clouds. On it was written: "A gift from the American people" and "in association with the Republic of Ireland." What America has to do with Ireland she didn't know, except for the fact that the largest portable phone company in the country was owned by Irish nationals. She didn't know why. Olivier had wanted to buy a franchise from them, to get out of accounting for other people's businesses, have something that was more their own. Work for the Irish. Better than working for the Americans? "*A ma chè,*" Olivier would say, sucking his teeth, "*tout blan se blan.*" What did it matter? He'd say, "Those foreigners are all the same." She wished they'd had other things in mind, escape routes and exit strategies. They'd set their eyes on nothing but a future in which everything would go according to a fabricated plan that they believed in more than in reality itself—or that amplified it. What was real was the sound of the tiny pattering footsteps from the children running through the house, pretending that they were invisible, giggling. What was real was the warmth of their bodies piled together under the covers of the too small, big enough bed; the everyday rhythm of things.

She had seen the babies' bodies. But where was Olivier's?

She could only close her eyes against the madness all around her, the long lines, the perseverance of everyone pretending that life was going on. Let them believe that this was living. She would remain in the shadows, trying to follow the orbs into that place to which they went as they dissipated into thin air at the end of a trail that usually brought her footsteps to stop at the base of a tent wall behind which she knew was a body lying in rest, the face an impenetrable mask of features contorted to reflect the pain or peace of the last moments before breath stopped. Before the day was out, the vultures would come, taking out the dead, throwing the bodies away like sacks of coal; the lucky ones were enveloped in a bedsheet, or bagged. The others were taken out in the clothes they had expired in, without the washing of the body, the scrubbing of feet, without the women's hair being tied back and wrapped, the men's faces being shaved and oiled (all the things she hadn't done for her three, for the boy, before they took him away). Then would come the picking over of the belongings, then the tent, then the space itself. There would be fighting, biting, kicking. Then the camp manager (if there was one) would appear and decide, if the volley of slaps and punches had not been enough, to settle the matter of the dispersal of goods and space.

Inevitably, there was a pecking order, so it was better to learn to fight. She didn't know how she'd gotten the space she had, what hands had brought her there, erected the tent with the American/ Irish logo, put a weaved mat inside for sleeping, a plastic jar for water, and a torn piece of paper in the bottom of a bowl with a wooden spoon weighing it down. It took her weeks to see the piece of paper and the words scribbled in pencil on it: "*Nou se wozo.*" She took the piece of paper, folded it, put it in her bra as if it was a currency she needed to protect. *Wozo.* Reed. Olivier used to call her that. You bend but you don't break. You bend. Don't break. Reeds feed on water, multiply. She'd never seen any reeds die. But maybe this was why they stood in marshes, lived between worlds, stuck in mud. Like her now, resigned to living on air, stuck on the mattress with her thoughts, and the tugging in the pitch dark of night. Why couldn't it leave her alone, with its little fingers and insistent pulling? She had had enough of that tugging for a lifetime. She thought she would never have a full night of sleep again after the third one came, so small and puny Olivier thought the girl would die within a week. But she didn't. "*Wozo,* like you," Olivier said. But under certain conditions, even *wozo* dry out, perish.

The third time the tugging happened, reminding her more and more of what she wished to forget, she knew it was there for *her*: it was no accident. Was it one of the orbs that she followed through the camp in the late afternoons when she found the energy to raise herself from the mat on the floor of the tent? What was it? What was she? Other camp dwellers had begun to ask her as her clothes turned to rags and her skin scaly from lack of washing. Some time had elapsed or maybe no time had elapsed. No, yes, some time. Long enough that she had had to cut off some of her long hair because she could not keep it as she had, oiled and braided. She contemplated cutting it down to the scalp, like a mourner. She was a mourner, wasn't she? She had seen some rural people do this, when her grandmother had died, for instance, and she had been brought back for a day of burial: all the old women had shaved their heads. They looked like old men, she thought. She stared. "Stop staring," her aunt had said. "They look like old men," she had said in turn. Her aunt had shrugged: "At their age, what does it matter?" She thought that today, after Douz, maybe it didn't matter that she was still a young woman. She felt old: the flesh of her body hung on her bones like a coat hung on a peg in the wall. She was an old woman: she could shave her head. But she wanted to wait a while longer, in case Olivier returned. In case he was still alive. The only way he could recognize her would be by her hair: it was her last distinguishing feature now that her flesh had become flaccid, her cheeks hollowed, her eyes smile-less.

At some point, the hands that had gotten her into the tent came back and shook her gently from sleep one morning to give her a washing down near the place where the women beat the clothes of dirt when water was scarce. Women's hands took the dress off her that had begun to stick to her skin (they had to cut her out of it) and gave her something new to wear (Olivier would never recognize her). She panicked when they took her brassiere off and the piece of paper fell out. She screamed until the hands gave her back the piece of paper after she had been dried off and returned to the calm shade of her tent. She held the scrap of paper close to her until she fell asleep that day. She slept through the heat of the day in broad light.

Did spirits prefer cleanliness? Had she known this? She had avoided washing and taking care in case her three tried to find their way back to her. She didn't want them back, not the way they were now: bloodied and broken, empty, lifeless vessels. She didn't want them back. (She wanted everything back. Everything.) Olivier. Where was he?

The third time the thing came to tug at her at night, it did something that only she could recognize: it tickled at her feet. It was something the second had started doing, when the girl was about three or four, because the girl had learned the relationship between her mother's sensitive feet and bringing her out of bed, and into the kitchen to fix breakfast. She startled when she felt the tickling. Said, "Is that you, *chérie*? Is that you, dear?" Wide awake, looking around in the darkness.

She wondered how she could be sure that it wasn't one of the orbs playing a trick on her. What if they were trying to get her to follow them into a world darker than this one, a world in which Olivier could never find her? (Of course, she didn't know if Olivier was in the world from before, her world in between, or the world somewhere beyond, with the orbs.) She needed a way to be sure. She stayed awake all night, wondering what she could do to test the spirit, all the while talking to it in whispers, in case it was the third child, her first-born, the bloodied mass, still alive, taken away to have a crushed limb removed, returned to her in a shell of bandages and splints, come back to her, seeking comfort. (She'd taken care of him, lips and fingers trembling all the time, until he, too, had died, a month later, his body thrown away with all the dead.) She apologized for abandoning their bodies without ceremony. She felt a wave of heat flow over her from the side of the mattress. She imagined forgiveness because she couldn't imagine what a child's wrath might feel like; and hadn't it tickled her? No angry child would do that.

In the morning, she decided to go look for bowls, water, salt (didn't they say damned spirits clung to earth because they had ingested salt?), a candle. "Going to wash, finally?" someone sitting on a handmade bench in front of their tent said to her, matter-of-factly (thinking she was looking for salt as a replacement for soap: salt cleansed, purged, disinfected), not looking up to see the determined expression on her face. She was going to catch some ghosts or find her daughters—one or the other. She collected six small plastic bowls (the kind she might have used to feed cereal to the three in the morning, while she watched on, amused at their earnestness while they ate), one for each of them, and for her grandmother, who might be watching over them (her, and the family), she thought, and a catch of fresh rainwater from Loko. Loko was collecting it in an oil drum he'd lidded with planks of wood shorn into a circle. The candle was for protection, and for hope, whatever happened, whatever revealed itself in the dark, trying to tickle her feet or tug at her arm, whatever or whoever it was. It took all day.

When she was ready, she set the bowls, half-filled with water, around the circumference of the mattress. In three, she placed a half teaspoon of salt. The malevolent ghosts would play with the salt water; the others would seek the fresh water. Why she'd thought of water, and salt, she wasn't sure, but if she thought about it, the tugging had started after the washing, sometime after that. There had to be some connection. It took her all day to prepare: to set the bowls in a half circle around the edges of the bed; to salt three of the six bowls. She repeated to herself the reasoning that malevolent ghosts would gravitate to salt and that the others (one of the girls?) would seek the fresh.

When she thought it was dark enough, she lit the candle, then laid herself down on the mattress and feigned sleep (could they know if she was awake or not?). She wanted to see what would come. Her mind raced, then quieted; then she listened to the ambient noises all around her. The camp buzzed like a market at high noon: she heard the slap of dominoes against a plank some men had set across their knees for a table; animal grunts; the flap of fowl wings; babies crying; mothers cooing; smelled the stink of rotting flesh—fruit, animal, or human—she couldn't distinguish anymore. She fell asleep. Then the tug at her arm came, then the tickling at her feet. She woke, opened her eyes slowly. Saw her, the little girl, one of hers: she smiled for the first time since this purgatory had begun.

The girl was dipping her hands in and out of the water bowls. Both the salt and the fresh. What did this mean? She shrugged to herself: maybe nothing mattered; the old sayings couldn't mean anything since the world had broken in two—before the Event, and after the Event. She saw a shape moving, not the whole girl. "Is that you?" she asked. "Is it you?" There were giggles in answer. Then small, translucent hands dipping into the bowls. She looked twice. There was not one but two, two pairs of hands, going in and out of the water, upsetting the bowls, spilling the water. There would be salt marks in the morning, in the dirt, staining the mat around its edges: proof. Two: The girls? Their two? (Where was Olivier?) Her grandmother was not there. (Where was she?) She had not seen or heard her for so many years; had not thought of her or laid a glass of fresh water before her picture frame in the house on the altar for the ancestors. Two pairs of hands: of different sizes, shades of brown. Hands she knew like her own. The two, come back to her. If there was another, she refused to see him, though she could feel him, for the first time since he had disappeared, some six weeks after Douz. She felt her heart pulse, surge. She apologized to them. "Be quiet," a man said to her from another tent. "There are ghosts everywhere: What makes you think yours have sought you out?"

"Leave her alone," another voice said (it was Loko, the kind old man with the rainwater).

She saw only glimpses of what they used to be: their lithe, thin limbs; shadows of smiles; the tapered fingers she thought suggested artists rather than functionaries, like her. Mostly, she heard their giggles. She told them how sorry she was that she had left their bodies like that, in the dust and dirt, that she had run away (but not far enough, not as far as Olivier). She didn't know where she was, really; she knew only that she was far from the home they'd had (did it still exist?). Did they know where their father was? Did they know? They giggled in response.

She tried to get close to them, to see them. She brought the candle as close to the shapes as she could (without burning them? Could ghosts—were they ghosts or spirits?—*burn*? Nothing more could happen that had not already happened). She smiled in the darkness: they seemed to smile back at her.

They were crouching close to the back of the tent as if they had somewhere else to be, backing away from her, smiles on their faces. (Were they smiles, or masks, she couldn't tell.) Where were they going—to Olivier? Could she follow them? How would she find her way back? She tried to ask them but all they did was giggle; then, suddenly, they disappeared, and she found her new dress soaked in the water from the bowls.

The bowls were in disarray all around her, the light from the candle distorting their roundness into oblong shapes that cast strange shadows. She lifted the candle higher, turned around, did not see the lit wick catch one of the string fasteners that was meant to keep intruders out. She watched as the tent caught fire, transfixed by the blaze eating through the logo: "A gift from the American people."

Fireproofing might have been nice, she thought, absentmindedly, taking the folded piece of paper out from her brassiere, the paper on which someone had handwritten in pencil, "*wozo*"—the word reminding her elusively of Olivier, a word whose meaning she had forgotten.

As she pondered what the word could mean—something about bending, not breaking—she heard a tear in the fabric of the tent behind her, watched without understanding as a knife blade pierced through. She watched the blade cut mechanically, then saw a young man's face peer, a face she did not recognize, followed by an old man's, whom she did: Loko, the man in the camp, a few tents down, who left her rainwater every day. There were women, too: Ma Lou, the market woman, a younger one who resembled Ma Lou about the eyes, and an even younger woman who vaguely resembled the young man who had peered through the breach first, following the blade of the knife, who appeared to be with child.

She was not alarmed. She smiled at them, then turned back to the growing flame, the sudden appearance of these faces daring her to hope. She added the piece of paper inscribed with the fading word to the blaze working its way up to the ceiling of the tent, as their hands reached for her. Now that the girls had gone, and Jonas, too, to find Olivier she thought, she turned her back on the benevolent intruders, not knowing what she should do next, reach out, or up, to bring him, all of them, back to her.

SONIA

Port-au-Prince, Hotel de la Montagne Noire, January 12, 2010
Dieudonné knew that something was wrong shortly after waking that morning. Jonas, the son of Olivier, the man who kept our books, was a little boy of eleven years of age, who could run like the wind and dreamed of being a soccer star. He had already come and gone before making his way to school, with a basket full of avocadoes and orange-fleshed mangoes retrieved from Ma Lou's stand in the market that we would give to the hotel management for indulging our presence. Ma Lou always gave us the best she could find, and the hotel manager radiated pride when she set out the fruit in the hotel lobby to show the foreigners the bounty of our land. We felt less shame, too.

Jonas had fulfilled his errand quickly, as if a spirit were clinging to his heels, giving him unseen force to move through the congested streets, hop on and off the tap-taps, run up the hill to the hotel where we had a room to ourselves, away from the clients, swirling dust like a dervish as he ran back down the hill, early, early in the morning, before the sun had fully risen in the sky, and Dieudonné had turned to face me from his bed and said, "Something is going to happen to that boy, to all of us. We're all going to have to run soon." He seemed half-asleep, entranced on the edges of a dream, or a nightmare, so I ignored him as his eyes closed and his mouth stayed open after he made the pronouncement, as he drifted back to sleep. He had known that something was wrong, was going to go wrong. He told me later that he could sniff it in the air: a too-clean smell that comes in the minutes before a hurricane or a thunderstorm, when the skies are clear and crackling with electric energy, before the winds pick up and snap fronds clean from swaying palms whose rhizomes grasp the earth like tentacular fists, as if fearing to be uprooted by the squalls. A too-clean smell where there should have been only the usual stench and smoke from the burning of garbage heaps gathered at the edges of the street and set to flame there before children like Jonas made their way to school. Not that such order could be counted on, but people tried.

He was confirmed in his suspicion that things were off when he saw the short, pear-shaped, walnut-skinned man in the dark suit and hat, with a white shirt straining across the reach of his bulging, pregnant-like belly, sitting at the bar, a few feet away from the kidney-shaped pool. It wasn't the man he'd told me was his cousin, Richard, who was in town only for a few days and who he had said wasn't anyone we needed to worry about. Richard thought only about himself, according to Dieudonné. He was an important man overseas and didn't have time to think about the trouble he could cause others, though, like most men, he caused trouble along his way anyway. No, the man in question was not Richard. Nor was it Leopold, another distant relation whom I knew only from the way he raked his eyes over my body every time he saw me, attempting with his gaze to penetrate through skin and bone as if my soul would release itself to him, and only him. No, not Leopold. The man eyeing me was much older but voracious in his attention. He stared at me as if I was the round, reddish-green apple he was avariciously biting through that morning. He held the apple akimbo in one hand, preciously, between bites, while the other hand rested ceremoniously on the head of a cane shaped to resemble a duck, or a swan, with two eyes made of red stones, one on either side of the head. The animal head of the cane peered through the gaps between the man's plump fingers. The sight of it was chilling, as if it might turn into a snake at any moment and strike us dead.

I saw Dieudonné shiver from across the bar when, later, the man lit up a thin cigar. He gave me a look across the counter and I could see in his eyes that we were thinking the same thing. *Gede. Se gede ki la*, the god of death. We read each other's thoughts. Dieudonné kept watch on the man, as if to protect me from imminent danger, but the man never moved from his seat, never sent over rum, or wine, not even water.

.

That afternoon, a few times, when the man with the cane had seemed to disappear, Dieudonné would start to relax. We both would. But whenever we thought the danger was gone, and our muscles slackened, the man would reappear, as if to tell us to stay on our guard, to be vigilant, be ready to flee.

The confines of the hotel seemed unsafe, though we did not know why, and we had planned to leave at the first opportunity, but it would take the rest of the day. I had labored all night, and there were things to wrap up before we could leave the hotel for the day, so that all the clients felt taken care of, satisfied. One always had to leave them with an air of normalcy, as if no transaction had taken place the night prior. Later, we could leave and get some rest, elsewhere. Perhaps the mysterious man who made us think of Baron Samedi would move on to the pool, or to a lounge chair; once, we saw him sitting at the bottom of a staircase leading to the second-floor rooms. But the next time that Dieudonné saw the man at the bar, sitting opposite me, and staring, he was tapping the tip of his cane impatiently against the large rose tiles of the courtyard. Was it a Morse code to the underground? Worse, the man was always smiling. At times a smirk, at other times a full smile, teeth bared. A jackal. Were we imagining things? Reading too much into the man's appearance: the hat, the somber suit, the cane, the slight limp when he walked away and disappeared, if only briefly?

Something was wrong. We both could feel it in our bones. Whatever it was, was already happening, we were sure of it. We simply could not see what it was, could not completely prepare for it, as it swooped down on us, all at once. Dieudonné checked and rechecked his phone in case it was someone in my family trying to reach us, my sister, Taffia, or my youngest brother, Paul. I felt Taffia was all right, but Paul had had us all worried for some time. Whenever we went back to the neighborhood to visit my mother or get some help with our accounts from Olivier, a man with a beautiful, morose wife and three beautiful children, including Jonas, the boy who ran errands for Dieudonné and Ma Lou, Paul watched us closely, too closely.

Lately, Paul had been obsessed with the Makout and asked Dieudonné if he was one of them. Dieudonné said nothing, smoked while sitting on his motorcycle, and tried to ignore him, like we all did. Paul took to sitting on the porch when we came, with his back turned away from us, as if he were spying on the girls his age down

the street, when I knew that he was eavesdropping on our conversations, between Dieudonné and me, or Mama and Tatie, as if
something said might open the door to that other, darker world he
thought might solve his problems.

Tatie had told me what Paul had confessed to her so many years
ago, about the priest touching him. Had that been why Paul, puny
and small, the runt of our litter, kept to himself, closed off, sullen
and angry? Had the worst thing already happened to him? Was it
happening to him? Was something else about to happen? We didn't
know, and we didn't want to wait in the hotel to find out.

The feeling haunted us all day, just as the bellied man with the
cane did, appearing, disappearing, reappearing, making us itch to
leave, to get away.

.

Even later, as we were attempting to get out of the city on motorbike,
the hotel fallen, the roads blocked, buildings that we had known all
of our lives now in pieces, neither dead nor living accounted for, we
wondered if we should have done more to acknowledge that death
itself had entered the doors of the hotel (Baron Samedi? The man
with the cane?), if we should have given a warning to others. How
we had made it out was still unclear.

We had been in the elevator with Leopold only minutes before,
stepped out into the lobby, then had decided to escape the hotel
to get some air, anywhere, and then, then, the minute we reached
Dieudonné's motorbike parked under a tree some fifty feet away
from the winding road that led up the mountain to the hotel, the
ground beneath us swayed and undulated like a carpet being shaken

in the air to clear it of crumbs after a meal. We were the crumbs, lifting, weightless. We reached for each other's hands as we rose up in the air. We heard a great thunder and then, suddenly, the hotel had risen, then fallen in on itself like a cake of many layers.

We reached for the tree against which we had left the motorbike to steady ourselves, wrapped our arms around it, the motorbike on its side at our feet, but our feet still there, still there, on the ground. Everything around us heaved, covering us in a heavy coat of dust.

Dieudonné had moved instinctively toward the rubble, maybe thinking of Leopold, with whom he'd exchanged a few terse words on the elevator, telling Leopold, in a glance, to leave me alone. They might have been related, but I came first, always came first. I clasped Dieudonné's arm and the tension in his muscles faded. He did not leave me to return to the collapsed mess in search of Leopold. He turned to look at me. "What happened here? What is happening?" There was no time to dwell on all the day's misgivings. They had, at least, brought us out of the hotel and into a clearing.

When we had sufficiently recovered, we picked up the motor-bike from where it had fallen at the foot of the tree. It was still working. We made our way, in fits and starts, through the debris littering both sides of the road leading down from the hotel. I clung to Dieudonné as I had always clung to him, depending on his knowledge, his certainty. Yet, as we looked out into the blinding dust, seeing the big houses at the side of the road flattened and twisted, their tall walls broken and tumbled, gates broken open with fissures in the ground beneath them, we both wished to be back in that place of uncertainty earlier in the day, that wretched, itching feeling of foreboding. Now that we could see what had happened, any discomfort might be easier to bear. Anything better than what had happened, was happening, anything but having to look upon bloodied and broken bodies, some we knew from the hotel, who had been coming in for shifts, others we never knew, littering the sides of the road all the way down the hill.

I perched on the back of the bike, wrapping my arms around Dieudonné's torso as I always did, and I thought of the scent of all the other men I had been with as I worked the hotel, and other places, discreetly, so that I could still hold my head up when I returned home to the neighborhood.

I couldn't call it home any longer: I had met Dieudonné at seventeen (he was a good ten or fifteen years older than me), left at eighteen, and never looked back except to see my mother, Taffia, and Tatie, to check in, nothing more. I brought back money to the neighborhood, some staples for the kitchen, whatever could be useful. My mother, sister, and aunt counted on me: despite the whisperings in the neighborhood, whatever my younger brother and father said, or did not say. I did not turn my back on them. I knew what was being said about me. It was all true, after all. I was a fallen woman, even if I did my work in the high-paying hotels and private homes in the hills. In a way, I had followed in my mother's footsteps, had not gotten any further than being a servant in a rich man's house. The only difference was that I was not invisible to these men: they wanted me. I made them pay for their desires. No one would take advantage of me the way they had my mother and other women, their servants. One day, those payments would help us get out of rich men's beds; out of the big houses where the help looked down on me and the wives were always absent; out of the island.

Unlike all the other men, Dieudonné, even slick with sweat, had the scent of a grandmother's *mamba*, a peanutty, spicy, homey scent.

The smell comforted me as I burrowed my nose into the nape of his neck and clung on to him for dear life as he gingerly maneuvered the motorbike through a terrain we had crossed many times yet seemed foreign, down the hill and across the city to the neighborhood where my mother and siblings were, to make sure that, like ourselves, they had survived.

As we trekked slowly down, the dust in the air stinging our eyes and layering itself as it fell on our skin and clothes, I felt Dieudonné's heart skip a few beats, then thump quickly, six times, then stop, then another six, then skip again. I pressed a hand flat against his chest, above the cage enveloping his heart, and directed all the energy I could muster toward his irregular heartbeat. I wasn't sure that this would do any good since I had left the church so long ago and was sure that God had turned his back on us, given our lines of work. But who else could we count on? I was conscious of the fact that my hands were clasped against his chest in a cross shape, as if I were praying over him.

Make no mistake: I *was* praying over him.

I was praying for his heart to slow down, to keep beating, regularly.

I was praying for his heart, our heart, not to stop.

.

When we first met, Dieudonné told me that he had been born with a heart defect. At first, I thought that he had meant to say that he had an enlarged heart, but the way he explained the matter to me, it was that the heart had extra parts to it, extra flesh and vessels. I wondered how he had found this out, having no family to speak of, no money for medical care. He told me a story about his heart stopping when he was ten or eleven. How an uncle, his mother's brother, who had been banished from the family for being *masisi*, but had means, had taken him to a private hospital for children; they'd taken pictures of his heart and shown him where it had grown an extra part, when he was still in his mother's womb. Nothing to be done, they told his *tonton*. It skipped a beat once in a while. Nothing to be done about it. He would have to take care, build himself up, become strong.

The night after they had told him the news about his fleshy heart, Dieudonné lay in his cot in the hospital and marveled at his broken heart, not exactly broken, but bigger than normal, different. For him, the enlarged heart explained so many things. It might mean that he could love more or better withstand loss. He'd already lost his mother. He did not know where his father had gone. The uncle from Jérémie came to retrieve him and took him away from the big city for the rest of his schooling, forced him to exercise on the beach, using his body as a weight, everything natural. He built his body up, hiding himself beneath the brawn. It was good that he did so because by the time he needed the muscle behind a fist, he'd discovered that he was like his *tonton*, putting a little too much cologne behind the ears, for other boys, rather than girls. Until, of course, me. I was a *sister*, a *kòmè*, and when he said this to me, I heard those words differently, felt them sink into my bones, deeply. Immediately, we were to each other like fingers of the same hand, eyes in the same head, right and left orbits that made one. There was no other way to explain what could not be explained. We had found each other.

That unlikely meeting had taken place in a club one night, a club for people like us, and for foreigners. We found each other by the rhythm of our feet, nothing else, had not even looked into each other's eyes to see the person behind the movement until we were facing each other, like the lovers we would never become. Unlike lovers, we had practically nothing to learn of one another. We seemed to have emerged from the same womb. We were the same: *marasa*, twins. We looked up from our dancing feet, into each other's eyes, and smiled.

Dancing led to talk, intense conversation, seeing oneself in the other's soul. Dieudonné told me about himself, his single mother, and how she had lost everything, even a piece of her mind, when his father left them and still they saw him walking about town, the relief at knowing that he had not died or disappeared, the pain at knowing that he could smile and laugh, away from them, and had created another life with another woman, other children (for there were many). His mother had died prematurely, old at a young age, but happy in a way, because she knew that her brother, even if he was *masisi*, would take care of her son in Jérémie, and because losing peace of mind had led to losing that piece of mind that made her more aware of her pain. He told me about his job as a fixer, how he could get anything for anyone: car service, drugs, fighting cocks, favors intimate and not so intimate, anything. I told him about how I had traded on my looks since the time I'd discovered that my father was not my father, that I had a half sister by another father, and that I wanted, one day, to be a mistress rather than a maid, to have a rich man's wealth but not his ring on my finger, none of his children. We came to an agreement right there and then: he would look out for me, be my go-between, make sure I didn't have to do anything I didn't consent to do. Then, eventually, eventually, if everything went right, we would get each other out of the game.

He dreamed of a house far away from the road and high in the hills above the capital, in Kenscoff, a house like the rich men owned, where they kept mistresses, or vacationed with their families. He wanted a house like that, no mistress, no children, for himself and chosen family. He described it in such detail that I could see it in my mind's eye, could see myself there. As I thought myself into his dream, felt myself inside of his life, his speech stopped, and I found myself floating there, within, as if in a painting. He continued, "You understand, don't you, that I'm M?"

He had not needed to say it. If you were a hustler, you were always in some way M, queer, even if you didn't know what that meant, had never touched someone of your own sex with desire, or love. I nodded. Told him about the other women I worked with, how we depended on one another, for *everything*. I didn't explain the fact that there was a choice in this for me, that I actively *chose* the women with whom I shared intimacies. I suppose I was deceitful, because I didn't want to break the spell of our meeting, but I was careful to let him know, as we entered into our contract, that he needn't bother brokering paid services for me with women, especially with foreign women. This was my private business. He could think of it what he wanted. I knew that women could be as brutal, as callous, as deceitful; but I still needed an arena of hope and so I chose women, my women, and they, in turn, and for the same reasons, chose me.

Riding the motorcycle across the dust bowl of the city, I thought of the first time my arms had enveloped Dieudonné's sinewy body on that dance floor, so many years ago, and squeezed him even more tightly. His heart responded by skipping, twice, the second time more lightly than the first; then, his pulse raced without stopping and I grew more afraid than I'd been in the moment at which the hotel collapsed thunderously behind us, more afraid than when I thought his hand would never reach across the girth of the tree that, in the end, must have protected us from harm. It, too, was still standing. I closed my eyes against the destruction, leaving Dieudonné to maneuver on his own, as I thought of my mother, sister, brother Didier, and Paul. What had become of them down in the valley of the city? My mind wandered vaguely over the irony of the moment—the black sheep of the family coming to the rescue with her equally suspect knight in shining armor leading the way. Yet with everything collapsed and in shards, who was coming to the rescue could matter little. All that mattered was that we were alive, and on our way.

I clung to Dieudonné as we made our way through clouds of dust, all the while fretting about who I had become, might never be. I hoped that, for today, who I was would be enough for my father, mother, aunt, siblings. As more and more people emerged, ghost-like, from the darkness at the side of the roads, some of them with streams of dark liquid veining their way down the contours of their heads, others crying, and throwing up their ashen arms into the air, I hoped that, whatever they thought of me, we would find everyone that mattered, alive.

.

My mother had always told me that she wanted me to do something more with my life than work in a rich man's house. It was too much work, she said, tiring work, she who had worked as a live-in domestic before she was married, before we were born. Work that broke down your body and your mind. You had to be ready at any time of day or night to get out of your bed and do the things you were asked, whether it was to clean, to cook, or to run an errand. You rarely got any time off, and depending on the morals of the family, you could be asked to do things you never had a mind to do. She didn't spell it out for me, but I knew she meant sex. I never asked if that had happened to her. I imagined that she wouldn't have worked so long in the same house if something had happened there. But I remembered faintly that there had been a succession of houses before she got the job in the house in which she found steady work, when we were all very small, and that my father had once been put in jail for going over to one of those houses and starting a ruckus, though he'd been let out of jail after a few days.

I went to work with Mama once, when I was about ten, before it became Didier's job to follow her to market and to run errands. He was a year or two younger, Paul and Taffia not yet born. My mother had said she needed an extra pair of hands, but I think she wanted to keep me out of trouble. I had wanted to stay home sick from school. But my mother put the back of her hand on my forehead, nodded, and said, "*Oke, ann'ale.*" By this she meant, Okay, I feel something, but you're coming with me. Going with her was better than going to school, I thought, since I could avoid the mean girls in the yard, which, in the end, was all I was striving to do.

We went to market on the way and bought fresh fruits and vegetables for the house from Ma Lou, whose husband had died when he was young and whose rich son lived overseas. Ma Lou still had a smile for everyone, was everyone's mother. Back then, going to market was one of my favorite things in the world to do despite the press of bodies, the flies, the overwhelming stink of sweat emanating from the cane-cutting men who'd set up rows upon rows of purple stalks against the wheelbarrows they'd used to bring them to market, and were whittling them down to carrying size; despite the large women sitting low to the ground on quarter stools, who'd been sitting in the heat for hours already, having set up their wares while the sun was still hiding beneath the lip of the horizon. Secretly, I envied the women, though I knew it was thankless work. I envied their ability to sit in front of all the mounds of fruit and vegetables, all the colors, the illusion of abundance it gave to passersby, that the large women and their children never went a day without eating, never a night to bed with a gnaw in the pit of their stomachs. My mother batted my arms when I slowed down too much or stared at the bounty laid out before us. She shoved the wicker basket we had brought to carry the goods back to the house into my hands, piling things into it as we went, so that I would have something to do.

My mother was spending money that had been given her by the lady of the house; she had to be careful. She was more careful than if she had been buying for us; every penny had to be accounted for as the lady of the house would ask her the cost of every item. My mother had had a few years of schooling before she started working in the big houses. She could read a little and write a little. She could count with numbers. When she went to market, she carried a little notepad with her and a tiny pencil that had been salvaged from a wastebasket in one of the houses, sharpened with a knife by my father down to the metal holder for the rubber eraser at the other end. She had had it for years, and now she wrote down with it the cost of what she purchased. Some of the market women eyed her with suspicion, as if she was a spy for the government, and sometimes did not give in to her demands for a lowered price. Ma Lou was different, though. She and my mother got on well. Ma Lou gave her the best prices, when she could, but that was our neighborhood market. Not all markets were the same, nor all market women. My mother would simply walk away from those who wouldn't haggle and move down the line, where there was always someone else selling more or less the same items a few feet or rows away. That day, we went to a different market from the one in our neighborhood and to a house I did not know.

When we reached the house, my mother found that one of the children of the house had been left in her care for the day, in addition to her usual duties. She was not pleased. The girl looked like an advertisement from a magazine. She had pressed hair and peach-tone skin without one sign of a blemish. Her skin was so taut that it seemed that the bones of her face were polishing the skin from the interior. I had a desire to pass a thumb against the protrusion of one of her cheekbones to see if she was real. When I looked at her closely, though, I noticed that we bore a faint resemblance. The girl looked at me and I could see from the look in her eyes that she thought the same thing upon seeing me. My mother looked back and forth at us, frowned, and sent me to the servants' quarters, where the night maid was sleeping.

The little girl was waiting to be played with, but my mother wanted me to help clean the fruits and vegetables we'd picked up. She told the girl that I would be done in about a half hour. Then she closed the door to the second kitchen, the kitchen most rich people have at the back of the house, not using the one that guests see in the house itself that always stays fresh and gleaming, as if it were staged. We started unburdening the basket of its contents, sorting things out according to what needed to be cleaned right away and what could be put in a bin for later use.

Mama filled a sink with water, added a splash of bleach, and then filled a basin she had cleaned, twice, with soap and water and had set out in the sun to dry, with clear, clean water. I had never seen anything so beautiful as the steel of that basin and the clear, clear water in it. I would have bathed in it.

We set to work. We both had gloves to wear. My mother scrubbed each fruit and vegetable in the sink, then handed it to me to rinse in the basin; then we put them on a clean cloth to rest in the sun until we could wipe them dry and stack them in bowls and clean plastics the lady of the house had gotten out for that use. We then opened the door to the rest of the house and walked to the first kitchen, where we put out a few things for the household to enjoy. The rest, anything that would be cooked for a dinner or made into a sweet, stayed in the refrigerator of the second kitchen. When we were done, I was allowed to play with the little girl of the house, but by then, she had lost interest in me. Another little girl from her school had come by and all I could do was watch them, aware of my plain dress that had been stained from dirt in the market and from the bleach solution splashing on it in the kitchen.

The girl looked so much like me that I felt like I was watching a movie of the life I could have had. I was on one side of a one-way mirror with no way in. I looked down at my simple dress, simple shoes, and was embarrassed. It was to be the beginning of wanting more than I could have, which turned out to be so much less than I had imagined, until I met Dieudonné: a desire to be in a rich man's house. I made my way back through the house with the intention of reaching the courtyard where my mother sat, peeling potatoes, to ask her if I could continue to help. In my mind, I was telling myself to hurry to the courtyard before I was found out, but my steps betrayed me.

Traversing the house, I slowed down as my eyes took in everything there was to see. It was the first time I had seen so many beautiful things accumulated in one place. Multicolored sofas that could seat at least twenty people, love seats and rocking chairs, all fitting into one room; electric lamps with opaque shades covering their bulbs, some made of glass, others of cloth; decorated ceramic dishes on glass end tables and a matching coffee table that were all spotless of fingerprints (surely, the dutiful work of my mother and the maids of the house). I picked one up with two hands and inspected it more closely, then set it back gingerly on the table where I had found it. I looked up and brown faces looked back at me from paintings that were so vivid with color that I felt as if they could transport me into another world, one even more fascinating and filled with beauty than the living room in which I now found myself.

My mother had never told me how beautiful the house was, or if she had, I had not been listening. The walls were high, painted an alabaster white. There were matching drapes pulled back on either side of a white window with angled glass shutters. I had never seen anything like these before and tried to open and shut them with my fingers. The panes of glass had been free of prints before I had come along, and I tried to get them spotless again by using the edge of my skirt to polish off the finger marks. Then I turned back to the room and noticed that they had a statue of the Virgin, a small, painted plaster reproduction, sitting on a small stand covered with a pink cloth in the corner, hidden behind the sofa. At her feet, three gold rings had been laid, and a small bowl filled with what smelled like rose water as I got closer to it and peered down. I was surprised to see all of this. I turned back into the room to see if anyone was watching me. I would have liked to take the statue with me, but I had nowhere to store it.

Years later, I would remember this moment when Taffia, my little sister, narrated to me the story of a popular Mexican telenovela she and others in the neighborhood gathered to watch at the end of some afternoons, after work and before nightfall, at my aunt's, after she had acquired a television. The heroine of the telenovela, called *Frijolito*, would lose her job when she was accused of stealing a statue of the Virgin Mary from her employer's house. I thought about how my mother would have lost her job if I had done the same. No more school for Taffia and Paul. No more little sweets after Sunday Mass and a plump chicken every other week when my mother was home and had the time to fry one up, making enough for my aunt, and others on the street, enough for some leftovers for a few days into the start of the next week. I had crept back silently through the house, back through to the door leading to the second kitchen, back out to the courtyard where I sighed a breath of relief as soon as I saw my mother.

"*Sak pase?*" she said, looking up from her work at me.

"*Anyen,*" I replied, looking away so that she could not see the guilt in my eyes. I didn't want to tell her that I was embarrassed by my plain clothes that showed shadows of old stains, and that I had wandered through the formal part of the house inspecting the luxury items on the walls and tables instead of coming straight through the yard.

"*Vin' isi pou ou kab ede'm.*"

I went to her, grateful that I could help, but wondering about the little girl who looked like me and all the wealth surrounding her. I looked at Mama.

Mama wiped her hands dry on the apron covering her legs. "Let me see how you are doing." She pressed the back of her hand against my forehead as she had done earlier that morning. "*Ou pa gen lafyèv ankò.*" She smiled. "You'll be able to go back to school tomorrow."

"I like it here," I said, thinking about how I could lose myself in the riches every day, staring at the brown faces in the paintings and imagining that I lived in the house. I wanted to ask about the girl. "Mama, did you notice that girl looks like me?"

Mama frowned, looked away. "Here is not for liking. Here is for working." She handed me a blunt knife, then pointed to the potatoes. "I peel, you cut, and then put them in there." She pointed to another steel bowl, as clean and polished as the one we had used earlier. "I am not bringing you here again."

Later, much, much later, I would find out that the girl from the house and I shared the same biological father. It was the reason that man I had grown up thinking of as my father had had that fight long ago and served time in jail. I never saw the girl again; I heard that she had been sent away to school in Canada; but I remembered the house, the paintings, the colored sofas, the gleaming counters of the inside kitchen. I knew, then, that I could either clean houses for the rest of my life, like my mother, and live the same risks, or be the woman that the lady of the house feared, and get paid a higher wage in return to be kept away. The choice seemed that simple, and not really a choice. I was what I was, but I thought I could change my destiny, eventually. Then Dieudonné came along and solidified a new dream. We would hustle, and one day buy that house in the hills, and no one would have to know what we had to do to get there. What we had learned from the hustle was that once you got to the top of the hill, no one cared how you got there.

Once I asked Dieudonné how he made sense of our relationship. He shrugged and said, "I like it because there is nothing physical between us and yet we love each other. What greater love could there be?" I nodded in assent but wondered if we could have made a child together, wondered whether this would have changed things, our social status, how it might have enabled ease of movement through the world. The difference a child's love could have made, whatever we *chose* to call ourselves, whomever we chose to take to our beds. I would have let him have his male lovers, if he needed them, the way I needed the touch of a woman after the long days of laboring beneath men who could not see me. We could have made a home separate from all that. It would have been a different life, one I could have worked to make, but I knew he did not think of it, and did not share the fantasy I had created for us in my mind, an appendage to the house in Kenscoff he had described during our first meeting, in that conversation that never came to an end.

Still, I also knew that I had made some of the decisions I had because, deep down, I didn't want children, had seen the way Taffia and, especially, Paul fought to keep some shred of innocence. After Tatie had revealed his secret (and the secret of so many boys in the rectory) to me, I thought of Paul differently, tolerated his sullenness and strangeness, because something in us was the same, sullied. The country was too harsh, the despair too profound for me to want to bring a child into it. The hotels offered a way out, at least out of the squalor of the streets below. It wasn't honorable work, but I could take the money from these fat men who paid to lie with me, take the money and build something for myself, Dieudonné, my mother, my aunt, Taffia, and anyone else who might want to join us, something respectable (did I think of Paul?). I could become mistress of my own house. I didn't have to be the girl looking into a mirror back at myself. The girls I worked with had all kinds of ideas for new businesses. We planned to merge and partner, create an underground empire. We could pool together our money, buy houses in different parts of the city, of the island even, be free. I clung to these thoughts, the impossible alternatives, when there were moments, pauses, spaces in which to cling to the impossible as a way to get through the endless days, as I clung to Dieudonné in the midst of utter decay and destruction. I suspected that most of the women who had been working the hotel that morning had died within the walls of the building, as it collapsed heavily, as we'd walked away toward the motorcycle, leaving all the eeriness of the morning behind us. There would be no more whispers in the night, no more secrets to lay bare like the inside yolks of eggs after boiling. They had died but the whispered secrets would live on within me.

If we had made a child, I thought, as we drew closer to the neighborhood. If we had had a child, it, too, would be dead. I thought of Jonas, who had gone running down the hill that morning, before the sun rose, wondered if he had made it to and from school, if he was running, where he might be, whether his father, Olivier, was out looking for him. If he was, still. If we had had a child, looking out on the sea of destruction on both sides of the road, I was certain that he or she would be dead now. Thank God we had not made one. Thank God.

We moved into what seemed to be arrested motion, an atmosphere thick as molasses, not knowing what we would stumble across next. Dieudonné brought the motorcycle to a halt next to my father's collapsed house and I swung my leg over the bike to reach what firm ground there was left to reach, one hand remaining clasped to his.

As we came to stand next to each other, buttressed against the ebbing heat of the motorcycle, surveying the fallen house, we both knew that all we could do now was search for signs of life.

RICHARD

Port-au-Prince, Hotêl de la Montagne Noire, January 9, 2010
Without water, let's face it, we're nothing. We are born with a makeup of 75 percent water that diminishes with time. Until we dry up. If we stay in good health, the content of water in the body stays above 50 percent and doesn't fall below 45 percent even if the cause is gross obesity. It's a strange fact, but the fatter you are, the less water there is in your body, proportionally. The thinner you are, the more liquid. In all cases, water is needed to survive, so that joints remain flexible, supple, articulations and digits in shape, flexible. Boiled water is decontaminated, for the most part. Pure water, in certain parts of the world, is harder to find. It's used, there, rather than for drinking, or cultivation, to light the homes of the wealthiest, as in India, where huge dams have been built to divert water to energy plants, flooding the land of the peasants, who depend on both land and water to grow food. The powers that be import their food and the peasant farmers starve to death, or die of thirst, or hang themselves. The dams are so huge you would think Brobdingnag, where Gulliver landed after his foray into the world of the Lilliputians, does exist. Looking out onto those dams, as I've done in my travels, you feel like a gnome, puny and minuscule. Kilometers of land were flooded to

build them, to make the water recirculate where the earth had not placed it naturally. I know you've never heard of the farmer suicides, but they've happened, hundreds, thousands of them. I don't know how many—I'm not paid to keep those numbers in mind—but it's a lot. Anything you drink, filtered water has been added to it. But pure, filtered bottled water in the Third World? It's not that easy to find. In a general sense, it's a luxury. If you are the last remaining of the dispossessed, you can make a rock soup and whatever else you can get your hands on. When I was young, we boiled the water, let it cool, poured it into clean glass milk bottles, then set them in a fridge or a cool place. There was no other choice.

It was here, in Haiti, as a child, that I learned to recognize and differentiate grades of purity, to appreciate them. Little did I know that it would serve as the key to my fortune later, after I left the country and made my way in Europe. I learned to recognize the degree of purity in water by the odor of boiled water. When I had my first glass of filtered water with the priests running the board-ing school where I was placed as an adolescent, I felt transported into another universe, somewhere pure and clean, far from mounds of stinking garbage that lined the roads, far from the smoldering heaps that perfumed the dawns. One day, we were given glass bot-tles with labels that indicated that the water they contained came from Switzerland, by way of France, with drawings of glacial moun-tains devoid of populations: a country of empty space. From that moment, I thought only of that other world, and of the properties of water. Everyone needed it. I could be a savior and become rich. The truth, of course, was that I thought more about becoming rich. As you can surmise, not much has changed.

When I met Patricia a little over ten years ago, she was drinking that water that had converted me in adolescence. I took it as a sign of a common destiny. She was then—as she has always been, despite the two pregnancies—thin, elegant, with a mocking air as if she didn't have the time to think about whatever was going on around her. I loved her instantly. Later, when we were married, I noted that she didn't drink enough water. I should have known from this that the marriage wouldn't hold.

I was in front of the executives in an office close to the Champ de Mars and my thoughts were beginning to crowd. I was missing the funeral of my eldest daughter's mother, intentionally. Missing my daughter, Anne, herself, who would return to her internship in the US within a day or two, go on to her first job in the field somewhere far away. The funeral had provided a convenient excuse for my own return to Haiti, which I had left behind long ago, but all I had done was continue to work, make my deals. Had I started to speak out loud my reminiscences about my wife, Patricia? What had I told them? I looked around the somber faces assembled at the table. The silence was dizzying. Some were leafing through the prospectus that the head office had prepared for them. Here, everything was still done on paper, in the old way. No one was looking at me, a sign that I had spoken out loud about my personal problems without noticing; the other executives didn't want to embarrass me by calling attention to the fact. Some cleared their throats.

"*Bien!* Good!" said Michel, the local manager at the head of the meeting, a little too loudly. He smiled at me thinly, prodded, "Maybe we can all take a little time to read the information over and reconvene tomorrow?"

"Yes, yes." I was grateful for the intervention. "I'm convinced that our company can make a breakthrough here. We all *so* need good water." I had yet to imagine how to sell the concept of individual water bottles in a country where half the people did not have hard currency, *kòb*, as my mother would have said. It was virgin territory. It was necessary to advance, penetrate. The key had to be to start at the top and then let things trickle down. Trickle-down economics—the American method, and who, here, did not want to become an American, however much they protested interventions and occupations? The method of gathering the droplets from rainwater that no one had the time to gather in large barrels no longer worked. Here, in the city, more was needed. Modernity. My thoughts were starting to come together. I was speaking out loud. Everyone seemed relieved to see me regain my senses.

"Good, good," Michel said, getting up and slapping me on the back amicably to stop my speech. "Let's continue tomorrow. Thank you, Richard, for this opportunity. We're very grateful." All said in an impeccable French.

I shook his hand, then that of each person at the table. Although I already knew that I wouldn't recall their names, for the moment, I had saved face; but then I decided to hold the bull by the horns, and go in for the kill. I would not leave that room without the contract. "Why leave for tomorrow what you can do today?" I said.

The Haitian executives assembled all watched me with a doubtful air, as if, after this morning's performance, they were all sure that they were dealing with a madman escaped from an institution. I simply smiled at them to make them feel better. I had already shed the sober dark blue Parisian-style suit, with its narrow, matching tie, in which I had arrived in Port-au-Prince. I was dressed in a relaxed style, what I imagined could be described as "Caribbean style"—white cotton shirt over khaki pants and handmade leather sandals. I felt comfortable. I had forgotten that, in Haiti, businessmen liked to dress like Frenchmen. Dressing in a relaxed way, as I had, could be taken as a sign of disrespect. But these days, it was important to take an anti-colonial stance rather than a "French" one. Everything that was American was good, whether it was the second-rate rice sent by the barrelful by NGOs, white and translucent, without any taste, or the boxes of instant macaroni in which could be found packets of dehydrated cheese of a striking orange color vaguely reminiscent of the color of rust, that tasted like cardboard. The *macaroni au gratin* that the old people used to make had become a relic of the past, a luxury, because the American products, even when they were bad, when they needed to be bought, were so expensive that they acquired a fetish value. In other words, despite the fact that my product was French, I told them, I knew the importance of selling the "American Dream," and the more I spoke, the more I saw the faces of the executives relax, saw them buy what I was selling. They forgot how I had gone off the rails minutes ago. Some might even have thought that I had done it on purpose, that it was part of the performance, the sales pitch—to play the overworked manager one minute, then the playboy on vacation the next, illustrate by example the good that my product could do.

Michel looked relieved. The meeting over, he shook my hand solidly and slapped me on the back. "Well played," he said to me in a low voice, "well played." To the others, loudly, he exclaimed, "I think that our friend here has shown us the future. This will put Port-au-Prince on the map. Brothers, shall we sign?"

There were skeptics in the bunch, but they all nodded. As soon as it comes to money, businessmen don't retreat when you show them the earning potential. They all know you have to strike when things are hot.

Dieudonné arrived to collect me in a somber-looking suit. He had gone to Anne's mother's funeral and returned. The look on his face registered his disapproval. I ignored it. I had a few days to rest before returning to Paris. I had signed a contract for millions of dollars to sell bottled water to a starving, thirsty people. My bosses would be pleased. Whether we could move the merchandise was another matter. For now, the most important thing was the exclusivity of the contract. I wanted nothing more than to retreat to my hotel room, swim in the pool, drown in the rum punches I had stopped drinking abroad but that signified home. Forget everything, even Anne and her deceased mother. Forget what had truly brought me here.

I wasn't the only one having a good time by the side of the pool next to the hotel bar. Every afternoon and late into the night, the businessmen, the high-class prostitutes, the drug dealers, the "pretty people," the chosen ones from the working dregs, the young people without occupations from rich families, the artists seeking patrons, and others seeking something like love, or its facsimile, converged in the mountain, protected by the tall trees, kept safely out of the sight of the lowly poor. Every night, it was a circus. You wouldn't have thought that this was a Third World country, one of the poorest. It was more like Las Vegas, which I had been to once or twice: the excess, the debauchery.

The pool at the Hotel de la Montagne was in the form of what the people called a *pois rouge*, or red kidney bean. The food was also

Haitian: rice boiled together with those same red beans until they stuck together, *riz collé*, or red bean sauce, *pois en sauce*; herring or chicken in a spicy sauce called *ti malis*, little devil or pleasure, that made the tongue dance. At night, there was a buffet with *bananes pesées*—flattened and fried plantain disks—and all kinds of other delicacies of the island. Everything was done with flair, refined, with the tables covered in white linens and serviettes so white one could imagine the cleaning women hitting the cloths with all their might after soaking them in bleach to make the coffee, wine, oil, and Tabasco sauce stains disappear. I saw the women through the evidence of their labor and I missed them in an indistinct way, as if they had been my mothers, and, in a way, they were. The dining room was a few paces beyond the pool, under a canopy. This gave the impression that both spaces were linked, that you could go from a dip in the pool to a formal dining experience, though this wasn't entirely true. But you could slip into one of the poolside tables and be served a glass of punch and plates of fried shrimp with a red sauce that was sweet, *à l'américaine*, mild, on the side.

I swam the length of the pool with long strokes and every time I came up for air, I could see a young man dressed in Hawaiian shorts, that is, shorts that reached beyond his knees to his calves, while his bare chest browned in the hot sun, dark glasses on his nose, eating an entire plate of the famed deep-fried shrimp all on his own. I watched as Dieudonné shook hands with the young man and, after he made a gesture of cordial salutation my way when he saw me looking over at them, sat next to him. They resembled each other.

I did a few more pool lengths before deciding to join them. When I pulled myself out of the pool and advanced toward them, the blue towel reserved for poolside use in hand, drying off one arm, then the other, they were deep in conversation. I had some trouble piercing through until, finally, the young man decided to reveal to me his identity.

"Leopold," he said to me, putting out a hand without the intention of standing up. The lack of formality rubbed me the wrong way, but I hid my irritation from them by nodding, then by pretending not to see the offered hand and continuing to dry myself, first my legs, then my back.

"He's our cousin," Dieudonné said to Leopold, and cracked a smile, "from over the water." The two men laughed. We did all vaguely resemble each other. Then, Dieudonné turned to me, "How did the meeting go?" He had changed out of the suit he had worn to the funeral and seemed to have gotten over the fact that I had been absent when I had said I would be there. He wore sandals, linen pants, a summer shirt open at the collar, revealing a thick golden chain.

I took my time to reach for a chair from another table and spread my towel over it to dry in the sun; then I sat myself down and made a sign to the bar boy to bring me over a drink. I wanted to get good and drunk as I normally never allowed myself to do.

"*Bof,*" I said, feigning indifference. "Sometimes it goes well, sometimes not so much. But this time the deal went through."

"You're in business, then?" The young man tried to hook me into a conversation. I could not place his accent.

"Where are you from?"

He smiled at me, closed the lighter with which he had lit a cigarette dangling from his fingers, and placed it back atop the carton of smokes.

"From Trinidad. And you?" He gestured at the pack. "Would you like one?"

"You speak Kreyòl well for a Trinidadian." Then I nodded and extended my hand for a smoke.

"My people are from the mountains of Paramin, in north Trinidad. The people there came from Haiti back in the day, so they say." He waved his cigarette in the air. He seemed too young for me to take seriously.

I glanced at Dieudonné, who was smoking his own cigarette quietly as he watched a young woman at the bar. The bar was a meeting place. A place for games and exchanges. I had forgotten that part of local hotel life. Members of different social camps mixed as if they had always done so, even though, when morning came, they withdrew to their corners and distanced themselves from one another to regain their worlds, their people, as if they had never collided, flesh never touched flesh. There were those who felt the mixing unfortunate. I overheard snatches of conversation from the elites frequenting the hotel:

"One has to tell the truth. Things can't continue like this. We have the right to an exclusive domain, by God!"

Another man chimed in. "All that needs to happen is to implode the bottom of the city, the port, the shantytowns, everything, and, *voilà, la comédie fini.*"

"*Pouf,*" said the first man's wife with a flap of hand. "*Ni vu, ni connu.*" The French phrase might be translated as "out of sight, out of mind," but here it had the macabre implication that if you were never conscious of someone, you were freed of the guilt of their disappearance: never seen, never known.

"It's already this way," one of the other wives added. "All these people, these ants, *sans-papiers.* Do you remember? We used to call them 'without-mothers' not so long ago."

"We mustn't confuse things, dear," said one of the men, taking the hand of the woman who had just spoken in his own. "The 'san-manman' were armed thugs. The 'without-papers' are simply poor people, the offspring of illiterates, who don't know how to get to the town hall to register their children, of which they have too many, one has to say." He insisted on this final point with a shake of his head, eyes wide.

"You're right," the woman said in a honey-laced tone. You could tell from their body language that they had been together a long time. I noted that the assembled members of the group were all of different shades of brown. The first to speak was rather dark, like the pit of an avocado. Some of them came, perhaps, from groups who had climbed socially after the "Black power" period; some called themselves "*noiristes*."

"Make everything disappear?" said another as he swiftly grasped his glass and took a swig from it. "That would be quite difficult. And anyway, we might be swept up with the others." He smiled wickedly. "We would need a very selective method, no?"

It was already difficult enough to tell the difference between those who felt that they naturally belonged in the four-star hotel and those who took pains to appear as if they could not possibly belong at the bottom of the mountain.

Dieudonné turned around to look at me, then turned his glance to the young man who resembled him, us. He pointed at Leopold with the lit end of his cigarette. "Leopold is in business, like you."

"Business? What kind of business?" What I was thinking was that a man his age could only be a hustler. I turned away from eavesdropping to focus my attention on the two young men, my distant relations.

"What would you like?" Leopold beamed, opening his hands wide.

I smiled back without following his lead, took a drag from my cigarette. I shrugged and took a fried shrimp from Leopold's plate, passed it through the American sweet sauce, and stood up while eating it. "They're beautiful, aren't they?" I said, without distinguishing between the shrimp and the women at the bar. Dieudonné frowned and turned his glance back toward us.

Leopold tried again. "What do you sell?"

"Me?" I smirked at them both and then I made a definitive gesture toward the pool. The ash fell from my cigarette. "I'm into water!"

"Are you serious?"

"Yes, I'm serious." I was slightly insulted. Who could not be serious when it came to water? I thought. Especially here. "You see," I continued, letting the words linger, "here, like where you come from, or in Bangladesh or Timbuktu, water is dear—it's expensive, and everyone needs it. The problem is that not everyone can afford it. You understand? It's my challenge to package something that everyone should be able to raise from the earth but can't—they have other things to do—and to sell it back to them, as if it had never been theirs in the first place. I'm selling convenience, purity, the essence of life itself." I let myself get carried away.

Dieudonné was preoccupied with a young child, an errand boy. The boy, too, looked familiar, like I had been when I was the boy's age, thin and clear-eyed, fast on my feet, not as I was now, paunchy. I thought I heard Dieudonné say my mother's name, as he spoke to the boy, and felt torn between the two conversations. I nodded to Dieudonné and glanced at the boy, whom he was holding by the shoulder.

"This is Jonas," Dieudonné said. "He runs errands between here and the market for us. He knows your Ma Lou." I looked into the boy's face and saw myself as I once was.

The boy smiled toothily and waved. I raised my hand with the cigarette, wanly, thought of the mother I had neglected all my life, resented even, when I was this boy's age. I missed nothing of the market, its pungency, its thickness. Still holding the boy by the shoulders, Dieudonné told me Anne would be leaving the country soon, a fact I already knew. I shrugged and said I would catch up with her later.

I had missed the funeral. I had not even planned on sending flowers or taking money over to the family as an excuse for my neglect. He told me Ma Lou would want to see me. I would call her, I said, and felt no need to see her. I no longer thought of myself as having a mother. She had birthed me, this was true, taken care of me those early years, but I had rebirthed myself. I was my own mother.

.

January 6, 2010

I should have been on vacation, seaside, with the family, like we do every holiday break, a few weeks after school let out for the kids, for the December break. I have two. Well, three, but there, in France, only two: a girl and a boy. Usually, I close the office for one or two weeks and then I catch up with them. I always loved that period when I was alone, before the vacation, making my own suitcase, taking the train solo. Sometimes, I left pretending that I was a single man, seeking an adventure, but the memory of the children's laughter, Patricia's smile, always made me forget forgetting. I looked for what I might bring them from the train station or a stop on the route, candies for the little ones, some magazines for Patricia that she hadn't already gotten for herself. But nothing unfolded as expected this time. This time, everything was already disordered. The compass we'd become for one another was no longer working.

I had been going in one direction, and there I was, only a few weeks later, going in another. I settled into the plane seat that would take me back to the shores of my birth, closed my eyes, and tried to shut out the cacophony of the passengers finding their way into their narrow seats at the back while I sat snuggled in first class, stuffing their too large bags into the overhead bulkheads. I took a deep breath. I wanted to throw everything into the abyss of this flight through all time zones. If only the flight could have lasted for eternity.

I wanted to leap out of my own skin, become a werewolf, or a *soucouyant*. Leave my life behind, like a heavy coat, shed it all and fly away between the shards of light in the night sky, stars and faraway bodies. I understood them, the *soucouyants*, their cries, desires, even their insatiability. I dreamed, once, when I was a child, of becoming like them: of flying away.

When my father died, and my mother found a place for me in a boarding school where they took me in for free because I read five years beyond my age level and had a mind like they didn't expect to see in the child of a market woman and a cobbler, I seized the opportunity: I fled. Little by little, I put distance between myself and my mother. A few times, at the beginning, I didn't go to meet her when they told me she had come for Sunday family time; I pretended that I was sick or had homework to do. She always said she understood; she said she knew I was destined for great things and didn't want to get in my way. My father was gone. There was no one to work against or make proud. I did not think of what this might do to my mother. I ignored her. With my own life in tatters, I realize now the turmoil I must have caused her. For someone like me, you understand, it's not easy to admit having lost control. It's like this: when everything becomes chaos and disorder, you begin to understand that control is only illusion and repression. I built my life on the drunkenness of ambition, without listening to anyone, even those I considered my life's great loves.

Let me be blunt: I'm rich. I have a beautiful apartment in the sixteenth in Paris, and a second home on the north coast, in Trouville, on the sea, a house that my wife's uncle, a widower who survived his wife for more than twenty years, without children, left my wife after his death. We were the only inheritors. I seized the opportunity to purchase an empty lot adjoining the property, and I undertook renovating and enlarging the little house to transform it into a real refuge from the fast pace of Paris. I imagined my children and their children playing in the yard, children with curled hair, golden, skin tones of all colors, their eyes green, gray, sparkling brown, overflowing from the joys of living. Patricia laughed when I spoke to her of it, even when I showed her the plans and the architect came to consult with us in the Paris apartment in search of clarifications and, of course, money, lots and lots of it.

We'd never spoken of having children, Patricia and I, yet we had two: Richard Jr. and France. I imagined that there would be others when Patricia recovered from the difficulties of her childbirths. But she never bounced back. Being a man who could transmit his genes only through the intermediary of a woman—my woman, any woman, as you like—I didn't want to leave the choice only to her. She knew it, fought me, and took her precautions. When I understood this, there were moments when I could have killed her. Instead, I yelled. It was ugly, dirty. I made her ingest my inflated, ego-driven thoughts like so much waste tossed upon a garbage heap. I forgot, in the meantime, that I loved her, that I wanted her. I simply thought that it was a matter of dominating her. That's how you win in business, how you stay ahead of the pack. I didn't know how to do otherwise. I'd always won. Sometimes, I've learned lately, you have to lose to win. I didn't know how to lose.

Looking back, I can see that I inflicted a form of slow torture. Not directly, not physically, but living with me was a form of abuse, I would say. I can see that, now that she's discovered my secret. Now that she's left. I couldn't foresee what was about to fall below my nose like two fried eggs on my morning plate, that morning like any other only a few weeks ago now, a morning when the children got ready for school and I was to drop them off after breakfast. Next to my plate: divorce papers.

Patricia sat there, as she did every morning, *as if nothing was happening*: a queen in her palace. I had to admit that she played her hand well. She had undertaken the operation like someone used to managing a large enterprise having to liquidate everything to save herself, her investments and investors. She peered at me over her glasses for a moment (she was reading the daily newspaper).

"I'm leaving you," she said, in a normal tone of voice, as if she were announcing that we had run out of milk. She continued: "I'm taking the children. I'm going to the summerhouse, but I want you out of the apartment. It's the easiest way to leave things." She was looking at me. I made no sign of understanding. She went on: "You hear me,

Richard? We are leaving you." Who was this "we" she was speaking of? She couldn't be speaking for the children, could she? Her voice had become a little sharp. I would have liked to modify her tone as if she were a tape, controllable, to rewind. She continued, "You can stay a few days, but I'd prefer that you were gone by the weekend to make things easier."

I drank my coffee quietly and watched her. I didn't know what to think. The children were buzzing around, in their rooms, in the bathroom, finishing their morning preparations. There must have been something that I had missed. She was hiding an ace in her pocket and I didn't know what it could be. For her to be so serene, without stress, it had to be something big, something that I couldn't undo. She watched me, tried to unmask me. I had trouble hiding the unease beginning to gnaw at me, to bother me. What could it be? I chose to hide my perturbation. I shrugged. "Is this a joke? Are you joking?"

"You know me, Richard," she said calmly. "I don't know how to play games."

She was telling the truth. She had never liked games, races, playing the stock market, not even playing with the children. That she did, but begrudgingly, because it could not be avoided, and made for a serene household. Now I could admit it: we should have avoided having them.

I tore my eyes away from her to watch the kids, who were floating through the rooms of the apartment without truly under-standing how their world was about to change irrevocably, even if they had understood the situation before I had. Reality hit me. I returned to watching her, all the while masticating a corner of toast. The jam from the grandmother on the first landing had a bitter taste in my mouth though it was thick and sweet. The bread seemed tough, like cardboard. I realized, slowly, that she had been feeding this vision of the future for weeks, maybe even for months. Finally, I understood that I had been betrayed, profoundly betrayed, that she had included the children in this without their realizing what was going to transpire. She had beaten me to the finish line when I had not even seen one in the distance. She was stronger than I was, and I had not recognized it. I swallowed this with some difficulty. I did everything I could to seem composed.

I stood and passed the table to gather up the children, and I saw the glimmer of a smile take hold of the corners of her mouth. She knew that she had won. Me, I was still trying to understand how she could have pulled it off.

While I drove the children to school, and they persisted in buzzing with questions I half attempted to answer with a nod or some mumbled words, my attention was turned fully inward. I wanted to know what Patricia might have found that rendered her so sure of herself, more sure of herself than I had ever seen in our common life.

When the children got out of the car with their schoolbags dragging on the ground, and while they waved to their friends already arrived, I felt my body turn cold, as if I had been struck ill. "Eh," I yelled after them, "don't drag your bags. You'll wear them out." I couldn't have cared less about the bags and what could happen to them by their misuse. They were replaceable, like their little shoes and their coats, all the stuff that having kids brought with it. Watching them as they receded into the swarm of lithe arms and legs, I understood with a jolt that they had already become much older than I thought. I had the tendency to think of them as still being in preschool or kindergarten, at the start of things, but they were already a few years into elementary school; they had friends I had never met, even if I had been told their names. Then, now, in a fatal, sweeping gesture, Patricia had announced that she was going to take them away, forever. I would never know my children fully, not really.

I watched them careening like birds in the schoolyard until someone behind me became impatient and started to sound their horn furiously. I had forgotten that I was in the drop-off/pickup lane, the zone for transitory transfers. I put the car back in drive and then followed the road that led to my office. It was important to move forward, not look back, though I already imagined myself pleading with Patricia, kneeling before her, supplicating her not to do what she had been dreaming of doing for some time. This image before me of myself vanquished, flattened, gave me vertigo. What was happening to me? I was still feeling unbalanced, feverish, everything capsizing around me, even the road, dropping even more, as I realized that it was the first time that I had felt so concretely something of the love I carried deep within me for my children. Instead of a feeling of exhilaration, the sentiment was a nauseous ball caught in my throat.

As I arrived in my office, that ball threatened to swell and explode. I couldn't respond to the usual civilities and I buried myself in my office while making a sign to the secretary not to disturb me, not to allow anyone in. I needed to think. I didn't know what or how to think any longer, or how to function. What did Patricia know, that I didn't, to be so sure of herself, so convincing in her departure?

I was ruminating on this when the secretary, Stephanie, peeked her head into the room. I hadn't even opened the blinds. I was in the dark, like a pouting, sniveling child, asking myself how I would solve this unfathomable problem. Stephanie had brought me water, as usual; I almost never drank coffee or alcohol.

"Sir," she began, a hesitation in her voice.

"Yes?" I straightened up in my chair, pretending everything was fine. But nothing was. The space was heavy with my sadness and my disarray. "What is it?"

"The water," she said simply.

"Ah, yes. The water," I repeated, like a simpleton. "Let's take a look."

She brought me a pitcher filled with our own water, to start the day, and, next to it, a competitor's sample. I put on my glasses, but I didn't have the taste for this silly game that had been my bread maker for these many long years.

"Thank you, Stephanie," I told her, while pretending to examine the packaging of the new rival. I made a gesture simultaneously indicating that she could leave the room.

"Sir?" she murmured.

"Yes?"

"You're forgetting that you have a meeting with the marketing team for this product in a half hour."

Yes, I had forgotten. Not only the meeting but the file. The file was on the table, at home, surrounded by the remains of breakfast that I had left there, without thinking twice about it, probably right next to the divorce decree awaiting my signature, which was going to wait a long time.

I frowned. It was essential not to let on that I had let myself be affected by a domestic problem. How many times had I fired subordinates for reasons as banal as a lack of attention in the office due

to their distraction over their personal affairs? I never even asked
them to explain what was going on. The office had to come first.
Business first. One had only to look at the shelves lining my office walls—which I showed them as I made a little speech about
priorities—filled with national and international prizes. Trophies,
plaques, certificates: I had received all known accolades. I wanted
only this from my team: absolute success, and along with that came
absolution, no, a dispensation from all domestic responsibilities. In
the end, that was the sphere of women, and of children. And children were, of course, the responsibility of women.

Stephanie looked worried. She had already heard all my speeches
and I knew that she couldn't care less about them as much just as I
couldn't care less about the personal lives of my staff. It was one of
the reasons why I found her likable. Patricia had once accused me
of committing adultery with her. Nothing of the kind would have
ever come to my mind. She was lovely, certainly, but having an af-
fair in the office with one's secretary was such a cliché, not my kind
of thing at all. Anyway, I loved Patricia, whatever she thought she
suspected. Truth be told, I respected Stephanie because she had no
fear of me, which perhaps gave the impression that I cared for her.
What I cared about in the office was reliability, efficiency, loyalty.
She had all three. Which is hard to find. *La femme de ma vie.* It's an
expression you can use only once or else it is meaningless. I didn't
have to think about it. It was a fact. That one was Patricia. Stephanie, other women, I never gave them a serious thought. "Stephanie, you wouldn't have a copy of the file to lend me, would you?"

Stephanie stared at me. I sensed disapproval in her gaze, but she
didn't miss a beat. "Of course, sir. Right away," and she left the office
to find the papers I needed. I knew that the only file that existed

was the one that I had forgotten. She was going to reconstruct the key pieces so that I wouldn't have to be embarrassed in front of the competition. She knew how important it was for me not to lose face, never to lose.

Without thinking about it, I took the bottle of the competitor in hand and drank it in one go. I had an extreme thirst. Then I drank half the pitcher of our own water while holding my breath. I was so thirsty. A thought crossed my mind: the competitor's water was a bit more mineralized than ours. The thought distracted me from my current troubles. Aside from that, no difference. I took another swallow of water, swished it in my mouth as if tasting a vintage wine. My taste buds awoke. Perhaps not all was lost. Maybe I could set to climbing back up the slippery slope. Maybe I could find a way to undo whatever it was that had made Patricia's actions possible. I reasoned: I would return home at the end of the day and I would use all available arsenal to change her mind. It was not a woman, *my* woman, who was going to defeat me like this. I was a master of negotiation. I took the competition's bottle in my hands to better examine the packaging. It looked American: attractive, colorful, showy, a bit over the top. The kind of packaging designed to make children beg their mothers at the checkout stands for an impromptu purchase despite the fact that it was only water. Just water: I could have laughed out loud if it didn't involve millions.

In the boardroom, the other executives were, like me, ready to launch the offensive. They hoped to win but they knew deep within themselves that they'd already lost, otherwise we'd be speaking to them through third parties, likely their attorneys. They were here because they were hoping to win something; that we might all come out of it winning. This was the art of negotiation.

I took a moment to compare the waters, theirs to ours. Stephanie played along by pouring large glasses of each. I pointed out the
subtle differences between their product and ours, the mineralized
aftertaste of their sample. Of course, I said to them tactfully, that
little bitter taste at the back of the throat might please some. (The
art of conquest is always to know to whom you are speaking.) I
spoke to them of water: fresh water, seawater, the water we come
across in the country during family vacation, far from the city, the
water from elsewhere that we suspect of being poisoned, the water
our grandmothers gave us right out of the faucet that we gurgled
down with pleasure, to please, despite the metallic taste left by the
pipes. Water was, finally, a need for purity for some, a *madeleine*, a
mnemonic, for others. I took the sample bottle in hand; I caressed
it as if it were some precious progeny. I flattered their modern, hip
packaging, and then I administered the coup de grâce: "Sirs," I said,
"I'm prepared to offer you a deal: your packaging, our water—or,
even, your water and your packaging, as you like, but our name.
Does this satisfy you?" I'll spare you the details. We shook hands
across the table, took notes down regarding the accord, and a beautiful future spread out before us all. Competitors became friends.
Where there is conflict, there are also the seeds of resolution, somewhere. It's a matter of finding them, those seeds, the spark of the
possible. In this case: mutual profit.

It was with this conviction in mind that I left the office for
home, sure that I simply had to find the common ground between
us, between Patricia and myself, to undo the disagreement, the dis-
cord, the divorce papers still preening on the kitchen table.

But that night, for the first time, there was nothing waiting for
me when I returned. I didn't find the children's clothes dropped

haphazardly, as they usually were, a little bit everywhere, nor did I stumble across their schoolbags, nor my wife's cellular that she normally left on the table in the foyer, at the door of the apartment, as if she assumed that once she had crossed the threshold, no one should bother trying to get ahold of her. The phone rang at all hours, vibrated left and right, but she left it there, ignored it. I was often the one who went to see who had called her and reported back. She was a woman beyond reproach, or so I thought, with nothing to hide. With a kind of insouciance, I had failed to imagine that she might betray me or risk an infidelity, but the thought did cross my mind when, as I arrived in our bedroom, I saw that she had taken the vast majority of her clothes and that, on her makeup vanity, she had left, instead of a written note, her wedding ring. She had severed ties.

I went quickly, quickly, into the children's rooms. There, too, many things were gone. I opened the drawers of their dressers: underwear and socks gone. She had organized things impeccably, which meant that she had had this planned.

I returned to the foyer to search for the cellular, as if, maybe, she could have left it behind, left an indication of an eventual return. I had the thought that she might try to call me on it, to give me news of the children, to explain everything, to explain to me what I could do to make things right, what I might have done to alter this outcome. I searched for my own cell phone and found it in an outer pocket of my suit jacket. I looked at the display screen: no messages, no texts. I plunged the phone back into the chamber I had pulled it from and set back to searching for my wife's phone where she usually tossed it on the foyer table amid the accumulated mail. I was still thinking in those terms, "my wife"—an expression that she

had always found objectionable when I introduced her as such at
business meals and gatherings where her only role was to make a
good impression on my behalf. Patricia provided me with an entrée
into a world that preserved its prejudices against brown men. Even
in business, the persistence of old ways of thinking preserved this
out-of-date banality, but in the face of reality, one had to fight fire
with fire. Patricia was for me a fire that I used to blaze through
the closed universe of the bigwigs of French society, but she was
also a flame that activated and captivated my desire. I never looked
too deeply to understand why. We suited each other. She had been
looking for someone who could bring her out of the closed and
homogeneous world of high society. I was her way of fleeing while
I kept her, economically speaking, in that world she was hardly
prepared to leave behind. I was her way of displeasing high society
without losing anything. When we were married, multiculturalism
was in vogue. Marrying a black man had a bit of cachet. Children of
chestnut or bronze hue, with golden cascades of lightly curled hair,
were fetishes in advertisements. The exchange was thus mutually
beneficial. I didn't think more deeply than this. And why would
I have? People got married and divorced every day. No one asked
questions anymore. I rose in the company year by year. I became
one of the highest-placed executives in the trade of global water. I
managed the office of international affairs and I found them new
paths for commerce, especially in the Third World, a world that was
developing quickly. Being from a former (very former) colony of
France, I was useful to the company. I was for them like an inform-
ant is for the police: I wasn't one of them, but almost.

   I found the cell phone beneath the pile of mail. It was there,
like the wedding band she'd left behind, abandoned, an accusation.

Right away, I looked for an indication of messages. There was one. It was a few weeks old. It was dated back to a weekend when I had found Patricia's conversation particularly bizarre. Well, perhaps not *bizarre* but enervating. She wanted to know what I thought of our life as a couple, what the future might bring, if I was counting on her to have another child (her: "There's no question of that"; me: "Why not? Wouldn't you like three?"), if we were going to purchase another vacation home together somewhere more chic, more "bourgeois" (she: "Maybe in the Caribbean?"; me: "And why would I go back there? To that damned country?"). I had always dreamed of having something in the South of France, preferably in the Camargue, near the sea, far from the tourists, or on one of the salt ponds there with wild white horses prancing in the marshes. I had never discussed it with her. I never spoke to her of anything beyond the house and the kids. I didn't think she had much to tell me from her side of things either. I found Patricia beautiful. That's all. That simple. She had given me two children who looked white as snow despite the brown of my own skin, the color of mahogany.

And so, yes, Patricia's cell phone had an old message on it. She must have listened to it and then marked it as "unread." Because of the date, I suspected that it had something to do with the disappearance of the family (suddenly, I was no longer thinking of them as "my" family; they had become an abstraction). I found the message and I pressed the button to listen to the recording. I put the phone against my ear and listened attentively. The connection was not good. I could barely hear the person who was speaking. And then, in a few seconds, I heard her. That voice a ghost from my past. I blanched.

"Richard," the voice was saying, "I'm trying to track you down. *Richard?* I'm sorry. I know you don't want to hear from us, from me. But"—a hesitation—"but . . . I thought you'd want to know that Maman, I mean, my mom"—hesitation; spitting on the line—"is dying. I mean, I know you know this. What I mean is that the doctors are saying that . . . it's the end. I thought you would want to know. I don't know if this is the right number. I don't think she'll make it to the end of the year. I wanted to thank you for all you've done . . . I mean, for paying for . . . I thought . . . I thought you might want to say goodbye? This is . . . this is"—another long pause—"your daughter, Anne."

It was Anne, the child of my first union, not a marriage. I had left her behind with her mother, a long time ago, when I was still a teenager. I eventually paid for her studies in Haiti, and for some internships in the US so she could complete her degree in architecture. But how was it possible that she had gotten Patricia's number? It could only have been through me.

I had forgotten, after all my time outside, that islands are little worlds unto themselves, that no one is too difficult to trace if one isn't careful. It had been a grave misstep to forget such a thing, even more to pass on Patricia's number at all. But how had the number found Anne? I rummaged the drawers of my memory. Ma Lou, my mother? Possible. She knew everyone. I tried to remember when I could have made such a colossal error, and I recalled that I had used this number once when I had placed a large bottled water order to be shipped to Haiti, that I had given the number to my fixer, Dieudonné, who is also my cousin, and who knows both Anne and my mother. Had he given Anne the number?

So, little Anne's mother had died. I had never confided in Patricia this part of my past that now came to haunt me.

I was disoriented. I found myself on the canape, still dressed in my suit the next morning. I hadn't even taken off my shoes. I heard Patricia's voice telling me to keep my feet on the floor, to set a good example for the kids. But it was the voice of a ghost. Slowly, the previous evening came back to me, her absence, hers and the children's. She had often told me to keep my feet on the ground, as if to warn me of imminent danger. I never listened to her. I preferred doing things according to my own mind. It was in this way that I had been successful exporting water. You have to admit that I have been successful, very. To convince countries rich in natural resources and nothing more to part with those, and even offer to mine them on their behalf, then sell them back a "product" that always existed in their own ground, you have to be good. To convince, in this case, an island of its need for water, you can't do this kind of work with your feet on the ground. You have to be able to take risks.

I remembered Anne's voice on the cellular. Anne, the daughter of whom I never spoke, who was a shadow belonging to the past now blanketing the present heavily. Had she really called?

I sat on the sofa, my head in my hands, elbows against my knees. The children gone, their smiles and morning quarrels silenced. The apartment emptied of its vitality. Patricia had taken them to the summerhouse, which was near to her parents' house. She was close to her mother. I took ahold of myself in order to call there. I placed myself in front of the window overlooking the street below. Pigeons were flying from one roof to another. The sky was dark, cloudy, a gray that could make one cry. I felt low. It was not a natural sensation.

It was her mother who answered. "Yes."

"I'd like to speak to Patricia."

"She's not here. Who's calling?"

"Listen. I'm in no mood for games. You know very well who it is."

"She's not here."

"Where is she?"

"I really have no compelling reason to tell you."

"I'm still the father of your grandchildren, in the name of God."

"As you say. But, apparently, you have others."

The remark shut me up.

"Thank you," I mumbled. I hung up. If Patricia's mother was aware of the cause of Patricia's departure, then they had spoken about why Patricia had suddenly turned up at the summerhouse in Trouville, with the kids, and without me. The house was the only thing that Patricia owned outright, in her own name. She had chosen to withdraw there because she knew it was the one space in which I had no true legal rights despite the expansion of the house I had financed. If she didn't want me to set foot there, she could keep me from doing so. But still, the children belonged to us both. She couldn't keep me from them.

I still held the cellular in my hands. I was thinking of calling back again but I didn't know what to do. Patricia had outplayed me. To ask for custody of the children was like asking to take them into my charge, and she knew that I didn't know how to take care of them by myself. I had never tried. I wouldn't know what to do with them. I wasn't equipped. Anne, in all this, was simply a confirmation of my incapacity, though I'd never wronged Patricia. Anne was from before. I decided to give myself time to come up with a counterplan. Surely, Patricia's mother would let her know I'd called as soon as I'd hung up. I was sure Patricia was there, since there would be no other reason for her mother to be spending anytime in the summerhouse by herself. I imagined the children playing in the yard. I heard them running in the grass, laughing. I imagined them throwing themselves against one another, stumbling lightly, the sound of the tall grass brushing against their clothes, imagined the northern winds against their cheeks. But here, inside, deep within myself, I felt a heavy weight, heavy as the caissons from the Second World War lying in the ocean beyond the house, resting there permanently like whales who had lost their sense of orientation once they had been thrown out from the sea onto the shore. I knew that I did not have the strength, in the face of that history, my own, to face Patricia there.

I resisted the desire to take the train to Trouville. After my discovery, later, Dieudonné called on my own phone to tell me that Anne's mother had passed on, the body being flown back to Port-au-Prince from Iowa. Would I come? By then, Patricia had left me, and I said yes, yes, but only because I wanted out, to flee. It hit me then, as I said yes, that a part of my own past had died, and with it, a part of my future. Dieudonné's call gave me the excuse to leave everything behind.

Before leaving, I listened again to Anne's message on Patricia's cellular. I noticed that her voice faintly resembled that of her mother, that girl I had once loved so long ago but whom I'd left at the first opportunity, telling myself that she would do well enough on her own. I sent back money for the child without ever asking after her.

I saw the girl once, on an impulse, while on a business trip. I had asked her mother where she sent her to school. The school was in the Tabarre section of Port-au-Prince, an area for the not-so-rich

rich, what we call the "petit bourgeois." Her mother not belonging to the social class of the parents of the other children who attended the school, Anne was a little to the side. I watched her in the school-yard while sitting in the large back seat of the car Dieudonné was driving at the time. She was thin. She vaguely resembled a cousin I had known when I was small. Her school uniform was visibly a secondhand concoction, the color faded and the fabric stretched as if it had been worn by several generations of thin students without social status. I made a mental note to send funds so that she could have a new one. As I made a sign to Dieudonné to pull away, she turned around. She was far from us but I had the impression that she was looking straight at me despite the distance, despite the imposing nature of the black car in which I sat, that she recognized me. She did not smile. She only looked. She ignored everything around, except me. Then, as the car started to roll forward, she raised her arm and made a little wave of the hand, as if to confirm to me that she had seen me. I couldn't help but return the wave through the window, and smile. Her body remained devoid of emotion but she continued waving until we lost her from sight. Dieudonné looked back at me furtively in the rearview mirror.

"*Se konsa*," he said, without explaining what he had understood. "*Se yon bèl ti fi.*"

I nodded. I was too moved to utter a word.

Yes, I thought, she *is* beautiful. And she's mine. Proud, I sent more money to her mother, all the while continuing to feign indifference. But I didn't claim her. I never claimed her.

Men like me, who had children strewn all over the country, who put them in pensions above their social class in the capital, if they could, were a norm in Haitian society. What was perhaps a little less usual was a businessman, a *blan*, a foreigner, who had to wipe away tears from his eyes after having laid them upon his progeny, a girl, at that. After this experience, Dieudonné and I became more familiar. I half-heartedly renewed family ties. He became my regular fixer, the one who greeted me at the airport when I came back on business. He would report to me on Anne, though I never went to see her as a child again. I came to trust him. Maybe it was not so much blood that tied us but simply that he knew my secret.

Dieudonné, God-given, one of these new God-fearing names that cropped up in the late twentieth century as Haitian mothers seemed to place trust in the only place that it could thrive, on the heads of their children, in some future tense. We were cousins, but I didn't know much about him, and didn't know how he had come to be named, which was not unusual in Haiti. He was trustworthy, that was all I knew, but now I asked myself he if wasn't responsible for the leak, if it wasn't he who might have given Anne Patricia's number, since I had used it once to place an order for a water shipment to Haiti. I hadn't seen them, Dieudonné or Anne, Anne's mother, or my own mother, for that matter, for at least ten or fifteen years, though I paid for things when called on—Anne's education, her mother's medical treatments, at the end, travel. It was the least I could do or the most, to absolve myself.

The last time I had seen Anne in the flesh was when I had gone down to help Anne's mother register the girl for an internship program in the States. Anne's mother had a brother in the US; the rest was a matter of finances. I was proud of being able to do it. Everything got done with the least amount of gestures and words. I had a few papers to sign and Anne's mother poured me a two-star rum in the brother's cramped apartment, diluted with some mineral water that I had brought them from my company, before I departed practically as fast as I had arrived. If I remember correctly, I had timed things so that I could take care of a distribution matter. I'd almost forgotten how I meshed business with personal affairs, or confused them.

It was Anne, in the end, the little Anne who had become a grown woman, who brought me back to reality, to the real world, the one I had left behind. And like that, I found myself on a Boeing 747, going "home," if "home" for me could exist still after all these years of imposed, no, chosen exile. I thought of Anne, then of Patricia, then of my shattered life, as I sank into my first-class seat and awaited liftoff.

.

Port-au-Prince, January 12, 2010
I don't know if it was the effect of the discussions I had been overhearing for the past days, lounging by the side of the pool, watching all the glamorous people come and go, watching Dieudonné and the striking woman by his side, whose name I came to know was Sonia, make their deals, or if it was the effect of the narcotics I had finally allowed Leopold to supply me for the last days of my trip wearing off: my thoughts had regained the memory of Patricia and the children, who would be returning by train to school this week, now that the New Year was dead and gone, and I wondered if Patricia had gone back to our Paris apartment.

I would be leaving in another day or so, so I asked Dieudonné for a driver to take me out of the city, for a plunge into the ocean. He was busy with Sonia at the bar, and an older man with a cane

who was eyeing her, them. None wanted to be disturbed. I saw the
boy, Jonas, again, too, the boy to whom Dieudonné had introduced
me, one of my first days at the hotel. The boy had come into the hotel
with a full basket of fruits, a basket the details of which tugged at my
memory like my mother's face. I watched the boy leave after a tussle
between Dieudonné and Leopold, Leopold taking back reluctantly
a package he had wanted the boy to carry down the hill. Dieudonné
thrusting into the boy's hands a fistful of blue candies the management always kept readily available, imported, ironically, from
England, cool mints, they were called, transparent and wrapped in
a plastic that made a distinctive sound as it was untwisted and the
candy released. Some of the candy falling from the boy's hands and
landing softly on the tile, to be swept away by an efficient, self-effacing
maid whose face no one would remember. The boy running, fast, to
catch the tap-tap that would take him back into his neighborhood,
then make his way to school. The left-behind candy a sign that
there was still some innocence in the world, so easy to sweep away.
I could see that in Dieudonné's protective gesture toward the boy.
It made me think of my children in France, made me feel the guilt
I would not admit carrying when I thought of Anne and how little
I had protected her. I wanted to clear my mind. I thought for a moment of going to see my mother, but it was fleeting. I dismissed the
idea by telling myself that it would startle her to see me. I decided
that the sea would be a fitting substitute. The sea: our common
mother. Why try now to repair the past?

Though we left early in the afternoon, there were cars and
traffic jams and it took a couple of hours to reach the sea. The
driver Dieudonné had hired for me, a man named Lucien, who
in another life was an engineer, got around the jams he could. In

this way, I saw certain areas of the city that I didn't know well. Neighborhoods that seemed peaceful with their little gardens behind low cement walls, the houses painted in bright colors: pink, green, blue. Other quarters were less well kept, the houses made of rough, rain-stained wood planks, one on top of the other, piles of garbage spilling grossly onto the streets. In some areas, people seemed to know each other well, while in others, you could feel, even passing by, a tension in the air, and in the closed faces of the traveling market people carrying their wares on their heads, alerting all of their passage to attract customers. I had the impression of zigzagging through the city, uptown like downtown, seeing my city of birth through a pane of glass, as if beneath a globe. We were following other cars that were inching forward with the same aim as ours, while others were queuing behind us. I still couldn't get over the number of luxury cars furrowing through the city streets.

"Since when have there been so many cars?" I asked Lucien.

"It's been a long time since you've come home, Mr. Richard," he replied, his tone betraying some measure of exasperation.

"Yes, but still. Haiti is supposed to be the end of the line. It should be like Cuba, with old cars." I watched a Hummer pass us on the left, followed by a Beamer. "Look at them go."

"That's progress," Lucien said, watching me in the rearview mirror.

I gazed back at him. We measured one another.

"Yes," I said, finally. I turned my gaze back to the scene beyond the car while he focused on getting us out of the capital as quickly as possible. I opened the window. Despite the strong odor of waste and sweating bodies, there was a slight, cool breeze coming from the bay. The afternoon had lost the freshness of early morning in which it still seemed possible to smell the overturned earth of laborers, to imagine flowering seeds. I tried to detect something of the kind on the breeze, the trace of a dream. Maybe I only wanted a hint of a return to a lost childhood moment.

We were headed to Sea-View, an old plantation along the coastal highway north that had been converted into a beachside resort for foreigners and moneyed locals alike. A Frenchman had married a mixed-race woman from the Port-au-Prince bourgeoisie, and together they had converted the plantation at the end of the 1960s. They had built seaside cabanas and manicured the sand along the shore to make it seem like a Miami-style resort with rocks and newly planted palm trees that delimited the property so that peasants could not stumble onto the premises accidentally. Despite these efforts at exclusivity, young men from the neighboring villages found ways to trespass into the domain with fresh conch for the tourists by coming onto the property from the water rather than by land. They smoked fresh conch in their shells on site. The managers looked the other way, since everyone was happy. Everyone won.

The road leading out from the capital had been pitted and broken, but our effort was rewarded when we came upon the ocean erupting suddenly above the road like a pearl from its shell. The rays of sun shone above. I thought of Anne, of never taking her to the sea as a child while my other children were now sitting on the banks of the North Atlantic ocean.

When I would finally speak to Anne, I didn't know. How to explain to her that she had dialed the wrong number weeks ago; that it was my wife who had picked up the message but had not given it to me; that my wife had known nothing of her existence;

that the call itself had thrown my life upside down and that my wife no longer wanted to see me and that, for me, Patricia, my children, the beautiful apartment in the sixteenth arrondissement, were all that mattered; that her mother I had forgotten long ago, and that she, Anne, aside from the memory of her little pointed, sun-filled childhood face, no longer occupied much space in my thoughts; that I had missed the funeral on purpose, taken a business meeting instead?

The day remained wonderful and hot, the air humid and sticky. On the beach, there were other businessmen, families. Lucien disappeared to get a beer with the other drivers waiting for their charges. It had been a long time since I'd felt myself so free, so alone as well. I thought of how my mother used to take me to the sea, when I was small. I entered the water like the child I once was.

I don't know why I was thinking about my mother; it might have been the waves, the water lapping up against me, into which I entered, carrying me. At my age, it was rare to feel completely stripped, naked. My mother had truly known me, deeply, and I had spent a lifetime fleeing from her and all that she represented. She, only, could have made me see clearly through the money, my need to climb to the highest pinnacle of society. Despite all her sacrifices, she had gotten little out of them herself. She wanted me to live well, with both feet firmly planted on the ground. This thought drew me more deeply into the water. I started to swim toward the horizon line. Then, as suddenly as I had started to propel myself through the water, I stopped, my legs paddling beneath the surface.

I turned to face the beach and I could see little children racing up and down the length of the dark sand without parents worrying over them. They were far from the bustle of the congested metropolis that I had spent a couple of hours traversing. I realized then that that was all that my mother had wanted for me, for Anne, and for my other children, had she known them: the liberty to find oneself on a beach, on the island, without having to ask anyone for permission about where one went or why. My mother had wanted to get out of the grind of poverty. Money, for her, when it came right down to it, served only to this end. There was no reason to stockpile it, to amass a fortune. I took a deep breath and plunged into the water's depths.

The water was clear. I could see fish swimming by from behind my goggles. There was coral and white, white sand. It was an underwater paradise. I could have stayed there forever but I felt something or someone calling me back to reality. For a moment, I thought it was my mother's voice. Then, Anne's? She, they, were speaking to me in Kreyòl. I felt as if I had lost my native tongue. I hardly recognized the words. It was a language I hardly used, even in business, where everyone spoke French, or English. But as in the folds of a dream, I understood the message. The voices wanted me to assume my responsibilities, not the ones that were easy for me but those that were the least comfortable: to find Anne, to explain her to Patricia, to make sure that my other two children knew their sister.

I felt myself swell with pride at these new thoughts, and like a newly inflated balloon, I bobbed up to the surface of the water.

In the hot, humid air, I exhaled and then inhaled, like a newborn. It was a new day. I was certain that I could dig myself a new opportunity, a second, even third chance. I felt a smile creep over my face, idiotically. I couldn't help myself. I stroked toward the shore until I could meet the ground, then I climbed onto the sand, which, despite my efforts, sank beneath my weight, step after step. The sensation of dissolution made me laugh, like when I was a kid. I saw Lucien on the shore raise his head in my direction. He had a cigar in hand; it seemed ridiculously small from where I was standing. I thought of Dieudonné, that I owed him something more, as a confidant, as a relation. As I continued to climb the sand in search of firm ground, I made Lucien a sign with my free hand that all was well. My other hand, like my feet, was busily inching me closer to firm ground.

Then, I heard a roar, a roiling, as if a drum circle had started. I had thought that we were far from any village life. Perhaps it was a demonstration on the adjacent former plantation land, for tourists? But the sound was louder, more acute, like something had detonated, burst. I saw Lucien throw away his cigar and rush toward the sand, in my direction, his face falling in a long grimace. The other drivers were also on their feet, running toward their charges. They were gesturing but I could not understand the meaning of their movements, and at the same time, my feet found firm land and I rose up, out of the sea. I advanced toward the chair where I had left my clothes but everything around me started to move. The roiling continued.

People who had been on the shore rushed toward the ocean. In the cabana next to the beach, the guards were seeking a radio station. Then, everyone seemed frozen in place while I heard the voices, again. They spoke to me calmly, *pa tounin*, don't turn back, and I had a moment of confusion, of disorientation.

I could still see Lucien moving toward me from a distance; he seemed to be jumping up and down, in place, like we used to do in gym class when we were kids. I did not understand what was happening. The roiling seemed to be getting closer. The people who had rushed past me into the sea had disappeared. Then, with my pants in hand, my shirt still perched on the back of the chair, I turned to take another look at the horizon, but all I could see was water, water everywhere.

An immense wave had followed me up the shore and onto the beach, like a many-armed giant caterpillar or crab, a spurned goddess for whom rituals of appeasement had long been forgotten. She scooped me up vengefully and swallowed me whole, along with all that stood in the path of her violent, stormy mouth, leaving nothing until her needs for ravishment had been satisfied. I followed down into her belly, my lungs filling with seawater as I fell, weighing me down. My last thought was of Anne, as a child, waving to me in the schoolyard, of Dieudonné saying, "*Se yon bèl ti fi.*" Then, all there was, everywhere, was water: water, on all sides of me.

LEOPOLD

Port-au-Prince, Hotel de la Montagne Noire, January 12–16, 2010
When the lift jolted and jarred before sending him, weightless, up against the metal ceiling of the elevator, he had been thinking of Sonia, of doing something he had never dared to do in the brief time of their acquaintance over the last few years, meeting her whenever he was in town and connecting with Dieudonné, his distant Haitian cousin, who had become like a brother. They had ridden the elevator up and down between the hotel lobby and their respective floors almost on a daily basis, and each time, the floral scent of Sonia's perfume inundated him in the same wave of desire he had known for years, from the first moment Dieudonné had introduced her, around a pool not unlike the one everyone had to walk around to reach the reception desk here, as if leisure were the most important thing to those who frequented the hotel, as, often, it was. He had thought, fleetingly, on the rare occasions she was not accompanied by Dieudonné, of running his hand along the S curve of the small of her back, of inviting her to his room. However, out of deference and respect for Dieudonné, but also because he realized that this was what she expected from all men, which is to say, not much, without distinguishing between them, he had fought off the urge, tucked both his arms, clasped, behind his back. She

conveyed her low expectation with the side glance she offered him when their paths crossed, the way her head tilted in the opposite direction from where he stood, the way her oval eyes moved toward the lit numbers of the elevator car, watching for the next stop, her floor. The second thing that had stopped him was Dieudonné, tall, lean, dark-skinned, who, at times like these, seemed to forget that they were like brothers and stared at Leopold with a chilling lack of emotion. The coldness of the stare conveyed more than a brotherly love for Sonia, something deeper, oceanic, a feeling he, Leopold, had never felt before for a woman but was beginning to understand in that moment of folding his arms back behind him, holding back, biding his time.

The last time he had run into them, together, on the elevator, he had wished them both a good night, and smiled when they looked back at him. Her left eyebrow rose up, as if she did not expect such jovial familiarity without intent, from a man, from him, though, of course, there was intent behind it, a need to be distinguished from other men. Dieudonné nodded, waved back, then steered Sonia out of the elevator with a hand placed above her right hip, grazing but not touching her. Familiar but not quite possessive. Leopold recognized the gesture, the way he himself hovered over merchandise before handing it over to the highest bidder, the way he had earlier that day, very early in the morning, when he had intercepted Dieudonné's errand boy, Jonas, as the boy was preparing to leave the hotel for his neighborhood. He'd tried to get the boy to take a bag of narcotics down the hill to one of his pushers in Bel-Air, but Dieudonné had slapped the bag out of his hand before he could reach, stunning both him and the boy. It had been their one and only fight. Dieudonné had smiled at the boy while his eyes stared icily at Leopold, then given Jonas some extra money and some hard rock candies wrapped in blue cellophane from a jar at the front desk and told him never to mind, that Tonton Leopold had older, bigger boys on hand to run his errands, that it was a joke. Jonas had hesitated, looked from one to the other, then taken the money, the blue candies, smiled, and waved goodbye as he started his run out from the hotel and back down the hill to an awaiting tap-tap that would return him to his neighborhood and to school, where he would forget all about the bag, the slap, the reprimand between the cousins. Thinking about the morning, Leopold felt a whiff of resentment against Dieudonné and wished he had made a bid for Sonia after all, then felt a wave of shame, dampening his desire. He did not want to be like other men to Sonia, men who bought and did not know what to do with her, who did not know how to cherish her. She was a treasure, even if she sold herself to those who could afford extravagances. Could he afford her? He had smiled at the thought. Of course, now, he could. But he did not want to buy or possess her. He wanted to woo, to be chosen. That was a power he did not have but could grant, if she chose. If she chose him, that is, if she so wanted.

He had watched the two as they had gotten off the elevator, Dieudonné's arm a shield against Leopold's attention, the sinews taut, defined, a man who had known labor but who walked through a four-star hotel with the telling ambition in his stride of a person who desired to own the hotel someday, to be more than a glorified errand boy. A man like himself, Leopold thought, recognizing the cockiness in Dieudonné's walk of a man who passed through, didn't belong, but knew how to dress for elevated surroundings: white linen shirt, pressed brown dress pants, smart leather shoes polished to a high gloss to show no sign of wear. Despite his desire for Sonia, he was stilled by how striking a couple the pair made, and that recognition made him less jealous, less possessive.

"Beauty" could be the only word that came to mind as Sonia and Dieudonné floated out from the elevator earlier that late afternoon, she looking back at Leopold, Dieudonné, in shadowed profile, waving goodbye, the exchange over Jonas not altogether forgotten, before he, too, looked away, away from Leopold.

.

Bumping into Sonia and Dieudonné in the elevator had made him think of another time, long ago, the first time—aside from the sight of his own mother's face—he had encountered beauty so essential and pure it could not bear the ornament of words. Only ten, he was no longer as innocent as the age would suggest. He had already survived hunger; sustained a knife wound inflicted in a street fight with youngsters only a few years older than he was; tasted liquor; been made to feel the pillow-like weight of a woman's breast in a brothel on a trip into Port of Spain with his father; fed plump rats as if they were pets; seen grown men shot on two different occasions; learned to swear like a sailor, until the day his mother heard him utter one of the offensive words, caught him by the seam of his collarless shirt, and smacked him so hard that he receded into a sullen silence from which he had yet to emerge some twenty-two years to the day later.

Something small, sacred, and quiet had emerged from the sand. All around they emerged, still viscous and formless from beneath the dunes, while their behemoth of a mother had gone back ponderously into the depths of the ocean. The hatchlings now strove upward, one by one, cut their way out of their leathery shells, squinted into total darkness for sight of the horizon line, and the scent of salt that signaled the sea, their mother's lair, the lure of a future to which they lurched eagerly, without question, their long, narrow flippers, the length of their still small bodies, propelling them out of the hole of their birthing, stumbling over each other, forward, into what there was to be of life.

They would come to live a very long time, these sea turtles, most of them, maybe sixty, seventy, even a hundred years of age, perhaps longer than any human watching them now. Leopold had stood there, mouth agape, as he listened to the guide whispering to them details about the leatherback turtles' lives, showing them what tourists paid quite a bit of money to see each spring season into early summer, the mystery his mother had hinted at before sending him off on this late night adventure, one of the few times she had permitted him to stay out past his bedtime.

It had been his uncle George, his mother's brother, who had flashed a red light so that he could see, along with the other Boy Scouts (a group into which he had then recently been admitted, to save him from the streets), the movement emerging from the shallow pit in the sand, above the shoreline. In retrospect, what had washed over him was the wonder of seeing the blue-black carapaces emerging from the depression, each sporting symmetrical white lines spaced a few centimeters apart and rimming both the shells and flippers, the heads dotted white, the dark eyes opening and closing languidly. It occurred to him that even in darkness, this was first light for the hatchlings, their first contact with air. The beautiful singularity of this fact took his breath away.

His uncle, waving the flashlight, explained in whispers the wonders of the deep-diving turtles, why tourists paid good money to come to their island to witness what they, living here, could see for free. Uncle George explained how the leatherbacks could swim great distances, from ocean to ocean, had some kind of built-in sonar system so they could tell which way they were going, and always, always, if they were female, returned to the sands of their mothers. If they were males, they never again would leave the sea, unless they were caught by predators, or poached by humans, which amounted to the same thing. Leopold listened absentmindedly as he watched the weak-looking hatchlings stumble in the dark toward the water. It was hard to believe that they would one day be a few feet long, hundreds of pounds, and be able to dive over a thousand meters down into the belly of the ocean, collapsing their lungs and bodies to withstand the pressure, conserving oxygen and slowing down their blood flow.

"They can also control their body heat," Uncle George had said, keeping the flashlight low against his body so as not to scare the hatchlings. He explained how the leatherbacks' blood coursed from their hearts to their limbs through a circuit of vessels that ran counterclockwise, transferring heat from limbs to veins and back again in such a way that their extremities remained cool and their core temperature above that of the water in which they found themselves. If they got too hot, their systems backed up and reversed the blood flow into the limbs to cool their cores. They were self-regulating machines living practically all their lives in the ocean, feeding from her, and voyaging across the bodies of water without a care for borders or boundaries. What was more, they had been here before humans, before anything existed, even before dinosaurs. They'd survived the Ice

Age, continental drift, volcanoes erupting below and above ground, asteroids. They were the first superheroes. All that, and still, like most things, they began puny and fragile, scared, scrambling.

Some of the boys in the group broke away and started to careen down the sand.

"Boys! Boys!" Uncle George first whispered, then yelled, when they ignored him. It was clear that all they wanted to do was stomp out the new life.

Uncle had whistled for backup and out of the dark emerged other burly men in green khakis, also on the beach guiding tourist packs. They ran to and pounced on the boys and moved them back above the dunes. The boys were wriggling and yelling in the bigger men's firm grips. Despite the intervention, two of the hatchlings had been killed and lay lifeless, imprinted in the sand, while eight more continued their frantic pulling against the grit of sand, the first sounds they ever heard the violent laughter of human children as they strove to get themselves into the salt water that would become home for the rest of their lives. To them, Leopold thought, as he looked on quietly, firm land would always vaguely remind them of danger.

·

Leopold hadn't thought of the hatchlings in a long time. He'd watched Sonia leave the elevator to enter the lobby draped in a yellow dress, and the memory of the hatchlings had arisen from a dark recess in his mind as the doors shut against her lithe frame receding into the light of the lobby on Dieudonné's arm. He had not followed them out and, a few minutes later, found himself still in the elevator, ruminating, because he had changed course, decided to head back up to his floor, then, as he approached it, pressed the L for lobby again, thereby prolonging his time in the confines of the elevator by several minutes with his indecision.

As the elevator came to a full stop on his floor, he felt the box jolt. He thought nothing of it at first, since elevators in this country were usually slow, owing to spotty maintenance and the humidity that gnawed at everything. But after the jolt, as the door to the elevator should have slid open, he felt instead the walls of the elevator tremble, the door start to open, then stall, tremble. Then, all around him, he felt the building sway. It was an eerie, surreal, strange feeling. It was as if the metal box were trying to remain still in the middle of an oceanic wave. But this wave was unlike anything he had ever felt. It was powerful yet invisible, and neither he nor the elevator could fight it. Then, as suddenly as the trembling had begun, he felt the tension of the box give way before it plummeted at high speed, and he felt his body spike abruptly into the space above his head. The rush of adrenaline, something like fear but not, was sudden and immediate. His mind careened and he thought of becoming reptilian, what it might feel like to be able to collapse lungs and limbs to survive, dive a thousand meters below sea level. All the while, as he remembered the hatchlings again, his body plummeted brusquely (or did it float, up, into the ether, while it was the car that careened down?) into a dark nook that bore no resemblance to water or to sand.

When his body came to rest at the top of the steel cage, it was as if everything was occurring outside of time, outside of space. Nothing was as it should have been: the elevator was no longer moving: it had become an encasement (later still, he would come to think of it as a casket, an embalming place): his body was against the ceiling and one side of the cage, when it should have been grounded on the carpet below; the palisades of what had formed clean, straight walls were now caved in as if some unlikely giant had surged out from the hills, descended upon the hotel, found the cage, and punched the sides in a fit of rage. The light had gone out but there was a draft where there should have been none: he could feel the air washing down from above. The top of the elevator box had cracked like a pierced tin can but remained sealed all around. Leopold felt pain shoot up his arm before he saw that it was broken: he could not move his fingers. Nausea moved through him from the bare bottom of his stomach and up the back of his throat. He felt like retching, but nothing came. He became light-headed from the pain, the darkness, the shock of finding himself against the top and side of the elevator with a broken arm above him, the blood, dripping. Nothing around him was where it should have been, including his body. The box of the elevator had turned and twisted, as he had, then come to rest on its side so that, after he had reached the ceiling and the box came to a stop, his body slumped and slipped from the ceiling to a side, but now it no longer mattered what was up or down. There were four sides around him, some of them bent into odd angles, the closed doors now sealed shut from the impact of the fall and twisting of the metallic sheets of the enclosure. He was trapped, a sardine in a can, involuntarily committed to solitary confinement. His arm throbbed.

There was light streaming in from the fissure in the ceiling, from somewhere, but he was not sure if it was real or artificial. The lights in the elevator itself had gone out. From time to time, there came human sounds, but they were so indistinct that he wasn't sure if they were cries or thoughts, noises he only wished were real.

He wondered what it would feel like to be a sea turtle now, to know the secret of survival beneath the water, to plunge deeper down knowing how to survive for a time without the need for air, collapsing into a smaller mass, having faith in an inner circuitry designed for collapse in atmospheric pressure, not being afraid of cold, of heat, of darkness.

Despite the shaft of light shimmering through, his mind was struggling to compute what may have happened. An explosion? A collapse caused by an engineering error? All he knew was that his head was where it should not be, and that his arm was growing numb, even as he could see it bleeding, and that he had better find some way of securing it before the arm bloated and became useless, unsalvageable, like so much else. He was thinking of the fragility of the hatchlings he had seen on that beach at ten years of age, so long ago now, it seemed.

·

He was thinking of how he had described the scene to his mother when he had gotten home, so excited that he had said that he wanted to become a marine biologist, and his mother had clapped her hands and exclaimed, "Like Jacques Cousteau!"

"Like who?" he'd asked.

"The man on the American free channels," she'd replied. "The Frenchman who swims with the dolphins."

Like his uncle George, he'd thought then, and some of his older cousins. They told stories of fishing expeditions in the higher

Antilles and the schools of dolphins. Yes! he'd exclaimed. He would be the Trinidadian Jacques Cousteau, and make her and his departed father proud!

"Don't worry about your father," she'd said. "He's long gone, and he isn't coming back." Those words were true, though he didn't understand them then. Then, even later, he forgot about Jacques Cousteau and about becoming a marine biologist.

Forgetting didn't take long. Not long at all.

Four years went by and he was back on that beach with a different purpose and a different crowd—poaching the turtle eggs as soon as the behemoth mothers took their bulky husks back into the sea. Not giving the hatchlings any chance to emerge, digging up the eggs with his bare hands because it was important not to damage them.

He didn't think about the hatchlings anymore, only that the eggs could fetch a dollar or more apiece on the black market, and all he wanted then, more than anything, was enough to get out of the old neighborhood, out from under his disapproving mother's thumb, and into the world.

His thoughts drifted back toward his mother.

She'd become hard, her face gaunt, no longer beautiful like he'd thought when he was a small child. She'd become less hopeful, didn't believe in him like she used to. But then again, he didn't give her much cause to believe—got in trouble, ran with a bad crowd, drank, stayed out all hours of the night, even got a girl pregnant, then pretended he'd never met her before. He'd done this even though he'd chased after her for weeks until he could get her to open her legs, then took advantage for a full month without using any protection, since he had been her first. He walked away from her like he couldn't hear her speaking when she told him she was pregnant with his child. Didn't even ask her if she needed anything, needed him. Nothing. Just became stone-faced and looked right over her shoulder, as if she wasn't even there, as he did when his mother confronted him, slapped him, boxed him about the ears, as she told him what the girl's mother had told her.

Slapped him hard, two times, three. But he didn't even let a tear fall. He looked right past her, with both hands in his pockets, and waited, holding his breath.

He thought only of the big sea turtles that never returned to shore, the male ones, like his father, that went far, far away, made their way into the churning waters, and never, never, ever came back.

.

Musk and flowers. That was what he remembered when he came back to the world of the black box in which his body was coiled. The smell as the two most intoxicating creatures from the hotel had gotten off the elevator into the lobby earlier. He'd felt an urge to follow them, before he'd changed his mind and decided to go back up to his room, Sonia and Dieudonné, the two of them looking as if they knew something about eternal life that no one else could know, a knowledge that transcended the here and now of the hotel walls, the roles that each of them played. Leopold had dreams, too. He thought wanly about the money accumulated in his bank accounts, of the influence he could use to buy her away from whatever held her to the place, a ghostly apparition stalking the halls as if she owned them.

He had noticed the way she walked on thin high heels, not quite stilettos, her back straight, not a trace of hesitation or vulnerability in her spine, day after day, her dresses the color of bold tropical flowers floating above her anklebones. At night, she was clad in white from head to toe. He could tell from the way she carried herself that she had measured the effect, knew that there was nothing more elegant than a mocha-colored woman draped in the color of light against a sky full of pinprick stars glowing above their heads, walking through the halls. If he didn't know where she had come from, he knew what she was, why she was there almost every night, like a permanent fixture, an unofficial hostess, with her perfect teeth framed by rouged lips, her eyebrows arched, and each lid brushed with a smoky film of powder accentuating her almond-shaped eyes. She was like him, from less than humble beginnings, a hustler, a survivor.

This and much more he remembered as his body remained suspended, or at rest—it was hard to tell which—while all around him walls had shifted and slanted in.

.

Leopold liked to believe that he was master of his domain, ignored the fact that he had only half the knowledge of most of the men with whom he did business and even less than half their experience. What had always counted most, he thought, was resilience and ingenuity. Like when a boy realizes one day that he has seen his father's back receding through an open doorway for the last time, that he will never see his father's face again, the last sighting the back of the father's balding head, the lines etching the skin at the base of his neck creased and folded by the pressure of a starched, discolored collar. Like when a boy discovers that smuggling a sweet-smelling grass stuffed in cigarette packs or folded in wax paper inside sardine tins and taking them down the hill hidden within a leather schoolbag that smarts as the weight of it bounces back and forth against growing muscles, he'll return from school with a wad of bills, minus the grass that the older boys will take from him and roll to sell again.

He was part of a chain, watched and learned who gave what to whom and when, who got more money on the chain than someone else, who got caught and how. He never got caught; he moved up the chain, started handling less weed and more cash, and set up his own operation before the age of sixteen. He ruled the house with his two older siblings long gone before him and three below him, his mother and grandmother still in the house, asking him no questions. When the Father at his mother's church asked when he was returning to service, the odd time he went there with her, at her request, for Mother's Day, or her birthday, or New Year's, when the Father asked when Leopold was going to stop killing everyone around him with the stuff he sold, he replied: "Stop trying to be my father. I have no father." He stuck out his chest like a rooster, spat, never taking his eyes off the priest, giving him a big-man look that normally scared off other men. But the Father only smiled, and sighed.

One day, when Leopold dragged himself to church with his mother once more, the priest said to him, "Leopold, you'll come back. And when you do, I'll be here." He watched his mother's face close up as she looked away from him, as she wrung her hands, and as the Father took one of hers in his and held it as if he had never spoken a word to Leopold. "Thank you, Father," she said, quietly pious, like a child.

.

Like a child, Leopold thought, as a pain erupted, flame-like, through his body.

He remembered the noise before the walls of the elevator car folded in, a thunderous clapping, remembered the stories some of the older cousins who had been raised outside the island told of their time as snipers in an American war, how they returned filled with hallucinations and would walk down shadowy streets when they could not sleep, turning their fingers into imaginary triggers and squinting into the darkness, yelling, "Rat-a-tat-tat," echoing the sound of the machine-gun fire they said they could still hear in their dreams.

He thought he had heard something like a bomb go off, the way they did in the science fiction films he'd watched, glued to his seat in the theater at the mall when he was a teenager, not so many years ago; when commando units, towns, villages, whole worlds exploded into smithereens across the screen, and he and his friends would whoop in excitement, never imagining that any such thing could happen to them. They were safe on the island, at least from such things as this.

There was a moment, earlier, it could not have been more than a second or two, when Leopold was floating toward the ceiling as the metal car of the elevator plummeted down, floating up toward the plastic panel separating the fluorescent tubes of light from what was soon to become a cage, that he thought of his mother, of the pained, tight-lipped smile she carried uncomplainingly through life. He could see her now, sitting low in front of a pile of something that she needed to shuck, shell, divide, sack, and label. Getting ready for market at sunrise or at twilight, that was how he remembered her. She was like Ma Lou, the market woman who always remembered him when he returned to Haiti, the mother of the French businessman Dieudonné had introduced to him by the pool, Richard. He had not become rich like Richard, but he was on his way. They were all hustlers, every one of them.

He might never see her again.

The reality hit him at the same time as dread knotted itself in the middle of his stomach and rose nauseously toward the back of his gullet, at the same time as the lights flickered out, then shattered, and the steel sides of the car folded inward incomprehensibly toward him. Paper would have crumpled more easily, he thought, distractedly. Then he felt the sensation of his broken right arm, the pain.

His next thought was to find a way to extricate himself from the box. He strained to pull himself upward toward the light and shaft of air in the ceiling, to see what lay beyond. He peered through the opening and saw in ruins what had been the hotel lobby. A bellboy he recognized as someone he had liked in the hotel, even hired for mundane tasks from time to time, lay slumped against a broken wall, a bloody gash on his head, his eyes open wide. The boy was dead. Leopold felt like gagging. A fine dust covered everything in sight. He did not see anyone else though he did see cloth, fabric, bursts of color piercing through the debris. Were there people there, wherever he saw color? If so, beyond the dead bellhop, he did not know how many more there might be. Everything was broken and misshapen, beyond recognition. What could have happened?

Then he felt a wavelike sensation, a wild shaking, and everything before him moved a few inches back and forth. The broken walls undulated, snakelike, shaking loose more dust and debris into the air. The debris filled his nose and lungs, as the elevator shook from side to side. It seemed stuck as if it had nowhere to go. The dust made him gag and fall back into the box, but not before he had seen some movement outside: some men cloaked in white dust appeared to be running across the roiling floor with a terror animating their faces so that they looked ghoulish and frightful. Still, the sight of the men comforted Leopold as he fell back into his cell, his broken arm following him limply downward. Falling, not knowing whether backward or forward. Earthquake, he thought, as the tremor continued. Earthquake. Who would have thought?

He knew only because he'd felt one at home, days ago, before the trip, the day after Christmas, while drinking a rum punch in the countryside with his uncle and two of Leopold's children, whom he never saw outside of the holidays, whom his mother had convinced him and the girls he'd gotten pregnant one after the other—the children nearly the same age—to give to Uncle George and his wife, the same man who had shown him the hatchlings as a child but was only ten years his senior. They couldn't conceive and were desperate for children of their own. The boys were ten and eleven, respectively. Neither knew he was their father. They'd all felt the earth shake, watching small figurines move as if nudged by an invisible finger across the surface of tabletops in the living room, then laughed, as the earth's shudder came to an end and everything was a few inches away from where it had been before. But this, this here, was no laughing matter. He wondered if anyone out in the world knew what was happening to them in this godless, godforsaken country, so much like his own.

He cursed the land and its people as his arm burned and throbbed. Cursed the grandmothers and all the children running about barefoot.

.

When Leopold became serious about trafficking, the Hotel de la Montagne had become his favorite place to land: it allowed him to dream. Everyone was accepted—drug runner like presidential candidate, scholar or NGO worker, UN personnel or hip-hop star. As long as you *looked* respectable and could pay your bill, no questions were asked: everyone mixed with everyone else.

The hotel was perched high on a mountain with a breathtaking view of the city and the port beyond it during the day. At night, it overlooked a dense, quivering darkness since electricity was sparse across the capital. Leopold breathed more easily every time the hotel's taxi-car climbed up the hill and he could see the railing of the covered patio restaurant come into view. Just beyond that would be the hotel itself and the rooms hidden away behind high white walls as if the whole place were a secret compound for the privileged few who could afford to be sequestered within them. Every stay, Leopold felt as if he had arrived.

When he'd started his business, sixteen years ago, he would never have dreamed that he could have checked into a place like the Hotel de la Montagne. Even seven years ago, he didn't have a pot to piss in. And here he was again, in a room as small as the cell he was thrown into when one of the jobs he'd been hired for by one of the older boys went bad and, for the first time, he'd been the accessory left behind. He did six months of prison for petty theft then since he had no prior record. At the end of his sentence, he emerged from the jail with a tattoo, the news from his latest girlfriend that she was expecting a girl (the only one of his children who knew he was her father), more street cred than he'd ever had before, and a taste for blood. He outgrew the outfit that had betrayed him, left them behind, and started another crew. He didn't marry the girl but started leaving her money from his jobs for the baby growing in her belly, determined that this time, this last time, he would not lose out on another chance to be a father. He was twenty-five, then, getting too old to mess around with things that could matter in the long run. He was too old to follow someone else's orders. Too old to get caught on raids. Too old to father children and drop them off at some relative's house and be called "uncle" by his own children for the rest of his life.

He was a small trafficker but an effective one. Used the old parallel trade routes for his smuggling—fishing boats between countries to move merchandise along with fruits and handmade crafts. Officially, he was in the import/export business, a cultural worker; unofficially, he was the best drug dealer anyone had seen for years. For several years after he'd served his six-month sentence, no one on his crew got caught. His reputation grew. The little girl was born early on. They named her Mathilde after a children's book character popular at the time. He spent a lot of time with her, and her mother, though they never got together again. The woman married but she and her husband let him continue to see the child, because each time he came, he left an envelope filled with money on the kitchen table. They didn't dare ask where the money came from because his fortune was their fortune. Letting him see the child was a small sacrifice, and he turned out to be a doting father, when he was around, which was not all the time, even seldom, as the years went by. But still the envelopes with money were delivered so no one, except for Mathilde, uttered a complaint.

Then he got a message from one of the big islands that his services were being requested. He went from island to island meeting with other drug dealers up the Leewards, then across the Windward chain, until he found himself in Jamaica. There he learned about the goings-on in Haiti, where his mother had always maintained her maternal grandparents were from, and he remembered that they had been part of a group of elders who still spoke patois, or Kreyòl, like they did in Haiti, though many denied the connection.

He learned that there was a bursting drug market in Haiti since the Americans had taken out Noriega. He nodded when he heard about the trade routes by water that could be used between northern Jamaica and southern Haiti, and from there by ground into the capital, which was protected by a smaller, rocky island at the mouth of its bay. It suited him perfectly. He even liked the idea of a return to an ancestral land. He assured his new clients that he would be effective, deliver what they wanted, and some Panamanian rum to boot. They laughed at him. "Don't you know those people claim they have the best rum in the world?" He hadn't tasted Haitian rum yet, had never set foot in the mythical world he'd heard about only from his mother and her parents and, occasionally, at Carnival time, because it was the place that had ignited their dreams of liberty invoked during their Canboulay, early versions of Carnival, when the slaves took to putting the cane to fire in search of a way out of violent exploitation and into freedom. That was how he made his way, finally, to the biggest catch of his life, to the land of the *bosal*, the wild ones, the Africans who refused to be collared, who refused to thank the masters for their chains as if cuffs were bracelets.

If he'd practiced thrift of necessity in the mountains of Paramin, where his mother's grandparents were from, in Haiti, he'd learned the true meaning of resourcefulness. Some things were the same as back home—the toys made for children out of bicycle parts, empty spools of thread, socks stuffed with torn clothing shaped into dolls. Some things he'd never seen before: old tires cut up and made into the soles of sandals; handbags made from candy and chewing gum wrappers; a girl's skipping rope used to guide a mule; a common gurney-type chair contraption used to carry those whose legs were of no use to them or who had none; plastic colanders of different colors hung helter-skelter on otherwise barren walls of living rooms and dens, taken down for use in the kitchen whenever needed, then scrubbed clean and placed back on the walls like totems or heirlooms, as if they weren't the common items for everyday use that they were; fresh, deep-green banana leaf used to keep a plastic jug of water steady on a girl-child's head. Nothing wasted. Despite this ingenuity, there were still signs of grinding poverty, the barefoot, the infants wearing torn, dirty T-shirts without underclothes, wandering through the streets seemingly unconscious of their nakedness. He thought of his own children, of how despite never taking care of the boys, he had never considered that he might need to worry about their being clothed or bare, never worried that they might be snatched off the street or mistreated. It made him think of Mathilde, who looked at him with an undoing innocence, a trust that he had done nothing to earn. Even if the unthinkable *did* happen where he was from, such things were invisible or unclear: there were no obvious signs of vulnerability. Later, he was to learn that even the children of the wealthiest could be at risk through kidnappings for ransom. Knowing about the precariousness of each member of the society, the uneasy seesaw on which everyone existed, endeared the place to him. It became a second home in which he came to be unquestioned.

He could come and go as he pleased.

He could remake himself.

.

Sounds that made him think of a song reached him from some-where beyond. A slow humming, as if the elevator music were still running, muted, almost dumb. Singing? he thought. Now?

The last music that had played in the elevator that he could re-member was Michael Jackson—Michael before his fall from grace. Michael moonwalking across stages around the world, smooth as silk, moving like no one had seen anyone move before, or so they thought, even though Michael was copying Cab Calloway and Fred Astaire. Michael before the high-pitched yelps had become obses-sion rather than soulful expression. Michael when it was still cool to be Michael, when everyone wanted to be like him, parading, even around the hood, with one glove on, or garish knockoff red leather riding jackets.

MJ's death last summer had come as a shock, rippling around the world, especially the black and brown worlds. Leopold had even seen some late-night drag queens pop up along Murray Street off Ariapita Avenue in Woodbrook, Port of Spain dressed up like MJ in homage. These men saw no irony in the stockings they wore below slim-fitting pants, their pouting, rouged faces half-hidden below worn fedoras, done up in heavy makeup melting in the heat, the most skilled dancers among them clad in skintight clothes, a black armband wrapped around a forearm, performing awkward "robots" on cardboard platforms laid across the same sidewalks on which they normally hustled straight-acting, God-fearing clients, as if it were 1999 and the King of Pop were still alive, not waiting for resurrection. No one bothered them that night. People drank and watched, clapped when the performances were especially good, and shed a tear or two for brother Michael.

Leopold's broken arm felt as if it was going to burst out of the seams of his bloodied shirt. He was still in the dark, growing thirsty and hungry, wondering what would happen next, what he could do to help himself.

The thought of invention made Leopold start to palpate his pockets with his free hand. His phone still had a small charge but no connectivity. He could use it for a light. He tested it by flashing the screen overhead until it prompted a faint cry from beyond, from someone who saw the light dancing. The cry gave Leopold's heart a small leap of hope; maybe he would be released soon? He was too frazzled, too anxious, his mouth too dry, to attempt crying out in reply. Besides, the cry seemed far, far away. But he had heard it and his light had been seen. He held on to the thought of rescue, continued the inventory of his pockets: some matches, a rolled cigarette, a box of gum with a cellophane window containing a few pieces still, a ballpoint pen, a linen square he had come to learn to use instead of a sleeve to wipe his nose, the card key to his hotel door. He wasn't sure what use any of these objects might serve. The spidery despair that he had temporarily held at bay crept in.

He contemplated the key to his hotel door. The door he wished now he had been opening for Sonia. For the first time since the car had fallen, his body down with it, he wondered what had become of Sonia and of Dieudonné. He had not gotten off the elevator with them but gone back up to his floor, then down again, time enough for them both to leave the hotel. Was that what had happened? He did not want to think of either of them covered over in the dust he had seen outside the elevator, did not want to imagine that some of the bursts of color belonged to them. Or maybe they had been out there, Dieudonné's body pressed up against Sonia's, holding her safely beneath him, his body a barrier against falling walls. Could Leopold have been that body? That savior? He savored the thought, took out a piece of gum, closed his eyes, and dreamed of it. Yes. He used his phone clock to time chewing half a piece every hour. Three hours had gone by, or maybe four. Sometimes he forgot to check the time or spat out the gummy substance because it no longer had taste or seemed to be dissolving in his mouth. Sometimes he forgot to chew as he contemplated his life, what he had left back in his own island and what had brought him to this one.

He thought of the boys who knew him as uncle; of his daughter's open smile—so much like her mother's, the woman he once thought (until he set eyes on Sonia) he should have married, but never did; of his social circle, the men on his crew; of his mother, whom he avoided because he could never explain to her what he did for a living, was ashamed of himself for becoming so much like his father, of whom his mother had always said: "Don't grow up to be like him," and who, to his great shock, he had, in ways, become. Was he, like Michael, going to die asphyxiated in a small chamber lacking air? Was he going to be missed by anyone if he did die? His children hardly knew him. He had alienated his mother, the truly God-fearing people of her congregation, the priest. Leopold shuddered against the metal of the box, straining to better hear the noises coming from beyond, signs of life he wanted desperately to rejoin.

"*Ki moun ki la?*" he yelled out finally. Who's out there? There was silence, then a knocking. Leopold yelled out again, then the pain in his body surged. Silence, then more knocking. There were people out there and maybe they were acknowledging his presence. But before he could try again, Leopold passed out, from the pain or too little oxygen, dreaming of dancing across a stage in Moscow with a Michael Jackson clad in a bright, tight, gold lamé suit.

When he came to, he heard a voice say in French, "*Y-a quelqu'un là?*" He didn't know what the words meant so he said what he had learned to say when he didn't understand another's language.

"*Wi,*" he said. Then, louder, "*Wi.*" Insistently: Yes. Yes.

"Okay," the voice said. "We'll be getting to you soon."

Leopold heard steps outside the box, then against its sides. A face peered at him from the other side of the crack in the elevator's distorted ceiling, followed by a light washing over him, blinding him. "Okay," the voice now attached to the face and light said, "okay. You're next. We're getting to you."

Relief washed over him. He wouldn't be trapped in the box forever. He was going to be rescued, see his sons maybe in the summer, rather than wait a whole year before seeing them again.

The head disappeared. "We are coming," the voice said, but it seemed to be speaking to someone else. Another survivor? Who was this "we"? Leopold thought. He hadn't been a "we" for a long time. What "we" would extract him from this mess? How had he gotten himself in such a jam? Through no fault of his own, he thought, this time, through no fault of his own.

Could it be Mozart that he was hearing?

Leopold thought that he was hearing the slow dirge of the Requiem. He had been listening to it recently, downloaded it onto his phone, a fact he would never have admitted to anyone. Small earbuds lodged in his ears, he would go about his business listening to the drawn-out musical phrases, inundated by the feelings of despair wrung from every note. He wasn't listening to dancehall or rap or American hip-hop. Only Mozart made sense now that he was trying to become cultivated. Mozart. Rachmaninoff. Bach. Occasionally he switched to jazz—Miles Davis, Coltrane, Cannonball Adderley. Volatile composers who had known and wondered at the meaning of life, infused it into their music. These were the beats that he walked to even as he palmed greasy bills in exchange for the packages of weed, white powder, and pills he sold.

Above him, the shaft of light had disappeared. It was night and things were growing calm, quiet. He could hear a jackhammer in the distance, closer still, a man, moaning a prayer. He wondered to whom the voices belonged.

No one had returned for him since he'd spoken to the face attached to the headlamp. No one had attempted to renew contact.

He was starting to feel clammy, despite the heat. He felt hunger more acutely. He'd peed several times already but that didn't tell him much about how much time had gone by. He thought about drinking what he had spilled, decided against it. But he had to pee. He rolled to the opposite corner of the box on his good side, peed into the carpet. Felt shame. Rolled back to where he had been, facing away from the stink of his own urine. The car had become a cell. Primitive. The pain in his body was growing stronger. Now, a splitting headache, nausea, a dry, sticky mouth. Panic settled in. Maybe he should try to get out. It was time for him to think on his feet, like he always had. Doing so had gotten him this far. Not far enough, he thought.

The elevator frame began to shake. Leopold thought he heard the rat-tat-tat of a machine gun firing. A civil war? He rose and struggled to his feet, using the caved-in sides of the elevator frame to steady himself. He strained to hear the source of the noise and movement. An image of a scarlet ibis nesting in a mangrove tree came to him from far away, an outing with his daughter, Mathilde, when she had turned four and become curious about the world around her. He'd convinced her mother to allow him to take the girl as far as the Caroni Bird Sanctuary, thirty minutes out from town. "Won't be long," he'd told her, shrugged. "To show her the birds."

.

Mathilde had been bored in the boat ride as the guide showed them snakes twisted in the tree branches or took a small crab from the water and held it in the cup of his hand. She slumped against the side of the boat and wiped at her face as if the heat was too much for her, squashed her sun hat down across her forehead, scowled at him.

He smiled at her, despite himself, scared that this small girl would reject him. It was a new feeling. He hid the fear, sought to please her with bribes of snacks and promises of how beautiful the scarlet birds would be, though he could hardly remember himself what they were like. He hadn't been out to the sanctuary since his own father had taken him when he was small, small.

Then they were in the clear of the swamp and drifting slowly into a mangrove bay. A huge tree with a canopy of green rose up into the sky. The guide told them that they would wait now, and they did so, quietly, with the motor cut off, bobbing up and down the surface of the water in the boat. After a few minutes of calm, suddenly, black dots moved across the sky toward the tree, became larger, then red, as they came closer and closer. The girl rose up on an elbow. "Look, Daddy," she said, pointing to the birds, then looking back at him to make sure he didn't miss anything, "look!"

He sat closer to her and they watched on as the tree filled with the long-beaked, long-legged birds, as they clumped their scarlet bodies in the leafy green of the tree. "It looks like Christmas!" Mathilde exclaimed.

He laughed a low, guttural laugh, experienced the kind of mirth that arose only when he felt unguarded, which was seldom.

They stayed in the boat a while longer, swaying with the wind atop the water. The birds squawked unintelligibly. Then, as startlingly as they had arrived, they began to rise up, extended their long wings out and jumped off the verdant branches into the air and flew away in group formation, as they had come, but away from the marsh out toward the sea.

"Where are they going?" Mathilde lamented.

"I don't know," he said, his arm around her small frame. She slumped against him, warm, trusting, a tiny mass he had created in a forgettable moment that would now last a lifetime.

"They'll be back," she said to him, in a tone meant to be comforting.

He kissed the top of her head. "Of course," he said, "of course."

She fell asleep against him as they turned back toward the park. He held her against his shoulder as he paid the guide a fat tip.

The man tugged at the bill in two directions as if testing it for elasticity. "Thanks, chief," he said, tipping his hat at Leopold, out of respect for his notoriety.

He felt the light weight of Mathilde as she shifted against his shoulder, nestled in for warmth. The night air had become cool and he hadn't brought out a sweater for her. His face flushed, hardened;

he was not entirely a father. He nodded at the man, assuming the mask of his reputation. Held Mathilde close and walked back to the car, wondering what he might do to secure his place in her world, a place that money could not buy.

.

A face he had seen earlier in the night reappeared above him, the light still clamped to his forehead.

"*On est là,*" the face shouted, particles of dust slowly drifting down through the light.

Leopold nodded, sank back to the ground.

Then, everything happened quickly: the sawing through the walls of the elevator, being lifted out in a leather seat that reminded him of a child's swing in a playground, his arm being placed in a sling, multiple hands pawing at his body, checking for other breaks and lacerations, water, cooling, poured over his mouth, down his throat, the gulping for breath. The only person he thought of, then, was not Sonia, who had flitted through the hotel a butterfly-vision, but his own daughter, Mathilde, imitating the flight of the scarlet ibis every time he came to her mother's home to pick her up, giggling. He shut his eyes and thought of her as the noise of chaos surrounded him.

A rush of air enveloped his body as he was taken away on a gurney to a temporary medical facility for foreigners. He raised his head and looked at the fallen husk of the hotel from between his feet as it receded from sight. He wondered if Sonia and Dieudonné had made it out. For a moment, Leopold thought he saw the diaphanous golden robes of a beautiful woman, a woman out of his reach.

With this thought alone, he let his head fall back. A hand rested on his good shoulder. "Good man," the voice from before said. "It's been a few days. You made it."

"Yes," he responded, closing his eyes, thinking of Mathilde. But he had no real idea how much time had gone by.

Later, he would find out that most of the people in the hotel—the moneyed, the NGO reps, the UN personnel, the stars, the wannabes, the prostitutes, the fixers, the musicians, the cleaners and servers—most of them had died. He didn't know about Sonia, Dieudonné, or their other cousin, Richard. It would be weeks, even months, before the tallies of the dead would be written up, survivors found again. How had he, a foreign trafficker, living far above the station to which he had been born, outrun such a thing? There had to be some reason, something greater than everything that his life had led to until now. For Mathilde, he would give up the life, this good life, the money, the power, the ability to infiltrate sectors of society that had always been off-limits, scuttling in like a crab, startled and anxious, crawling back and forth on the edges of its claws.

As they had lifted him out of the debris of the elevator, the fallen and crumbled walls, he had felt no anxiety, no fear, a quietude descending upon him as he let himself be led away by the men who had extracted him from the car, a waylaid sardine. He thought of watching Mathilde grow up, of the cost of being present and what dividend the sacrifice might supply. He thought of the scarlet ibis in flight, and of the gain of being grounded, standing below them.

He slept. He didn't know for how long but in what seemed like no time at all, compared to what had turned out to be more than a day, not hours, in the confines of the elevator box, he found himself on an emergency charter flight back to his island, his arm set, his hunger and thirst satiated.

No one at home had known he had been gone or what he had survived. Forty-five seconds followed by hours, days of waiting, dreaming, trembling, then being dug out, flown home on on army rescue flight.

Only his mother asked about his arm in the cast and sling, asked why they saw more of him than before, asked why he returned to the church and shook the hand of the priest he'd disdained as a much younger man. He shrugged and explained nothing, took a job at a local resort, became the best pool man they had ever seen, made legitimate money, stopped hanging out with his crew, didn't touch a drop of alcohol, took no snuff of any kind, drank water all day long. Only water. Dropped weight. Became lean. Ate green. Became vegetarian, almost vegan. One step away from being a Rasta, if only he could believe in such a thing as a god.

Everyone thought he had lost his mind or found it.

Once in a while, he thought of Sonia and of Dieudonné, even of Richard. Wondered what had happened to all that beauty, and depravity, wondered which of them would be more likely to survive. He kept away from everyone but his children, Mathilde and his boys, and his mother. Now he looked into his mother's worn, lined face and saw the beauty still there, forgave her his father's failings, and for the first time understood her smothering love for what it was, for that feeling that had washed over him in the confines of the elevator when he thought he might never see Mathilde grow up, never see her innocent face again, had longed even for its disappointment in him. Understood a mother's pain, at last, in a way that few men could. Recognized his own frailty when he looked up from his shave and inspected his handiwork in the mirror, forgave himself, closed his eyes, breathed in deeply, thanked something— whatever it was that had looked out for him and thought fit to give him this second chance.

TAFFIA

Bel Air, Port-au-Prince, April 2010

When the new *Frijolito* episodes aired again shortly after the New Year, Tatie's parties started up again. The neighbors crowded her living room, bringing offerings of Prestige beer, *guanabayana* juice for the children, and smokes. Some of the younger set watched from the windowsills. They stood outside and hung their arms over the bottom of the window frames, making comments at the television and gesticulating wildly when the action on screen became intolerable. I don't know if it was because the actors were Latinos or because their names were so much like ours, but everyone loved *Frijolito*. The basic storyline was familiar too: a young woman from a disfavored family—her name is Margarita, or Litzy—falls pregnant after going on a date with a wealthy guy, Nacho, short for Ignacio. Neither of them can remember sleeping together because the guy's friend, Lucho, who reminded me eerily of my younger brother, Paul, who also wants the girl, slipped something into their drinks at a bar. For the rest of their lives, they try to get back together, sometimes successfully, sometimes not, and poor little Frijolito, the son, grows up without a father, though the wealthy guy's brother, Francisco, also wants to get with the girl but never can. We could all relate to that. The girl is a maid in the rich guy's house, too, which is how they meet. I sometimes fantasized about who we might be if we were in the world of the soap. Because my mother worked in a wealthy house in Pétion-Ville, I sometimes thought I could be Litzy, but I lacked the glamour or appeal. In my world, Litzy was either my sister, Sonia, or my friend Selena, from school. I didn't know enough about Sonia's life away from us to reconstruct a soap world around her. Selena's Nacho would, of course, be another classmate, Stevenson, and Lucho would have to be someone shady like his friend Junior, willing to do anything to get what he wanted. If I was Litzy, then I had no idea who my Nacho might be, but the rest of the players would be the same and Francisco would, of course, be Didi, my older brother, always trying to do the right thing, except that he obviously wouldn't be in love with me. He would be with my best friend, Kassy, so we could all be family to one another. That way, I would never have to lose either of them.

We were waiting to walk over to Tatie's to watch the show when the earth swayed. Kassy was supposed to meet us there, Paul and me, but we never saw her.

They say I screamed for two days. I don't remember doing that, screaming. But I do remember what I saw and what I didn't want to see. Things I wish I could forget: walking to get home; all the ash covering the jagged fragments of buildings. If it weren't for the constancy of the hum, the craters you had to watch out for but couldn't see below your feet, mincing forward, it could have been Carnival. A throng of bodies moved through the unnatural snow, their faces frozen in grimaces, lips and eyes encrusted with the white flakes, some gesticulating, looking like chickens after slaughter, white plumage smeared with red. They carried the remains of neighbors, of kin, on their clothes, like tattoos on their skin. The dust covered over the red with white absolution. Only the screams remained, piercing the whiteness, followed by the gloom as night fell, suddenly, blanketing pallor with darkness.

We made it to Tatie's house before our own. It was rubble. I knew from the squares of cloth I could see peering above the debris that resembled pieces of Tatie's clothing that she was beneath, gone. That's when I let out the first scream. Paul was beside me. Later, Paul said that he had imagined a flying carpet as the earth uncoiled beneath our feet, like we had seen in cartoons, folding and unfolding. Was this how it felt to be a caterpillar before being enclosed in a cocoon? For seconds, we felt no contact with the earth beneath our feet. We levitated. Paul said that it had made him feel free for moments, rather than fearful. Then, when our feet came into contact with the earth again, we felt our knees buckle beneath the weight of our bodies. Then all of reality rushed back, and it was this material reality that was unrelenting, the inability to fly, to lose the chains of existence. I was not the only one screaming. Everyone around us was making noise. Paul peered around and noticed young men moving with determination through the streets, through the debris, pointed them out. He would join them later, not even days later, and enter a sullen darkness from which it would be difficult to pry him.

After a pregnant pause, as the earth settled, I let out another scream, but this one ended in a word: "Tatie!" Paul stood still at my side, not uttering a word, stunned by the sight. He looked like he might want to throw up at the sight of the body; then, he steeled himself. I could see it from the way his body clenched, the fists he made hanging limply at his sides. Tatie had been flattened by the fallen ceiling with her rice and beans left intact on the stove, burning.

Her house, where so many gatherings had taken place, had sunk into a crater, and all the other buildings on the block, including our house, and blocks on end, had toppled, slabs of concrete askew, the people moaning all around, limbs like unnatural branches protruding from concrete, from the dust. People who had been laughing and fighting one second were reduced to lifelessness, their bodies tossed by the side of the road until a truck could pick them up and take them away, later, much later. The sound covered us all, like vibrating wings of some giant hummingbird. In school, I had learned that hummingbirds could beat their wings seventy times per second. The sound from my own throat joined in the hum. Didi would have called it Armageddon, the battle for souls at the end times in the Bible.

Paul said nothing, did nothing, until an older man waved him over to come help. Paul followed the man and did as he was told, helping, over several hours into the night, to uncover a neighbor's boy from the debris of Tatie's house, a boy who ran errands in the neighborhood, for Sonia too, back and forth from the hotel high above the city. The boy's leg was smashed to pieces. One of the men made a tourniquet out of his shirt, in attempt to save the boy's leg, and as he did so, I could see that in Paul, a fire was brewing. I looked away as the boy's father appeared out of nowhere and took him from Paul and the other man as they emerged from the broken house, the boy's eyes wide with terror.

It would be a long, sleepless night, but whenever we looked up from a task we were assigned in the street, we saw movements and countermovements amid the bedlam: there were loose bands of boys Paul's age wandering through the melee of broken buildings and bodies. I could see the shape of things to come.

Paul and I walked from Tatie's house to ours after we had done all that we could do there. When we arrived where the house should have stood, I did not recognize the heap at my feet. Paul had to pull on me and say, "This is it." He pointed out to me our father, who was standing in the street, staring at us.

My father swayed in front of us. He was covered in white dust and the rims of his eyes were thin and red. He tried to say something to me, but no words came out of his mouth. When I reached for him, to ask after Mama, a slow stream of blood made its way from the top of his skull down the side of his face, ceremoniously tracing a red line through the white. I thought of Baron Samedi, the god of death. My father looked like a *zonbi*, his eyes empty. I stepped back. He stepped forward, stumbled, held himself erect, gazed in a faraway direction, tears pooling along the length of the red rims. "*Sak pase?*" he mumbled. "*Sak pase?*" I pulled him to me despite the fact that I knew he had come out of a rum shop. Paul, who had been following silently, looked at us embracing, then away. He seemed to be looking at moving forms running down the streets.

The snowy ash continued to fall. Everything seemed to be moving extremely slowly and at high velocity at the same time. I could not tell which: there was a buzz in my head that grew in intensity. My head pivoted slowly to the right: I looked down the street. My head pivoted quietly to the left: I looked up the street. Where was Mama? I saw snow, blocks of rubble, smashed cars, and oversized chickens running wild, flailing their plucked limbs, screeching, though their heads had not been cut off. Some of the people bled. Some of them had round mouths that gasped for breath, looking like my father. Dozens of fathers ran down the streets with bleeding heads, bleating for their children, calling out for their wives, fathers who smelled like tafia, for which I am named, or who looked like bakers, or vodou priests, blanketed from head to toe in white dust. There was only a feeling of coldness at my side, though the air was laden with end-of-day humidity. Cold heat and sweat. Then, a hand clasped me out of nowhere, warm, familiar, pulling at me. I turned around and it was Sonia standing there with Dieudonné behind her, his shirt wet through with sweat. They were breathing heavily, covered in a fine dust. I was so glad to see them. I hugged Sonia. Dieudonné took over the care of my father. Sonia took my hand and we walked with Paul in search of my mother. Later, much later that evening, we found her with Ma Lou, trying to console the woman who had lost her children, who was waiting for her husband to return with the third one, the one Paul had helped to free.

The work of trying to save the dying and move the dead began that first night, before the dust had begun to settle. Even useless people like me worked at moving rubble with our bare hands until our fingers and feet bled. Every time we released a body from the tangle of steel and debris, every time one of those bodies heaved for breath, we felt a little lighter. This went on for a few days as we scrambled to find water and food, and first aid for those bleeding to death from crushed limbs. I will not lie: there were mercy killings. Older men took care of those and did not tell us what they did; they would say only that a soul had been released back to the ancestors, before carrying on. I helped to shroud the dead. Sonia and Dieudonné came and went, using their motorcycle to help with errands as they could. Mostly, they came, and they went. There was no time to ask questions or request a giving of accounts. Everyone did what they could, in their capacity.

Among ourselves, the neighbors on the street, we had decided where to pile the bodies for when the trucks would come for them. We did not know when they would come, only that they would. For days, where we were, deep down in the entrails of the city, no one came, so we started to organize camps in open spaces, where nothing could fall to crush you. This is how we came to be at the foot of the cathedral, where the market used to be, a market turned into a camp.

It took days for any sense of order to return to the streets. What bodies could be retrieved were wrapped in bedsheets and grouped together, Tatie and the neighbor woman's two girls among them. In a few days, they would be carted away by a truck and dumped, like refuse, somewhere outside the city limits. Later, much later, Paul would find out that some of the dumping grounds were the same locations that the Makout had been instructed to use by the Palais National to relieve themselves of their victims so many decades ago. I don't know why this detail was important to him as he relayed the information to us. I felt dread as he told us. Paul seemed to feel nothing except a sense of expectation. He had plans, was biding his time until he could meet the night prowlers he studied from the confines of our tent in the market camp, boys like him who had escaped unscathed and now walked against the flow of the crowd, who knew how to take what no one was willing to give them freely. When the foreigners came with their medical supplies and bloated bags of rice, throwing the goods at the disorganized crowds, those night prowlers had already helped themselves, Paul said, and could be seen cackling at a distance, making bets on which old lady would be trampled by the crowd or which middle-aged man would be beaten down by a foreign service officer holding a long stick for a weapon. Paul shook his head as he told the stories, but he seemed to admire those boys, his new friends.

.

This is what we were left with: a small bundle of clothes (two shirts that belonged to Didier, one of Paul's shirts, some skirts that belonged to Sonia, a housedress that had belonged to Tatie, blue with red flowers, some underwear, Papa's suit and two pairs of his slacks, different sizes of T-shirts); some pots and pans; a hair press; Mama's palm Bible with our names written on the inside flap in coarse pencil; the photo of all of us together; Mama and Papa's wedding photo, folded and out of its frame; a cushion from the couch; a bag of rice; the blue box of recorded music that Didier had sent me that I had hidden away in my pillowcase, and the head-phones. I hadn't listened to the music for a few weeks; the charge had died. In the camps, eventually, there were stands where you could recharge just about anything. I took it there and a young boy recharged it for me and I would pass it around the tent at night when there was nothing else to do. I went back with Paul a couple of times to look for more belongings, but before long what little that remained had been picked over for anything of worth, moved or sold by whoever found them, and I gave up. The street vendors, Ma Lou included, set up shops in the tent city and we learned to adapt together, barter, sell, take good care of what we had left, and keep a sharp eye on everything else so that it did not walk away and out of our space. If something disappeared, you would never get it back again, and you tried to forgive whoever took it, reasoning that they needed it more than you did, even if that couldn't be true. We

helped Sara, the woman whose boy Paul had helped to free from
Tatie's fallen house, settle there, in the tent city, a few spaces beyond
us, where we could keep an eye on her. Her husband came to find
her there, some days later, with their son, but, within weeks, left
again. After a time, when we realized the tent city was not going to
be a refuge but was to be our home for a long time, just taking care
of ourselves became a heavy burden.

When the rains came, we sat on the sleeping pallets we had
managed to bring into the tent city, thin things you couldn't call
mattresses but that made it easier to sleep against the ground. Loko,
the old man from La Gonav who made a living from collecting
and selling rainwater, showed us how to put out as many recepta-
cles as we could to gather and store the rainwater so that it would
stay relatively fresh. He started making rounds and delivering small
quantities of water to those who couldn't collect their own. When
the waters rose high, we tried to hold as many things off the ground
as we could, including the neighbors' children, who might drown if
they were left to themselves. I tucked my skirts into my waistband
and waited the storms out.

The rains were a blessing and a curse. Blessing because it was
free drinking water from the gods when collected. Curse because as
the water pooled and stagnated in the muddy rivulets of the camp
paths and ran off into the ditches and mixed with the water from
the outhouses, flies swarmed and illnesses spread. The days after
the rains were always ones of low morale. For me, things got better
only when Sonia returned to stay and didn't leave again. She stayed
because Dieudonné had decided to head west, toward Jérémie, to
see how his relations were faring there and if it might be a place to
go. After he left, she was quiet, distant.

In the meantime, as I waited for things to get better, I got organized. I watched the old ladies in the camp who still had all their senses and their strength. They washed clothes on Monday and put them out to dry on long strings they had put between the tents or tied between trees. Tuesday was for water. They went themselves or sent children with a variety of plastic bottles they'd managed to find. Wednesday was for bartering: water for food, food for a piece of clothing, clothing for medicine, and so on. Thursday they went out on expeditions to see what they could find beyond the tent city, including survivors from their families. Sometimes this went on through to Saturday, when they'd return at night to make meals, to pray, to think. Saturday was cleaning day. From them, we learned to sweep the earthen grounds of our square plots as if they were home, and the space leading to our cloth doors. Like them, we collected trash that had been strewn about close to our dwellings during the day by people who didn't live there or didn't think about the fact that this was where they put their heads down at night. Paul was another story. One day, he simply walked out of our tent, saying he would be back in a few hours. Instead, I saw him falling in step behind a pack of boys that roamed the camps at night. I confronted him about it once, when I had some strength, fearful of what he might become, and he told me not to worry, that some of the boys he knew already from the days he would venture into Cité Soleil, so he was allowed to trail, and then to join in as the boys walked into abandoned stores and houses, taking what they fancied or needed. Nothing special, he said, taking things for the taking that we all needed. Mama didn't know what to say because some of the things he brought back, some days, were useful. It was hard to say, now, or ask where the things had come from, so we said nothing.

A month or two after our camp started to look permanent, a manager was put in charge by some foreigners. They came and gave him a better tent with ventilation and a solar cooking space. They set it apart from the rest of us so that you could tell he was the manager. Three people could live in that tent easily, all with their own space. Without giving it a lot of thought, the tent city dwellers started to put the trash out in the space between the manager's tent and our rows. I think we wanted to give him a reason to want to stay away from us rather than feel we'd been looked down upon. At the same time, it made his tent seem less glamorous, perched as it was behind a growing heap of trash.

Sunday, we sorted the wash for Monday and put our few things in order by our beds, on stools or little stands, if we had managed to find or make some. Then the women went to Mass, either to the churches in their old neighborhoods, if they were still standing, or right there in the camp if there was a priest or pastor, or even a *houngan*, a healer, willing to hold a service. If they went back to their neighborhoods, it could be a long journey, but they were also glad because they were getting out of the squalor of the tent city for a while, even if it was back to the areas where there was nothing left to look at. Those were days for dreaming, and hoping, and giving thanks for what was left, if you had it in you. The remainder of Sunday was for rest and drawing up plans for the next week. Other tent cities probably worked differently, and within them there must have been variations, but I trusted the elderly women because they had lived long enough to have gray on their heads. To me, this was an achievement as significant as getting a high school diploma or, as Didier had done, having the faith to move to another country to start over. Getting old couldn't be a matter of simple luck.

I walked through the camp, watching as each person acted out their rituals of the day against all the despair and fear they felt. The smallest of the children were playing together. Old men traded dominos on boards laid across their knees. There was nothing else to do but keep an eye on one's dry corner of the world to sleep in before having to start the search for food, water, loved ones. It was hard to believe that only a few weeks before, all I had been thinking about was school matters, going to the clubs, and whether I would have friends or a date for a school dance. It was hard to believe that my life and that of my family was reduced to a small tent, no belongings except the blue box, and waiting. It was hard to believe that Tatie was gone and would never return. It was hard to believe that only a few weeks ago, all I had cared about were things like my name and soap opera storylines and getting invited out by popular girls and that, now, we were in a telenovela ourselves, hoping to awaken from a dream. Most of the time, all there was to do was think, about the life we used to have, the life we used to want to escape, which now I realized was so much better than what we had been reduced to, waiting in the camp.

.

They hadn't been expecting me, so my mother had named me for what she thought was the last lining of her belly, though there would be one more after, even less expected. I came out dark like the rum made from the leftover dreg from sugar and molasses factories, dark and sticky like a sweet sold for two *kòb*, not even two Haitian dollars, in the roadside market stalls. But I also could have been so named because, by the time I was born, my father was a *tafiatè*, a booze head, and tafia was his favorite drink. That didn't mean that I was his favorite, though.

I would never name a child like that, as if it had no future, but I changed my mind for a time after they started showing *Frijolito* on television. For a while, with everyone planning their day around the early evening show, it seemed glamorous and endearing to name a child after food or drink, after a little bean, or grains of rice.

I think my father has a preference for Didier, who lives *lòt bò*, in the States, and for my sister, Sonia, who's the lightest colored of all of us. Me, he doesn't think much about; Paul, my younger brother, even less. Don't let them tell you that only the rich care about color. Down here, below, it makes a difference, too. Paul seems to think so, anyway. Dreams of how he might be noticed since he can't change from dark to light, though I've seen some people do it with a soap you can get in the fancy markets that looks like it's made for curing infections, a big cross on the wrapper, but is for lightening shades of brown. Paul dreams of a revolver, aviator glasses, tight blue pants, and a shirt that will show off his growing biceps. He's told me so. He's growing a mustache. Told me once how, with a gun, he'd blow a white man's brains out or his worst enemy's right toe, show all of us. I don't have the heart to tell him that what he dreams of, like so many dreams, will be nothing new.

The whole color thing I figured out from observation, but also from watching the telenovelas after Tatie inherited an old fourteen-inch box television from the house where she did the housekeeping in the early fall of last year. It was like something that should be in outer space: a black box with a crystal-clear screen and stereo speakers that made everything sound like it was happening right there in the living room, *krik eh o krak!* It sounded so noisy to me. I like music but not noise. I don't like it when you have to hear everything your neighbors are listening to as if you're right there with them in their house. We didn't even need a radio because we could hear the one next door and we could yell over for them to change the dial if we didn't like the show they were listening to. Sometimes, they did. It took Paul and two of his friends to haul the old TV down from the house in Pétion-Ville and into Bel-Air because it wasn't the new kind with a sleek, flat screen. It was bulky and wide with a fake-wood veneer around the screen, but Paul was in good shape, running in the morning, and at night, before going to bed, I watched him do more than a hundred push-ups and sit-ups on the floor of his room. At meals, he took all the extra meat available as if, because the rest of us were girls and women and our father was seldom home for dinner, anything extra we might have was his. He consumed as much meat as he could, when it was available, which wasn't often, sometimes to the point of throwing up. When there was no meat, he ate all the extra vegetables there were and neither my mother nor Tatie said anything. Tatie pursed her lips and told us later that Paul had a secret, and that because of this secret, we should give him a wide berth, excuse his bad behavior. He couldn't help himself, she said, but maybe, in time, he might change, be less angry, channel that energy into a positive direction. We could only hope.

Tatie had a celebration when they brought the television down. She made rice and beans for everyone and she killed one of her chickens, then broiled it in a spicy *ti malis* sauce though it wasn't Sunday. One of the neighbors brought over some *bananes pesées*, fried green bananas, and someone else made some chips from the flesh of *lam veritab* pods, which are supposed to give you strength, but we eat them because they're plain tasty. Papa brought a few cans of Haitian beer and Tatie made some strong cups of coffee to distribute among those crowded into her two-room house. Even Paul, who had long ago stopped doing anything with the family, stayed. We had a feast. The screen of the television was snowy and we still had to play around with the metallic ears; the sound spat and we had to turn it up real loud to make out the voices. But despite the low quality of the sound and picture, it was satisfying to be the noisy ones, for once. I didn't live there, but I took satisfaction in the fact that Tatie was the center of attention and that the neighbors were in her house. Every week after the arrival of the TV, we continued to gather at Tatie's house in the late afternoons to watch the news, sports, and *Frijolito*. Even Paul continued to come. Tatie claimed that the telenovelas were make-believe, but they didn't seem so unreal to me. Experiences of deceit, lust, illegitimate births, and murders were daily occurrences in all of our lives. It escaped me at the time that these were melodramas. They seemed to me more like dramatized documentaries.

Watching the telenovelas, I learned a few things: people prefer to lie than to tell the truth even when they are good people; it's sometimes better not to know who your real father is because you could be rejected or disappointed when you find out who he is; rich people scheme as much as poor people, only they get rewarded for it; if you're a boy, you're always considered attractive even if you're short or psychotic; if you're a girl, you have to have long hair, preferably light in color with waves in it, and you have to have a big bust, otherwise, you'll always be a best friend, if that; in some worlds, there is no such thing as brown girls and if there is, you have to be lighter, like Sonia, to be worthy of a second look by white or brown boys; fast girls of any race are curvaceous and loud—they get attention, but they're seldom loved. I began to understand why Sonia was so popular. It was pretty clear that it wasn't being nice that got her admitted to the big hotel up in the hills with the view of all of Port-au-Prince; and that job guaranteed that she would never get married in one of those big weddings in the telenovelas, with a long, flowing white dress and flowers in her hair. I never saw girls like me on those shows, with their short hair oiled in twists and shiny soapstone skin; flat-chested, skinny, tall girls with flat feet. If they appeared at all, they were in the shadows, hidden in dresses with skirts that reached below the knees; they were cleaning and cooking or tending to crying babies. They wore their hair in plaits or covered with a head rag. They were anything but glamorous. They were part of the decor. My brother Didi always told me that I was beautiful from the time I was small, but watching the shows in Tatie's house, watching how the neighbors reacted with their grunts of approval and thigh slaps when the beautiful girls came on screen, I realized that Didi had been lying.

The void between Didier and me had become wide and dark in our rare phone conversations. I didn't know what to say to him anymore. "I'll send you some music," Didi said, sometime over the summer. "It's a tiny box and I can put all kinds of things you'll like on it. You'll be the envy of all the kids at school." It was understandable that Didi thought that sending me music would make a difference. It was our link, the way we talked to one another, through lyrics and words. It was all that was left of our connection. He knew I wanted to be a writer; he wrote songs.

He sent me the box, but I didn't use it in public. I didn't take it to school because someone was sure to want to beat me up for it, or I'd give it away out of fear. Didier had been gone only five years, but he seemed to have forgotten what it was like to live here, for people like us with wooden pegs and twine for locks. He was living in another world. In that world, he was supposed to be making money to send back to us; this was all that he understood and all he thought we wanted.

I consoled myself with the songs he had put on the box, trying to decipher the deeper messages they implied. There was a popular song about safe sex. There was no reason to worry: I didn't take those kinds of chances. Boys were mostly a nuisance and not that interesting. Another song with a jazzy beat laid over a reggae sound talked about people suffering from lack of clean water. But the one song that made me cry, unexpectedly, by myself in my room, was the one Didier wrote for me on his guitar, about women who work tirelessly despite the misery all around them. It made me think of my mother, Sonia, Tatie, Ma Lou in the market. Didi was telling me to hold strong but I didn't know how I would, who I might become. In the neighborhood, when people ask you how you are doing, one of the ways to answer is to say, *map gade*. I'm watching. It means that you are waiting, looking out, observing to understand a situation before acting. Sometimes, nothing changes as you watch on, but you have to have your eyes open. Looking away doesn't help. What was Didi trying to say to me?

I cried a little bit before I took the headphones off. They were keeping me from hearing the noises from the neighbors, the radios and the TVs blaring, the crying babies, and the roosters cawing, the hens pecking at the ground, and the panting dogs with not enough to eat. I would come back to the music later.

I carefully wound the earphone cords around the blue box until the metal casing almost disappeared. Then I hid both inside my pillowcase. I had no idea how I would make sure that the battery remained charged. Didier had forgotten about that, about the lack of chargers. I supposed that in the world in which he now lived, everything was within arm's reach. We had to go to a neighborhood shop to pay someone with a charger to recharge the one phone we had between us.

Didier's music box arrived in early fall. I stopped listening to the music sometime in December. The weeks in between were filled with Didier's silence, school, and the gatherings at Tatie's to watch the telenovelas.

I became more popular at school because of Tatie's TV. I could finally compare notes with the girls who had TVs at home already, whose braids were always tied not with the cheap *bobo* made of elastic and colored balls but with silky ribbons, the girls who never had to get fittings for hand-me-down school uniforms but got theirs brand-new at the beginning of the year from a department store. They were not the kinds of girls who would ever come to my house. But I could pretend that they might when I jumped into conversations about the story lines of *Les feux de l'amour*. We talked about Jack, Ashley, Victor, Victoria, Traci, Isabella, Brad, and Katherine as if they were people we knew. We knew more about their lives than each other's: their tempestuous love affairs, their betrayals, their deceptions. But it was sometimes a difficult charade to keep up. I hadn't been watching the shows long enough and the stories all seemed to blur together. There were blondes and brunettes, and the occasional brown person (usually the maid or chauffeur or the person cleaning glasses behind a bar), and that was about all. They all looked alike, too, which made it easier to understand how infidelities might occur. But the dramas were the same. There were

WHAT STORM, WHAT THUNDER   147

older matriarchs and patriarchs who resembled the elderly couples in the bourgeois families in the hills, and then there were younger sets falling in love with the wrong people, usually someone who was poorer than they were, or somehow related, or dying. That could have been true of anyone we knew so it seemed real though the sets were outlandishly rich, even when the characters were supposed to be poor.

Poor people on soap operas always have enough to eat. In many scenes, they are seen eating something that the rich people find disgusting, but they still have food. Poverty on these shows means that you live in two rooms instead of two floors and that your walls are painted a putrid green or yellow and usually they have nothing hanging on them. The rich people always have paintings in gilded frames and sculptures on stands. Rich people's decor is always ponderous, like their words, and the looks on their faces when they find out that the love of their life is as corrupt as everyone else they know, or themselves. Rich people also like rooms with windows. Their neighbors live so far away that they don't have to worry about anyone peering to look in: they have views, usually of rolling hills or of horses running wild in the distance. Poor people don't have windows at all, just their four walls and a door. Rich people have a lot of furniture made out of dark woods. Poor people have soft-looking couches covered over in cloth. I preferred the cloth over the wood, but I kept that to myself. Could I aspire only to a different kind of poverty elsewhere? Poor people tend to have crucifixes hung prominently over their doors while rich people hang paintings of their great-grandfathers, the men they honor because they left behind their wealth. Was it possible that Didi's apartment had only wooden furniture? I wondered if he wouldn't rather have ended up in a green-painted box than in a room with windowed doors from which he could see trees while playing his guitar. It would all depend on whether he could find a rich blonde, I thought, some blonde who didn't have to be blonde, wealthy like the women in the soaps who lingered beneath the paintings of their great-grand-fathers, whispering to them their secret desires and schemes as if their money hadn't done enough. It turned out that the poor prayed to the wrong gods and the rich didn't pray at all: they demanded.

"What do you think of what's happening to Jack?" one of the girls asked me at recess one day, as if she were speaking of a boy in our class. But I knew better: it was a test. She was talking about soap opera Jack, brooding dirty-blond, blue-eyed Jack with a beauty mark on his cheek and a cleft in his chin, builder of a multimillion-dollar cosmetic factory, a factory like the one Tatie had worked in. She had followed her husband to Canada for two years, only to come back with horror stories about the stink of the factory, the scary substances that burned the skin, the coworkers who took sick leave and never came back because they were undergoing cancer treatments from which they would never recover. For all these reasons, she had come back to Bel-Air when she'd had enough money saved to build a little house on a small plot of land belonging to her husband's family. He didn't complain. He liked having somewhere to go in winter. He had another woman up north now and came less often, but Tatie didn't care. She had her house and she didn't have to wear makeup anymore.

It was late fall and we were all sitting on one of the low concrete walls lining the courtyard rectangle below the classrooms. I played with a fray in my skirt. I furrowed my brow trying to remember what had happened to Jack in the most recent installment of the soap. I could not recall. Giving up, I finally said, "It's terrible," hoping that that would cover any plot twist.

"Terrible? What do you mean?" Selena, the popular girl, said. "He's getting married to the love of his life! What could be better?" She looked at me like I had two heads.

"Well," I said quickly, to cover up, "who knows how long that will last? Can she *really* be trusted?" I flung a hand over my shoulder like one throws salt for good luck while cooking, and I clucked my tongue like an old woman though I had been fifteen for only a few months.

Selena stared at me, then turned to another girl. "What do *you* think?"

"*Ou chape,*" another girl to my right whispered into my ear, then took my hand. There was nothing unusual about that. Girls held hands at recess. Boys did as well, until a certain age when wrestling took over as the best means to display affection. Girls had no such ways of letting off steam. The girl who had taken my hand was Kassy, a dark-skinned girl like me who lived in a brick house painted bright pink with a stoop and a brick fence setting it off from the street. She had a guava tree in her yard; her mother made jams from the fruit; they also had a rooster, and three chickens. Kassy's grandmother liked to sit on the stoop with a pipe in her hand and never answered when you said hello, though she might wave back; she was deaf. Kassy's father was a small businessman and her mother was a seamstress. No school uniforms bought at market for her, but also no hand-me-downs. Her mother made everything she wore. Maybe that was what made her so beautiful, one of a kind. Kassy's hand in mine was warm and inviting. I smiled at her.

"You don't know a thing about Jack," she said matter-of-factly.

I shook my head, no, discreetly.

"Neither do I," she whispered, and we giggled until the other girls realized that they had been left out of the conversation and that we were ignoring Selena.

Selena liked to be the center of attention. She was the daughter of a businessman, like Kassy. She was one of the girls whose parents paraded her around in an SUV so that you could see only the top of her head as they passed by, except that she wasn't rich enough to remove herself from our company. She acted like she thought she belonged elsewhere, and we all followed suit. Maybe we wanted to be her. Maybe trying to be like her would be the closest we would ever get to being like the women our mothers worked for, like the women in the television box. Selena tried to be like them, and we tried to be like her. It was the way things were.

Sometimes, the boys would come by while we were talking and flirt with us. Sometimes we ignored them, but other times we didn't. We waited for Selena's cue. She picked the boy, or boys, she wanted, like a queen bee, and then we would know that we could enter into conversation with the other ones, the ones she had not picked. The boys did the same on their side. There was clearly a boy leader. His name was Stevenson. He was a rough-looking guy with a head shaved on the sides and a strip of curly Afro down the middle. His shirt never seemed to stay tucked in his pants. He rolled one side of his pants up to his calf and left the other one long. And he smoked. He walked right up to Selena one time and asked her out to dance at a club along Route de Delmas and Selena looked up at him from her seated position and let him sweat. She didn't answer at first but asked him for a pull on his cigarette.

Then she asked him for cigarettes to be shared all around. He gave her four cigarettes, never moving his gaze, never moving one inch from where he stood, which was less than a foot away from her crossed knees. After he handed over the cigarettes and took another drag from the one he'd already started, he spat on the ground, then wiped his mouth slowly, deliberately, suggestively.

"*Et alors?*" he asked, making an open gesture with the hand holding the lit cigarette. "I won't ask twice."

"You just did," Selena said, looking down.

He seemed piqued but stood his ground. She had the upper hand.

Selena looked back at him defiantly. She was holding her own cigarette now, not sharing it with anyone. "*Pourquoi pas,*" she said, then, looking away again, "since you ask so nicely."

Kassy stifled a laugh. I grasped her arm to keep her from laughing out loud.

Stevenson had a reputation for being wild, possibly a drug runner, a petty thief, the kind of boy other boys look up to for no other reason than their fear of him. My brother Paul was leery of him but watched him, too, like all the other boys.

Stevenson was usually followed around by a gaggle of boys, but there was one in particular who was always by his side, Junior. We didn't know who he was junior to, but he certainly acted like Stevenson's lackey. He followed him around like a puppy dog that had lost its bone. Hungry and lean, Junior was searching for something to hold on to and he had found it in Stevenson. Junior eyed me while this transaction was going on between Selena and Stevenson, but I looked away while still grasping Kassy's arm. When Stevenson and the boys were walking away, I stole a glance at Junior. He gave me a sidelong, cold stare. It sent shivers up my spine.

"Don't worry about him," Kassy said, following my gaze. "He wouldn't know what to do with a girl if he had one." She laughed, then pecked me lightly on the cheek before pulling me away by the hand. I laughed with her, but Junior was still staring at me, and under his glance, something turned in the pit of my stomach.

I remembered these moments like sweets, lying beneath the tarp of the tent in the camp, after Douz. It seemed so long ago, but it was only a matter of weeks since we had been so carefree and oblivious of what was to come, so innocent and so careless. So young and naive.

·

It took a few weeks to become accustomed to the tent city below the cathedral, to draw a mental map of its snakelike paths, to create an order in the mind of where things were: the latrines, the place where water was dispensed, food dumped, the tent where medical supplies could be gotten, the spots to find others we knew from the neighborhood, the people to stay away from, the paths on which to make one's way to and from the tent. Paul had the idea to tie one of Mama's kerchiefs to the top of our tent so that we could use it like a polestar, a true north in the middle of the messiness of the camp.

One day, after I had made a few rounds of the aisles of the tent city I was familiar with, I looked for Mama's red kerchief floating above our stall and started to walk toward it. I was looking up and didn't notice when someone put himself square in the middle of the narrow dirt path that had been made uneven by the rains. By the time I looked down, the man had me by the arm.

"You're here."

"What?" I looked up at the man whose face was in shadow, the sun overhead, behind him. It was Junior, the boy from the school-yard. I hadn't seen him since the day we girls all went to the club on Delmas to which Stevenson had invited Selena, where we got a first lesson on what it might mean to become women. Now, he was smiling maniacally. He was even thinner than I'd remembered but he was wearing a clean shirt, a bright red bandana tied around his head. "Let go of me," I said.

"Not now that I've got you where I want."

A chill went through me. I remembered the night in the club and his insistence then, the way the boys acted as if we girls were prizes, things to possess. It made us feel like telenovela stars but it was also terrifying. We knew where babies came from.

At night we heard screams and all of us knew what they meant. They weren't screams of despair any longer but something else, like when dogs are kicked, or worse. I thought of a song I had heard recently, in the camp. It was a catchy tune, so catchy that you might miss some of its finer points. What the singer, a man, says in it is that if you give a girl a drink, a cheap imitation juice that cost twelve cents, and a bit of peanut butter that also costs twelve cents, then the girl owes you a dance, or something more, because you gave her twenty-five cents worth of stuff, meaning: a boy can buy a girl for a quarter. Just because we're poor, it doesn't mean that we're not worth something, I'd thought, walking away from the song and the boys gathered around the boom box, laughing at the words and slapping their thighs.

"What do you want with me?" I struggled against Junior's grip, tried to loosen my arm out of it. He held on firmly.

"There's nowhere to run to, is there? Where were you heading? I can walk you back. You know these places aren't safe." He said the words "these places" as if he didn't have to live in a tent city. I wondered about that. Out of reflex, I looked up at Mama's flag above our tent, as if it could save me. Junior's eyes followed me. "That your tent?"

"Just leave us alone."

He laughed. "It's only you I'm after." He let go of my arm violently. "Who are you anyway? Go. What do I need with you?"

I stumbled backward, started walking in the opposite direction to make it look like I hadn't been moving toward the red flag, though I knew he now knew it was ours. I heard him laughing at my back, then calling out to a friend. When I couldn't hear him or see him if I looked back over my shoulder, I tried to look for the flag again. There was too much heat, too many flies, too many bodies. How long would we be without a door to our name, without locks, having to spend every day looking for food and water, depending on the foreigners to come with their trucks of provisions that were not what we needed, or reserved for a better class of people? How we longed for the clear, bottled water they put up to their lips nonchalantly as they peered at us, smiling hesitantly, playing with the children, who always welcomed attention. How we longed for a return home. By the time I reached our tent, I found Mama plaiting Sonia's hair like she used to do when we were little girls. They both smiled at me when I entered the tent. My heart warmed. I forgot about Junior. We had lost so much but we still had each other.

If I had known what was to come, I would have found a way to sleep without thinking, without wondering about the future. Before, things were challenging, but we had the roof over our heads, our concrete walls, Tatie's television with the soap operas, the school, the treks down to Route de Delmas where we could imagine that we were part of a better-heeled, hipper crowd. There was helping Mama to wash the clothes, fishing Papa out of the rum stalls, listening to the music on Didi's blue box while dreaming of his world up north, watching Sonia in her fine dresses in her rare appearances on the block with Dieudonné and his stern face, watching Tatie make dinner when Mama was too tired, her eyes fixed on the pots as she dreamed of her Prince Charming or of the hairdressing business she would one day have. Things were complicated, in a way, but they were simple in another.

·

By the time the outing to the club on Frères rolled around after the encounter in the schoolyard with Kassy and Selena, a few days into the brand-new year, I had forgotten all about Stevenson and Junior, especially Junior. I was only looking forward to a rare night out.

Mama sent Paul with me so that I would stay out of trouble. I didn't know what good that would do me; Paul almost never spoke to me, though our rooms were next to each other at home. He hardly spoke to anyone since Didier left five years ago, when he was twelve and I was ten. By that time, we had already stopped counting on Papa, who spent more time in the rum shops than at home, and Sonia, too, already had left. Paul kept to himself, but he still listened to Mama, so he came to the club with me. I arranged to meet Kassy there; she was also going to be accompanied by her brother.

We dressed up. The boys wore clean, striped rugby shirts and had cleaned their Converse shoes so that they seemed to gleam in the night darkness. We wore tight jeans and bright-colored tube tops. I had my hair redone in tight twists; Kassy had hers in braids, tied back. We had agreed to meet the rest of the group at the corner housing the Pétion-Ville cemetery. The road forked to the right on Frères, and we were going to walk the rest of the way, stopping at other places along the street to see if anything interesting was going on as we made our way to the club. I was secretly hoping we'd run into my sister, Sonia. I hadn't seen her in weeks.

"*Li pap la*," Paul told me as he checked out the girls on the street and combed back his hair with his pocket brush. "So don't look for her."

"Why not?"

Paul frowned at me. "Don't you get it? Sonia doesn't have time for stuff like this."

"Then why are *we* going?"

"Because we're not Sonia." He walked ahead of me and joined the other boys.

"Who's Sonia?" Kassy asked, hooking her left elbow into my right one. She smelled of perfume.

"My older sister," I said quickly. I didn't want to explain about Sonia, so I changed the subject. "What is it that you're wearing?"

"Some stuff I found lying around."

"Just lying there?"

"Yep. Lying around minding its own business, asking to be worn."

That meant Kassy had "found" the perfume in a real market and "found" some way to walk away with it. A rare find, indeed, since most pharmacies had everything in locked cases and you had to ask an attendant to bring out what you needed, even the cheapest nail polish.

"You didn't!"

"I did." She nodded. "Doesn't it smell good?"

I took my arm out of hers to run my hand lightly through her braids, brought back the tips of my fingers to my nose, inhaled the perfume, and nodded appreciatively. She laughed, and her laughter rang out. Then, just as quickly, the boys already much ahead of us, the other girls forming a cocoon around us, our arms were once again interlocked, with our heads thrown back, light as air, ready for anything. We were becoming best friends.

The music drowned out our laughter and chatter as we entered the bar. The bass was louder than anything else. I could hardly make out the melody. It didn't matter. What mattered was that we had made our way and that, for once, the party was not going to happen without us. Selena was perched on a high stool at the bar, surrounded by the other girls. Kassy and I took spots on the dance floor, and hand in hand, we gyrated in front of the bandstand, hoping that one of the musicians would take note of us. There was nothing so romantic as a musician, especially an older one who had perhaps gone as far as the Dominican Republic and back.

We felt beautiful in our tight jeans and tube tops, like the girls in the music videos we saw on the television. We had rouged our lips and put on eye shadow we made ourselves from coal mixed with the chalky tablets of dry watercolor paints they gave us in art class at the high school. We closed our eyes and held hands and imagined ourselves far away, in another world, a land of plenty, where our every desire would come alive and love would find us. Most of what they played in the club sounded like rap or techno. It had a hard beat. We didn't listen to the words. We didn't care what they said. All that mattered was that we felt alive, like kids anywhere. We went to the bar to retrieve drinks in small cups that the boys paid for and then went back to the dance floor.

Suddenly, there was a loud scream and bottles smashing. The tight crowd on the dance floor swayed like a riptide and I lost my footing. Then, another scream. Yelling. The boys got agitated and I heard the sound of rubber soles screeching against hard cement. Arms flailed.

It was Selena screaming.

I had been standing on the dance floor, eyes closed, grooving to the beat, but now my eyelids flickered open against their will. I had been too happy where I was. Sweat dripped down my temples from my forehead. Kassy had let go of my hands and was facing the bar, standing on her tippy-toes to see above the heads of the others who had crowded all around us on the dance floor.

"*Sak pase?*"

Kassy waved me back. Wait. She strained some more, then started to push her way through the crowd. I strained up too and saw some boys fighting. Stevenson had another boy in a headlock and was pounding down on him with his fists. I followed Kassy through the crowd.

The other girls had already stepped away from the bar. I tried to make my way through the crowd, and as I came up to see if I could spot Kassy, I found myself toe to toe with Junior. He was smiling. I was frowning.

I peered around Junior to see the fight. "Aren't you going to help Stevenson?"

A wide circle had formed around the two boys while the bar owner was rallying his security, two young men no bigger than Stevenson and the guy he was fighting, to break up the fight and lead people out onto the street. The owner was yelling at them to stop, threatening to stop admitting teenagers into the bar, as if there was any way to stop us from coming.

"He's got it." Junior folded his arms against his chest and blocked my way.

"I'm trying to find Kassy."

"What about me?"

His voice chilled me. "What about you?" I replied sassily. "Can't you see that they're trying to get us out?"

"Look," Junior said, "if this is the closest I'm going to get to you, so be it. You don't give me the time of day at school and you don't give me the time of day in the neighborhood. So, I'm making you aware. Putting you on notice."

"On what? And what do you mean 'in the neighborhood'? I've never seen you close to our house." I knew Junior lived somewhere in Bel-Air, but it was a big sprawl and some people came from adjoining areas. I didn't know where everyone lived. Panic set in beyond the brawl in the club. Was Junior following me? Did he know where I lived? Mama always told us girls to be careful of boys like Junior who never let up, who were like bees to honey. You do them like this, she would say, smacking one palm against the other. Like *marengwen*. You flatten them like mosquitoes, stop them from buzzing around. *Rete yo nèt*. Stop them square in their tracks.

"Come on." He cocked his head to the side and ran his tongue over his lips. He squinted so that all I could see were his long eyelashes, the eyelashes that the other girls at school always talked about as being dreamy and sexy. I'd never noticed them before. Junior might have been a catch for someone else. He was stocky, muscular, a bit on the short side, on the light side of *café con leche*, a kind of muddy brown that always made me think of *kachiman*, the color of cashews while they still hung from the sour bulb of fruit we liked to suck on in the summer. His hair was longer than the norm, curled against his head. A *griffon*. A red man who thought he was worth more than others. "Come on," he repeated, "you know you want some of this." He pressed himself against me. I could feel his muscles, and other things. I tried to push him away but the crowd behind me pushed back. They all wanted to get out. I held out my hand to keep from falling and it fell like a spring against his chest. He smiled. I pushed myself away. The palm of my hand came away slick with sweat. I grimaced and wiped the wetness against the back of my jeans. "*M'vle sòti*, Junior."

The crowd pushed against my back again and I found myself looking eye to eye with Junior. I could see a flame there of something disturbing, dark. I looked away, afraid, and pretended to be looking for Kassy still. I felt a hand, the thin fingers of a woman's hand, encircle my wrist and pull me sideways through the crowd. Kassy, I thought. I felt relief and allowed myself to be pulled through. Junior fell away and I heard him say, "If that's the kind of people you hang out with, you'll find time for me." I heard him let out a cackling laughter, saw him turn back toward Stevenson, the muscles bulging out from the side of his neck, and then he started to fight along with some other boys who had had enough of dancing and wanted to let off some steam. The rest of the crowd was scattering, spilling outdoors. The owner was putting away his bottles and telling the patrons that the police were on their way, though we knew they would never show up. There was no police. Security guys were pushing people out onto the street.

When I finally made it outside, the air, though warm, felt cooler than it had felt inside. I took a deep breath. The hand around my wrist let go. I fell to the ground, my hands on my knees, breathing heavily. Then I straightened up, half smiling, expecting to see Kassy. Instead, I felt a stinging slap fall across my face. I looked up. It was Sonia.

"I don't ever want to see you out in a place like this again."

Tears welled up in my eyes, both from the pain of the slap itself and from the fact that Sonia was looking at me with such fiery anger. I had not seen her for weeks, not even for Christmas or New Year's Eve, and this was how she was greeting me?

"But, Sonia, we were just out having some fun. Mama let me come with Paul."

"And where is he?"

I had lost track of Paul between the dancing and the drinks.

"I don't know," I babbled, looking down, tears streaming down my face.

Sonia stood close to me and her hands came up to my face as quickly as they had when she had slapped me. She wiped away the tears with her two thumbs. "You don't want to become like me," she said, quietly, "do you?"

I didn't know what to say. Despite what people said about her, and how she made a living, I worshipped Sonia. I didn't care what people said about what she did. I didn't care that Mama prayed for her at church and tut-tutted and walked into a different room when she came to give us money and sweets. I didn't care. If I could be like Sonia, I would be like Sonia.

I looked at her. She had tears in her eyes as well. "Don't cry, Sonia. You'll make me cry more."

"I'm sorry I slapped you. I was scared for you. What was going on in there?"

"I don't know."

"Okay." She waved at her friend, Dieudonné. He was a tall, dark-skinned man with a shaved head, an easy stride, and a serious face, skin shiny and luminescent as polished black coral. I didn't know much about him, just that he treated Sonia well. "We're going to drive you back. Dieudonné has a car today instead of the motor-bike. Do some of the other girls want to come with you? We'll take you all home." Her eyes swept the crowd, but she had been gone so long that she didn't recognize anyone.

"Kassy?" I said meekly. I looked around the crowd and saw Kassy's braids weaving through. "Kassy!" I yelled out louder in the direction of the braids.

Kassy emerged through the crowd, excusing herself left and right with a girl in tow. It was Selena, who was crying and shak-ing. We followed Sonia and Dieudonné to a side street; then Paul joined us out of nowhere. We all piled into the back of the car and left the scene.

Dieudonné drove without speaking to any of us. At one point he removed a cigarette pack from his breast pocket, took a cigarette from the pack, and lit it. He continued driving, all the while let-ting the smoke out the window as he careened through the streets, avoiding the potholes. He knew how to drive, I had to give him that.

I shrugged at Kassy, then fell back into the seat and stopped worrying because Sonia was there with us. Selena blubbered on about how Stevenson had misunderstood something she had said to another boy and things had gotten out of hand. Kassy pretended to listen with some sympathy. I looked out the window as we were driven back home to Mama, while feeling the weight of Kassy's hand against my elbow and Sonia's worry reaching from the front to the back seat of the car.

Sonia, of all of us, had found a real way out, through her beauty and her smarts, though most didn't realize how smart she truly was because of her line of work. Sonia meant "wisdom" in ancient Greece. Didi had gotten out with his music. And the rest of us were waiting for rescue.

·

The night it happened, something worse for me even than Douz, that would mark and change me even further, forever, I had forgotten about Junior grabbing me on the winding path of the camp, a few weeks after we'd gotten there, after the earth had swayed, destroyed Tatie's house and swallowed her up in it. I had forgotten about how he had shown up in the club and taunted me aggressively, his eyes full of fire. I had forgotten what he'd said about Sonia and the likes of her, meaning that one day, I would have to give in to someone like him, that I didn't have a choice, would have no choice. It was spring already; some months had passed, and we were getting used to our new life in the camp, Sonia, Mama, and me.

We usually went in twos to the latrines at night, but nothing had happened for a while and the latrine ditch was not far from us. I walked alone toward the ditch, finding it in the dark by its stench. When I was done and walking back, someone, a man, grabbed me in the dark, lifted me off the ground and carried me away. There were many hands. One over my mouth and another around my waist. Two holding my feet and two more holding my hands. I fought against them yet marveled at how one man could be an octopus. But there were three of them. They stuffed a dirty cloth into my mouth so no one could hear me scream. Two held me down while the third tore off my underthings. They were stronger than I could be. This wasn't how it was supposed to be. In the soaps, even when a man does something like put a substance in your drink, there is love and there is fire. Here, there was only fire, a burning as they tore through me and discharged themselves of something more burning than fire. *Kadejak.* My mind reeled. Rape. It was happening to me. I could not do anything, my hands held back above my head, my legs held apart. When the first one trembled into me, writhing and moaning, he whispered in my ear: "Thought you could get away? I can do whatever I want with you. We own this camp. *Bitch.*" He spat out the last word with emphasis, as if he'd practiced. The voice was Junior's. He stank of sweat and urine and something else I would later come to identify as the seaweed-like scent of semen. They stank of feces, as if they'd all three been hiding in the latrines, waiting for whoever came that way; that night, it happened to be me.

Junior stopped talking and did to me what he'd been wanting to do since the night at the club. He was brutal in the delivery of his desire, as if he wished me to know down to my marrow the depth of his humiliation at being refused. The others repeated his performance, a reminder that I had been reduced to nothing, a reminder that the safety we had established by banding together with our neighbors and watching out for each other was an illusion, a delusion. Walls made of tarp and cloth would never keep jackals at bay. When they were spent, they threw dirt on me and I lay there, wishing for the earth to open a second time, to swallow me whole, to take me to wherever Tatie had gone with her hand still on her stirring spoon. I yearned for the taste of her rice and beans upon my tongue instead of the sourness that filled me now.

After some hours, when the morning dew stirred from the heat of the rising sun, I rose too. This was before troops of women would descend into the camps with clipboards and pencils, taking down information from whoever would speak about their assailants. One of them was Ma Lou's granddaughter, Anne, and I would watch her and those other women curiously, wondering if what had been done to me could have happened to them, somewhere else. But I never told, especially later, when I realized that I was pregnant and it was too late to get rid of it.

When I knew I had the baby growing inside of me, I stopped eating the camp rice. A part of me wanted to starve the thing though it clung to me for dear life, clung to me like the man-boy who put the seed in there without asking me what I thought about it and then disappeared back into the night. Paul, too, disappeared for a while, but he came back to find us in the camp.

.

Then there was the day, seven months after we'd reached the camp, three months of which I was already pregnant, that Paul, Sonia, and I were all together, sitting in front of our tent while a woman named Anne was making rounds in the camp, taking down information from tent to tent about what might be needed, who might have been assaulted, when we saw her, a few tent openings down from us, throw down her pen and papers and cry out, "Fire! Fire!"

We looked up, alerted by her alarm, and saw the smoke coming from the tent of the woman who had lost all her children, the two under Tatie's house and the one left to die with her under the tent by the husband who left and never came back.

Sonia told Paul to fetch his scouting knife and after he did, we ran over to help Anne, who was running around looking for water. Paul cut through the tent and I could see from the way he did it that he had done it many times before. But instead of dwelling on this, I helped him and Sonia tear at the fabric of the tent until it gave and we saw the woman turning away from us, following the path of a flame making its way across the roof of the tent. How she had started a fire, I could not guess. I saw upturned bowls, puddles in the dirt, and only a little water left in a container, not enough for what was about to happen, on the dirt floor of the tent. I imagined everything going up in flames, then the flames spreading from tent to tent, our tent too, destroying the little we had left. I stepped decisively under the tarp, wrenched the woman back from the flames while grabbing the only cloth I could see, a worn bedspread strewn over the thin mattress she used for a bed. I threw the cloth over her, shielding her from the growing flames, Sonia grabbing her around the waist, and we stirred her out of doors. Then Anne appeared, followed by Loko and Paul toting a large container weighing them down, its contents spilling over from both sides. Doused with the rainwater, the fire was over in an instant, before it could spread to the neighboring tents. We held the woman between us, Sonia and I, while Anne canvassed what was left of hers in the tent to take. Paul helped Loko retreat with his container. Loko was shaking his head, bewildered. I felt the woman shiver beneath the bedspread I had wrapped around her. She had an odd look on her face, a smile that was not quite a smile, her gaze far away, as if she did not understand what had happened, what had almost happened. Anne spoke to Mama, gave her what was left of the woman's belongings, then Mama told us we would make space for Sara in our tent. We didn't see this Anne in the camp after that. She left while others came.

After Sara came to live with us, Paul was quiet, even more quiet than usual. I looked at him by the light of the fire at night and pondered things that seemed impossible before. I wondered if when he had disappeared, he had done things like what was done to me. When the misdeeds of the pack of boys Paul ran around with had circulated (and by this time there were many), their already terrible acts were amplified through innuendo. There had been a rumor that Paul had started carrying a knife before he was eleven years of age and used it to menace girls when they found themselves walking alone from school. Others rumored that he had never been the runt of his class but that he had bullied others rather than been bullied, joining older boys in rounds that included beating up elementary school kids and stealing the lunch sent with them to school. The more the rumors grew, so did Paul: his skinny frame became lean with sinew and muscle; that glow at the sides of his temples from the sun gleaming against the deep prune hue of his skin became the contours of scars received in a knife fight that no one remembered having witnessed but that everyone swore to having heard talked about; the quick saunter of his gait, an effect of dread, was reinterpreted as swagger. No one remembered Paul as he had been: thin, scrawny, hardly worth a second thought. The acts under cover of dark, in unexpected circumstances, anointed them with dreaded superpowers: they became werewolves bathed in moonlight. I stared at Paul and wondered. He was the only one who dared to look at my belly all those months and went to fetch water from Loko in my place when the load became heavy, as if he understood something no one else could. He was the only young man I saw in the camp doing things that women do; perhaps this was because he lived in a family of women. The only one who didn't yell insults at women walking by like the other men did, especially when the women were foreigners or white women. But still, I wondered. Anything was possible now that didn't seem so before.

After Paul came back to us, I asked him why he was so quiet. What I wanted to know was what he had done with those boys, what was true and what was not. He mumbled something about wanting to be remembered, a legend in his own time, a cowboy, a werewolf, a Makout sowing fear from his satchel. But then, he said, he'd come to realize that there was something wrong in what he and his roving band of boys were doing. At night, he said, sometimes he couldn't sleep, because ever since Sara came to live with us, he felt like something or someone was tugging at his clothes, a heaviness. When he thought about it, he felt a nausea overtake him to the point of dizziness. I listened to Paul but said nothing. There was nothing to say. The days, weeks, months ran together after a while, punctuated by events, large and small, that changed the fabric of our lives. They changed even to whom we might be connected thereafter.

Eventually, someone else took over Sara's tent, built over the remains of what was left there. Maybe if we had not saved her, she would be less alive now, though she was not completely herself, telling us that her son and daughters were there with us in the camp, hovering about, visiting her at all times of day and night. This thought seemed to make her happy, so who was I to say that there was no one there? Who knew about these things? How could I know?

.

Some months from now, a year that started with the splitting open of the earth and so many deaths will end with my son born in a tent, by the side of the road, in a camp below the broken cathedral, where the market used to be. He will be small and scrawny and will have a good pair of lungs. Sara will tell me that he reminds her of her son, the one Paul helped to save but who then lost his leg and died of gangrene. She will say nothing of her daughters. Sara and Mama will help take care of the new baby, as I am afraid to look into his face and see his father there. Sonia will say that he reminds her of a child she had wanted but never had, so she will avoid his cries when she can, and wait for word from Dieudonné so she can leave this, us, all behind.

.

When we used to come to market, before Douz, we thought that God was watching over us. Now, when we walk by the crumbled remains of the cathedral, we know there is no God left, or else he's gone elsewhere. The cathedral is where the big weddings and government funerals took place. I would see beautiful people going in and out, and the building was so beautiful with its rose-and-yellow-painted walls rising into the sky and the round windows that made it look like a ship with portholes stranded on dry ground. I had dreamed of having my wedding there one day, when I would marry a rich man and be taken to a house in the high hills overlooking the valley of the city. At night, even then, though, it wasn't so glamorous. There were hustlers and pimps and women walking the sidewalk, but in daylight, it was a fairy tale. Now, there isn't any difference between night and day. Daylight is an illusion. I wonder why this has happened to us. Not just to my family, but to all of us. This is where we live now.

We are in a tent at the foot of the broken cathedral, waiting.

All there is to do is wait.

And wait.

Wait.

Douz: when something terrible happens to you, it feels like a dream at first. Not until the pain and the panic settle does it seem real. This is what I will tell Didier when he returns, and everyone will nod. I see them there, gathered, Sonia, Mama, Dieudonné, Paul. They all know. Didier will nod as well. We all know—however it is we will ourselves to move through this: afterward, the terrible thing never goes away. It dims but remains, lurking, an uninvited guest, a leech. The more you try to forget, the more it hangs on. One side is scissor to the other, back and forth, conjoined, not able to leave. The feeling uniting dream and pain lasts eternally, but you yearn for the return to a blank space, the in-between suspension between the two before they came to be jointed. You yearn for the sweet, open-eyed innocence, the comforting warmth of the blankness, to never become aware of the jointing itself, of then having to live in the after, always, remembering the before.

DIDIER

Boston, Massachusetts, late December 2009

And I heard a great voice out of the temple saying to the seven
angels, Go your ways, and pour out the vials of the wrath of God
upon the earth.

And the first went, and poured out his vial upon the earth; and
there fell a noisome and grievous sore upon the men which had
the mark of the beast, and upon them which worshiped his image.

And the second angel poured out his vial upon the sea; and it
became as the blood of a dead man: and every living soul died in
the sea.

And the third angel poured out his vial upon
the rivers and fountains of waters; and they became blood.

—The Revelation of Saint John the Divine 16:1–4, King
James Bible

Armageddon: the end times. I have read these words every week, from the moment I stumbled across them in a Bible I found in the taxi. I've become religious. Not so unusual for a Haitian, but unusual for me. I was an agnostic before, though still I like my *rara* and my *ti danse*, like everyone does, a little *rasin* music, when I get nostalgic, that I pluck from my guitar. But when things started to fall apart after the first-year anniversary of my arriving in Boston, and nothing was coming through, the gigs drying up and the false friends going their way or back home to Daddy's house in the plush hills and I was left alone, without proper papers, reduced to having to drive a cab when someone would lend me theirs to put in some hours when they were off the clock, I took to reading the Good Book. There was nothing else to do, after a few weeks of late nights and having college kids throwing up in the back of the cab and the cabbies stiffing me on tips so that all I could cover was the expense of the fuel, watching old ladies smother their dogs beneath their armpits while others threw their pets out car windows on busy highways to dispose of them, and then getting beat to an inch of my life in South Boston for being the wrong color at the wrong time in the wrong place. I did all there was left to do: I got religion.

In the neighborhood where I live, Mattapan, it's not hard to find a church, every kind of faith you can imagine from Catholics and Methodists, the old-time religions, to the new convert Baptists and Episcopalians. I wouldn't be surprised if there was even a mosque tucked away behind an unassuming storefront next to a shoe store. Haitians will believe in anything that gives them hope.

When I was home, in Haiti, hope came not from believing in gods but from the rhythms I plucked out from my guitar. That's a religion too—the sound you can make with your own body, your mind. You only have to take a walk through any market, look at all the fruits piled up and the women grown rotund from having to sit there, under the heat, day after day, selling their wares, to believe there is something akin to a God, or gods. Looking at these women, you have to come to the belief that there is something more than the toil and the mercilessness of the choking humidity. Whatever there is, there, imprinted in the pupils of their eyes, their tenacity, their goodwill, their vulnerability, ripening under the sun: this is something of what others could call God, whatever God there is. I learned this watching my mother exchanging with a woman about her age in our local market. Her real name was Anne, but we called her by her husband's name, Ma Lou. She had had a son who had disappeared long ago, after her husband passed. I saw her only in the market, did not know her life beyond it, when my mother would take me along for errands to hold the basket in which she placed the things she bought, both for us and for the women in the hills for whom she worked.

Ma Lou was a strong, thick-bodied woman, colorful wraps always about her head, protecting her hair, and wearing skirts and dresses of many folds below the waist that she used as smock and makeshift carrier while helping her clients as they chose their fruits and vegetables, moving her products from one basket to another, to skirt, in response to their whim. I watched the choreography of her movements, which were seamless and fluid despite her girth, with awe, when I was a child of about ten or eleven, and as I grew older, I admired her and all the other women like her, so close to the earth that they seemed dust-laden and ethereal, like the ballerinas in little girls' jewelry boxes, as dainty and as precious. They were women who seemed to want for nothing and gave all. As I grew older, I would come to the market with my mother's basket and my guitar on my back, and as Ma Lou filled the basket, I would sit, waiting, plucking at the strings of my guitar, serenading the *madansara*, who sometimes sang along, or hummed, if it was something original that I was working on. I realized only later that they were my first loves, these earthbound, dusty women, my first audiences and inspiration. Back then, even amid political violence and deprivation, hopes dashed over and over again, in the market, everything seemed so simple, so neat, beyond the tentacles of the mighty who would want to crush us: a woman's world with other rules. As the women moved among their wares, their skirts billowing red clouds of dust, clucking at clients who were brusque or impolite, sometimes at each other when one undersold the other, I learned what it meant to be present in the everyday, to hope for things that were simple but nourishing. Still, I felt I needed to leave. I recognized, however at home and safe I felt there, that I was not, and would never be, a market woman, or, even, as a man, a cutter of cane. I needed to write and play my songs. To do that, I needed freedom from the land that had borne me yet would suffocate me with the dust these women swept up in the dance of moving between sacks of beans and towers of avocado, kicked up between feet and pleated skirts. The women of my childhood were dreams, long-ago apparitions, ghosts.

Since I've come to this white, snowy land of hard stares, where I've learned that to speak with an accent and walk within a dark skin means that you have to keep your head low and your tongue quiet, I've fumbled in the dark for anything to hold on to: cigarettes, alcohol, women, and, now, the Bible. I read the Bible before I go to sleep, and when Sunday rolls around, I go to Sunday school with the five- and six-year-olds. I sit in the back of the room on a low chair with the children looking back at me, tittering every few minutes, and I ignore them to listen intently to the explanations of the Bible verses they're given in answer to the questions they ask.

When we read the story of Moses parting the Red Sea, one of the children asked: "Why didn't the sea swallow them up?" When they were told it was an act of faith, one of the little boys muttered: "I wouldn't have walked across."

The teacher overheard him, smiled, and said, "Then you wouldn't have been saved."

The boy frowned and folded his arms across his little barrel chest. I could see that when he grew up, he would be like me, asking questions and walking away from authority. I smiled.

When the children discussed the distribution of the loaves and fishes, they asked, "Was it magic?"

The teacher, who was afraid that some of her pupils had *vodou-isants* parents, spoke cautiously of the absence of magic in divine intervention.

"It's like God has superpowers," one of the little girls said, "like Superman!" I couldn't keep myself from laughing out loud at that.

But when we got to the story of the end times, they didn't have much to say. One of the little girls told a story about her mother telling her that the hole we were making up in the sky was getting bigger and bigger and one day we would all fry up like little dirt worms lost on the pavement after a rain, getting burned to a crisp by the sun. "The end times are now," the little girl said, solemnly, frowning. We were all dying a slow death but didn't know it, her mother had said.

"How cheerful," the teacher responded with a barely cloaked note of sarcasm in her voice, smiling against the vision of annihilation painted in all our minds by her pupil. "It's true that one day we will all go to a better place," the teacher said, "heaven." She added hastily, "But we can lead happy lives in spite of ozone depletion."

I raised my eyebrow and looked across the heads of the children and met the teacher's eye. Did five- and six-year-olds know what the word "ozone" meant? Did the little girl who had spoken even understand the word "death"?

The teacher coughed, avoided my glance, and cleared her throat. "The point is that we have to be very, very good, like at Christmas, when Santa Claus comes."

"I thought Santa Claus wasn't real," one of the little boys said, turning to the boy at his left.

"What are you saying?" a little girl whispered, reproachfully. "Everyone knows Jesus and Santa Claus are the same thing."

"They bring you presents," said a fourth one.

The teacher could see that she was losing control of the class. "It's simply a story about how we have to be on our best behavior or very bad things can happen."

"Like not getting any presents at Christmas," one boy said.

"I don't know about your house, but that happens at my house all the time, no matter how good you are," another boy said.

The teacher snapped her children's Bible shut, grimaced. "Any more questions?"

The hands shot up, and I left the room with my lost-and-found King James Bible in its grainy black leather binding tucked under my arm. I had my own questions to ponder, but I had to get back to work, to driving the jitney cab.

·

And I heard the angel of the waters say, Thou art righteous,
O Lord, which art, and wast, and shalt be, because thou hast
judged thus.

For they have shed the blood of saints and prophets, and thou
hast given them blood to drink; for they are worthy.

And I heard another out of the altar say, Even so, Lord God
Almighty, true and righteous are thy judgments.

And the fourth angel poured out his vial upon the sun; and
power was given unto him to scorch men with fire.

—*Revelation 16:5–8*

It's in the cab that I find out what it means to be black in America.
How "black" people think I am. Black here doesn't mean what it
means back home. It isn't only a color or the idea that your ancestors came from Africa and reinvented themselves on a stretch
of land out in the middle of nowhere, or what it became after the
Revolution, something every citizen became, something cultural,
to celebrate as free sons and daughters of a new nation of infidels.
It's a label they slap on you, and if you accept it, it's a resignation.
It means you'll never amount to more than what white people tell
you. If you cross the wrong ones, then watch out: you'll be shov-
eling snow for the rest of your life, calculating when not to put
some dry salt on patches of ice in order to make them fall, the only

power left to you a pettiness right out of a high school playbook: spitting, swearing, mumbling under your breath, trying to get their girls though you'll never rest in beds like theirs. That's what it's like for a black man in America, even if you don't think of yourself as black. You look the part and you get the role. It's as simple and banal as that.

In all of this, I haven't figured out how people come about thinking that they're white. I look at the people in my cab from the rearview mirror and I wonder what makes them white besides the pale color of their skin. I've seen people who look like them all my life back home, and none of them thought they were white, even if they didn't think that they were black either. They thought they were better, but they didn't think they were white. They knew who their grandmothers were. I peer at these pale people in the rearview mirror every shift I have, and I try to guess what they are. My own exercise in radical racialism. I rarely, if ever, come up with "white." When they ask me where I'm from because of my accent, which I can make out only here because everyone else around me sounds to me like they speak with an accent, and I, too, work hard to understand them, when they ask, I don't blink; I tell them: "Haiti." In the next breath, I say, "And you?" Their eyebrows always shoot up. "Me?" they ask, incredulous, a tone of condescension creeping into their voices. And almost always, inevitably, the stock phrase: "I'm an American!" Ta-dum! As if this is always obvious. Depending on the day and whether I'm feeling brave or not, I keep going. "Yeah," I say. "Everyone's American, but what are you, really?" Sometimes they turn away, sallow skins flush with anger—anger is pink on pale skin—and spread their newspapers wide open so they can hide. I turn up the radio. NPR. That's how I get my news and better my vocabulary. If I want to piss them off even more, I whistle as we whiz through the streets. Some people you want out of your cab as quickly as possible.

I'm usually talkative, you see. Not in an annoying, over-the-top kind of way, but I have people skills. In the first days of driving the cab, after a few lifts, I realized that I was supposed to be as quiet and as invisible as a fly. If I talked too much, the women clutched their purses a little closer to their bodies. The men glared at me through the rearview mirror, thinking I was insane. Some of them said to me: "Just drive," their faces aglow from the light of their cell phones. So I did, though sometimes I forgot about their need for my silence and hummed with the music on the radio. You're thinking that doesn't sound so bad, maybe those people were in a bad mood, maybe they wanted a different kind of service from the kind I was delivering, maybe they expected service to be smooth, efficient, given with a smile and that's that, like people in Haiti in big houses who think out loud about the help as the help scurries all about them, sometimes even asking the domestics to agree with their assessments of the poor beyond their gates, the people they call "the masses," the very people the help's wages go to sustain.

Surprisingly, some of the worst offenders give fat tips. Not the businessmen who think you should be shining their shoes and getting a whole dollar for a tip, but the ones who litter back there and complain about the smell of others. It's the nice ones you want to worry about, the ones that schmooze you up and talk about "the man" and so forth, who ask if you know where to get a good joint, or, failing that, if you can spare a cigarette. Joints I know but I tell them I could get fired and can't help them out, though this isn't a real job. They don't know that. What they don't know won't hurt me.

The worst fares are from the ones who come into the car with their pet dogs. Little rat dogs: terriers, Pomeranians, Chihuahuas, wieners, cockers. You name it, they have it, in zip up carriers or with their heads hanging out of handbags as if they're a blanket these people are going to wrap around their shoulders, like live minks. The only little dogs I like are the Jack Russells. They look like the dogs on TV shows, like the dog on the comedy show about psychologists running amok in their personal lives who's smarter than the stars of the show. When I'm not reading the Bible, I watch a lot of TV in my off time. What else is there to do? Jack Russell owners tend to keep them on a leash. Some are talkative, some are not; they don't cause trouble. The other passengers with dogs seem a bit crazy to me. They're kinder to the dogs than they are to people. They bark on the phone to their associates and lovers, bark at me. They tip like shit. They act like they care more about their little dogs than anything else in the world, but they care about nothing more than themselves, and appearances. Some of them feed the dogs in the car from little hidden treat bags they keep in a pocket though the back of the cab has a clear sign that says: "No food." I guess dog treats aren't food to these people. I pointed this out a few times at the beginning but simply got nasty stares for my trouble, as if I'd taken a mother's milk out of a starving baby's mouth. These people don't know what it means to starve.

After a while, I started envying the dogs, though, the poodles and the ones that looked like little mops with miniature ribbons tied into the hair at the top of their heads. They had homes, and treats, and some kind of sick love that meant that they were carried off the ground in a satchel or purse from one place to the next. My goodness, these people with their trench coats and fancy boots, their shades, and their ability to hop in and out of cabs still have to pick up dog poop. This is a city ordinance. Those dogs bring them to their knees, literally. Those dogs are the kings and queens of the city.

But I know all this is an illusion, as so many things are. I realized it the day I was coming back into the city on the highway from a long fare that had gotten me a twenty-dollar tip. I had been behind the same cars for a while, had memorized their decals, noted the ability of the drivers from the way they rushed traffic or braked when they got too close to someone ahead of them. There was a low-riding red hatchback about three cars ahead with the head of a dog popping up and down in the back seat; the driver was gesticulating and looking back. I assumed he was on the phone with someone. There were cars with whole families, little kids turning around to give me the finger. There were the single girls, whose minds seemed elsewhere, driving with a mission but weaving up and over the middle lines, checking their text messages. There were the loose guys in the big trucks, with their arms hanging out the driver's side window (they always drove Fords as if it were the only brand around), true patriots, the good old boys, men I wouldn't want to meet in the dark, especially those who had Confederate flag bumper stickers. I hadn't been here long, but I knew that spelled trouble. I was watching all of them, thinking about the fact that there were other cars behind me, with drivers doing the same, watching ahead and wondering about the lives all around. I was making my way, intent on getting the cab back without a scratch.

That was my motto with the other guys: without a scratch. They knew they could trust me, and I got the cars more frequently that way, from at least half a dozen guys. Driving was becoming more and more of a regular gig. But there I was on the highway, thanking God for granting me the good luck to pick up this ride and pondering if I could afford to get a drink out that night, when something incredible, no, I mean unimaginable, happened. The low-riding red car that had been a few cars ahead of me swerved in and out of its lane. Sitting up in my seat, gripping the steering wheel in both hands, placing my foot on the brake, I got ready for whatever came next. The traffic slowed only a little bit and then more cars started to swerve, and I saw that there was a dog in the middle of the highway, trying to figure out which way to go. It was a big dog, a longhaired setter. The dog had been thrown out of the red car that had kept going. I was too far to stop and grab it, but I could see it ahead in the lanes, running, confused, stopping, turning around. A car that hadn't seen the commotion came up behind me, to my right, and ran over it. At first the dog was stunned, popped back up, hobbled a bit; then another car that hadn't seen it ran over it again and that was that—roadkill.

It wasn't the first time I'd seen a dead dog on the highway, or I guess I should say, dog parts. Sometimes you see something that resembles a furry femur on the side by the median. You wonder how it got there, where the rest of the animal might be, but then you forget and go on. Highways are like that: they don't invite stops and speculation. Things happen. Shit happens. This time, I *knew* that someone had thrown a live animal out into oncoming traffic, as if he had wanted to *see* the animal dead, punish it for some misdeed rather than give it away to someone who might care for it. It was no mistake.

I had seen only the back of the head of the guy in the red car. Hadn't seen if the arm throwing out the dog was white or brown. It was a shadow like so many shadows. The car had had stickers of skulls on its rear bumper, and a university crest. That could mean anything and nothing. Cars changed hands like tissue here.

.

After that day, I eyed my dog customers with suspicion. I pointed out that the "No food" sign included dog food. I told them they'd better be good to their dogs and not be putting on an act. I envied the dog owners too, the companionship, the loyalty they got from those dogs. At home, dogs ran the streets aimlessly in search of food. They were a breed I'd never seen anywhere else: tan dogs with small bodies. It was hard to believe that they were descendants of Cuban dogs that had been trained to track and kill enslaved Africans, to dismember them alive. I supposed that this was why no one looked after them. Generally, in Haiti, man and dog ignore each other. We have a quarrel with the dog as a species. We don't want them around. We kick them when they're down. They've become too much like us, in a way. They remind us of our weaknesses. The people who keep dogs either have them to guard their houses, though some who travel to the exterior quite a bit, mostly women, they have them as pets. Those women are bored to death with their lives and shower those pet dogs with unrestrained adoration. They barely speak to their maids and give the leftover food to their dogs while the maids starve on the little corn porridge they're allotted. Those pet dogs don't last long. The heat usually gets to them and then the whole household has to hold a silent vigil in the backyard. These are the same women who never even ask after maids who disappear from work. They prefer to think the maids (women like my mother) are lazy rather than wonder if perhaps one of their children has taken sick. They take an afternoon off from their social calendar to bury their dead *dogs*, but the maid loses her job if she has to bury a child.

If I could afford it, I thought, I would have a dog. It would ride up in the front of the cab with me, in the passenger seat, and stare back at the clients. *Watch out*, it would seem to say, panting: *I'm watching you; one wrong move, and I'll bite your head off!* I would even let it bark if it wanted. I would feed it dog jerky—pet food would be allowed in the front of the cab. If it had to go to the bathroom when I was on a job, I would excuse myself with the client at the back of the cab and pull over and let it out to do its business. But if I had a girlfriend or a *ménaj*, I would make it sit out on the porch in front of my house. I would let it howl at the moon before treating it like a person. I would say to it: "Look, I'm the boss; dogs are dogs and people are people." But I also would let it know that God is dog spelled backward and give it its props. Who knows, God might be in one of them, judging us, laughing, watching us pick up its poop. "I'm the boss," I would say to it, "but you've got to atone for what you did to my people, God-dog; you have to prove that you're man's best friend and I'll be your friend too, *dakò*? Okay?"

But I couldn't afford a dog. Dogs were for bored people and I was not bored. Just poor. Dogs needed space. I needed space. If I were a rich man, maybe I would have a dog. An outdoor dog that was free to run around and have its own cares. If I were a rich man, I wouldn't have time to think about these things.

I came home forlorn the day of the highway incident. I even forgot to return the car. I couldn't think straight. The man I'd borrowed it from, Guy, my best friend, an African American born and raised in this city, had to call me looking for it. He and his wife didn't live that far. He walked over to get it. I told him the story of the dog over a finger of three-star Haitian rum I kept in the kitchen pantry for when I had guests, which was never. Guy was the first, though he and his wife, Julie, had had me over a handful of times to their place. I told him the story of the dog. He laughed. I stared at him. I didn't think it was funny. I should have recognized then that Guy and I weren't wired the same way.

"Welcome to America," he said, swallowing the rum in one long draw and grimacing as it hit the back of his throat with a slow burn I knew all too well. "America, where people are as liable to let their dog loose on the freeway to get rid of it as to give it to a neighbor. Why would you want to make a neighbor happy? Love thy neighbor as thyself." He bent forward, over the coffee table separating us, and wagged a long index finger close to my nose. He was already buzzed. "Remember that a neighbor here in America is a stranger. You have to watch out for number one."

"Number one?" I asked.

"Numero uno, buddy." Guy pointed to himself. Then added, with a slur, "The guy taking up space behind your eyeballs."

That day, after Guy went on his way without giving me any part of the tip I'd brought back from the last run because he'd had to come over for the car and drive it home, I realized that America was like those wealthy women back home: bored out of its mind and careless to the point of cruelty. I continued to drink on my own, swished the rum around my mouth, felt the alcohol tingle against my cheeks. I took a second shot, then a third.

Numero uno, Guy had said. I'll be the dog, I thought. Someday, I'll be the dog. Not one of those little measly Cuban castoffs slinking around in the streets looking for a morsel to eat but a mastiff sitting in the front seat of my car, barking its head off at the cowards that dared to cross its path. A dog with a mission, unlike the ones that sat primly in dainty bags, fed by hand like a chicken in a coop, one morsel at a time.

A top dog: the one that poops where it wants, runs free, protects hardworking, tough women, barks atop heaps of sweltering garbage, that no one dares to even throw a rock at.

.

And men were scorched with great heat, and blasphemed the
name of God, which hath power over these plagues: and they
repented not to give him glory.

And the fifth angel poured out his vial upon the seat of the beast;
and his kingdom was full of darkness; and they gnawed their
tongues for pain,

and blasphemed the God of heaven because of their pains and
their sores, and repented not of their deeds.

And the sixth angel poured out his vial upon the great river
Euphrates; and the water thereof was dried up, that the way of
the kings of the east might be prepared.

—*Revelation 16:9–12*

Then there was the day I wasn't grateful enough. I was in a bad mood because I hadn't gotten a shift in a week, and no music gigs either. I'd been borrowing money from anyone I could, a little here, a little there, getting food from the corner store on credit, trying to keep track of everyone I owed, praying that a job would come my way. Then Guy called, asked me to meet up with him in the dead of night, take his cab and drive out to South Boston. "Man, are you kidding? You want me to get killed?"

"Nah, nah," Guy said, "nothing like that. You'll be fine. These are friends of friends; they're in a bad spot and need someone to get them out of there. I can't go because I have the boys tonight."

Guy had been divorced and his first wife, the one before the current one, Julie, had been giving him a hard time about seeing their two boys. He had twin boys with the first one and twin girls with Julie, like the only thing he could make was twins. At the thought of the boys, the chance to spend a little time with them, I relented. I hadn't seen my own family for a few years by then. I missed them. I thought of my younger brother, Paul, who was lacking direction, who came of age when our father grew more and more distant, spending most of his time in rum shops.

Paul was eleven years younger than I was, almost another generation. Before I left, he was on the brink of adolescence, sullen and withdrawn. The sweet boy I had known when he was small, who held my hand to go visit with the women at the market while I strummed my guitar, avoided me. That had started after I'd had a bad reaction to his showing me a photograph from a library book of a Makout. I understood immediately the attraction, but Paul did not understand the danger. The men looked smart in their dark blue uniforms, their pressed slacks with red stripes running down the sides. They were fit. Many of them were middle-aged, even older than our father. The men had single round guns strapped to their midriffs, like the tall white men with chiseled features in American Westerns who spoke in monosyllables. A few years before the photograph, when Paul had been about nine years old, and our mother had asked at the dinner table what he wanted to be when he grew up, he'd said, without hesitation, a cowboy. Now he thought he'd found out that there had been cowboys, right there in Haiti, with red handkerchiefs around their bulging necks, like Lucky Luke and his white, ten-gallon hat. What could be better than that? I hadn't known what to say, what to explain. Paul became obsessed with the photograph, wanted, for his birthday, aviator glasses and a shiny black revolver like the ones he'd seen in documentary footage of the time they called the era of Papa Doc.

Paul was too young to remember a time when a *makout* was no more than a satchel that peasants wrapped around their torsos to carry goods while making their way in the mountains, too young to know the fear that some carried in their bones when *tonton* was put in front of that word to transform a man into the most feared uncle you could ever have, too young to care, and I was too weary, too preoccupied with my plans to depart, to take the time to explain. I should have. Paul was too young to remember even vaguely the men called "*chimè*" or "*sanmanman*," rebel boys, "haunts" they were called, or "without-mothers," who had motorbikes and rapid-fire machine guns rumored to have been delivered straight to the front doors of their shacks by the first in command. At that time, the first in command lived out on the road that led to Tabarre, rather than the road to the Palais National the invaders had had built, claiming to help build the country. Some of these boys who received gifts from their removed, highly placed patron lived in places that didn't even have doors, but Paul didn't seem to know this, or care, if he did, places that were poorer than where we lived. Some of the shacks had florid, worn sheets that hung limply across doorless openings that led into one-room dwellings with beaten earth that pooled and muddied during the rainy season, instead of wooden planks or tile, for floors. These boys, like him, even the ones they called "motherless," still lived with their mothers, mothers who could no longer look them in the eye for fear of what lurked there, mothers who did not recognize the hulking bodies that once hung from their tits. These boys grew up to be men with scars and broken limbs that sometimes healed at odd angles, which they used to good effect when they decided to leverage threats with stories about gun battles or even murders they said they'd committed. I told Paul that some of these stories were apocryphal, that boys retold or co-opted things they'd heard in the street to make themselves seem tougher, that most of them didn't make it past the age of twenty-three to tell their tales, but nothing mattered: it was not enough. I should have taken Paul with me, but it didn't occur to me at the time, and we had grown too distant. I forgot about Paul, focused only on my younger sister, Taffia, and on myself, getting out. When I departed, Paul was left to fend for himself, no man in front of him and no younger male sibling coming up behind him to think about. Boys need fathers, or at least older brothers, or they need someone to father—to grow straight, not crooked.

"I'll go," I said. "You'll owe me big." I was thinking of money, but it turned out that Guy would owe me a lot more than that. I was lucky to be alive after that night, lucky to be able to do anything.

When I got to the address Guy had given me, driving his cab, I flashed my lights like he'd told me to do, to let whomever I was picking up know I was there. I slowed the car down. I waited in front of the triple-decker clapboard house, but no one came out. After a few minutes, I decided to go around the block, try again.

Still nothing. When I came around the third time, I caught a flash of white from some sneakers moving swiftly through the dark, followed by the sound of baseball bats raining down on the hood of the car. A band of men with their faces hidden by ski masks had descended onto the car. I gesticulated for them to stop. I glimpsed red hair and freckles, ruddy cheeks, and the coldness of blue and green eyes showing from beneath the outlined edges of the masks. Damn it, I thought, what did Guy get me into? I was getting ready to simply drive through them when someone opened the driver's side door and beefy hands came at me, latched on, and dragged me out of the cab. I'd never heard the word "nigger" used so many times. I didn't even have time to ask them why or ask them to stop. I tried to shield my face after I felt the crack of bone and the searing pain that followed. I left my middle exposed. That's when they cracked some ribs. I curled up in a ball and tried to wait it out. Prayed. Thought of my mother and Taffia. Hummed songs in my head that I'd wanted to put on a iPod for her that I'd found in a cab, songs she was too young to remember, from past generations, that made me feel less alone, that I thought might connect us still. It was the first time I'd felt so alone in Boston, so bereft of home, so . . . so . . . *black*. Until then, I thought black Americans partly imagined the recriminations, the anger, the fear, that it was all ancient history that they couldn't get over. That night, I learned what their lives were like, shared the fate of dark skin. I was in the wrong place, at the wrong time, the wrong color in a shadowy night.

When they were done with me, they smashed a couple of the cab's windows, and one of them tossed me back into the driver's seat.

"Get outta here," he said, "and tell whoever sent ya that we'll do worse to him if he ever comes back into our hood." It dawned on me that the incident hadn't simply been a case of driving while black. There was something more to it. Guy had let me walk into a trap, and the fact of my color had made it easier for those men to do what they did, nothing more. They'd been expecting me, or someone like me.

The men left, but I couldn't see anything. One of my eyes was shut and dripping blood. My hands were swelling up, and I couldn't breathe. I dialed 911 on my phone, gasped to an operator what had happened, and waited. By the time the ambulance reached me, I had passed out, and the next thing I knew, I was waking up in a bright white room. At first, I thought that maybe I'd died, but soon the pain overwhelmed me and brought me back to my senses. I looked down at my body and noticed the clean white bandages. I was in an emergency room.

Guy called, a day later, deep into the night. A nurse held the phone to my ear because my hands were all bandaged up and too huge to hold anything.

"What the fuck," I said into the phone, apologizing in a whisper to the Irish-looking nurse, who smirked and looked up at the ceiling. "What was that all about?"

"Man," Guy drawled, "if I had known it was going to go down that way, I wouldn't have sent you in there, I swear."

I heard the words, but in the pit of my stomach I knew they couldn't be true. I knew that he'd put me out there like a yellow canary in a mineshaft. He'd talked himself into thinking it was okay because I was Haitian, so I should be used to this shit. I was expendable. He didn't say anything like that, but I could feel it, down deep into the marrow of my bones. The knowledge made my body go cold. "Do you realize what they did to me, Guy? They fucked me up!" There was a sigh on the phone.

"I've already talked to the doctors and they say you're going to be fine."

What? He'd already talked to the doctors? Was he my father, or something?

"I'll pick you up in the morning and take you home, okay?"

I didn't say anything. The nurse looked at me with piercing eyes. I nodded that I was done. She took the phone away, closed it.

"You need your rest," she said. "You need to stop thinking and get some rest." I looked at her freckled cheeks, the plumpness of them, the wisps of red hair escaping from the ponytail tied back behind her ears. I felt like I was in a movie.

"The men who did this to me could have been your brothers," I said.

"Sir," she said, looking at me evenly, her eyes betraying that she understood what I was thinking, "I don't have any brothers." She had a cross around her neck, a small silver thing with a miniature Jesus on it. She saw me look at the cross, then turned back to her busywork of straightening the sheets all around my body.

"Do you believe in God?" I asked.

She paused, stared at me with her sea-green eyes. She made me think of a cat I'd once seen at a girl's house, a calico with pale green eyes that squinted at you as it prowled around.

"Yes," she said, "yes, I do believe in a supreme power, God, whatever you want to call it." She laughed. "I'm Irish. What choice do I have? And you?" Her tone had shifted: it was warm, familiar, as if we were strangers in a village that we both called home. I wondered if it was working in such close proximity with broken, wounded bodies that gave her the facility to cross barriers, if she was asking if I was Irish too, or if she meant did I have a choice in the matter of faith. I looked deep into the nurse's eyes, all the plump flesh straining the cloth of her nurse's whites, the slight cleft in her chin I supposed had also been her father's, the earnestness with which she moved and tucked the sheets around my body so that I felt strapped against the bed. Everything ached.

"Can I have more drugs?"

Her eyebrows shot up.

I closed my eyes. She must have been thinking that I was a drug addict.

"Aspirin," I hastened to add, sighing, "for the pain."

She hurried around the bed. "Of course. The call interrupted my giving you these." She took a small paper cup from the side of the bed and emptied the contents into my hand: two codeine tablets. I swallowed them. She resumed tucking in the sheets, the conversation we'd started forgotten. "You get some rest." She stepped away from the bed and started to draw the curtain that formed a half circle around the bed, isolating it from the others. I could tell it was the dead of night from the quiet all around me. She smiled at me. I took courage from its warmth, but I was starting to fade from the drugs.

"I believe in Dog," I heard myself say, groggily. I saw her nod, frowning. I'd meant to say, "I believe in God."

.

And I saw three unclean spirits like frogs come out of the mouth of the dragon, and out of the mouth of the beast, and out of the mouth of the false prophet.

> For they are the spirits of devils, working miracles, which go
> forth unto the kings of the earth and of the whole world, to
> gather them to the battle of that great day of God Almighty.

> Behold, I come as a thief. Blessed is he that watcheth, and
> keepeth his garments, lest he walk naked, and they see his shame.

> And he gathered them together into a place called in the Hebrew
> tongue Armageddon.

> —*Revelation 16:13–16*

Almost a year ago now, after I got home from the hospital and was convalescing in my apartment, I had my first theological conversation with door-to-door Jehovah's Witnesses trying to sell me on their good word. They came through the neighborhood every once in a while, offering enlightenment, the "good news," as they called it, and copies of their publication, *Watchtower*. It made me think of the Tower of Babel with paranoia attached to it. They were waiting for the world to combust, to save as many people·as possible for the new earth that would come into being after the Second Coming.

The Jehovahs believed that only 144,000 people would be saved in the end times, not one more or one less. How they thought that would get sorted out, what would happen to the remaining billions, who would be found so deserving and who not, I didn't know. The best you could do, according to them, was to lead a righteous life and hope you'd be allowed into the new, earthly paradise, while the chosen ones had the opportunity to flee, to become angels in an unearthly place.

I normally wouldn't have let them in. I usually closed the door
and always felt guilty when I did, wondering if they were taking it
badly, if their feelings had been bruised like mine in the cab, wanting to have a conversation and realizing I needed to be invisible,
nonexistent. I thought of them as misguided, that they hadn't read
a real Bible except the one they'd made up that made them feel better about the world. But something about the relentlessness with
which they swept through the neighborhood made me curious to
understand what they thought they knew. I was also bored, cooped
up in the apartment, recovering. The Bible and television were not
enough.

The Jehovah's Witnesses, a couple, asked me: "Would you like
to hear the good news?" "Pain is the work of the devil," the woman
said, scanning my face as if I were already possessed. "We can relieve you of this pain if you'd let us in," the man said with a note of
eagerness in his voice, sensing a hesitation in my stillness that he
took for opportunity. "Won't you let us in, son?"

"Why not," I said, holding the door open and showing them
into my sitting area next to the kitchen. "Would you like coffee?"
The pain I was in was no reason to forget good manners. Being gracious made the pain a little more bearable. There was nothing more
Haitian than offering strangers a little coffee, as if they were family,
as if there was no such thing as a stranger once they'd crossed the
jamb of your front door.

Her hair was cut short and straightened by a hot comb. I wondered if hot combs conflicted with her religion or if she made ex-
ceptions, prioritizing surviving in a white world over the state of
her soul. She would have looked beautiful with natural hair cropped
close to the scalp. I wondered what her religion had to say about

the plight of black people, outcasts, how it taught about Exodus. They took the coffee though they eyed it suspiciously once it was placed before them. They amused me. I started to forget about the incident with the car, being jumped, the pain radiating through me, the hospital, Guy picking me up and letting me know with grandiosity that he had taken care of the hospital bill. The truth was that I needed to talk to someone, anyone. They happened to be available. I thought that maybe they could make sense of why things were happening the way they were, if, like me, they thought the world was truly coming to an end.

I wondered how the woman coped with going door-to-door for her religion. I looked back and forth between them. The man was lighter-skinned, orange-toned like a peach, thin, but jovial. They made me think of Laurel and Hardy, except that they were black, of course. I assumed she needed him for protection. He was along for the ride, not so committed. It gave him something to do and a way to hold on to her. She was hiding who she truly was, hoping to find herself in one of the flats they visited, as she converted others to her way of thinking.

"You from Haiti?" she asked.

"Yes, yes I am." I smiled toothily. "*Ou pale Kreyòl?*"

She shook her head back and forth, vehemently, no. "We have nothing to do with that devil place."

I felt as if I'd been struck again, except by one of my own. It hurt more deeply than the blows I'd been dealt. The pain of the cracked ribs seemed comforting at that moment. I had the sudden urge to throw them out, but I couldn't move quickly enough. "What kind of God-fearing people are you? You don't even believe Jesus is Jesus, for Christ's sake!"

The man's face dropped. Things had soured. It was all I could think to say. They let themselves out.

That morning came and went: I couldn't get up off the couch. The bruises and cuts were healing but I felt desolate, bereft. I wanted them to return but didn't have the guts to call the number stamped on the back of one of the magazines they'd left. What would I say? Uh, spiritual intervention needed? Baptism by shower requested? A little exorcism to beat back the devil's work? I didn't know what to say or to whom to say it. After a few days laced with a codeine buzz, bemoaning my fate, I decided to start reading the King James Bible I had found in the back of the cab again. It was better than no company.

The King James Bible isn't the Bible I grew up with, but it suits me fine. I found it practically shoved into the fold of the back seat, as if someone—God? Jehovah?—had wanted me to find it. I asked the guy who had lent me the cab that night about it, about putting it in the lost and found, and he pushed the leather book back into my chest so that my hand held it there as if in prayer and said, "You look like you could use the good word." He was a religious type. I nodded, took the book with me, and started reading it that night. Then I started going to the kids' Bible study class on Sundays, when I was free.

I started with the Old Testament, struggling through the arcane names, trying to understand where the action was taking place, and when. I was surprised to realize that so much of it was taking place on the African continent. The flight from Egypt, all of that, on African soil. I was all the way into Exodus when I stopped reading. I had left the people in the desert as stuff they could eat started falling from the sky. I wondered what it was. The book said manna.

But it seemed like snow to me. They were eating snow in the desert. It made me laugh. First Moses parting the ocean, God engraving two slabs with thunderbolts, then the wanderers finding sustenance from snowflakes falling from the sky. I closed the book and put it away on a shelf bolted into the wall above the couch and left it there. I reached for it when Trebek wasn't doing it for me anymore. I didn't know any answers to the *Jeopardy!* questions, but I thought the Jehovahs might return. I could prepare for the next encounter. Have questions to ask and answers to give.

It was a quiet time, too quiet. My phone wasn't ringing off the hook like it used to. Guy must have told the other drivers I was laid up. I started to worry again about how I would pay the bills. I would have to venture out for groceries soon too. I took the Bible back down from its perch and started reading from Psalms. I had a dim recollection of my mother doing this when I was a child, me sitting in her lap, her Bible in front of us, reading slowly, painstakingly, each word underlined with a tracing finger. "You'll be a better reader," she'd told me then. "All my children will read, write, and do their numbers in their head." She had gone to school long enough to learn the basics, maybe two or three years, not much more. I remember looking down at the pages of print, wondering what it all could mean.

I still had the same feeling of swimming in type as I read the Bible, now in English instead of French. I paused at words as my mother had, my index finger tracing the path of my hesitation. Sometimes, being an immigrant is like being illiterate. Not only do you have to learn a new language, but you have to learn new codes, cultural ways, mind yourself, stay out of trouble. A paperless, immigrant alien has to be even more careful than one with papers, has to stay on the right side of the law, remain beyond reproach. I can be anything you want: your chauffeur, your errand boy, your "yes, sir, no, sir" boy. It's close to being a servant, a jump and a skip to having no name, nowhere to land. The lack of place to call one's own gives me vertigo. Or that could have been the codeine. I was on the last pill. The codeine gave me a weird feeling, like my brain was filled with dense cotton and my limbs could detach themselves and go off in their own directions without me, a satisfying feeling of floating in space, above and beyond pain, a good feeling.

I was in the middle of contemplating the ceiling when a knock came at the door. I imagined the Jehovah's Witnesses on the other side, having returned to forgive me my insolence. My mind was foggy and my steps unsure as I rose from the sofa and made my way to the door, but inside, I was ecstatically happy. The sensation of my chest rising with expectation felt strange. I held my ribs with my left hand. My side was still stiff and sore; it was taking time to heal. I opened the door with my free hand. My face fell when I saw it wasn't the Jehovahs. It was Guy.

"Fine way to greet a brother," Guy said. He was holding an animal, one of his hands covering the creature's face as it whimpered and pawed against Guy's thick body. I peered at it.

"What is that?"

"Apology gift, motherfucker, if you bother to let a brother in." He smiled that winning smile that he claimed got him all the girls in Cambridge he wanted, despite the fact that he was already married, for a second time. I always wondered if his boasting was for show or if he did step out on Julie, a fine-looking walnut-brown woman who had had difficulty recovering from the birth of their twin girls four years ago but still had a soft look in her light brown eyes that made one think of forest animals that preferred to keep in hiding rather than be seen in the light of day. When I looked at her, I always thought of how lucky Guy was, thought about how I would never walk out on that, and wondered how Guy did.

"You can come in," I muttered, opening the door more widely and moving aside. "But I didn't ask for a dog."

Guy stepped in, turned to look me square in the face, so close that I could feel the tobacco-laced odor of his warm breath hover beneath my nose. "Look, you can either take the dog or I can break its neck right here and put it in the trash."

I took a step back. There was a pause in which neither of us moved or said anything. Guy broke the tension with a coarse laugh, then slapped me, hard, on the shoulder. I winced in pain. He went into the kitchen. I heard the nails of the dog's paws as they hit the linoleum and it padded around. Guy rummaged in the fridge while I stood there, dumb, at the door. I stuck my head out the door and looked up and down the tree-lined street for the Jehovah's Witnesses, but the street was quiet. A cat in heat screeched. I wondered what it was doing out in the cold and closed the door, then turned back in to face Guy. The puppy came running up to me as I did so, then relieved itself at my feet.

Guy emerged from the kitchen with a soft drink can in his hand. "This all you got?" Then he took in the scene of the puppy flopping on the carpet, smelling its own pee, looking up at me with large, pensive eyes, and barking in a high pitch. "Can't get rid of him now," Guy said. "He thinks you're his dad."

I ignored Guy. The puppy was not so bad, I thought, except that he had peed on the carpet. I went to find some things in the bathroom to clean the mess, returned with a wet rag and some all-purpose cleaner the last occupant had left behind. I was living in

an apartment Guy had secured for the cab drivers. It was basically a
crash pad and those without papers could live there without being
disturbed. I had been alone there for a while and hadn't yet made it
home; I was still finding items previous occupants had left behind,
as others would one day find mine. The puppy ran around me as I
cleaned. I felt the dampness of his nose as he tried to sniff around
the spot. He nipped at my fingers.

"No," I said, putting an index finger down on his muzzle. The
dog stopped, looked at me, sat down, then ran off and peed elsewhere. I started the same procedure all over again until I found a
big empty box from when I'd moved in and put him in it, in the
kitchen. He was too small to climb out. He whimpered plaintively.

Guy had settled on the sofa while I did all this, talking and not
talking to me, maybe to himself, dialing through the TV channels with the remote control. "You don't have shit. Where's your
cable?"

When the puppy finally settled down, I went to sit in the chairs
where the Jehovahs had sat opposite the coffee table, their backs to
the television.

"What do you want?"

Guy put the can of pop down on the table between us. "I don't
want nothing. Just making things square."

"You think a dog makes us square?"

"Why not? I thought you liked dogs. I thought you were a bleeding
heart for dogs. I thought you'd like him. He'll keep you company so
you don't have to moon over Julie."

I bristled at the comment about Julie. "I've never . . ."

"Don't even try." He waved me off. "I know what I know." We
glared at each other across the table still littered with the *Watchtower*

magazines from my recent visitors and the orange pill container of prescription codeine tablets.

Guy picked up the bottle of pills, fingered it, peered at the label, and squinted to read it. He unscrewed it as he looked at me, then popped one in his mouth. "Potent stuff, but not as good as what I sell."

I stared at Guy. Where did he get off popping my pills? "I need those."

Guy waved me off again. "I can get you this and more anytime, just let me know."

I had a strange feeling of moving out of my body at that moment, and a rising anger filled the space in my chest. I wanted to smash Guy's smug face in. I wanted to do to him what he'd let happen to me.

"You think coming and handing me a dog is going to fix things," I managed to say through gritted teeth. "Get the fuck out of my house. *Deyo!*" I said other things too. I started cursing him in Kreyòl and that seemed to frighten him, so he took his can of pop, told the puppy to have a good life, and let himself out.

"You'll come back when you need me," he said over his shoulder. Then, quietly, he added, "They always do." Through the living room window, I watched him walk away in that tight, straight-legged way of his, like he was holding a cork between his thighs. My sudden aversion toward Guy erased everything I'd thought I knew about him until these last days: family man, company man, brother.

The puppy yelped. I guessed that he was hungry. I made a makeshift leash for him from some loose rope I'd used during my move into the apartment, when I'd secured the overfilled boot of a cab I'd borrowed for the move. I put on a coat and walked out into the cold of the day with the puppy strutting behind me as if he had always known me, to find us both some food. I called him Siwo, because his coat, which had some rich brown undertones when it was hit by light, reminded me of molasses. When he slumped from exhaustion, I would call his name and his little tail would thump back and forth but he wouldn't look up until he was good and ready. His behaviors also reminded me of my father, when we would need to fish him out of rum bars and he was not yet ready to go. It was time to return to reality, to take responsibility for myself, to stop waiting for saviors to come out of nowhere with their fishes and loaves and snow falling from the sky. Life was not a Bible story.

In the last days of my convalescence, I don't know if it was the codeine or an overactive imagination, but I began to feel a presence in the apartment beyond the dog. Even Siwo felt it. In the middle of the night, when I imagined there was a large man walking through the room, the dog would first bark, then whimper. The man was in my dreams. I felt him, hovering. He would stand there, in the middle of the room or the hallway, and look at us, but when I would open my eyes and try to confront his gaze, he was never there. When I thought about what he looked like, the only image that came to mind was a recollection of a photograph I had seen of my father when he was a young man.

In the picture, he had been wearing overalls, a light blue shirt, a straw hat like the peasants wore when working in the field. He was working construction then. He hadn't known my mother long but had built a house of bricks for them in Bel-Air, which was still the house they lived in today, but when he had built it, there were no neighbors all around. He built Tatie's house too, my mother's sister.

Since she lived alone after leaving her husband behind in Canada, where they had both worked (she hadn't bothered to divorce), the family and neighbors congregated at her place. Taffia, my little sister, had written me that Tatie had gotten a television; now people gathered in her living room once or twice a week to have a meal together and watch a soap, a game, or the news. In the photograph, the city was beginning to spill over its edges. My father looked strong in the picture, not yet the drunk he would become. He was the morose type. My father was my age in the picture. What would have happened had he stayed sober? Would he have moved us out into a better area; would we all have made it through high school; could Mama have quit her job cleaning and cooking in the houses of the rich? Where might we all be now? I wondered if I would be strumming my guitar on a back porch or in an open yard, with my own kids gathered around me, if I would never have left the way I did, never have wanted to see this mysterious place in the north where we thought lives were so much better. The reality is that it's cold here.

The figure that came at night wasn't well. I could feel that. He didn't look like my father. I could never see his face. But I knew it was him, or some part of him, paying me a visit. I didn't know what to say to it. I didn't know if it came from the future or from the past, or from somewhere that belonged outside of time. I let Siwo bark at it, protect me. I imagined bumping into it on the way to the bathroom. I was afraid of it and started talking to it to make myself feel better. "*Papa, sa wap fe la? Koman ou ye?*" Daddy, what are you doing? How are you? "*Ou gayen kek bagay pou di'm?*" You have something to tell me? "*Dimmwen sa ou vle di.*" Tell me what you have to tell me. Then I would strain to hear a message but heard nothing. The presence came and went and seemed pleased to have been acknowledged.

Once the codeine tablets came to an end, the presence left, taking with it the heavy feeling. That was ten months ago.

I got better, resumed my normal activities: scouring for gigs, filling in extra shifts for other cabbies (except for Guy, whom I shunned as much as I could), scoping out the girls in Cambridge who were looking for a quick and dirty lay. Siwo came out on the rides and sat quietly in the passenger seat next to me. He barked at clients he didn't like and I didn't let them in or told them to get out if they'd already sat down. I let them curse me but didn't give two shits. Siwo was looking out for me. He was the only thing for which I could thank Guy. I told him so the one time we crossed paths at a cab stand while I was dropping off a car and going on my way with Siwo on the leash. Guy looked surprised to hear me say it. He smiled, nodded, then walked away without saying as much as a word. I didn't miss him much, but I missed Julie and their girls, the sense of having a borrowed family when they invited me over to dinner. It hadn't been often, but I missed the visits.

I faded the isolation away with the sound of the guitar. At first, my fingers were stiff, the strings needed tuning, but muscle memory took over and I was off and away, forgetting and remembering all at once, replacing what I didn't want to face with what I wanted to feel—lightness, joy, the intense immensity of life. That's what music always did for me. The power music gives me, that I felt the day the first guitar I would buy turned up in a shop in one of the old buildings close to the port, and I turned over money I'd made on my own for it, greasy, grimy *goud* that I'd been able to save over several years. It hadn't been enough money, and I promised the shop owner that I'd come back, run errands, do whatever was needed until the cost was paid. It was how I learned to hustle, frequenting pimps and prostitutes, and realizing that they were artists in their own kind of way. Like trapeze artists in the art of life. That's how I knew what Sonia was up to before anyone else did, despite her quiet, despite the way in which her eyes always looked away when she talked, like a girl who could never lose her innocence. I'd noticed that the man she lived with, Dieudonné, was similar. He was all muscle, and at first, I thought he was her pimp. I almost tried to fight him to get her back, out of that life, but then, when I stood in front of him, toe to toe, man to man, looked into his eyes, all I saw there was bewilderment and innocence, as if I were looking into the eyes of an eight-year-old. I looked from him to Sonia, who was holding his hand, her eyes pleading with me to let them go, and stepped back. I did. I let them go. I would never understand what they were doing together or what they were doing, period, but I did understand how they were innocent of what life had led them to, pure.

I strummed the guitar in the kitchen while Siwo howled in the living room. Thinking of how I'd started on the guitar made me think of the prostitutes down by the harbor in Port-au-Prince, the way they closed their eyes when I played. They said it let them dream about where they'd rather be. I tried to imagine what other lives they might have had. There was always someone, some man, they'd tell me, who needed them, and the women always had to give themselves up to the fantasies the men carried with their pockets full of change. I had promised them to grow up to be a different kind of man but I wasn't sure if I had.

To console myself, sometimes, back then, I went down to play in the market below the cathedral. I played to the market women sitting on their low stools as I had to Ma Lou, to their errand boys, boys who reminded me of Paul when he was still young and innocent, holding my hand when it was I who ran the errands, not dreaming yet of aviator glasses to hide the sullenness in his eyes. I wondered about all we did not know about each other, even as we crossed paths in and out of the market, how little I knew about these women's lives.

Playing the guitar in my living room made me think of Sonia, which made me, in turn, think of Taffia, and how to preserve her, which made me think of Paul, who seemed no longer to have any innocence. All he had was pent-up, unexplained, unexpressed rage. He made it hard for anyone to get close to him. I could think only of saving Taffia, as if she were all that remained of us, or would remain. I started composing a song for her, remembering when we would write together in the house—me working on music, her on stories we would get her to read after dinner. The song wasn't coming together, then I remembered the blue iPod someone had left behind in one of the cabs. I called Julie and asked her if I could come over when Guy was out. She startled when I asked, getting the wrong idea. I quickly explained that I wanted to make a present for my younger sister, but I didn't have the equipment, that I'd bring over the CDs and be quick. She could leave the music on her computer if she wanted or erase it. "You owe me something after that stunt Guy pulled," I said.

She paused. "Okay."

For a week I went over to her house during Guy's shift and played with the girls while I downloaded music, made copies, played it back, until it was perfect, until it was me in a little blue box, letting Taffia know I was okay, or not so okay, but thinking about her, pleading through the songs to have her hold on to a better time, when we were all together, dancing in the living room, not worrying about all there was to worry about, happy to have each other. That was before we spent those nights looking for our father in the rum shops, before he abandoned us altogether.

Of course, once the music stops, the gnawing workings of the mind resume, sentinels keeping watch or rats feeding on gray matter. I wondered if this was happening to Taffia, to all of them. I sent the blue iPod as soon as I could, with some of the money I was making from the taxi drives, not telling them anything about where the money came from, letting them imagine what they wanted about my good life.

New Year's came and went. The year 2009 became 2010 and I expected nothing much to change.

.

Cambridge, January 12, 2010

And the seventh angel poured out his vial into the air; and there came a great voice out of the temple of heaven, from the throne, saying, It is done.

And there were voices, and thunders, and lightnings; and there was a great earthquake, such as was not since men were upon the earth, so mighty an earthquake, and so great.

And the great city was divided into three parts, and the cities of the nations fell: and great Babylon came in remembrance before God, to give unto her the cup of the wine of the fierceness of his wrath.

—*Revelation 16:17–19*

I heard about it over the radio while driving out of Cambridge one early evening in the new year, after ending my last shift for the day.

I'd stopped for coffee at my usual spot, where the college girls who liked to live dangerously knew to find their rides. I was waiting for one or the other to happen: a last hire or a hookup. It was late afternoon, not too cold but crisp. We'd had some snow since the New Year. A girl came first. We went to the taxi I was driving and I asked her where she wanted to go.

She said, "Your place."

I said, "No, yours."

Siwo whimpered in the back seat, then lay down.

"Okay," she said.

I knew better than to let the Cambridge girls see where I lived. We both knew what she wanted.

"Is that your dog?"

I looked at her. I'd seen her around, eyeing me. She wasn't like the usual college rides. I nodded. "He's my dog. He's good, doesn't bark unless he doesn't like you." Dark, short hair. Dark eyes. A small frame. She dressed like she was a punk or something like that, all in black, white T-shirt, ankle boots. I was getting too old to keep track of the trends. She had eyeliner on, no eye shadow, a touch of mascara that made her eyes pop. She didn't smile. She asked me if she could smoke. I told her she could if she opened the window and let the ash fall outside. She obliged. I drank my coffee with one hand and steered the car with the other. It was like any other end of day, driving home, except for the girl in the car.

She sat in the front seat so I would know she wasn't a customer, or a customer of a different kind. I didn't think much about it. It was not unusual. I also got books from these girls, and vocabulary for my ever-expanding English. I was working on losing my accent, fitting in; it was an exchange of sorts. She looked out the window, hummed. I couldn't tell if she was nervous or careless. She was starting to pique my interest. I put the radio on.

She laughed. "You listen to NPR?"

I shrugged. "Doesn't everybody?"

She smiled, then looked away again.

The news came on and the announcer said it: "There's been an earthquake in Haiti."

I thought I had misheard. I turned up the volume. My breath left or held me. My brain said, No, not possible. The man repeated the news. I drove on automatic pilot. She had told me the address already. Brighton Avenue, in Allston, over the bridge, where the rows of brick apartment buildings let out mostly to students gave way to turn-of-the century triple-deckers painted in a variety of lively colors. Lively in contrast to the somber brick buildings in the neighborhoods preceding it. Muted in comparison to Caribbean colors, drab. A few pale yellows and greens breaking through the monotony of grays and browns, the usual colors Americans use to paint their houses. I drove there in a daze, head spinning.

"I'm not sure I can do this," I said, when we got there.

"Why?" She pulled a drag from her cigarette.

I looked at her, puzzled, pointed at myself. "I'm from Haiti."

She shrugged.

"Didn't you hear the announcer?" I pointed to the radio. "Earthquake in Haiti?"

"I heard," she said, looking at me with wide eyes. "I'm from Bangladesh. Floods, quakes." She shrugged. "Shit happens."

She turned away from me, opened the door to the cab, and put out her cigarette on the ground, let the door swing back shut when she was done. "Are you going to call home?"

Home, she'd said, as if we knew each other or were from the same place. As if my home was her home. Haiti. Bangladesh. Same difference, she seemed to think.

"Yes," I said, "yes."

She stepped out of the cab to give me some privacy as I tried to call. The signal wouldn't go through. I called a Haitian buddy of mine who drove with the cab company. "Nothing doing," he said, "nothing's getting through. All systems are down. We just have to wait." I opened the door to the cab and looked at the girl.

"Are we doing this?" she asked.

"Do you have cable?" I replied.

"Yeah," she said.

"Okay, then," I said. I thought I could keep watching the unfolding news.

"Come on up." She led the way into a narrow, tall building, after opening the gate to the backyard so I could leave Siwo there. It was one of the triple-deckers, one of those houses they made into multiple flats after the Second World War when soldiers came back and needed places that weren't too expensive to start their families. Then waves of immigrants took them over, one by one, while those who had become true Americans after successive generations drifted into the suburbs. A triple-decker has narrow stairwells and flats with tiny kitchens and claw-foot bathtubs and a bedroom or two and a living space. She unlocked the door, peered in, smiled.

"Roommate's out," she said. "Come on in."

It was the typical student apartment with mix-and-match furniture, a sofa with the depressed cavities where too many bodies had lain, the floor worn down in places to unvarnished, flinty wood, the kitchen sink filled with unwashed dishes, a smell of damp and mold in the air.

"This is my room," she said, leading me forward.

I was in some kind of a trance, worrying what a quake could mean, watching the girl's narrow hips advance, wondering what was going to transpire between us, what I was still doing there, how I might get away, get back home.

I was surprised to find her room tidy and orderly with furnishings that matched and curtains on the windows.

"I can only sleep in total darkness," she said, by way of explanation.

I nodded. "Me, too," I said, although I didn't know if that was true.

"You can leave your shit there," she said, waving to a chair by the bed. She dropped her leather jacket on the chair and kept moving. "Do you want something to eat? I'm starving." Without waiting for my answer, she moved back out into the common room and into the kitchen, where she proceeded to clean dirty dishes left in the sink.

This wasn't going to be the usual assignation, I realized. "The TV?" I asked.

She waved at a corner of the living room. "Under the blanket."

Tucked between the end of the sofa and a window, there was a box covered over with a throw. The TV was under it. It looked old. I grew worried.

"It works," she said, over the clanking of dishes and water, reading my thoughts. "We have CNN," she offered.

I found the remote control and sat in one of the depressions on the sofa, turned the TV on, and searched for the news. On CNN, there was a guy I'd never seen before explaining the science of tectonic plates. He wore a bow tie and had a grin on his face that seemed maniacal. He strained to make it seem possible that a quake could be a fun opportunity for a little science learning. My phone vibrated in my pants pocket. It was one of the guys from Guy's taxi company.

"Are you watching the news?"

"Yes," I said.

"What the hell is happening?"

"I don't know. We have to keep watching." There were several other calls like that one in the first half hour, then the phone went dead. No more calls. The girl was still in the kitchen. I heard the refrigerator door open and close.

"Do you like rice?"

"Yes," I said.

"Do you like stewed vegetables, chicken?"

"Yes," I said.

"Okay, then, I've got you," she said.

I heard the microwave go on and dishes being put out. I smelled the curried chicken and vegetables before she put them out on the plates and brought them to the living room, where she sat on the floor and put a plate in front of me and ate hers in silence, watching the television coverage with me. It was like we were old friends, though we'd never met before. It was like something in me felt I could trust her because she was from a place like mine. She was quiet, not asking me for anything. I ate like I hadn't eaten in two days. It's possible I hadn't. Sometimes, I lose track of time, especially when the nights are long and the rides scarce. You have to stay awake, somehow, wait and wait and wait. It's easy to lose track of things like food. I drink a lot of coffee when I take breaks and wait for the Cambridge girls. Not exactly nutrition. Empty calories. Sport. Diversion. She gave me seconds without asking. I turned the sound down on the TV. They weren't showing us anything important.

"Why aren't they showing us anything important?" I asked no one in particular, gesticulating at the television with one hand, holding the second serving of food in the other. "With all the technology they have, can't they show us anything more than these graphs and things? What the—" I felt like throwing the plate across the room, smashing it to pieces, but I knew I wasn't in my own place, and my mother had taught me better than that. But I did feel like breaking something.

The girl studied me. "Maybe we should get online," she offered. "Sometimes the news online is better, more up-to-date."

I nodded. "Yes," I said. "That would be good."

She smiled for the third time that night. She moved some hair out of her eyes. "Just let me put these in the sink."

But she did more than that. She rinsed everything we had used and put the dishes in the dishwasher, then put away the tubs of leftovers back into the fridge.

"Come on," she said, finally, not unkindly, as if she'd realized that I was like a wounded animal that could be provoked to unpredictable behavior. "Come on," she said again, and led me back into her room. "Bring a chair with you," she added.

I grabbed a chair from the living room.

"No," she said, without even looking at me, "get one of those in the kitchen. They're smaller. The other one won't fit in my room."

I found a chair in the kitchen, one of those cheap plywood things that's made to look chic but is simply a copy of something more expensive, and then I followed her into her room with it. She'd already put on her computer and found a livestream of the earthquake. The livestream was Canadian.

"You understand French?" she asked.

"Yes," I said, putting down the chair next to her.

"Thought so," she said, turning up the volume, and got up to close the bedroom door. "My roommate will be getting back anytime. No point in alarming him."

I moved over so that I was in front of the screen. They were about to show images directly from the capital. All they had were still shots taken in the dark from satellite feeds: the National Palace, the Palais National fallen, broken in two.

"That can't be real," I said.

The girl peered over my shoulder. I smelled spice and lilac, not an entirely unpleasant scent.

"I don't know," she said. I felt her hot breath on my neck. "Looks real."

"Photoshop," I said. "They can make anything seem real. That can't be real."

The announcer's voice was shrill. "We are trying to get as much information as we can," he said, in French. "Built by the United States in 1920, the National Palace of Haiti has fallen like a deck of cards."

"*Kou manman*," I said. In my mind, I was thinking, Armageddon, the end of the world, apocalypse. I wished that the Jehovah's Witnesses were there to talk to.

"Reports are that hundreds of buildings have fallen," the announcer said. "The capital is in disarray."

"The capital is in disarray," I repeated, slowly. I flipped open my phone. The battery was dead. "Do you have a charger?"

"Yes," the girl said. She took the phone from me and plugged it into a charger by the bed. "It won't take long," she said.

I nodded and turned back to the computer screen. They had posted a photo of the cathedral. It was in ruins. In pitch darkness. The cathedral perched only streets above the neighborhood where my family lived.

"*Non*," I said. "This is not possible."

"Everything is possible," the girl said.

"No," I said, too loudly. "*Non*."

The girl became quiet, still, as if she was waiting for me to explode. I wondered, in a vague way, if that was what she expected from me. I wondered how many men she'd gone home with who might have done just that.

Then she asked, "Mind if I light up? I'll open a window if it bothers you."

"Do whatever you want," I said. "It's your place." The world had already come to an end. A little smoke wouldn't kill me.

"Just trying to be considerate." She shrugged.

I nodded but I wasn't paying attention to her anymore. I was thinking of my parents, my brother, Paul, my sisters, of Taffia and the blue iPod of music I had sent her. I wondered where Sonia was and if she was helping them all or if she and her *tèt kale* boyfriend, Dieudonné, had finally lost their heads, left the capital, and disappeared into the countryside. I had a gnawing feeling in the pit of my stomach. My mind raced. I wondered if Paul was keeping it together, if my father was in a rum shop, oblivious, or if the ground had opened up beneath him and swallowed him. I thought of our mother. Of the girls, Sonia would have the best chance of getting out of this unscathed, I thought. She was probably somewhere safe with someone rich, keeping her out of harm's way, but could money save you from the effects of an earthquake? It couldn't hurt, I thought. I went to check the charge on my phone. The battery light was blinking off and on.

"It's going to take the time it takes," the girl said.

I looked at her blankly. She was sitting up against the wall, on the bed, thick pillows behind her. The bed was next to a window. She had an ashtray on the ledge in which she flicked ash. The window was barely open. I wrinkled my nose.

"Smoke bothering you? I can stop." Not waiting for my answer, she put out the cigarette carefully in the ashtray so that she could light it up again later. "We have a porch out back," she said. "You know, there's nothing you can do," she added, nonchalantly.

I went toward her. I was moving as if through a vat of jelly, as if every movement was costing me something. I wanted to leave the apartment, get back in my cab, drive home with Siwo, whom I had left running in the backyard of her house, but I was afraid I would drive too fast, kill someone. I was afraid that someone was already dying, over there, crushed by the earth. I didn't know what to think. An earthquake hadn't happened in Haiti for more than a hundred years. It was the stuff of legend and dreams. We weren't Montserrat or Saint Lucia or Guadeloupe. We weren't anything like those places in any way. The eyes of the world were on us and there was nothing to be seen. All lines of communication were down, lights out.

"Come here," she said.

Couldn't she see me moving toward her?

"Come here," she said again, moving the covers aside, getting into the bed.

She was still fully clothed, but she started undoing things under the covers while she looked at me, not smiling this time, her dark eyes fixing me, sizing me up, surgical. I took my cue from her and started undressing next to the bed. I stood there, naked, for a minute, not thinking, feeling shattered. I felt her hand take mine and pull me into the bed. "*Edike eso*," she said, in her own language. "There's nothing you can do. We're alive," she said. "We can do this. It will make you feel better."

She started to kiss me. I kissed her back. She stroked me. I stroked her back. She was smooth like a seal.

"You feel good," she said. She emptied words into my ear that I had heard before and others that were alien, translating them as she went. When I did things she liked, she said, "*Bhalo*." When she became excited, she said, "*Kub bhalo*." When I became too eager, she said, "*Ashte*," and I knew from her movements that she wanted me to slow down. But after a few minutes of this dance between strangers, with pleasure mixed with guilt assailing my every cell, after she guided me into her small frame and I grasped her torso, I forgot everything but what I had seen on the computer screen and emptied myself into her in desperation. My eyes closed tight, I saw a white fluorescence, felt ecstatic release, a serpentine uncoiling. When I was spent, I remembered where I was. I asked her if she was all right. "*Ami bhalo acchi*," she said. Just fine. She pushed me away and leaped out of the bed. I heard the shower running. I had started falling asleep when a thought jolted me awake. I hadn't used a condom. I didn't know the girl. She could have anything, be anyone. I could have made a child with her. I didn't know.

We could have made life while others were dying, I thought suddenly, thinking again about the images of the fallen National Palace, the broken cathedral. Guilt washed over me, the possibility of life in the face of death. I thought of the unremitting human drive for survival, the best and worst of it. I saw the faces of my sisters, and Paul's face. I thought of my mother, of my father. I wondered who would make it through this night alive, if the only person left to tell the tale could be the embryo I might have implanted in this girl with jet-black hair, who spoke to me in tongues.

I fell into a deep sleep, so deep that I did not feel the distant giving of the mattress as she came back into the bed. The scent of lilacs was stronger than it had been before. I didn't even hear Siwo as the girl let him into the house for the night. I felt only the sheets being tucked around my body. I dreamed that I was in a sarcophagus being led into a tomb.

·

The next morning, alone in the shower—the girl had left, saying, "Let yourself out," no sweet goodbyes, she had stuff to do, study hall or some such—reality rushed back in.

I thought about the chaos unleashed below ground back home, not knowing who, or what, was still standing. Beneath the spray of the water, I let out long gasps. I could hardly breathe. I felt like I was going to drown in the stream of water. I wanted to drown. I was splintering from the inside. I suppressed a scream by clasping both hands onto my mouth and turned my back flat against the cold tile that hadn't yet been pelted by the hot, streaming water. But then I needed the water as I felt the tears come.

I wanted to hide my tears from myself. I felt the heat coursing down my face; it soothed me and I stopped trying to hold back the pain, and the shame. The pain of not knowing what was happening to the family I had left behind to come to a world I knew nothing about, and could scarcely survive in, but pretended was better than what I'd fled. For once, I wasn't thinking of the grinding poverty, of all the work people did to keep their kids off the street, to escort the old women home before hoodlums roamed the streets at night, to get the old men out of the rum shops and playing dominos on their own porches, if they had any, to keep the bellies full and rage at bay. It had all been too much for me, the weight of it. The weight of them. The weight of not being able to do enough. If I was honest with myself, that was why I'd left. But now, all I could think of was anticipating their voices on the phone, the disappointed tones when I would say that I wasn't coming home, yet. The shame: while people were dying, I had been making love to a stranger, a girl who had picked me up the way men picked up Sonia in swanky hotels.

I had always judged Sonia harshly for what she chose to do, flanked by her faithful Dieudonné. The truth was always that I resented what she did, not because I thought it was immoral but because I knew that if Sonia had been born into a different family, she could have become anything. Worse even was the fact that Sonia was not only beautiful on the outside, she was beautiful on the inside, but no one would ever truly know how beautiful because of her occupation, like me with the jitney cab, the kind of work that made one disposable, invisible. The tears came like a torrent. I found myself crouching down into the bottom of the tub, the shower drops pelting against my back like small, explosive bullets.

I wanted to feel something like pain outside of myself. The water became so hot it scalded.

After the shower, I heard the roommate coming into the house but left the door closed. The roommate didn't come to check on who was there. Probably the girl and he were used to sharing the space with each other and other strangers. Siwo sat at the foot of the bed while I sat on its edge and placed the phone to my ear to listen to voicemail. No one from my family had called. One cabbie after another, all of Haitian descent, had called to find out if I knew anything more than they did and asked me to call them back. Some cousins in New York and Montreal left messages to say that they hadn't heard from the family. They also asked me to call them back if I heard anything. There was a girl, crying, who didn't leave a name. I didn't recognize the voice beneath the tears. I looked at the log of phone numbers and erased them one by one. I wanted to leave room on the recorder for important messages, some real news.

Dressed, I sat looking out the window, wondering what would come next. The streets were blanketed with snow and made ashen by the cold. Everything was gray and drab. I wondered how many bodies were trapped beneath gray concrete back home, suffocating, taking in their last breaths, or gone already. Within myself, I felt the way the world looked outside, gray and cold. Which was worse: to die pinned under a massive weight, or in a pocket of hot, humid air without being able to see light, or in the blue cold of a snowdrift like those at the side of the road below? To freeze to death or to suffocate, crushed? In the end, pain is pain, I resolved, in the terror of the last moments. My brain flashed on the faces of my father, mother, siblings, each face made more gruesome than the next in my imagination. I started to sweat profusely, to shake. I wiped away the beads of perspiration, tried to slow the fast beating of my heart. I put a hand on it, trying to calm the pulsing. I had become an animal reduced to instinct, a fight-or-flight response to extreme fear, even if the danger was not immediate.

I stood up, shook off the images of blood and gore traversing my mind, put the phone on vibrate, shoved it into the front pocket of my jeans, and went to the kitchen in search of some breakfast. As I did so, my mind returned to the computer in her room. I found a muffin to eat and returned with it in hand back to the computer in the room in order to pull up the websites I'd gotten news from late into the night. I started making calls. Talked to the cousins in Montreal, talked to the other Haitian cabbies. Some were crying, grown men broken. I fielded calls, swapped information. The lines were down but the satellite feeds were working. I asked someone to post a word about my family on social media, sent a photo. I relayed messages, but there wasn't much information coming back.

I grew frustrated. I took Siwo for a walk before heading back into the heart of the city. He seemed to sense that something was wrong, staying close to my side. We walked a long time. When we got back to the car, my fingers were blue with cold. I had forgotten to wear gloves. The numbness made me feel more alive. Death had slipped through the door of worry and I wondered who would be left, when the news came. I thought about the fact that whatever the news would be, what had happened had already happened. The girl was right. There was nothing that I could do now. I went back to my apartment.

After that night, the girl called me a few times when she wanted a free ride, and I went along with things because, well,

because it was the only thing keeping me tied to a sense of reality. This went on for a couple of weeks in which there was next
to no news. She told me about Bangladesh, of floods, the waters
swirling into houses, the loss of everything, having to start over
and over again. She said it with a quixotic smile I incorrectly
interpreted as pain. I remembered the soldiers sent to Port-au-
Prince from Bangladesh by the UN in 1994, to keep the peace,
they'd said. I told her about how they lined the docks on the
port, their rifles slung over their shoulders, pointing down at
tiny children clasping their mothers' hands, escorted back onto
land after their boats had been diverted at sea, attempting to
flee. I went over to the girl's place with Siwo, though she always wanted him kept outdoors; sometimes I left him in the
car, which stayed relatively warm. I never stayed the night again,
always going back to my apartment immediately afterward. I
thought we had some things in common. But I couldn't feel
anything. I was numb. I was wrong. The fourth or fifth time I
went over, we started to fight after I talked about my despair at
the lack of news, not knowing who was dead or alive, what was
going on with my family.

"That's life," she said to me, pulling a drag from her cigarette. "You
lose some and you win some." She was practical and full of clichés.

"How can you take things so lightly?"

"How can I not?"

"I don't know if my family is dead or alive."

"Some will be dead and some will be alive," she said. "Those are
the facts."

We traded barbs. I still hadn't received a call from someone in
my family. "How can you be so cold?"

She looked at me and I finally saw that the brown of her eyes was lifeless. Had her eyes always been this way? I hadn't noticed, these weeks that we had been together, rocking together, eyes always closed, not looking, feeling next to nothing.

"Sometimes," she said, very slowly, very quietly, very deliberately, as if she didn't want me to miss a word she was about to say, "sometimes, I do think that the dead are luckier than we are."

I jolted up from my seat and went for a walk with Siwo. We walked far and when I came back, I gathered all the things I had lying about in the girl's apartment. I had resolved not to return.

"Where are you going?" she asked.

"Back to Mattapan," I said, "to what I have left."

"There's always more and less wherever you go," she said. She couldn't help herself. "That's a fact," she said to my back, as if she held some secret keys to the universe. I took my stuff and Siwo and drove home to my apartment.

There were notes on the door when I got there. One was from the Haitian cabbie whose car I had, asking when I was getting it back to him, and adding that he hadn't been able to track down his family yet. Another one was from Guy and Julie, in Julie's handwriting, wondering where I was, and could they help. I imagined the Jehovah's Witnesses dropping by: "Have you found your people?" Then, talking to me about the devil. I had a vague recollection from their literature of the angels being cast out of the heavenly spheres into a lake of fire. The Caribbean Sea? The Atlantic? Lucifer, Beelzebub, Mastema. But if they had been angels, God had done this, not the devil. Siwo came up to me and put his head on my knee, whimpered. I stroked his head, looked into his wet eyes. If God were a dog, I thought, we wouldn't be in this mess.

The girl called a few times more after that but there was nothing left.

"There are reports of rapes and violence," she said one of those times. "Bangladesh is sending in women soldiers to help in the IDP camps."

I shrugged into the phone. What did it matter? A handful of brown women in a foreign country when the worst had already happened. Being brown and female might not mean anything under these circumstances.

"You win some, you lose some," I parroted back to her.

The earthquake changed everything.

Those first weeks and months, all any of us Haitians talked about was where we were, where we stood, when it happened or when we heard. Nothing else we might have had in common or not in common seemed to matter any longer. Just where we were when we heard the news, there or elsewhere, if we'd lost anyone, or didn't.

I always omitted where I'd spent that night though I came to realize so many people had been doing the same thing, trying to fend off death, or the fear of it, in someone else's arms.

So many post-earthquake babies would be born some nine months later, and then, after that, each month, for months to come, many conceived not in love, or even from despair, but from wanton violence, anger, revenge.

.

And every island fled away, and the mountains were not found.

> And there fell upon men a great hail out of heaven, every stone
> about the weight of a talent: and men blasphemed God because of
> the plague of the hail; for the plague thereof was exceeding great.

—Revelation 16:20–21

One of the things I've learned from driving the cab is that there is no such thing as community. Collectives are fabrications. Collective memory can also depend on which side you find yourself on. I'm sure we can't find a place on earth without its battle scars, its trace of human blood. Grenadians remember the execution of Maurice Bishop, followed by the day the Americans landed on their beaches. Imagine if you were one of the black soldiers descending on the beach to occupy; then imagine being the black person staring incredulously back at them: the point of view is just not the same. Jamaicans still mourn Marley though he was in a battle with himself far away from any holy land when he died. In Boston, they like to talk about the time the colonists poured the tea into the bay to protest a tax or something. They were letting Britain know that they were a free people. I'm sure some heads got broken over that. Today, the pole in Antarctica has become a lake thawing from global warming. In Tibet, monks and nuns are setting themselves on fire to send smoke signals, trying to get us to look at what China is doing to their people. But we all look away unless it's us, or someone we love, going up in flames. You don't know what collective you belong to until your own house is on fire.

Burials without ceremony, bodies dumped in mass graves to protect the living. I watch it unfolding on my TV screen. It had to be done. *Malpropre.* Untidy. The dead are so many they cannot be counted. There is no before, no way to think before. There is only the not knowing of how to put the before together with the now. Before is a distant memory. I am still waiting to hear from those I loved, before. Waiting to hear if I can say I love, still, or if everything will remain past tense, what it was: no beyond, no good-byes: simply after.

I sit on the couch and listen to the Jehovah's Witnesses, whom I let in when they come and knock at the door, ready to talk about their Second Coming. I nod and listen politely because I know already that after the nightmare, there is something neither dreadful nor beautiful: no spectacle, no reward, only suspension. They might need my help, these people, when their Armageddon comes.

OLIVIER

Camp Cocasse, Haiti, March 2010

In the span of forty-five seconds, one in every fifty good Haitians in Port-au-Prince died. Who knows about the bad ones. One assumes that they, too, perished, as shockingly and abruptly. What happened to all the fixers, the drug dealers, the prostitutes, the ones I saw all the children in the neighborhood looking to in awe, envious of what seemed their easy life, fine watches and gold bracelets dangling from their wrists, then turning to look at those, like me, who tried to stay straight, with almost nothing to our names? My firstborn, Jonas, hadn't started looking at us like this yet, wouldn't ever, though we let him run for Sonia, a neighbor's daughter for whom I kept accounting ledgers, who worked in the big hotel perched over Port-au-Prince that I heard fell like a deck of cards, and for Ma Lou, in the market. I had been afraid that he might be next to lose to the streets, or some other shady business, that he, too, would start looking at everyone with the eyes of a bird of prey, like Sonia's younger brother Paul, who paraded through the dirt roads wearing broken smoked glasses, as if he wanted to lord over us like it was 1977. All Paul was missing was a revolver and you could bet he would use some of us for target practice. Our Jonas won't grow up to be one of these men.

I wondered when I saw Jonas leave early that fateful morning to take a basket of fruits from Ma Lou up the mountain to the hotel for Sonia and her partner, Dieudonné, what might happen, especially if Leopold was up there. Jonas had turned eleven in the new year. We thought he was old enough to go straight there and come right back, but I worried because I knew that Leopold was in town, and when Leopold was in town, nothing good could come of his passage. But the heaving ground did not discriminate. Most of the dead, good or bad, will get covered up, covered over, become part of the pitch when the roads are fixed. I don't know if Leopold was one. No one will know the difference between the good and the bad. The bones won't give up the secrets of who they once were. And as fast as the dead are counted and buried, the money pours in.

It's been less than three months and there's been a mad dash for pledges from what they call the "international community" (what community there is, I don't know): millions from Cuba, Venezuela . . . Brazil? God knows from where. Hundreds of millions. Thousands of millions. Maybe trillions. Unbelievable that it took this— an earthquake!—to open the coffers, abracadabra!

Imagine if every single Haitian who lost someone could get their hands on some of that money, decide what they needed for themselves, their family? You could create a healthy working middle-class and, still, there would be millions amassing in a treasure trove behind them. But, of course, they won't allow that to happen.

They tell us, first, that we need to learn our lesson (death by hunger isn't enough), *then* that we need to build better infrastructure, *then* that we need to unlearn our corrupt ways, stop killing each other, have fewer dreams for our children (because everyone knows that we are a dreamless people), be good factory workers so that those who are already millionaires can become billionaires and billionaires can become zillionaires. In short, aspire down, not up.

A people who know what to do with nothing will know what do to with plenty, is my thinking. You can be sure of that. I only have to look at all the *madansara* at the sides of the roads and in the markets. I know they have a stash somewhere. After they pack up at the end of the day, the vast majority of them have a little *kabann* to go home to. They lay their heads down; they might even make enough to pay another woman a little something to clean while they're away, send the children to school and greet the children when they return, have a pot of bone soup waiting on the stove.

Ah, women like Ma Lou, they know how to pinch pennies, spread the wealth! You raised us, paid for our uniforms and schoolbooks, dusted us off when we fell, taught us our prayers, taught us how to tell the devil to fuck the hell off when we needed to (because the devil isn't always an enemy), showed us how to turn pennies into *goud* and *goud* into *dola*! Ah, the almighty American dollar. You women know. You taught us. You could turn this whole goddamn place around, bring us into the black, *literally*, and take no shit while turning the evildoers out of the market.

It's simple math: 2.5 million of us crawling around a maze of streets in a capital made for 250,000. Not enough pipeline to carry away all the shit that 2.5 million people can produce on a daily basis. Not enough potable water to service that 2.5 million. Not enough garbage trucks to haul off the refuse that 2.5 million can produce on any given day, piles and piles accumulating next to the produce being sold at market while everyone is running around doing something, but at least 70 percent are officially unemployed, the majority of the population under twenty-four years of age, and at least 50 percent children or people over seventy. An earthquake happens after decades of people wishing that they could "blow the whole place up" and—don't you know—the whole thing does blow up and we *can* start again, we *will* start again. How convenient! There is no other choice. We have to "build back better!"—as the *gouverneur*, our American benefactor, says.

Of course, no one knows for sure who this "we" might be. It doesn't include any of us boiling like groundnuts under corrugated roofs. The rich have sequestered themselves in the coolness of the hills ringing the valley in which Port-au-Prince sits, calculating how they might benefit from this unforeseen opportunity. Three hundred thousand gone is a *mercy*—so many fewer people to worry over, so many fewer miscreants to feed, to watch out of the corner of one's eye as they wash their progeny in water where pigs rut about, defecate, sex, and eat the shit of the 2.5 million who have come to call the city built for 250,000 their *home*. Imagine that.

By March 2010, the American government could give a fuck about butthole Haiti and its abject masses as long as they provide their "comparative advantage" to the world economy: pittance labor. Want to work for castoffs, no bathroom breaks, unsanitary conditions, with blowing the manager your only means of job security? Well, then, welcome to an American clothing factory in Port-au-Prince, with satellite campuses soon to open in Caracol in the north, and right here, right here, north of the capital, in this dirt camp, named Cocasse. They should have called it Canaille for the imbecile who thought up the name! They say thousands of jobs will open up—thousands! They say we'll be rich!

We might become the Bahamas, or Jamaica, even Ber-*mu*-da. We could tell people to fuck the hell off, get lost in the triangle. We might even forget about the Revolution and Dessalines. Toussaint L'Ouverture's name could die on the lips of French-speaking children in the Jura region of France, beneath the Swiss Alps. We'd all disappear, then, every last Haitian, never to be heard from again.

So, no, no millions for us. No, instead, the white saviors promise: fifty dollars to each displaced household, a hygiene kit, free medical care, a school for the children, food rations, potable water, which doesn't necessarily mean clean, first dibs on factory jobs with a Korean garment factory block that isn't even built yet, and last, some kind of shelter. The catch is that to get all that, you have to leave the capital, take transport to the desert, and wait there. They call this "decentralizing."

The problem with promises is that they don't come with guarantees; they can be forgotten or broken. They aren't worth the paper they're written on. In the desert, there is no paper. You go out there on a prayer and wait. I took them up on their offer for what was left of our family: myself, Sara, and Jonas. We had seconds to react, then minutes, hours that lasted like years, to think of our own survival, of Jonas. The girls were gone in a blink. No time to mourn.

·

Paper. The only thing I left behind. A little piece torn from an old envelope on which I had written a word of goodbye—*wozo*—reed, my nickname for Sara. I left the piece of paper, folded, in a bowl in the tent, so that she would find it after I left. Remember me, us.

·

As soon as I arrive in the rocky field of Camp Cocasse, I find that "shelter" turns out to mean a doghouse smaller than the shithole tent I had to leave my wife and son in, in Port-au-Prince, in the market turned into a displaced persons camp below the cathedral. The shack has got a metal corrugated roof that's hot as hell and no running water. There's a water truck that comes through once a week, but that's about it. The truck rumbles through at high speed, so fast that children and goats have to be snatched, quickly, out of the way, to keep them from being run over. A donkey was killed that way, fast, the first day: the driver snapped its neck and the camp dwellers roasted the carcass over an improvised pit. There was fresh food for several days, that time, but no one wants to end up a dead donkey.

We still have to make a run for it to piss or crap in holes after the porta-potties fill up and no one has the stomach to empty them, not even the *bayakou* (we have to both save ourselves and clean up our own shit, can't pass that on like we might have, before). There's no school (the camp dwellers will have to organize that for ourselves, too). Food rations are the usual blanched Arkansas rice we've been eating for years, and freeze-dried packets of gritty material reconstituted with boiling water that we pretend is edible. The hygiene kit is made for people who have nothing more to treat than paper cuts: some squares of cleansers, a glycerin to help with healing, some small bandages of different sizes, all in a waterproof box in case we get rained on (and we will). Nothing for people with cigar-cut amputations, or crushed extremities, or who had their heads bashed in from bricks falling on them. Nothing for someone in the state that my son is in. He would have to be nearly healed to come out this way, and when I left, it didn't look like he was going to make it. From the camp, the hospital is as far as the capital;

there's no way he would survive the trip. All that can be done is to fight off infection, hope he survives. In the meantime, I'm here for the work, to make money, or this is what I tell myself.

In Camp Cocasse we're five thousand souls in the arid desert. Soon, when word gets out about the factory that's being planned out this way, there will be thousands upon thousands more, but now, it's just us, out in the middle of nowhere, with no running water, no electricity.

It's dark at night, much darker than in the city. I can see the stars up above clearly. Fat lot of good that does me. *Fuck* the stars and *fuck* the US of A relief services.

I never even got my fifty dollars after I was shown to the door of my new lodgings, a shithouse in a long row of doghouses. They smiled when they dumped me in the camp, as if I should be *grateful*. The only cheerful aspect of the dwellings is that they're bright white instead of the drab, institutional gray of the tarps being handed out in the capital, tarps stamped: "A gift from the American people" or, alternatively, "in association with the Republic of Ireland." The Irish own the telecommunications in Haiti; they don't have to pick potatoes, or anything else, anymore. I wanted to buy a franchise a few years ago. We never did it. Would we be elsewhere had we done that? Would we be on a plane heading out to Ireland now? The dwellings are so white that it seems that perhaps the people who had them built had imagined that they were creating a colony on the moon, or on Mars. We are a colony, that's for sure, a petri dish. Welcome to Camp Cocasse: gateway to the intergalactic, medieval future.

After I settle in, the neighbor to my left gestures hello to me, a thick-bodied man who looks about ten years my elder. If I extend my left arm right out, I can practically touch him: that's how much space they give us, here, to "start over."

He smiles toothily. "*Pa mal*," he says, "*non*? I'll be able to plant a garden." I don't respond. Look at him blankly. I mean, what is his story? How is he going to create a garden without any water, out in the desert? I look at him as one looks upon a crazy man and resign myself to the fact that this is how people will function from now on, as if a boatload of crazy is preferable to contemplating suicide. Haitians don't kill themselves: we have too much to strive for, so much resilience.

How would you even kill yourself? Death by drowning is out of the question. Death by hanging, impossible. Razor blades, maybe, if you have any, but they're most likely dull, not even good enough for a close shave, too dull to cut clean through tendon and sinew. Pharmaceuticals also out—soft drugs maybe, the kind you smoke or imbibe slowly, weed, grain alcohol. You're more likely to die of heat exhaustion first.

If it wasn't for Sara, and for the *clairin*, moonshine, I'm sure that I would have found a way to do myself in by now. Thinking about the various possible and impossible means by which I could do it passes the time, keeps my mind nimble, preoccupied. My own form of crazy. I'm thirty-two. The same as the number of coups that Haiti has suffered in its two-hundred-year history. I don't know how many more strokes of the lash we can bear.

.

When I met Sara, I thought I'd be teaching her everything. I'd been *lòt bò*. I spoke English practically like a native. She was a country mouse, looked it, acted it. I thought I was grown when I met her, full of myself. I was a boy, damaging to women, everyone, everything. Violent with my disregard. Sara quieted me down, made a man of me. She taught me to stop dicking around. To get serious, not mess things up by not talking to her, plotting in private about things that would change her life, our life, to figure out how a woman's body worked, to love every inch of her, not just dig for my own pleasure. She taught me to think of her sex enfolding mine as a flowering. Me, the fleshy part of a mussel encased in a shell that opened and closed only when water moved through and over it: oceanic.

She taught me how to caress her before slipping in toward the light. How to love that as much, more even, than rocking together. It got so that holding her could give me a hard on. Like a teenager. Fuck! She'd laugh. Your friend is here. She wondered aloud what it was like to have a part of your body flagging desire. Men are vulnerable that way. I'd never seen my body through a woman's eyes, a curiosity. Boys are taught to think of their dicks as swords, sticks, tools of conquest, I said to her. She paused, her hand on it, gentle. This is not a testament to love? Nothing more than that, and I'd be gone.

My arms around her shoulders. Eyes closed. Bliss. My mind blown away by the simplicity of our communion. Yes, goddamn it, yes, I wanted to scream (like a woman, I'd thought then): I'm yours forever. I'll never put this stick of mine in anyone but you. I swallowed, hard. The wind gives us erections, I'd said. Oh, she said, sounding disappointed, her hand still on it. It quivered. I quivered. But this one, I'd said, this one is for you. She smiled, slid her hand farther between my thighs, then slipped onto me, into me. She straddled me fully, her hair a waterfall on either side of us. I suckled at her breasts as if they were coconuts fresh from the tree. When I came, both of us gasping for air, I knew we'd made Jonas, our firstborn, knew that nothing would be the same again. She collapsed against me. We were slick, wet. I remember holding the back of her neck in my left hand, the top part of her shoulders clammy already from the sweat evaporating, my right hand resting on the small of her back, feeling myself go limp inside her. Wanting to stay like that for all time. The wind, you say? What? You said the wind made boys "flag." Not like this, I said. And I felt myself swelling up again. She was still atop. She moaned. Her lips parted. I kissed her and held her tongue in my mouth, sucked on it as if it were a *kenèp*, sweet and tart. We went at it again.

I started to laugh. What is it? Eyes closed, smiling, still clasping me. You, my dear, I said solemnly, are no fly-by-night event. She whipped her long hair back, out of the way, squinted. No? No, I said, laughing still, you're a hurricane. She smiled, kissed me. Good, she said, I didn't like the idea of being any small gust of wind, getting your sails up. Ahoy, I said, pumping on an imaginary whistle above our heads. That was when I told her that I loved her for the first time, though I'd already planned for a future, planned to ask her to marry me. We could have made them all in one go, that first time, but it would take a few years for the girls to follow.

Hurricane. Waterfall. Falling and blown about. She upset my world and tethered me to this ground. I stopped dreaming of departure. Wanted only to stay and cultivate the soft, sacred garden of her body. *Wozo*, I said to her. You are like the reeds in marsh water that never break, only bend.

But I was wrong, like a drugged man seeing only the immediate present. When the third baby came, I should have taken them all across the waters, anywhere, and left this dirt patch, this damned, parasitical paradise.

·

All people seem to have on their minds now, after the disaster, is how to fuck each other. I should say men, not people, the jackals, the werewolves. It's the men who are fucking and the women, girls, who are being fucked over—some boys, even, but no one will mention that—in the middle of the night. It was happening in the camp where I left Sara and Jonas. I never should have left. We'd wake up to mornings of women wailing, the tears in the fabric walls of the tents apparent by daylight. Crowds would examine the tears as if a supernatural being had made them, a *lougarou*, a werewolf, but they were made with the cut of ordinary knives, not fangs, sharp fingernails, not claws. Among those seemingly dazed crowds were the men who had spilled through the tents, unwelcome and unannounced, brandishing their knives and swords, falling upon their prey as if upon soldiers in battle except that the victims were not ready for war, had already been to the gates of hell and back, and these *lougarou* took them further into the depths of purgatory. I spat on the ground, disgusted but feeling helpless. I looked away from the wailing women. I told Sara not to look but that was unnecessary; she was already in her own world, too concerned about Jonas and trying to forget the sight of our crushed daughters to worry about others, about herself. I walked away from the wails then, but they've followed me.

Some of us men have heard enough: hearing a woman's wails is like listening to a baby cry through the night. It sets you on edge.

We don't talk it over; we patrol the borders of the camp with sticks in our hands, walk the narrow alleyways between the makeshift houses in the hope of restoring order, offer some semblance of security to the helpless. It's something to do in the absence of radios and televisions and domino games. It's darker than dark. We're afraid sometimes, even us, men with sticks in our hands, between our legs, cigar blunts stuck between our teeth. It's difficult to tell shadows apart in the dark. In the dark, anything can be, anything can happen. We do what we can.

It's not clear if we're motivated to save the women and the children, or if we simply want to spare ourselves the wailing, the unending wrenching of tears. Enough already. Enough. It's tiresome, and tiring. Fucking exhausting.

I walk unstintingly every night, because there's simply nothing else to do in Camp Cocasse if you want to keep taking life seriously. Nothing to do but wait for the water truck—and it comes once a week—that and drinking *clairin* when there's nothing else to drink. I need to escape my own head.

It's while I'm walking that I figure out the solution to all this. I work the numbers, since this is what I do, used to do: all they need to do is pay us the reparations owed, going back to the Louisiana Purchase. I'm talking about the Americans. Forget the French, who still owe us the equivalent of 40 billion US, in today's dollars, to repay the indemnity they forced us to pay to get access to global trade after we'd *won* the Revolution. But it's the Americans who won in that deal, won big. *Big time.* Napoleon lost his footing in the New World and France went on, while America became the US of A. Without our Revolution, there would be no USA. No US. There would be no us, as we are today. All the Americans need to do is stop giving that $300 million a year to the Haitian government and give it directly to us, "we the people," for our dead; give it out to those of us still cheating death. They give us $300 million while our GDP is close to $7 billion. Where is all that money going? If only those of us who lost loved ones received aid directly, some piece of the billions being raised post *Douze*, each family would get a healthy five figures. Not enough to bring back the dead, but enough to get out of these shit hole places, enough to rebuild and try to start again. Then, maybe, there would be no plunder, no rape, no pillage. Plenty of time for leisurely, and consensual, fucking, if that's what people have a mind to do.

By the time the images of the earthquake devastation make the rounds of American households across the US, courtesy of the silver fox on CNN, clad in a leather jacket and tight gray T stretched over his muscled chest, half of American households—the 30 percent headed by single women, I wonder?—have given something to emergency relief agencies, the biggest of which declare within a few weeks that they *will not* disburse these funds for relief because "that is not our job." They cannot be preoccupied with the long-term activity of lives rescued from calamity, they say. Their main function is to invest funds in readiness for future disasters not yet come. This is news to the American households that believed that their well-known foreign rescue services were like Saint Bernards with little kegs of lifesaving alcohol tied around their thick necks. No such luck.

Fuck the do-gooders with their white crosses, with their little porta-penny boxes. You might as well pull over a billionaire on the side of the road and hand him all your extra cash and tell him to sacrifice the poor and destitute: he's doing it anyway, what are a few pennies more? Sacrifice the dead and their survivors—why not? Philanthropy is a form of necrophilia. The dead don't need money. They won't be able to tell whether they're buried head down or head up. Might even be headless, dismembered. They don't care. I mean, really, what the fuck? And the survivors are immobilized with grieving: What does money mean to them?

As I sit, alone, in the doghouse meant to be my home, the numbers obsess and haunt me: three hundred thousand gone. Some of them were fucking when it happened: that's for sure. Some of them were fucked with, never to be seen again. Some of them dreamed of fucking: no more dreams. And some of those who've survived are trying to *fuck* their way out of the nightmare of having lost everything. What will they call the babies born of this chimeric time? Miracle babies? *Goudougoudou* babies? Hope babies? Build-back-better orphans?

Whatever they call them, judging from the cries in the night, there'll be a whole generation of kids born from the despair of co-existing with a kind of death no one has ever seen before. Because death isn't the thing: it's the sheer scale of it. The numbers no one, not even I, can compute. The knowing that walking over some rubble, you might be walking over some corpses, and that some of those bones beneath might belong to you. Three hundred thousand. No roll of names. You only know if there's someone you can't find. But what about those of us who didn't die?

Really, what can all those people fucking away be thinking? Fucking doesn't make life more real: it only ensures another being will be brought into the world to be condemned to death. I didn't sign up for this when I became a father. You do your best to keep them alive, happy. You don't expect them to be slapped like mosquitoes, squashed like flies. Nothing I could do. There was nothing any of us could do.

If Sara were here, she'd tell me to stop saying the *f*-word. She allowed me to utter it when we strove long hours at night toward the light—the wonder of it. But now all I'm left with is the crude, empty shell of the word, its sheer violence, its reality: we're all fucked. Fucked. There's no way around it. No light to strive toward.

.

When Sara told me that she let those people take the bodies of our girls away because they were mangled and didn't look anything like our daughters, I told her it was okay. But it wasn't. I wanted to see them. They came into the world, out of Sara's belly, bloodied and slimy. I wouldn't have minded the blood. Of course, I didn't see what Sara saw. I had to trust her.

I had not seen the house collapse on my children, the house where everyone gathered to watch *futbòl* or the soaps. I was getting home from work when I came upon the street, the roads undulating like waves, to someone telling me that they had seen Jonas enter the house and thought he was still there, somewhere, beneath, because they had not yet found his body. I held on to hope, then. Sara was doubled over in pain, suppressing cries by stuffing the edge of her skirt into her mouth. The man who had seen our son pointed to the place where he thought he might still be and rallied a few other men to come help, including Paul, Sonia's brother, the one who went around wearing sunglasses, even at night. He was there with his other sister, the younger one, Taffia, their father, dazed, blood streaming from a gash on his head, standing not far behind.

I noticed that Paul's hands were smeared with red already, as if he had been painting a house. What had they been doing? Could Paul be trusted? These thoughts crossed my mind but had to be pushed away. There was no time to waste. No time.

We made levers out of anything we could find, but the make-shift devices broke against the far heavier pieces of cement and tinder blocks. I had to leave all the thinking to others, followed the leads of those who could maintain a sense of cold-bloodedness. Someone came up with the idea of lifting larger pieces of the concrete with men on either side of the jagged slabs, of having some of the men thrust smaller pieces beneath until a stack could be formed for leverage, a counterweight, and Jonas could be freed in that way. Paul was positioned to push smaller pieces into the stack, then to climb down into the hole next to Jonas when we had made enough room. He descended into the darkness and found Jonas slick with sweat, almost unconscious. My son was still breathing, shallowly; there was no time. The older man who had taken charge told Paul to inspect the boy's body, and he did so as he might have a piece of driftwood on an empty beach. He yelled back that one of Jonas's legs was pinned beneath the edge of a cement slab and that his jeans were soaked from blood. One of the other men, thin but muscular, scrambled into the hole, unprompted, tore off his T-shirt, and made a tourniquet of it where the leg was pinned, to stop the blood, to keep Jonas from bleeding out, then and there. "We have to do this quickly," I heard him say. "I'll pull the slab up and then you push the leg out from under the slab," he said to Paul. "Boy," he said to my son, "*kenbe*. We're going to get you out." The boy whimpered if he heard at all. Sara continued to cry by the side of the road. She was encircled by women now, Ma Lou among them.

It took three attempts before the leg was freed. We were successful because the slab itself was not attached to anything; it was a piece of wall that had fallen onto the boy, keeping him from making it out of doors. The boy went limp as he was pulled up and out, then placed in my arms. The T-shirt that had been used to make the tourniquet was soaked with blood, but it had worked. Maybe the leg could be saved? I dared not look too closely.

I ran toward Sara, but when she saw that Jonas was still alive, inexplicably, she turned away. I had no time to think, so I turned to follow others who indicated that an emergency triage tent had been set up in the port by US forces; I had to believe in them now, despite the ravages of history. There was nothing else, no one else. I did not know then that they had closed down the airport, were not letting others in. I was holding Jonas and realized, slowly, what the crushed leg meant: that he would never run again, never be a soccer star.

I ran as fast as I could toward the port and the floating hospital, away from the fear, telling my boy that it would all be okay. But it wouldn't be. The leg, they sawed it off. Without anesthetic, deep into the next day, or the next, or the next. I lost track of all time. When they did it, I held the hair on my head in tight fists: saving my boy's life an agony no one would want to visit. A few days before, I had given him a pouch filled with the marbles he'd asked for, for his eleventh birthday. I had sewn the initial of his name on the outside of the pouch. His childhood ended on that table; he passed out from the shock of the pain.

He wasn't the only one. Cigar-cut amputations left and right, no anesthesia. Screams everywhere leaving a buzzing in my head, a beehive of suffering. I wished he had died along with the girls under that house in the neighborhood on the first day, that I hadn't had to come here to watch. I turned away when they severed the leg, his screams a strange hum in my head that hasn't left me.

By the time we came back, Jonas and I, minus a leg, a vial of antibiotics to last six weeks in my pocket, another of codeine, and a bag full of clean dressings to change every few days, Sara had been moved to the camp below the cathedral. Ma Lou showed me where. Sara hesitated a smile when she saw me return at first, but when she saw the boy's stump, she drew away. I exhaled heavily. I needed her to take over. I gave her the boy even as I saw that the light in her eyes was fading. I didn't have the strength. I didn't have the strength. I knew that I didn't have the strength for what would come next. I rationalized that I would be more useful elsewhere, far away from them, charting a new course out in the wilderness, working on the future. At the same time, I also knew that my flight was a ruse to escape the truth that, like the girls, Jonas was going to die.

I did not think that Sara and I could survive the losses. I did not see how we could. I told myself a story about starting over, finding work, reuniting and finding a new house, elsewhere. I knew none of this would happen, but still, I went through the motions.

I left because I knew that Jonas would be gone before I could get back. He was listless, in shock from the surgery, hardly ate, had difficulty swallowing those pills, which were the only defense against pain, contamination, death. The wound was garish but the amputation had been done by battle-weary medical marines; he could survive. He would not survive. As the pills in the vials I had been given declined (partly because I took to taking some of the codeine pills myself), the skin above the bandages broke out in patches. I didn't know how long the antibiotics would work against the onslaught of microbes teeming from everywhere. I guessed that it would not be long. The boy's screams at the time of the amputation, calling out for me, his mama, rang in my head. I rationalized that death by infection might be easier than the steps that would have to be taken to save his life again; gangrene, if it came to that, sepsis in the bloodstream, working its way to the heart, a mercy. But I didn't want to be there when it happened.

·

People tell stories in this fucking desert. I hear the one about the bright light that some reported seeing over the bay before the earth swayed and arched her back like a woman copulating with the ocean. They say that our enemies set off a bomb underneath the bay, in the dark. Some of them say they heard the explosion, that it was heard from all points in the capital, followed by a bright light floating saucer like above the water, and the woman that was land arched her back, opened her belly, and everything set precariously on her flesh shook and came tumbling down. "Fuck me," someone says, hearing the story. That might have been me. I don't know. "No, fuck us," someone else says. That could also have been me. We all nod, pensively, lips tight, chewing on cinnamon sticks. Whether they set off something beneath the waters or the earth had had enough of us lying lazily on her back, the end result is the same: we—are—so—fucked.

Now, I may be swearing so much because (a) Sara isn't here to give me the slant eye to make me stop or (b) I've been drinking *clairin* to alleviate the pressure in my brain since I saw the way they cut off Jonas's leg. I'll say it again: there was nothing I could have done. It was going to be over before we even knew what to do. All I remember now—when I allow myself to think about it—is the way he moaned and moaned until the sound emanating from him was so steady that it could have been the motor of a clock: ticking, ticking, ticking. He moaned low so that he wouldn't disturb us or seem weak. It was important to him to seem strong. That was my fault, no one else's. How I could have left Sara to deal with that all by herself, I don't know. I didn't want to think of what I was asking of her: to watch our son die, after she'd already seen the girls die. By herself. Fuck. What kind of a man does that?

But me, I am no longer a man. I live in a doghouse; therefore, I am a dog, sitting where the Big Men who govern this country have dumped me, every one of them, whatever the color of their skin, a *blan*, meaning heartless, without color or feeling, hoping that the heat and the drought will make us all crazy enough to want to be factory workers instead of accountants, crazy enough to want to let the sun bleach our brains, blanch our bones, become not quite white but white enough to do what is asked of us without asking too many questions. It's what I deserve for running away, a coward, a scoundrel, a condemned man.

·

Clairin: I put it in his milk. Drops of the moonshine right in the milk, the way the old folks used to put rum in the milk of teething babies. I told myself it was so that he could get some sleep, rest, but it was the grating constancy of his moaning I wanted to stop. It wrenched my insides out. I'm ashamed to admit it. I wanted him to die. It would have been a way out, for him, and for me.

No, I did not abandon her completely. I asked Loko, the rain-water man who set up a station in the camp, meting out clean water to whoever needed it, to look out for her. I also asked Ma Lou to bathe her, dress her if necessary, keep an eye out. To keep her alive for as long as it took for me to get back. I knew already that the boy would be dead in days, maybe weeks. I was hoping they would all do what I'd asked. Loko was alone, glad for a task, some charge all his own besides collecting and disbursing his rainwater. He said that Sara reminded him of his daughter, whom he had left behind long ago in a village in the mountains of LaGonav. I have to be thankful for old men and their country ways.

We should all have stayed away from this godforsaken city. Loko should have gone back to his village long ago. I should have gone back to my grandfather's land in Jérémie, to the west, and made amends. I'm named for that land. Or, rather, I'm named for the swarthy Italian plantation owner who stole that land from beneath my grandfather's father, then told my grandfather tales of olive groves when he was small enough to sit on the old man's knee. My grandfather suckled on stories of olive groves, of planting saplings in the red earth, but in the end, he was just an overseer, tending to the man's coffee plants, watching over them, watering them, cultivating the crops, extracting the seeds, making another man rich. It's a tale as old as the first conquests. The Italian deeded the land to the children he had had with his real wife in Italy, left the bastards born of the red earth to cultivate the land; made the le-gitimates rich, while convincing the bastards that this arrangement was their saving grace: Wouldn't they be better off than previous generations? What would they know to do with a deed, ownership? Fucking capitalist imperialists.

Don't get me wrong: without the coffee plantation, I wouldn't have been sent to boarding school in the capital, wouldn't have had the English lessons, gotten my accounting degree at the state university, got work off and on from the legitimate merchants in the capital, trading on the plantation's reputation. But these were small contracts and they weren't enough. So, I supplemented by keeping the ghost books of those in the neighborhood with dubious occupations but no book learning, people like Sonia and Dieudonné. Even Ma Lou occasionally asked for my advice, though she could keep her own numbers. It never hurt to ask a professional, though my family background was no evidence that I knew what I was doing. My plan had been to buy out some of the five hectares of land, get it back, rescue myself and my family. But after I met Sara, my plans dissolved. I lost the trenchant edge of bitterness needed for revenge. I let go of my grandfather's land out west and held on to Sara in the capital. She was enough to tie me to the ground, to make me feel I was home, even without a piece of land to call our own. Call it a case of misplanning, of blindness or shortsightedness: we could have been sitting far away from here on our own piece of paradise had I followed through with getting my grandfather's land back. Instead, two of my babies are dead, one lay dying, and I have betrayed my wife, royally fucked her over because I was too weak to take back what's mine in the first place.

The world falls apart, people's babies die, their mothers are pulverized like squash blossoms beneath the walls of the houses they've worked a lifetime to build, and someone, somewhere, some fool, thinks it's a good idea to sit and make a pot full of *clairin*, God bless that someone. I'm thankful. Without the moonshine, I wouldn't be trying to muster the will to live, get back to the city, find Sara, try again.

.

I am walking in the desert, under moonlight, listening for *lougarou*. The camp people say that they are everywhere, scurrying, with their fangs and their bloodshot, yellow eyes. They come out at night. I hear a rustle, a scream. I stop to listen. A woman's scream? A child's? I recall Jonas tossing and turning under the heat of the tent. I remember Sara's glassy eyes, her soul torn out. I push the thoughts away. The screaming doesn't stop.

As I am walking my beat, alone, what happens next comes upon me all of a sudden, and then slowly, brutally. The stick I am holding is swiped out of my hand. At first, I cannot see them, but then I see that I am surrounded by five or six young men. One resembles Paul. How would Paul have gotten here? They start to beat me mercilessly. The werewolves have come. They exist, after all. The screaming continues, and I try to discern the source despite the pummeling. Is it a woman's cackle? The young men beating me are grunting between punches and kicks. They are young, young men, younger than I am, and stronger. They take me to the ground. I wrestle with them as if in a schoolyard. We tussle. Two take me by the arms, lock them back, and grind my chest into the ground. I hear a new scream. Could that be me? No: only women scream. The ground smells like garbage. *Fatra.* Garbage is the universal umbilical cord. They have me pinned to the ground. I know what's coming. I know. We all know. My God, my God, is this why the women scream at night? I feel a wrenching in my gut. They're younger than I am. Maybe twice my Jonas's age? Or Paul's age? Not much more than that. Half mine.

I hear the sound of feet. Someone else is coming. There is yelling. I hear older men's voices. The young men disperse, run. Where is there to run to? We're in a fucking piss-hole desert! All the little doghouses in straight rows. The young men run through the narrow dirt paths in all directions, howling. They run. And run. Laugh. Squeal. The pack of wolves leaving a pack of dogs behind.

"*Sa pa fè anyen*," one of the men from the patrol says to me as he helps me to pull up my pants, using his body to shield me from the other men in the patrol, who all look away, toward the camp, up the paths, toward the moon, examining their nails, pretending that they don't see anything. I am trembling. The men in the patrol surround me. Screams are still sounding in the night, left and right. One man stays by my side. "Are you going to be okay?" he says, as he walks me back to my shack. I shake my head yes, no. Yes. No. What does it matter? He places a hand on my shoulder as he leaves me at my door. He says a word to my crazy neighbor, who is sitting in front of his shack, doing nothing. They look in my direction, nodding. I crawl into the doghouse to flee their gazes.

I am no longer a man. I am of no use.

When morning arrives, I wait to hear the thunderous stutter of the water truck's engine before flinging myself out the doghouse door.

I know exactly the route the truck will take around the perimeter of the encampment, avoiding the latrines, heading straight for the first aid tent that has no first aid in it. I follow its course from within the camp; then I start running as it turns a bend. I meet it before it reaches the first aid tent. The driver cannot see me and before he can brake, I throw myself in front of the steel grate protecting the engine. Throw myself hard against the moving truck so that nothing will be left of me.

The weight of the truck, the velocity, is a shock. Picks me off the ground, drags me, before the driver realizes that he's hit something, someone, me.

"Damn," he exclaims, as I feel a weightlessness enter me. "Another goddamn donkey!"

Others come running, women snatching their kerchiefs from their heads and waving them in the air. All colors.

"*Sak pase?*" asks a *madansara*; I look at her from the corner of my eye. My chest has caved in, but I don't feel anything anymore. She's another Ma Lou.

"Damn," the driver says again, seeing that I'm not a donkey or a goat. "Damn, he's not going to make it to any hospital, even if I try," he says to no one in particular. He looks around at the gathering crowd, shrugs his hefty shoulders helplessly. "*M'pa kapab ankò . . .*" His words trail off.

Everyone understands the situation: we're all screwed, sitting like stray dogs in the blistering heat of the desert. "Damn," the water truck man says again. I feel his callused hands on both sides of my head. I remember the story of the donkey. This man has experience in the killing of livestock; I'm counting on it. There will be water today but no meat. The water delivery job is temporary, like they tell us everything is temporary. Do it, I silently pray. Please. Take me out of my misery.

"Damn," the driver says, again, his holy mantra in life as in death.

The thick fingers of his hands wrap themselves around my neck and jaw. In a moment, they will make the sharp gesture that will snap my neck bones smoothly out of place. There will be nothing more for me to do, nothing more to be done. Nothing but to thank the truck driver for his swift hands, for the relief he will have brought, for the water he brings to quench the thirst of the camp dwellers who will have to dig my grave in this desert they must call home now, all the while waiting for rain.

ANNE

Kigali, Rwanda, July 2010

I was not there when it happened. Like most people outside, I learned of it from the news, not even the night of the Event itself, but several days after, when one of my colleagues, Marc, a white Canadian on the building mission with me, in Kigali, brought me a newspaper with a photograph on its front page of the National Palace building fallen over on itself like an ornament on a wedding cake.

He pointed to it and said, "Isn't this where you're from?"

I peered at the headline, "Earthquake in Haiti," and then at the photograph of the broken capital building that had always stood, next to the Champ de Mars, facing Place L'Ouverture, framed by an iron fence at least nineteen feet high, interrupted every few meters by thick concrete pylons painted white, and an even taller ornamental gate that swung open to admit dignitaries (some, in the past, never came out). The fallen structure was a landmark. It had not always been there. But it had been there all of my life. It meant something. Now it was gone? I tore the paper from my colleague's hands.

"I'm sorry," he said, though there was nothing for him to be sorry for. It wasn't his fault.

I read about the death toll, estimated already in the several thousands of thousands a week or so into the calamity. I read about the buildings flattened, the rescue missions being deployed from Cuba, with others to join them from around the world, coming over from across the Dominican border and across the chain of mountains dividing the two countries, because the Americans had shut the airport, the most direct port of access. A chill went through me as I read, and I tried to call my grandmother, but she did not answer.

"I'm sorry," Marc said again, putting a hand on my shoulder and squeezing it lightly, but I waved him away and tried to call a different number from my cell. I called my father's cousin, Dieudonné, a fixer and driver in the capital, who always had the latest gadgets, but his line was also dead. There would be no response for several days. The problem could have been my own whereabouts, I conjectured, but later, I would find out that the problem was the damage on the ground, more severe than any photograph could convey (though the fallen Palais National was in itself a sobering reality), when I received an email from a fellow engineer on the ground, a Haitian American named Lucien whom I had connected to Dieudonné, who occasionally hired him as a driver. There was no message, no subject line, only a series of photos of the devastation, one after the other. I recognized vast open spaces of places I used to know: the church where I had been baptized marked by the cross of a crucified Jesus; my mother's house reduced to a flaked pink stoop decorating a pile of rubble; the hotel where Dieudonné and his girlfriend, Sonia, worked flattened to the ground.

There was a picture of my grandmother, Ma Lou, showing the broken stalls in the market beneath the cathedral, which was also collapsed, broken beyond recognition. I sighed in relief at seeing

Ma Lou's round, open face, her mouth open, her arms wide. I could see from her pose that she had been explaining what had happened when the photograph was taken. She was alive. A message followed saying that Dieudonné was also alive, then another stating that Lucien had witnessed a wave swallowing Richard into the sea since he had served as his driver that fateful day. The body had been lost to the waves, he wrote, matter-of-factly, so my father was presumed dead, another casualty of the Event. The next email contained two lines. "You should come back," it said. "What Haiti needs now is builders: that's us."

We had both received our degrees at the end of the previous year, Lucien's in engineering and mine in architecture, with the hope of opening a practice in Port-au-Prince. The problem, for us, was that we both had chosen to specialize in accessible eco-building, and the likelihood of being able to get paid for that kind of work at home was slim to none. This was why Lucien took odd jobs to make ends meet, but also to network, depending on his family in the US to send him money to keep him afloat while he remained in Haiti. Both of us had been hired, right out of our master's degrees, to work for NGOs in our first jobs. Lucien had been lucky to be hired by a Canadian nonprofit locally. I had been hired by a French NGO to work in Rwanda, where more international funds had been made available to rebuild the country after the ten-year anniversary of the genocide. I would be working on affordable mixed-use buildings, the kind that could house studios, businesses, and multigenerational family units in the same place. I was especially interested in building structures that would be useful to collectives of women pooling their resources in the new economies of the Global South, with microloans and cooperatives.

These were already popular throughout Asia and were becoming popularized in parts of Latin America along with notions of architecture for the people. Lucien specialized in water and sewage systems, on maximizing clean energy. We hoped to one day revolutionize building in Haiti.

It wasn't that there weren't Haitian architects and engineers who could do the job—UNESCO sites like the Citadelle Laferrière to the north demonstrated our long history of building structures that could outwit time; there were also the wooden gingerbread houses so well constructed that they had withstood termite invasions, the Revolution, hurricanes. The rich had had their mansions built back in the mountains, many designed and built by Haitian hands, but constructed of imported materials. But as the capital became overpopulated, mostly with poor and rural folks seeking their fortunes and in need of quick housing, building codes were not, could not be, observed, and structures were built of hastily fashioned cinder blocks, many of which were hollow in the middle, and one person would build on top of another, wherever there was room, in zigzag, up the sides of the hills encircling the city, between the valley and the higher reaches inhabited by the wealthy, one person's roof serving as another's floor. Building codes were reserved for people with means and running water. The rest took their chances. What would we be able to offer? I wondered.

Soon, the disaster vultures would descend on the island; things would spiral out of control. In our line of work, it would be the emergency shelter crowd we would see first, those with prototypes ready to go. Shelters had become a business opportunity, as more people around the world were displaced, made homeless and migratory by civil wars and famines. If someone, anyone, could roll out a compact structure that could house families of at least four, keep them dry when it rained, safe from the beating rays of the sun when heat swelled, and screened from mosquitoes—in short, designed to improve the chances of survival while minimizing the kinds of illnesses easily spread in the cramped quarters of an IDP camp—then that person would be not only hailed as a hero but guaranteed to reap the financial rewards for generations to come, all while having made the world a better place. We would have to watch helplessly as lesser-equipped professionals used the destitute to test their new products.

"Come back," Lucien wrote. "Haiti needs us."

It was Lucien who had been driving my father the day he disappeared, swallowed by the sea. It was Lucien who told me the details of the disappearance, and on whom I came to rely, later, when I tried to track people, starting the work of beginning again, of hoping.

I could have been there, for the earthquake itself. I had been there a few days into the new year to bury my mother. But I had already planned to be in Rwanda, after the funeral, and had left even sooner than I had planned because my father, my biological father, had said he was coming to the funeral but never showed. I was so angry. Instead of trying to track him—I knew Dieudonné would know where he was—I stayed on schedule, and joined the French architects deploying to Rwanda to build affordable structures where they were needed, because the country was now stabilized and accepting outside help, and it was the sole French-speaking country on the list of choices I had been given. Had my father unwittingly saved me with his failure to appear?

I told Marc of my mother's death, then, of my father's disappearance. He was the person I trusted in the group. He later came
back with one of the laptop computers and showed me how to
create a social media account. "This is the only place I'm seeing
messages posted," he explained. That was how I learned about who
had died beneath the rubble or who was still being searched for,
how I learned a majority of women at the head of national women's
organizations—Anne-Marie, Myriam, Magalie, Myrna—women
with whom I had had conversations about programs that would
provide women with training to work in masonry and construction,
maybe even get associate's degrees in engineering—had perished,
all of them, a whole generation of activists gone in a matter of seconds, decades of work wiped out.

It wasn't long before others on my team awkwardly approached
me to ask if I could track a coworker, a fixer, an intern, an in-law.
These requests were followed by emails from others I had known at
school, in the States, with contacts in Haiti seeking the same.

My first query, to track an intern who had been meant to join us
in the field but who had decided to take an extended holiday with
his family before beginning to work, was sent out like a fishing line
in still waters to Lucien. A few days later, his response read, "I'm
sorry, but all your contacts are dead. Your intern is alive but all the
contacts you gave me to find him are dead." The phrase rang in my
head for days: "All your contacts are dead." I understood immediately it would not be the last time I would have to read the phrase,
or some variation of it.

I took the names down in a notebook, and the names of whomever they thought might know that person on the ground, and I
would send out new queries, usually a few at once. Some of the

time, most of the time, I would find the person they were looking for, learn where they were, if they were on a list for evacuation, or not, if they were safe, or not. Nine times out of ten, like that first time, it would be the contact names who would be unaccounted for, those who lived in the country full-time, or who didn't have the means to live in houses with fortified, shear walls, and I would have to make another list, one for the dead, and yet another list for the phrases I could use to relay the news, all different depending on the degree of remove the dead had from the person who had asked.

The list of the dead grew day by day, week by week. I got through those days by focusing on the living, putting the list of the dead at the back of my mind even as the list grew longer. Still, death was with me like a cloak, a second skin. My mother, the person I was the closest to, had died—that was my personal earthquake. My father, a man I hardly knew, was presumed dead, or disappeared. I was on the other side of the world, in a country where so many had perished by their neighbor's hand.

·

The stories haunting Kigali's mountains—like the mountains themselves, down to the sienna brown of the soil—remind me so much of Haiti, preoccupy me as if they are my own. I take long walks at the end of each day, up a hill, in the direction of the city, trying to shake things off, to think clearly, objectively. I watch myself being watched. But it is not enough to use the little Kinyarwanda I know: *muraho* (hello), *bitese* (how are you), *murakoze* (thank you). I can't blend in. Don't want to. Don't want to become part of the fabric of things. Couldn't. Can't. Isn't part of the job.

One of the first places I visited after arriving in the country, to familiarize myself with the people, the history, before setting to work, was the Kigali Genocide Memorial. There, overlooking gardens, were immense concrete slabs covering the remains of 250,000 genocide victims interred in mass graves below. I was struck by the fact that it was the same number entombed beneath the fallen buildings in Port-au-Prince: a neat erasure of thousands could not be so readily contained as what I looked upon now, in a place where killings had been widespread and uncontained, where remains were still being found piecemeal and brought to the common grave for burial among the martyrs, if they were not already laid to rest in a yard or family grave, of which there were too many to count.

Is 250,000 a euphemism for "too many to be counted," a number at once unfathomable but easily understood, that can contain the horror and amplitude of the loss, because once one goes past this number, it would be impossible to contain anything more, the magnitude of it all?

As I left the museum shop, the cashier asked me, abruptly, "Are your parents still alive?" as if we were talking about the weather, as if this were a routine question to ask. I paused. Maybe, here, elsewhere, it *is* a routine question.

"No," I started by saying, thinking about my mother, who had passed away in December of the last year, then, "Yes," I continued, thinking of the father I hardly knew, whose body had yet to be found. I secretly worried that I might have been responsible for his death. After all, if I hadn't called to impart the news of my mother's passing, and asked Dieudonné to tell him about the funeral, he might not have gone to Haiti. He still hadn't come to the funeral. Why had I felt the need to include him when he had been so long

absent? Without those calls, he might not have felt compelled to
return; he might still be alive. Inaccessible, but alive.

"Yes, or no?" the boy clarified, frowning.

"I don't know," I said. "Some of them are dead. It's a long story."

"It's like that here," the boy responded.

"My mother is dead," I said then, matter-of-factly, a piece of
information I would never so readily have revealed about myself
to a stranger. But some places stripped you clean of the desire for
privacy. "My father is missing," I added. "Presumed dead. I'm from
Haiti."

"They speak French there?"

"Yes," I said. "Also Kreyòl and, increasingly, American English."

"Haiti. Where there was the big—?" The boy opened and closed
his arms wide, then made a wild pumping gesture with one hand,
up and down, then opened the other hand, mimicking an explosion.

"Yes," I sighed, "*that* place." Others to whom I'd disclosed where
I was from since my arrival didn't seem to know about the earthquake, or, if they did, it had not touched them. One person on my
building team had asked if Haiti was where a tsunami had taken
place. I couldn't blame them. Rwanda and Haiti were two small
countries so far away from one another that it was difficult to over-
come the distance. Two small countries struggling to come up for
air.

"*Wihangane,*" the boy said. He did look like he was sorry.

He fiddled with the bags in which he'd placed my purchases.
I wondered if he waited at the counter, daily, in thirst for conversation and, finding none, sat lonely with the ghosts hovering the
length of the slabs at his back.

"*Wihangane,*" I said, when I left the store. "*Murabeho.*"

"*Muramuke,*" the boy responded, as if I might return, but we both knew that I would not. In Rwanda, I found myself among a people in a persistent state of grief, which, in a way, made me feel at home. It had given me the room to grieve my mother before the next wave, once news of the quake reached me.

Of my family, I am now one of two remaining. Ma Lou, and myself. I don't know how to feel about this. I know that it is true. At times, especially when I think of my mother, I ponder if I, too, am one of the dead still seeking life, a *zonbi* unable to tell the difference between being dead and alive, if this is how those who were never found felt at the moment of their passing.

.

A few weeks had gone by after the quake when I found myself standing in front of the altar in the church of Nyamata, now a memorial—a church desecrated by the killings that took place within its walls—contemplating what was happening at home. In Nyamata, the people who had been slaughtered were gone but they had left behind traces of themselves, multicolored clothing, bangles and earrings, here a cup and there a spoon, a single left shoe without its mate, the leather stale and cracked. These people had been betrayed, slaughtered, vanished in the sanctity of a church, by their neighbors, their priests. I read the notes left on the altar by the grieving survivors. I contemplated the decaying flowers and faded penciled scrawl. I started seeing designs in my mind's eye as I thought through how the cathedral might be rebuilt to honor the dead while also being a place where the survivors could remember them in peace. I thought of a recent trip to Rome, the old crypts and monuments we were led through, of an exhibit some of us had been to of the Roman architect, originally from Venice, Piranesi, who drew the Roman ruins obsessively, over and over again, with a draftsman's precision, but never drafted plans for anything that could be built. Blue draft lines moved in a space over my head as I mentally redrew the contours of the fallen cathedral walls, rethought how the old could be merged with something new, something honorable, dignified, that would, like a vodou peristyle, intercede between the living and the dead. But it was all in my head; I put nothing down on paper. I wasn't even sure why my mind had turned to this impossibility of rebuilding, to a desire to build again, as Lucien had said, to be a part of what might come next.

I thought of my mother and where I had come from, of all the bodies buried beneath the rubble of unstable buildings, how those they once had housed had been betrayed, slaughtered by disregard just as the vanished had been cut by machetes. I knew at that moment of surveying the remains of the slaughtered that it was time to stop fleeing, to stop being my father's daughter, though I had never truly known him. It was time to return and face what was left, even if it was next to nothing. The ghosts would be everywhere. But the fact was that something remained, still, even in the rubble, something stronger than memory. Ma Lou, for one, was still there, holding on.

I knew then, standing in front of that altar in Nyamata, surrounded by the crumbling heaps of clothing that none had dared disturb, that I had to return, as Lucien had suggested, to Ma Lou, to the dead, to the ghosts of what remained. So I went back, six months after Douze, to be of help, to rebuild without building.

.

At the beginning of the return, every second, every minute, every hour, every day brought with it a new disaster. Everything was monumental, the losses so immense, so grave. It was already everything to have lost my mother, yet that maternal loss, usually so isolated and singular, became multiplied a hundredfold. The city was like a raw, exposed nerve delivered up to the winds and the dust swirling through the devastated and broken streets. HCB walls had collapsed in most of the residential buildings. Multistoried buildings showed cracks impossible to repair at their base; the top-heavy buildings without proper reinforcement merely settled into the empty spaces: it was simple physics, gravity. Concrete was cheap, had replaced wood since foreign powers had deforested the land; steel was difficult to come by, to import or make. There were no foundries to speak of. Commercial buildings were of a better grade, since their owners had employed qualified engineers (for there were some in the country who built their own houses low to the ground, without second stories, to code, as much as possible) and used flexible, imported building materials, and reinforced the columns, ceilings, walls. At the time, they hadn't thought of earthquakes but of buildings that could withstand high winds, hurricanes. Beyond the physical collapse, one could feel a heaviness in the air. Let me say it: one could feel the dead.

The most important person in my life, my mother, had died, and upon return to the broken city, I would have expected that everything else but her absence should have remained more or less the same: the walk to the market, the things I would find there, the people I usually said hello to on the way and back, my mother's house, how I arranged my shoes at the door, against my mother's own. But when I returned to the island, as I had observed in the photographs that Lucien had sent me by email, all of these things were gone. I did not have the comfort of a ghosted familiarity. The buildings had disappeared—the church where both my mother and I, in turn, had been baptized reduced to the pink-fleshed Jesus hanging limply, desolately, from a cross in the front courtyard, as he always had, more mournful now for his loss of a gathering place for the followers of his kingdom. We were all haunted. Everyone I met, even those who could still find a way to smile, to laugh, everyone was walking through death. It was all around us like a thick vapor, and it was hard to tell who was alive, who dead, hard to tell where one thing began and the other ended. I had to think of nothing else than what was immediately in front of me to do and pushed everything else aside.

Lucien had informed me that the government was hiring structural engineers to survey the damages, to see what could be salvaged of what remained. An architect would be superfluous, but I knew enough to be of use. When I found out that surveying entailed crawling into the fissured buildings, top-heavy with concrete and little lateral strength, which was to be expected after decades of building without seismic codes (the country was poor and there hadn't been an earthquake for over one hundred years, after all), and that only one hundred people had been rescued within the first few weeks, leaving the rest mostly dead and buried beneath the rubble, I opted for a volunteer position surveying the living to match them to viable dwellings rather than the structures themselves. I could not fathom walking over the bones, nor could I fathom the possibility of one of those structures falling on my head, adding one more to the count. I could be useful doing triage in the camps, coordinating who could go back to buildings either green- or yellow-tagged, indicating, after survey by the newly trained local engineers who would sweep through Port-au-Prince, neighborhood by neighborhood, the buildings that had had no structural damage and could be immediately reoccupied, and those that needed some work but had sections that could be inhabited. A green tag signaled that a structure had been inspected and deemed safe; a yellow tag signaled restricted entry and restricted occupation. A red-tagged building meant that it was unsafe and should not be inhabited at all. Some structures would have to be torn down entirely. If a whole neighborhood, or most of one, had been green- or yellow-tagged, and I could find a cluster of people from it, the task was usually easy. But if I was signaling that one or two houses on a block had been deemed safe enough, it was usually harder to find their owners. Everyone wanted to go home. Everyone wanted a home.

Inevitably, as when I had been trying to sort the dead from the living for colleagues looking for friends and acquaintances in the first days after the quake, I had to develop another list, one that corresponded to the more pressing needs of the people I encountered, and try to get them met by other NGOs and health services that could help them. Food was high on the list; finding other relatives was too. There was also the fact that some people would not return to yellow-tagged buildings for fear that an aftershock would send them tumbling to the ground. Sleeping under the stars felt like a safer bet, though the camps were growing increasingly insecure as the need for basic staples grew and what was being offered freely became meager and scarce. It was difficult to match need with the proper assistance—there were too many NGOs present, and not all of them knowledgeable of the terrain. I thought that being of the place would have helped, but my education and newly acquired class standing as a white-collar professional removed me from those I thought of as my community, especially those who had not seen me grow up from a weed, who weren't from my immediate neighborhood and did not know my mother or father's mother.

During those weeks, each morning, I emerged from a good rest in Ma Lou's small house; it stood tall in its simplicity, perched on a hill in Pacot, above the boulevard that hugged the coastline and ran through town, Boulevard Dessalines. She had moved there from Bel-Air some years back, maybe as long as a decade ago. It was perhaps why she had survived the quake, her house unscathed, and could return to the market day in and out despite the surrounding mayhem: she had someplace to return to that was her own, that she had made. It was not a makeshift shack hanging perched like a bird's nest above the heights of Pétion-Ville that were not meant for building. Those shacks fell like decks of cards, one on top of the other. The heights of Pacot were steep but not overbuilt, perhaps because they were next to tony Turgeau, where the established bourgeoisie lived, those not quite elite, but not everyday folks either. Ma Lou liked living there; it made her feel she was still in the countryside where she had been born and raised before coming into the capital. She took a tap-tap to work and had arranged with other women, some of whom worked for her, to store her wares closer to her stall.

Ma Lou was industrious and limited access to her personal world beyond the market. She knew everything to know about her clients and what went on in the city through the *teledyòl* or gossip that coursed through the markets as if on the back of a river:

it traveled from mouth to mouth to mouth, from market woman to market woman or from the mouths of businesspeople or state officials who met in the market and spoke of private matters as if the market women were made of stone or salt, as if they had no ears. The rich people also did this, speaking liberally in front of the market stalls, or their "help," as if no one could hear them, and the news of covert operations, shady deals, assassinations, warnings, traveled far and wide so that, often, no one could trace back the source. This was one way that the people in service, and the poor, kept themselves out of harm's way, harm caused by conditions other than poverty. The market acted like the spokes of a wheel from which all information retracted and radiated. In this way, everyone knew Ma Lou, but no one could get into her business; she lived too far from the center of the spokes. I left the house in the mornings after she did and rejoined her there later in the evenings, when we had both done our work. No one would have thought to link us one to the other, though it would not have mattered had they done so. Sometimes, we came home so exhausted from the day, from what we had seen or heard, that we said nothing to each other, prepared dinner and ate in silence.

Eventually, I met up with Lucien so that he could recount my father's final minutes in person. As he talked, I tried to imagine what it might have been like, standing on the shore, watching the waves get larger and larger. Then, how the waves might have hit my father's body with full force while he was still wondering what was happening, the ground shaking so that his foothold on the sand loosened until there was nothing to hold on to, his arms flailing ahead of him. What might it have been like to die alone like that? I wondered if my father had felt fear at that moment, how the features of his face would have rearranged themselves as the salt water enveloped his body and lifted him away from firm ground. "The water between us is all that we have in common, all that's left," Ma Lou had said to me on the phone before I'd returned. My grandmother said that Richard, her son, my father, wasn't gone, not until they found a body. I told her that it was better to assume that he was dead. "I bore him," she said, "and I will decide when he's truly dead." But something in her voice made me feel that she already accepted what I had: that we would never see him again.

I hadn't lived with Ma Lou before, though, of course, I had grown up knowing her after she came to my mother, introduced herself as Richard's mother, and told my mother how Richard had renounced her too but sent money back for her every few months. She handed my mother a swath of bills with a promise to be present after I was born, should she allow it. She was, without saying so, attempting to atone for her son's absence. She could be counted on, had integrity. She was not one of those who put a finger on the scale to make it seem heavier than it was, she said, forcing their clients to pay extra fees for their goods like some of the less scrupulous, younger market women did. My mother had said that Ma Lou's earnestness had made her smile. How different the child could be from the mother, she told me she had thought. They were never quite friends, but they coexisted for me. They were both my mothers. After the quake, none of the market women needed to tip the scales: prices climbed to outrageous heights by the day because of scarcity. Only the foreigners could pay.

As Lucien and I had predicted, those in our profession were busy trying to deploy the latest design in emergency shelters: round structures made of straw and mud, others made of recyclables that

could be collapsed or built one atop the other, still others indistin-
guishable from pup tents but claiming to be heat-resistant, each with
a distinctive advertising logo on its side that could be read from a
distance. I suspected this was for drones or helicopters, to be spot-
ted from up above. I watched as each of these structures was given
out to camp managers since none had been fabricated for use on a
mass scale but were being piloted instead, one by one. As small and
inefficient as the structures were, they became prized properties. One
camp manager who'd been given a narrow, collapsible structure on
two floors that could house his wife and baby son in an elevated bedroom while the ground floor was made up of a kitchenette and sitting
area, decided to run a white picket fence around the periphery of his
small lot, as if the distinctiveness of the structure was not enough:
he wanted to be sure that it would be recognized as the center of
camp life. In another tent city, the inhabitants were less tolerant and
heaped their garbage on the plot next to the shelter their manager
had been given, a solar-powered tent with heat-retardant walls, or so
he was told. The manager had placed his tent at a bit of a distance
from the gray-tarped wooden structures of the other unfortunates
and they, in turn, did not let him forget the cost of his arrogance. He
may have had light at night, but his tent smelled of the sewer while
rats ambled at night next to the structure, rubbing their matted fur
uncomfortably close to the walls of the tent. That manager was a
single man who had ignored the mounting heaps of garbage and fed
the rats with his own hands.

I looked away from such scenes to focus on the task I had at
hand to relocate camp dwellers. The people I interviewed regarded
me with suspicion, until they realized that I understood and spoke
Kreyòl, but until then, often, some would curse me to my face, as

if I were like any other common foreigner, a *blan*, or white person. Sometimes, usually when it was a man suggesting all manner of lasciviousness, sometimes violent—the things he would do were he free to do them, what he would do under cover of night, after the UN security guards had gone back to their bases, when I no longer had my clipboard in hand—I would respond. "Why don't you try, then?" I said to one calmly, in Kreyòl, after he'd said to the woman standing next to him that he would be the one to give me what I was searching for: a *bon kadejak*, (I paused before responding: Could there be such a thing as a "good" rape?). I glared at the woman. Was she his girlfriend, his spouse? Had she already had his children? Girls? If so, were they the issue of rapes? I hoped not. I pretended as if the exchange had not taken place and followed up by asking for their names, the location of their dwelling—a tent or a shack—and their needs. They did the same and answered the practical questions, all the while the man glaring at me through yellowish eyes, a sign of possible jaundice, perhaps liver problems. I wrote their answers diligently, in Kreyòl, in French, and in English. I told them someone would be getting back to them though I knew that only the emergency situations would be addressed immediately. All the rest (the need for food, clean water, basic medicines for minor ailments such as headaches and diarrhea—which would turn out, in only months, to be an indicator of something far worse that would wipe out thousands who had survived the unthinkable), as it always did, could wait.

Not everyone was suspicious; even fewer were aggressive like some of the angry young men who resented my ability to come and go out of the camp unscathed (as if I had lost nothing and they everything; and yet I had lost nothing, and everything). Sometimes my grandmother led me to someone she knew who needed attention and could not find it. This was how I came to know Sara. She told me she was waiting for her husband, and her children. I wrote the husband's name: Olivier. There were no children with her; was she hallucinating? An older man who kept an eye on her and who collected rainwater for a living, Loko, told me part of her story, how two of her children had died on the day of the earthquake and the third weeks later.

I looked at the woman. I could not imagine the burden of her loss. Where was her husband? I tried to ask what she needed. She moved slowly as if the air were made of molasses, waved me toward her invisible children and absent husband, as if the air could speak to me of them. My hands shook as I took down the details of need. I told Loko to bring her as much clean water as he could, so that she would survive what the other members of her family had not. I thought of Richard and his bottling empire: how he could have been of help now, but he too had disappeared, been washed away in the tsunami following the earthquake. Loko nodded in assent but his eyes looked grave, as if no amount of clean water would make a difference in this case, no prayer nor appeal to the gods. As Loko spoke, I noted that he wore amulets around his neck, strings of beaded necklaces made of seeds, pods, and small shells.

Sara reminded Loko of his daughter, he informed me. The first time he saw her in the camp, he thought that it might be her, that maybe she had crossed the bay from LaGonav after she had grown up. She was what he imagined his daughter might look like today, with her mother's dark sable skin, and his own father's large, round eyes, the tight curls of her hair like the small stones one found when picking through dried *djon djon* mushrooms, the mushrooms so black and dark that sometimes it was hard to tell them apart from the black pebbles they grew between. He enjoyed taking care of Sara in the camp, even though she could hardly speak to him. He had seen the husband, Olivier, in the camp when she first had come but the man had left, saying he would look for work in a camp outside the capital, where factories were to be built. Loko shook his head back and forth, said the man had never returned. Jonas, her son who had died in the camp, came to be a grandson for him, and he did what he could to distract the boy from his pain and dying with the spells and potions that he knew from his days as a *houngan*, a healer. Loko was originally from LaGonav. He had come to the capital after a disagreement with the local evangelist who damned anyone and anything associated with a whiff of vodou. "Well," Loko explained to me, "I had to leave." Maybe native medicine was all that could help now.

I listened to people like Loko every day I went into the camps, but his story made me ponder the loss of his family, the pain his daughter might have felt when she realized that he would never be coming back to LaGonav. It made me think of Richard sitting in the car that time he came to see me at the private school he had paid for, how I had waved and wondered why he never came out of the car to speak to me. The world of men, of fathers, was a mystery. Loko was one of the people whose house had been marked red— uninhabitable. He would remain in the camp for some time.

Ma Lou and I decided to keep tabs on Sara regularly, to see if there was anything we could do for her, keep her afloat. But one day, when we arrived to check on her, I saw smoke coming from the tent, left Ma Lou standing on the edge of the camp, and ran in, yelling to Loko for water, any water. A girl named Taffia, a teenager I had interviewed, whom I suspected had experienced a *kadejak* right there in the camp but would not say so, and her brother, were already running ahead of me. We stormed the tent.

Loko and I threw water on the flames until they were all put out. It was all over in minutes. The episode winded and wounded me: I was an architect not building any buildings, not a miracle worker. Loko showed a surprising preparedness for the tragic. He, along with Ma Lou, tended to Sara's burns, and I returned, alone, to Ma Lou's house.

I did not stop by the camp to check on Sara again but heard of her outcome from Ma Lou. Her burns had been minor and would heal in time. Other camp dwellers promised to take turns watching out for her. Everyone wondered about the husband who had left her there, with her last child's limbs turning black from lack of circulation. After her son's death, other parents held their children close and didn't let them out of their sight as night fell and the shapes of the tents threw oblong shadows across the dirt paths, making unfamiliar terrain seem even more perilous. They felt sorry for her, sorry for themselves. This pity motivated the care they gave her that she might not have accepted from anyone other than people who had been through similar losses and witnessed hers. Solidarity grew from a common wound.

So many people were telling Ma Lou their stories, as they always did, as Loko, and others, had told me theirs. At times, I thought her rotund body would burst from receiving them. After a time, I could no longer contain them myself: the stories of the deaths, the rapes, those who went crazy because they kept thinking that the walls were going to fall and crush them; people who would rather sleep under the stars and did not want to leave the camps even if offered something with walls and a ceiling for fear it would not stand.

After Sara's rescue, I started losing sleep. I walked in the pitch of dark, at three, four in the morning, and looked at the lists I had made in my notebooks. The lists of the dead, the living, the half-dead, those who needed help, those who did not go back, even if their buildings had been cleared, those whose houses had been cleared and who planned to reclaim them before someone else did. I talked to my departed mother in half sleep about these things, and I wept. I did not know that Ma Lou heard me. One morning she came to me in the dark, held my face between her hands, and said, "*Pitit, ou bezwen kite.*" You need to go. "I'll be fine," she said, "but you need to go." I cried, heaving into her bosom.

By the end of that week, I had packed my bags and returned to Kigali, to continue the work of looking at sites, drafting plans for new, affordable structures of various kinds, work on behalf of those who were surviving still, elsewhere, ready to lose myself in the work of forgetting, while those I worked for, and with, tried to remember.

.

Kigali, May 2012

I stayed away two more years, keeping tabs on Ma Lou and what was going on in Haiti in furtive phone calls, working through the loss, the absence of both my parents, and the ground of my birth that I cherished still. Even as I worked on drafts for new buildings to go up in Kigali and in the wider countryside of Rwanda, and others in the neighboring DRC—especially housing for women who had been cast out for being victims of civil war—my thoughts returned constantly to my own mother's last months and days, to what I had already lost.

In the ICU in an Iowa hospital, I had sat next to her, holding her
hand, and often fell into a half sleep in which I felt myself hovering
alongside my mother's body, as if I too were hooked up to the machines, laboring with each breath, stupefied, drugged, drowsy, floating within my mother's consciousness—wherever it was. It was both
a bodily and an out-of-body experience, as if death were already upon
us. Death, in this way, did not feel like anything I had imagined: it
was not dark and sullen but light and ethereal. Or perhaps this was
the purgatory they talked about in catechism—an in-between space,
suspended between our material world and paradise. In any case, it
felt womb-like, this floating, eerily familiar since we had both been
there before—me inside her, growing. But now I felt as if it were I
who was being asked to contain my mother, to breathe with her every
thought, every breath, to pull her through and weigh her down so
that she could remain in the land of the living. I was not sure if this
was desirable. She was a wisp of herself, like a small piece of cloud. As
I held her hand, the light weight of it was terrifying—because I knew
that there was nothing that I could do to save my mother, no, save
us—and yet it was a strangely comforting sensation, this buoyant,
drugged feeling, a confirmation of how we had once been one and
would remain so. Death came, slowly, steadily, on icy tiptoe, and, in
the middle of one of those nights, whisked my mother away silently,
so that the touch of her hand was cool, then cold, and the whoosh
of the respirator continued but there was no real breath there, a machine doing what it was calibrated to do, pushing air into a body that
was now a shell. It was nothing more than this, a husk, the vessel that
had once sheltered me. Something shifted within me. I felt buried
within a deep cottony receptacle, a muted cave. It was difficult to feel,
hear, sense. My soul was disturbed, my heart dislodged.

My mother died a few days before the end of 2009 and her brother made the arrangements to fly back her remains to Port-au-Prince. I accompanied the remains, alone. My uncle could not get enough time off work to come with me and stayed behind, with his family. He had done all he could, and more than most. Everything else, on the ground, had been arranged through Dieudonné, who met my mother's remains and me at the airport. I had tried to contact my father, then in France, against my better judgment, and did not hear from him until the last moment when he sent me a message through Dieudonné to say that he would be flying over for the funeral. But I did not see him there.

I hadn't seen him in so long that I thought that perhaps he had come and that, in my grief, I had simply overlooked him. I remembered only the man who came with Dieudonné to my school playground where I was out at recess, the man staying in the car and Dieudonné waving at me, so I waved back, but I did not go toward them. I stared at the man I had been told was my father and understood that he was the reason why I was in the new school where no one played with me at recess, where I missed being with my mother. In the old school, which was not as nice, the chairs worn, the books defaced and ancient, at least I had had my mother nearby because she had been a teacher there, and this made me feel less alone. In the new school, everything was shiny, resplendent, and you felt in the air that you were meant to be doing something important with your life, but there was also an emptiness in the way the other girls looked right through me and compared the brand of their shoes since it was the only thing that was not part of the uniform, though the shoes had to be navy blue or black to match. Richard had been in shadow in the car; I never truly saw his face, so, eventually, I looked away. Later, I saw Dieudonné at my grandmother's and he tried to explain my father to me, the way men explain to women the rules of soccer, and I did not understand much of it and cared even less. That was how much I knew about my father aside from what Ma Lou told me, which was not so very much, as he had broken her heart when he was sent to boarding school, and then proceeded to ignore her at the gates when she came with cakes and sweets for him and the other boys. I would never have done that to my mother, I thought, when I heard the story.

Yet when I was handed the newspaper with the headline "Earthquake in Haiti," my first thought had been of Richard. What had become of his body? I hardly knew him, but I nonetheless felt a wrenching loss, as if I had counted on something from the man who had cared enough to pay for my schooling but not enough to be my father, as if after my mother's death, he might have stepped in and rediscovered us, both me and my grandmother.

One of the advantages of having left ground zero for Rwanda was that the AP articles that came through European channels kept me informed. Being far away was helping me fit my broken pieces back together again, or at least move the shards around within me without cutting myself, helping me make sense of what I had seen on the television screens, what I had gone back to see for myself up close, a few months later: the images of the broken buildings, the losses, the dead and dying in the camps. I collected articles and read them voraciously late at night and early in the mornings, whenever we were not in the field. In a few months, and over the next few years, many of the traces of such articles disappeared, as if the reporting had never happened. Anything critical of US intervention evaporated. Anything that could still be found existed only if someone working on Haiti had had the foresight to archive it on another site.

The extent of the damage was massive, beyond anything one could try to imagine. I came across an article on the destroyed murals of Holy Trinity Cathedral, a church that had been built by an African American–led congregation in the days when it was rarer to have a non-Catholic, English-speaking church. It had beautiful murals decorating its walls, murals I had seen only once, on a school trip. The murals had been painted in egg tempera by Haitian artists with names like Obin and Duffaut. These artists had painted biblical scenes translated into a Haitian reality—Judas, the traitor, was no darker than all the saints, and the disciples were brown of skin. The Virgin Mary was Erzulie, also known as Ezili, attended by dark angels, scars upon her cheek; Jesus carried the Haitian flag as if it were heaven's flag; Christ's baptism took place under a waterfall, our own Saut d'Eau, where the vodou spirits live, bless, and heal. Among the masses, the Savior was shown to be anointed by the ancestors alongside the lowly, stripped to their underthings, the trees surrounding them girded for the gods, prayers made and unmade in the name of the living through the intercessors, the undead, the teeming nature all around, those things that cannot be seen or explained.

I saw them, that once, the fourteen murals bedecking the nave, the altar, the transepts; I saw us all as we would have been had we written the Bible ourselves: our beauty, our strength, our persistence. Like everything else, it could not last. Even amid chaos, thieves find work. Some shards disappeared in the first weeks after the earthquake into the hands of thieves who recognized the value of a piece of patrimony for foreign collectors. Or perhaps beauty is to thieves like water: a necessary thing, a human need. Or maybe, even, Obin lived on in the corner of an anonymous, tarped shack where the promise of a multihued world shone out like the lamp from a lighthouse showing the way into an uncharted future, taken not by the hand of a thief but by someone for whom a shard of the mural would be their only, rightful inheritance. In the article, a conservator from the Smithsonian who assessed the damage (only three of fourteen murals were left standing, and even those remaining were fissured and cracked) was quoted as saying: "When you have that little left, there's nothing you can do." Was there nothing that could be done? To commemorate the dead? To preserve what remained?

I read that there had been an earthquake in Italy, and an Italian architect I had known in college, but who had not contacted me after Douze, sent me an email about it and a worldwide event that was being organized to raise funds for the artisans of the region. The email explained that two hundred thousand rounds of pecorino would spoil if they were not used, so the global campaign had been organized to have them bought and used in a marathon of cooking a simple Italian recipe, with all the proceeds going back to the region. Two hundred thousand rounds of cheese. It was a kind objective, a goodwill gesture, but reading about it only made me sigh wearily. For every round of cheese, a person had died in the Haiti earthquake, and now I was expected to respond to this regional calamity while still burying our dead as if I, and others, might be "over" what had happened to us, as if the earthquake were far enough in our rearview mirror that we could have moved on by now. At least 250,000 people died and only their closest relatives and friends remembered who they might have been; they could not be recovered, not even their names. I, too, had been irrevocably changed, by my mother's death, my father's disappearance, the toll of the earthquake itself, and the visits to those in the camps some months later, especially seeing the disintegration of Sara, the woman who had lost all her children, and those, young and old, who had been violated in the camps, their faces etched by indescribable hauntings.

It was Marc who came to me about the international competition just announced for the rebuilding of Notre-Dame Cathedral, as he had come to me with the news of the earthquake. "You should enter," he said, dropping the printed page on the table before me, then walking away with his hands in his pockets before I could protest. "It's all you've been thinking about since you came back. You want to build something, or at least try. You want a Haitian architect to design something of the new structures."

I surveyed the announcement. He was right. It was something I could offer, something I was good at. I had been thinking about it since he had brought me the first newspaper with the picture of the fallen National Palace and cathedral. I had thought, then, that everything could be rebuilt, that it might be something I could offer. The Palais National had been designed by a Haitian architect trained in Paris, Georges Baussan, and the Cathédrale Notre Dame de L'Assomption, better known simply as Notre-Dame, had been designed by a French architect, André Michel Ménard, in 1881; he had brought to Haiti the "new" building method of using concrete walls when, until then, wood and stone had been the favored materials. So the buildings that fell were not all the result of Haitian complacency, or presumed incompetence, the methods and designs imported like so much else. I knew that though we had nothing so ancient as the Roman Forum, as monumental as Saint Peter's, or as jaw-dropping as the Sistine Chapel, we had treasures worth preserving. We had Christophe's Citadel (mercifully still standing since it was so far from the epicenter of the quake). We had the remains of the cathedral, the memories of the square sprawling below it where all the Sunday strollers used to assemble to show off their best clothes after churchgoing, exchanging the latest gossip and catching up on family news. That open space had turned into a market over the years but remained, still, a place of gathering. We had what remained of the murals of Trinity even with the pieces stolen or sold away. We had the ingenuity that built and painted these things, made them in our own image. What remained could not be measured by wealth, stature, monuments. Nothing rebuilt could replace what we already had made and could never forget. I started drafting the plans I had been thinking about since the trips to the genocide sites when I had first arrived in Rwanda, before my brief return to volunteer in the IDP camps, for a new cathedral, a Haitian cathedral, one that would commemorate the dead and sanctify the living.

Feverishly, I set to working on the plans. I looked at photos of what was left of the cathedral in Port-au-Prince, of the young people—mostly women—sitting beneath the broken arches far below the open roofline, some of them with babies in their arms, their hands outstretched to receive alms from the photographers. The scenes recalled the etchings of the Roman Forum by the Italian architect Piranesi, which I had seen in an exhibit during the tour of Rome I and some of the other architects had taken before the assignment in Rwanda. The question that lingered through each of Piranesi's drawings of ancient ruins seemed to be: Could any, should any, of these ruins be rebuilt? What had caught my eye in Piranesi's etchings was that the floors of the ruins were occupied by vagrants, people with no homes, nowhere to go. Similarly, etchings of churches and palaces beyond Rome's walls featured lone goats, or jesters, caps in hand, standing on top of cliff edges, appearing to be listening for sounds of mobilizing armies that never returned to the scenes of decrepitude and abandon they had left behind. In other scenes, the gentry walked through vast architectural treasures, seeming to declaim on the virtues of ancient Rome, but did so while treading upon the skulls and bones of the unidentified dead, presumably those for whom the ruins were once shelter. The figures in the etchings were so small that they sometimes needed to be seen with a magnifying glass to reveal minuscule jesters and courtiers, but also grave robbers, unaccompanied women, and Moors. Thinking back on these, I was struck by a simple realization, that there was a beauty and majesty to ruins: they lent testimony to the past.

As I worked on the blueprints, I also came across two vintage photographs in an online gallery of photographs archived in a private research university in Georgia, in the United States: the photographs showed two churches, side by side. One was of the cathedral in its infancy. The other was of a smaller, squatter building without much embellishment, labeled "old cathedral," though it had none of the majesty of the new structure. I vaguely recalled that there had been an older structure there, but not that it, too, had been a cathedral. In the photograph, the structure looked colonial, the kind of church built to convert natives, nothing more. In front of the two churches, there was a sprawling market. Both men and women were dressed in draping clothing from head to toe. It looked like an African scene, northern Africa, Tunisia or Algeria, in the early days of colonization, except everyone was dark of skin. Perhaps Tanzania? The Gold Coast? It did not look like Haiti. Maybe it wasn't Haiti. But in the same gallery, in different places, I came across the same buildings from different points of view, the same labels for "new" and "old" cathedral, and I was certain that this was Port-au-Prince, from a forgotten time.

Internet searches revealed to me that the older of the two buildings, the "old" cathedral, had been burned to the ground in the 1990s while our first freely elected president, a former priest, had been in office. There had been some kind of political falling out between warring factions. I didn't remember any of this. I was a child then, overwhelmed by all that I did not know, my mother's fears and struggle, my father's looming absence. The building had since been razed, leaving an empty lot below the almost majestic edifice to its right, Haiti's Notre Dame, a symbol of some not inconsiderable national pride. The "new" building was pink; it fit in where it was, pastel and Caribbean, but it might have been laughable elsewhere, in the heart of Rome, for instance.

This was what I came up with: a long arc drawn across the vellum paper, representing flight, volition, the desire to commune with God. I had erased the line, tried something else, put it back. The paper showed the lines of erasure and recomposition. I drew a circle with the altar in the middle, with seating areas in half-dome shapes extending to each side. Behind the altar, the half-circle space could hold a choir, or simply an effigy, whatever the congregation might prefer. As my fingers moved across the surface of the velvety-smooth paper, the mirage in my mind became clearer with every stroke. Thinking of the pink of the original building, I used pastels to bring some color into the drawing, to suggest people and objects, movement.

The new structure was in the form of a rosette, what Catholics liked to think of as the sacred rose of Mary, found in labyrinths the world over, remains from pagan rituals of prayer to the earth goddesses—the middle stone where one heard the angels whisper their counsel, the answer to one's pleading prayer—a circle for light and grieving, for rejoicing, and for prayer. The rendering showed the "new" cathedral structure erected downwind of the broken one— still majestic with its toppled, pink-hued walls. An unfinished, salvaged ruin. Keeping the broken walls as they were was a testament to those who had died, to remember them through all time. The debris would have to be cleaned up, the walls strengthened, but the broken walls should remain. I placed an iron-wrought fence around the ruins of the cathedral, as they had around the Forum in Rome. Here, as in Piranesi's drawings, the poor and the peasants were free to roam around the rotund new structure I imagined in the space of the place where the burned-down "old" cathedral once stood. Ruins had meaning: they revealed time like nothing else could, outlived bodies, love stories, everything. They should stand.

Satisfied with my work, I entered my submission into the competition with no real hope of winning. I was not working with a high-powered firm, and the reputation of Haitian-born architects was forever tarnished by the disaster, whether or not any of their buildings had fallen. I did it for the satisfaction of doing something, of imagining a better, less hostile future, where a God might still exist to watch over us.

JONAS

Port-au-Prince, Haiti

Douz: It's the number of days that passed since the first of the year
and the earth trembled, only half of which I was finally old enough
to blow out my own candles. Douz. Divided in half: it's the number
of candles Mama put on my cake, short five wicks for my real age,
because that was what she could borrow from the neighbor woman
whose children had all left her years before and never came home.
The number of cell phones they could have bought her by now. The
number of eggs that sit in an open carton on Ma Lou's stand at the
market, which takes forty-eight steps to reach if you forge through
the crowd like a chicken looking for her babies, hoping not to be
snatched up off the ground to be fried for someone's dinner at night.
The number of eggs we wonder at with wide-open eyes but can buy
only two or three of at a time if there's money in the house that week
or, if not, that we can only gaze at from a distance, while Ma Lou
makes us scatter away so she can deal with real customers, the ones
who come down in their cars and never even put a foot out to touch
the dust, who look out onto the market stalls from their perches and
squawk at their drivers to get this and that, inspecting the whole
dozen of eggs before purchasing it while Ma Lou yells: "*Pa manyen
ze'm!*" Don't touch my eggs! "*Pa kase ze'm!*" Don't break my eggs! "*Ou

touche, ou w'achte!" You touch, you buy! *"Dola, pa kòb."* We all know they have houses in Miami and Montreal, those people.

Douz: the number of ears of corn the crazy man who thought he was a cob had eaten after he was cured, then choked, thinking: "I know I'm not a cob, but what if the chickens don't know?" Papa told me that joke. Minus two: it's the number of friends from school I can count on my hands. The number of first cousins on my mother's side. The number of seconds I can hold my breath at the dinner table before Papa slaps me gently across the back of my head to get me to stop, and I burst into laughter. Mama says he worries after us like a woman. But like a man, he doesn't talk much, uses his hands instead. Times two: the number of seconds I can swim under water before coming up for air, watching the little school of fish with yellow bellies dart between my body and the distant, pointy pokes of pinkish coral reef stuck below, at the bottom of the ocean.

It's the number of pieces of blue mint candy I took from the dish in the hotel lobby that morning, after running an errand for Ma Lou and Sonia, the niece of the neighbor whose television I watch, sometimes, after school, and gave to the girl in my class I have my heart set on, once I got to school, all sweaty and tired from the morning run. The number of times that girl's older brother got shot at when one of his deals went wrong in an alleyway, but none of the shots landed on him, and he laughed and laughed and laughed, before his girlfriend left him, saying she didn't want to hear that laugh again. It's the number of blocks between the house and the school with all their hiding places and shadows. The largest number of points on a domino tile. The number of times my mother prays the rosary before she goes to sleep, round and round again, the coral beads dangling across the *mapou* brown of her fingers. Plus two:

the number of stations of the cross at church; the number of times
the little Jesus had to pay for our lives; the number of little thorns
I imagine dug deep into the flesh of his scalp and made him bleed
before he realized that no one was coming to save him.

Twelve seconds is all the time it took for the length of wall
separating the living room from the bedrooms in the neighbor's
house, where we all gathered, frozen in front of the TV, sitting or
standing, watching the late afternoon soap opera, to fall, while I
traced a vine-like crack climbing speedily across its surface. I wasn't
supposed to be there, warming the one egg that I had gotten from
Ma Lou's stall, running an errand after school for Mama, who was
waiting for me in our kitchen where she was making something for
us to eat. The girls were there, sitting on the tile floor, playing, then
disappeared into the ground. It's the number of times I cried out
for Mama until I realized that she couldn't hear me for all the other
children crying out for their mamas, both in the neighbor's house
and out in the street, everyone crying out for their mamas as if each
were the same person, reaching for my little sisters only to find air
in my hand, grasping, then hours of hearing them crying together
only for their cries to go silent, after a while, while I lay pinned beneath cement blocks, not knowing what to do, frightened.

.

Divided by four: it's the number of hours it takes Papa and some
other men from the neighborhood, old and young ones, to get me
out from under the broken wall, the number of fractures the medic
counts in my leg before he stops counting and turns to tell my father the bottom of it will have to come off.

It's the number of minutes it takes for me to add up that I'll never become a soccer star, never get out, go anywhere, have to be carried about for the rest of my life, in the arms of my father, who carries me as he follows the man with a cross on his back to a floating hospital in the port that smells like acid and is filled with people oozing on gurneys, crying, like me. Even later, it's the number of seconds, counting backward, it takes for me to pray to die as a man in a mask and green fatigues has other masked men grasp me while my father holds his head in his hands, some feet away from me, and the masked men saw at my leg, and when I feel the searing, I scream: "*Papa, ki sa…?*" Papa, what's…? Holding my breath, hoping Papa will walk over to the side of the table and slap my head, shake me out of this terrible dream. Later, when we are both back with Mama, who won't look at Papa and speaks to us only in riddles, it's the number of pills that the men who sawed off my leg gave him to give to me, every day, for six weeks, so that Mama will learn to count them out before he leaves, one white and two pink.

Divided by two: the number of weeks it takes for my father to decide he's had enough and tell us that he's going to another camp, ten hours away, where he can find work. I don't believe him, but what can I say? He looks away from my absent leg, as if it might still be there, and doesn't look me in the face.

Plus ten: the number of days it takes for me to realize that I haven't heard the laughter of my little sisters. The number of days it will take, after the am-pu-ta-tion, for me to be yanked up and away, right out from my body, like parachutists I've seen on television after they've thrown themselves out of a plane, pulling on the string to open up their chutes, then are yanked back, and up, before they float again toward solid ground.

Times infinity: the number of microbes that multiply and spread tentacles from the sutures holding together the seams of my missing leg, crawling through tissue, to blood, to my heart, and settling there, like displaced people needing to set up camp on land not their own, like us. Me, looking on my body upon the mattress, and Mama moving slowly around the bed where it lies. The pain, then, is dull, a faraway throbbing and flitting, like the flies buzzing. Mama swats around her face, not knowing it's me, too, floating about her head. Mama doesn't look at either of us: the me on the bed, or the me in the air. She can't see either of us, won't. I am flying in the air, laughing, not a care in the world. I can see my little sisters, too, playing hide-and-seek inside and around the tent. No one sees them but me and Loko, the rainwater man who sets a container of clean water at the front flap of the tent for every day Papa doesn't come back. The girls play around Mama but don't understand that she can't see us. Later, I'll see Papa, too, floating in the air, too distant to be touched. He doesn't seem to want to see me, us. I don't know if he can.

Douz: the number of tiger's eye marbles I asked for and got on my birthday, in the little pouch my father had sewn with the *J* for my first name, stitched below the drawstrings, though, that week, there was only enough money for *one* egg from Ma Lou's stand, crushed between my hands. Minus one: it's the age I'll be for an eternity with Mama murmuring her prayers over us, because there is nowhere else to go, no living room with her *dodine* to rock in, no Papa to swap stories with.

Douz: the number of fluttering kisses I give Mama about her head each time she goes to sleep in the tent, so that she knows: I'll never leave her.

MA LOU

Port-au-Prince, June 2012

That end of day at market, the day of the earthquake, I had not noticed, in the chaos of running back and forth, with everyone screaming, "*Alleluia! Alleluia!*"—as if it were the second coming of Christ himself—that my cellular had been ringing, at intervals, on and off. While the earth rippled, my little portable phone—the cheapest thing so that I could call my suppliers and receive the occasional calls from Dieudonné, from Anne—rang tirelessly like a chick that had fallen out of the nest, pleading for its absent mother, then went dead, like so many others. By the time I could give it any attention, I found I had several messages, days, weeks old. I listened to the messages. They were mostly from Anne, several days after the Event, asking me where I was, if I was all right, asking about her father, asking for me to call her back. Richard had not shown up to the church service for her mother, before the earthquake itself. But when I at last received the messages, and for many nights after, I had no way to call her back, no heart to find a way. Richard had gone earlier in the day of the Event to the beach. I assumed, at first, that he had survived, even though in my heart there was a tugging. Any mother knows when a child is lost, in spirit or in flesh. He had been gone in spirit for some time, so many years, not even returned when his father died, unexpectedly, of heart failure, and I had put him in the boarding school. But this leaving was different. He felt gone entirely, as if the universe had sucked him away.

After those first days, the days of cleanup, of mourning, some of us wore the white of initiates for weeks. Some of us danced, but our movements were dirges, not celebrations of life, as they said on the television reports, especially those from the outside who could not understand our assemblies, the swaying, the wearing of white in the bright light of day instead of black. It was all that could be done. There was no time: day rose and set but had nothing to do with *maten* or *aswè*—no day, no night. Mourning came to have only one meaning: letting go. I did not dance. I watched, but I did not dance. Instead, I stayed still at my post, wondering what faces I would no longer be seeing walking through the market: the husbands who had left their wives, the wives having affairs on their husbands, the children hiding from their persecutors, the destitute pretending that they were shopping for pantries that didn't exist. I understood: even if you have no pennies to buy, markets can make you feel rich: all the overflowing, colorful fruits and vegetables, the trinkets, the chewing gums in their miniature, vibrant packaging, the made-in-China items that no one has seen before and marvels over. Only those who can pay can have a morsel of it, the bounty. The rest of us are *banann*, like plantains made soft when boiled.

The days melded one into the other, light with dark. It was hard to explain later, when those who hadn't been here wanted explanations for delays. But there was no real way to explain. Reality was no more; time had evaporated. Those others were out of harm's way: they were safe, in the unreal world. Here, life and death were stripped to their bare elements. All that was man-made fell, including time, buckled into the sky with nightfall. The horizon met and we scrambled upon the surface of the earth like ants, instinctively, following shadows to find our way. That's all we were: shadows, paper cutouts cast large against sheets of receding light.

If I think about it now, this is all I can remember: the shadows of black ink moving against indigo-blue skies, and, as the night blanketed us, nothing but sighs and gasps, cries in the night mixed with those of roosters and braying donkeys for whom time had long ceased to matter.

When I finally got the cellular recharged, I found Anne. "It's not the first time the people have disappeared," I said to her, not knowing what question I was answering. "Not the first time. And it won't be the last: Mark. My. Words. You listening? You hear me?" Eccentric pronouncements of an old lady; it was as if the tragedy had made me a seer, as if I had a crystal ball and could see right into the future. I caught myself, thought of my Lou. "This one, no, no one could have foreseen it."

"Well, that's not entirely true," Anne responded, quietly, over the phone.

I stroked the stray hairs on my chin absentmindedly, comforting myself. Anne told me that she had read in the paper, after, that there was a Haitian *seis-mol-o*—yes, *seis-mo* . . . well, you know what I mean, someone who studies the earth and how it moves, all the layers crackling, folding, moving, who had predicted it. But no one had believed him. That's how unimportant we had become. I bounced a finger on my temple. "Who decided that?" I said into the phone, my voice high-pitched. "Who in the hell decided that?"

Even now, I think of all the lives that could have been saved. The little boy, the angel-girls, their mother, Sara, with the shadow of a burn on her face. The tall girl with the model looks with her lovelorn protector following her like a sleek Doberman. I think of all the people who used to come in and out of the market. Human beings. Leopold, whom I knew only from photographs sent by a distant relative in Trinidad, where some of our people went long ago, who came to make his fortune, selling his contraband on the edges of the market through teenage boys and staying in the big hotel on the hill. The hotel slid and fell like a stack of dominoes.

"Everything matters," I said to Anne. "I mean, everyone," opening my arms wide, though she could not see me, "*tout moun*. We, too, right here, right now." But who listens to a Haitian, a *nègre*, a black man, divining a catastrophe? Who could believe that a *nègre* had studied these things, in a university, and had a job studying Vilokan, yes, yes, that's what he was studying: the underworld floating beneath us, where all the dead go. Who knew that could be a job? I fell silent, listening to Richard's daughter. Her words confused me.

I felt the edges of my eyes crinkle shut. Concentrated, then released both eyes, opened them wide. Understood. "Who could have known?" I said again, against disbelief. After I removed my hand from the vat of rice into which I had sunk it, listening to Anne, white grains sticking to the dampness of my dark brown skin, I dipped my hand into a basin of water and the grains detached themselves and floated. I wiped my hand dry against the florid cloth covering my chest. A few stray grains bounced onto the cement below me. I gathered them up one by one, quietly, slowly, dropped them into the basin along with the other stray seeds.

A gust of wind descended. Stray bottles toppled; papers scattered. The edge of my smock lifted. I held it down, covered my skirt.

Held it with a strange ferocity, remembering that day, that minute I could hold nothing, when gravity was no more. Lifted my head up. Squinted into the sun. Lifted a hand against its hot rays, placed the hand, palm out, on my forehead. Fingers winglike. Could I fly?

"Listen," I said to Anne, my granddaughter, suddenly exhausted, feeling my bones pull on my flesh. I was thinking: We are particles in motion. This is why the gods can descend into us. My mother's gods. Lou's gods. The ancestral gods. Our gods. We must find our way back to them. No more rosaries and earthenware statues, no more churches that fall down around our ears. It's the, gods, the *lwas*, that allow us to see into things beyond us. Because everything has always been moving, falling. *Se konsa.* Why should the earth be any different? Why should it? It moves, just like us. It has no choice.

"We'll talk again," I said to her. "*Fòm'ale.* I have to fly."

·

Shortly after Douz, maybe a month or two later, a *kòmè* called to ask if I knew the cemetery on Route de Frères was being moved. "Moved where?" I laughed bitterly. "The whole place is a cemetery." Who thinks of moving a cemetery in these days?

The cemetery had always been there, or as long as I could remember since I'd come to the city, at the crossroads where Route de Frères and Delmas forked together, Frères running north and east beyond Pétion-Ville, Delmas running north and west, back into the city and up to the sea. I didn't know what moving the bones could mean, if the spirits would be angry, or relieved, but I knew I wanted my people's bones before the cemetery was moved. Lou's bones, even the bones of one of Lou's sisters, and those of two of her five babies, the two that had been planted in her womb together and emerged in the world fused belly to belly, and died as they were born, facing each other and away from the world. I fought so that I could take them back, cradle the bones, and bury them again. I fought to retrieve them before they were simply turned over and under, and forgotten, before the spirits could be disturbed from their slumber, so that they could be at peace and forgive us, should forgiveness be needed. Some spirits don't want their bones to be moved, watch over them jealously like scrappy dogs underfoot beneath the eating table. Some of them did not go in peace in the first place, did not want to go.

I explained all this to the judge, after they arrested me for trying to dig up the bones of my people, my own bones. How could I be arrested for digging up what had always belonged to me? He tried to get clever with me, the judge, tried to say something poetic and spiritual, said that the spirits were long departed and had no worries for earthly things the way that we did, that I was too sentimental, too old-fashioned. I raised my fist toward him and stood up after it. "Listen here, *ti'moun*," I said, forgetting that he had to be called "sir" and "mister." "Listen, child," I said, "you're too young to remember the first lesson: the marrow of the bone contains all the information you'll ever need to know. Yes, the spirits are gone, but they watch over the marrow. Those bones are not simply dust going back to dust, do you understand? They carry energy." I was speaking like a *vodouisant*, though I'd never set foot in a *hounfort*. No, I had begun to lose faith in a Christian God—I had begun to believe in other gods, Lou's gods. The judge looked at me quizzically. He hadn't expected me to be able to speak on my own behalf, to be as eloquent as more educated folks. But I've had books read to me, and conversations with my granddaughter, named for me, who knows all manner of things. Beyond this, I know things not in books, that only leaves and touching the ground every night before bed will tell you, the murmurs of the source of all, the earth and the rivers. You don't get cataracts for nothing: it's to see the paradise within. "Let me have my bones!" I yelled. After I said all I had to say, the man let me take them freely.

I got my bones but not all the bones were saved or moved. They destroyed the cemetery with plans to make a bus terminal, then a parking lot, but they've done nothing since they disturbed the bones except put up a fence around the periphery of what used to be the cemetery. When I walk past the lot, I remember. I am seventy-five years of age, and for me to say that I cannot remember when it was not there means it has been there for longer than I have been walking the dust of this island, since before the forests were cleared, when you could still smell pine in the air all the way down to the harbor. I feel the chill, the sadness. I feel some of the spirits lingering there, at the crossroads.

There was a time when the dead were revered. Those times are gone. We have forgotten what it means to honor the dead. Even before the Event, I have seen places where so many human skulls are left exposed to the sun, used to adorn artless statues, for candlesticks at the altar. Some call this art. I say that we no longer remember that this skull belonged to someone's sister, brother, mother, someone's child.

Over time, I kept the bones beneath the bed in my small house. The house that had stayed standing regardless of the earth's swaying and buckling. I thought long and hard about where I could find a new home for the bones. I thought of returning them to my mother's village, my village, even if it was not theirs. But at least they could rest.

There was talk, in those days of mayhem and half-baked solutions after Douz, of moving people back to where they had come from, to disgorge the city. I was not opposed to the idea. I was growing tired. My own bones ached from the daily grind of caring for others who did not imagine that I had any worries of my own. I added their worries to mine, but I needed rest, some time to think, or not think, only to be, without observing everyone, playing at rescuer when there was nothing, really, that I could do of substance. I assisted a few in dying more easily, brought staples to market that everyone needed to get along, but there was no moving forward, only back.

I needed to leave this place.

Long ago now, my mother had left me a small parcel of land. I had somewhere to go, back to where her bones lay, back to Saint Marc. I called Anne, who was all I had left, Richard's Anne, my namesake, and told her. If only she could come to help, I thought, but didn't dare ask. She was so far away, had returned once after the earthquake, to help, but it was too much for her: I sent her back. She called sometimes to get news of how things were going. "They're going," I would respond, but not explain the rest, the tumult, the disarray, the chaos, the hollow eyes I saw in the people coming now to market, the emptiness. She had her own life to live, out there, safe from all of this, I thought, after losing both her mother and her father. But not me, I thought, not me: I'm still here. I called, told her about the bones, which I had kept with me, hidden, all this time. There was a pause, a long silence, and then she responded that she was coming, coming back to bury the memory of her father, to bury the dead, to help me with the bones.

·

When I see Anne walk into the market, her appearance is to me like fresh water being poured into a glass. I am the container that has not known it needed to be filled. She is the water bringing solace, that does not know it needs to be contained. She is unmistakably mine, has Richard's gait, Lou's lopsided smile, the effusive gesture of hands that Lou tried to make Richard stop doing in case the other boys took them for signs that he was *masisi*. I don't know if my Richard was or not. I don't know. If he was, maybe it was my fault, for sending him away on the brink of manhood, after his father had died. It's difficult to become a man without a father. I plan to bury the bones close to the ocean, on my mother's land. Because I need to leave this place, the market, take my bones away.

I tell Anne where I want to bury the bones, and that we should take with us the girl, Taffia, her young son, not yet two years of age, and Sara. Sara did not have a chance to bury her dead, and the girl needs to cleanse herself and the baby of what happened in the camp. They are in need of ceremony, something all their own, away from the city and its repeating cycles of wounding. Anne nods: "Yes, yes, we'll take them too," and, like that, we hatch a plan. I am the happiest I have been since the thing that should not have happened, happened.

"Myself," I tell her, so she knows, "when the time comes, I want to be buried close to my mother, close to Lou, smell the sea salt of the ocean with my last breaths. I want to be away from the stench and congestion of the city, all that dust and haunting hanging in the air."

It does not take a lot to convince Taffia's mother and sister, Sonia, to let the girl come with us; they decide to come as well. The women are delighted to have a reprieve from the city, some time away. Me, the bones, my granddaughter —we are all going back to my home beyond the city, this city that has become a grave. I will show them all where we came from, before the before of the Event. I want to go to Saut d'Eau on the way up toward the coast. In the city, I had seen a fissured mural in Trinity Cathedral, the one with the dark-skinned woman below the falls split apart by the crumbling walls. I want to go there, *there*, to see if the real waterfalls still flow, because, if they do, I can believe in something again. Our bones, too, need a cleansing, to be released from all that they have seen and absorbed these last years of sorrow and strife. Grief resides in the marrow. This, I know. It's what weighs us down and pains us as we grow old: the grief in the marrow.

We leave a few days later in an oversized car. A rental, Anne calls it. That means that when she leaves the island, she'll give it back at the airport. It is like sitting in a spaceship. I haven't been driven in a car for so long I feel like a rich woman. Strange. The car even has air-conditioning, but we roll down the windows instead. Richard's girl smiles at me and I am thankful. "There's also a stop I'd like to make along the way," she says. I nod. Okay. I don't ask questions. Market women gossip but we don't pry, or cry. The women peer out the windows as if a new world is opening before them. Taffia's son sleeps quietly, nestled in her arms.

Anne has maps. She knows how to make her way through the city. When she gets lost, she's not afraid to ask. Tells us about her travels all around the world, to places I've heard of but never imagined. Places in Africa where they've also seen their share of trouble. Places in Europe where they've forgotten that they have, too. She likes to tell stories. We can sit back and listen, watch the countryside roll by. The women smile. I do not know what they are thinking as the broken city recedes behind us. Maybe, like me, what they are feeling is relief. I sigh. I'm coming home, Mama.

·

Saut d'Eau is nothing like I expected, and more. It's quiet since it's not yet feast time. There are a few other people, stripped to their underwear under the falls, moaning, praying, putting their hands out to the sky. I have my bones in a burlap bag in one hand, bouncing against my leg. I ask Anne and Sara to come into the water with me. They agree. Anne helps me navigate over the stones, get closer and closer into the foam. As the water hits me from behind and all around, I experience a sensation of cold running through me, then my body cries, shakes. I am grasping the bag of bones in the one hand and Anne asks me if I want to open it. We three open it together, let the water fall over the blanched bones, an anointing. Take the pain away, *Wede*. Take the pain, *Wede*. *Wede*. Take us. I feel the bones cleansed of every past sorrow as the water courses over them, over me, through us. I see tears come down Sara's cheeks as she says goodbye to her own. We close the bag. The bones must go home to the land. We sit beneath the waterfall in silence, watch Taffia carry the baby into the falls, where Sonia, stripped to her waist, anoints the baby and blesses him in the name of Wede, their mother watching from the side of the waterfall, hands clasped. For the first time in two years, I smile as my heart empties and receives grace. Sara looks at us with more clarity in her eyes than I have seen since the day of the fire. *Mèsi, Wede. Mèsi, Damballah.* My mother's gods. Thank you. Lou's gods. Thank you. I hear Anne make a prayer by my side for her own mother. We do not have her bones, but we pray over them as if we do.

Then we are back on the coastal road, and Anne makes the stop she wants. The signs at the side of the road announce a private beach resort, Sea-View.

"I can't go in there," I say.

"Of course you can," she says. Then, after a pause, understands me. I am just a market woman.

"You're with me. Come along now," she says to me, as if to a small child. Sonia comes with us, while the others stay behind in the car, Taffia feeding the baby.

I scramble out of the car and put the bag of bones in the boot of the car. I follow them into the resort. Sonia orders something for us to drink and eat and sends items back to the car for the others. We sit close to the beach and watch the waves. More luxury than I've had in a lifetime. Close by, there is a small white cross planted under a tree. When we are about to finish, Anne closes her eyes for a long time. I close my eyes too. Rest the bones.

"My father, your son, died here," she says, "two years ago, when the waves came up on shore."

"I know," I say. I remember feeling the loss, the gaping hole, like nothing I had felt before. I knew he had died in that moment because the grief of all the years he kept himself from us disappeared and only an open space was left where I kept his memory. A hole, a nothingness, a clearing. I take her hand, squeeze it tight, my mourning already done long ago.

"It's time to let go, rest, let go of these bones," I say.

Having made our peace with Richard, said goodbye, we return to the car and continue on our way.

.

After we bury the bones in my village, I sit on the ground above them. The men I paid to dig the holes scatter back to their lives, probably wondering what this crazy woman from the city has been doing with a bag of rattling bones, asking for their help. If I were younger, I would have dug those holes myself, dug them with my own hands, cupping the earth to feel the richness of the soil, to be tattooed with the henna red of it.

I watch the men go, the plaid of their shirts clinging to their backs, mumbling to each other as they depart, their shovels over their shoulders, balancing. I feel the wind pick up and caress my cheek. Then, I realize that it is Anne.

Feeling the softness of her hand, first, I startle, then I weep, long and hard, as I've never wept before, not even when my own mother died, so long ago now. I take her hand from my cheek and kiss the hollow of her palm. As I do so, I think of all those bones with no one to claim them, all the bodies found that were thrown into a pit somewhere on the outskirts of the capital, beneath the cleaned-up city, disintegrating, becoming foundation. I realize, then, that those who died may have been unclaimed, their remains abandoned of necessity, but never, never, were they unloved. For all of them, for us, with Anne's palm against my mouth, I weep.

ACKNOWLEDGMENTS

For the six months following the earthquake, I was on the road nonstop, delivering talks on the consequences of the earthquake for women and children, and the politics of reconstruction for the grassroots and general Haitian population. Every time I gave a talk, survivors of the ordeal would come to me afterward and tell me their stories, in Kreyòl, French, English, of those who perished, who were never found, or who had survived, fled. I also networked on behalf of survivors on the ground, connecting grassroots groups with resources and funds in the US. I would continue this work for the next three years; it would be my main occupation even while I still worked full-time as an academic and writer. What fees I was paid went, in whole, to a variety of grassroots organizations, including Zanmi Lakay, Ecole Bazilo Communautaire, Atis Fanm Matènwa, International Child Care, and Oxfam, among many more. Still, I did not plan to write this novel.

What changed my mind was a chance meeting with Trinidadian painter LeRoy Clarke, whom I was brought to meet by a mutual friend in 2013 in Saint Augustine, after having served as the writer in residence at the University of the West Indies the year prior. Clarke was completing a cycle of paintings begun in 1986, entitled *Eye Hayti . . . Cries . . . Everywhere*, but had never finished.

After the earthquake, he returned to the cycle and painted feverishly, long into the night, for nights on end. When I saw the series, it had approximately seventy-seven paintings of different sizes
(there would be about one hundred in the end, later exhibited at
the National Museum and Art Gallery of Trinidad and in Haiti).
Clarke had never been to Haiti then, not met a Haitian painter, yet
each canvas reflected a Haitian sensibility, Haitian realities of pain,
despair, hope, persistence. Upon seeing the paintings, I wept. I felt
the spirits in the place, the spirits of the dead.

I cannot say more about this meeting except to say that I con-
cluded from it that the stories that had been conferred to me after every talk and every reading I delivered in those early days after
the earthquake were a charge, a responsibility that I carried, that I
needed to do something with as a writer, a responsibility to the dead.

I give thanks to all those who shared their stories with me, usually
anonymously, who inspired the characters I developed, in Brooklyn/
New York, Massachusetts, Boca Raton, South Carolina, El Paso,
Maryland, Oregon, Seattle, Kentucky, North Carolina, Milwaukee,
and in Puerto Rico, Trinidad & Tobago, Saint Martin/Sint Maarten,
South Africa, and the list goes on, stories received from pool boys,
housekeepers, businessmen, schoolteachers, artists, fixers. Often, the
stories came without my asking, were delivered in unexpected moments. Listening for years, I realized later, was a big part of the process of writing this novel. Those conversations fueled me when the
work seemed impossible or too heavy to carry forward.

Though I was inspired by the stories I was told, and witnessed,
by my own returns to Haiti, to Port-au-Prince, Léogâne, Jacmel,
and LaGonav, over the four years after the earthquake, this work
remains entirely one of fiction. Readers will have to forgive any

departures from fact, historical timelines, or geography taken within its pages as a consequence of artistic license, that is, for the sake of the story. What I hope to have distilled from what I have heard and learned over these years are the layered and multiple effects of the earthquake on all whose lives the event touched, including my own. I hope that I have captured what was at once a national tragedy and one with individual dimensions. In the end, what I wanted to capture was the way in which lives were disrupted, what those lives may have been like, before, what might have remained, after.

I read a great many accounts of the earthquake from its beginning until several years in its aftermath. The first were AP news reports, many appearing in the *Miami Herald* written by Jacqueline Charles; I read Beverly Bell's *Other Worlds* blog, "Another Haiti Is Possible," which provided reliable information in the weeks and months after the earthquake on how average Haitians were affected on the ground. Most books published by university and independent presses on the earthquake crossed my desk for review, and I read most of them; of these, I would refer readers to Beverly Bell's *Fault Lines: Views across Haiti's Divide* (2013). Much was written in French and Kreyòl by Haitian writers in the form of short stories and poetry, most of which I did not read, not wanting to be influenced by any, but I did come across and review Yanick Lahens's *Failles* (2010), which I found most affecting. After a time, in order to stay within the cocoon of the story, I stopped reading texts on the earthquake, stopped reviewing the endless stream of academic production on Haitian subjects, post-earthquake, increasingly ungrounded in expertise.

I am grateful to readers of the first full draft of the novel, whose commentary was invaluable to me (they know who they are), and to my late mother, Adeline Lamour Chancy, for providing expertise on the Kreyòl for the final version.

A note on the Kreyòl contained in this work. Kreyòl is a living, syncretic language; as such it has known, and continues to know, many iterations, with variances that approximate transliterations into both French transliterations and English. It has been an officially recognized language of Haiti since 1987 but was codified with an official orthography in 1979—prior to this time, Haitian writers used their own variants (and some still do). That orthography, largely based on the French, has changed over time (for example, we once wrote "creole" as opposed to "Kreyòl"). My text follows the orthography set out by Haitian linguist Yves Déjean (Iv Dejan) in his 2006 book, *Yon lekòl tèt anba nan yon peyi tèt anba* (*An Upside-Down School in an Upside-Down Country*), who is an authority in the area of Haitian Kreyòl. This orthography is consistent with that more recently regulated and codified, beginning in 2014, by the Haitian Creole Academy (Akademi Kreyòl Ayisyen), of which Déjean was a founder. Any departures from this orthography in the text will be referential (i.e., referencing, in intertextual moments, earlier versions of Kreyòl in preexisting, published texts) or contextual (when a character takes liberties with the language as a living organ, i.e., their right to colorful and inventive speech).

Thanks to editor Jim Hicks, who published a short, early excerpt in the *Massachusetts Review*, and to the editors of *Il Tolomeo* in Venice, Italy, for publishing another, both in 2015. I am also grateful to editor Janice Zawerbny, whose keen editorial eye assisted me in streamlining and reshaping the novel into a form that met its promise; thanks go also to Tin House editor Masie Cochran, for lean edits that polished and tightened the final prose. Thanks to the

Morgan Library of New York for gracious access to their holdings on Italian draftsman and architect Piranesi. I am grateful for time spent in the company of Franca Bernabei and Bill Boelhower, with whom I saw a retrospective on Piranesi during one of my many forays to Venice to visit them; over the many years of our friendship, they have offered me a home away from home and sustenance, artistic, intellectual, and personal, through difficult times.

Born into a family of musicians on my paternal side, I also listened to a great deal of music while writing this text, but perhaps none was more significant to me than Sade's single "Bring Me Home" (2010) and BélO's "Timatant Nan Wout" (2005)—both literally brought me home. Terence Blanchard's "A Tale of God's Will" (2007) was also a constant companion through the years of writing and rewriting.

I wish, finally, to give thanks to: my ancestors, especially my great-grandmother Aricie César Lamour, a market woman who owned a business in the original Marché de Fer of Port-au-Prince in the early 1900s, and my mother, who joined them in early 2019; the *lwas*; and all the spirits now departed who visited LeRoy Clarke's studio in Trinidad. Without these presences, and their precious guidance, this novel would not be.